The Chameleon's Shadow

By the same author

THE ICE HOUSE
THE SCULPTRESS
THE SCOLD'S BRIDLE
THE DARK ROOM
THE ECHO
THE BREAKER
THE SHAPE OF SNAKES
ACID ROW
FOX EVIL
DISORDERED MINDS
THE DEVIL'S FEATHER

and

THE TINDER BOX
CHICKENFEED
(Winner of the Quick Reads Readers' Choice)

MINETTE WALTERS

The Chameleon's Shadow

MACMILLAN

First published 2007 by Macmillan
an imprint of Pan Macmillan Ltd
Pan Macmillan, 20 New Wharf Road, London N1 9RR
Basingstoke and Oxford
Associated companies throughout the world
www.panmacmillan.com

ISBN 978-0-230-01566-1 HB
ISBN 978-0-230-01602-6 TPB

1 3 5 7 9 8 6 4 2

A CIP catalogue record for this book is available from
the British Library.

Typeset by SetSystems Ltd, Saffron Walden, Essex
Printed and bound in Great Britain by
Mackays of Chatham plc, Chatham, Kent

Visit **www.panmacmillan.com** to read more about all our books
and to buy them. You will also find features, author interviews and
news of any author events, and you can sign up for e-newsletters
so that you're always first to hear about our new releases.

For Marie and Sarah

Shadow – In the theory of C. G. Jung (1875–1961) the dark aspect of personality formed by those fears and unpleasant emotions which, being rejected by the self or persona of which an individual is conscious, exist in the personal unconscious.

Oxford English Dictionary

Traumatic Brain Injury (TBI) – Some common disabilities include problems with . . . behaviour and mental health (depression, anxiety, personality changes, aggression, acting out and social inappropriateness).

Wikipedia

Murder victim 'beaten to death'

THE BODY OF A MAN, discovered two days ago when police were called to a house in south London, has been identified as that of Martin Britton, a 71-yr-old retired civil servant who worked for the Ministry of Defence. Friends and neighbours said Mr Britton hadn't been seen for several days. The decision to enter the house was taken after police used a ladder to check the bedroom windows.

A post-mortem examination carried out yesterday revealed that Martin Britton died from head injuries. 'He was beaten to death in a violent attack,' said Det Supt Brian Jones, who is leading the inquiry. 'We believe it happened on Saturday, 23 September, and we are asking for anyone who was in Greenham Road on that date to come forward.'

Neighbours describe Martin Britton as a 'charming and courteous' man who became 'something of a recluse' after his partner died last year. Det Supt Jones said Mr Britton may have known his attacker. 'There was no sign of forced entry,' he added.

The Superintendent refused to confirm whether this murder is being linked to the death of Harry Peel, a 57-yr-old taxi driver who died from extensive head injuries two weeks ago. Mr Peel lived less than two miles from Greenham Road and was found in his bedroom by his estranged wife after she became concerned that he wasn't answering his mobile.

The police have enlisted the help of the gay community in the search for Harry Peel's killer. A one-time soldier in an armoured regiment, he worked for several years in the docks before becoming a cab driver seven years ago. He was a regular visitor to the bars and clubs in his area.

Searches by scenes of crime officers are continuing at the Greenham Road house.

Eight weeks later

THE CONVOY OF armoured trucks, led by a Scimitar reconnaissance vehicle, had been visible for some time to the four Iraqis who crouched in what remained of the upper storey of an abandoned roadside building. The road – part of the highway that linked Basra to Baghdad – cut a straight path across the flat desert landscape, and the group's elevated position and long-range binoculars had allowed them to track the convoy from the moment the lead vehicle breasted the distant horizon.

The heat was intense. Shimmering mirages produced *trompe-l'oeil* reflections in the tarmac, and one of the insurgents captured the effect on a DVD camera before zooming in on the turret of the Scimitar. He could make out the helmeted heads of the two soldiers on either side of the 30mm cannon, and of the driver below it, but the vehicle was still too far away to identify their faces. Another insurgent pointed to a telegraph pole in the long line that marched beside the road and said there would be two good minutes between the Scimitar passing the pole and the explosion. Time enough to capture British soldiers on film before the home-made culvert bombs on either side of the highway obliterated them forever.

The cameraman expected to see complacency, even arrogance, on the faces of the coalition oppressors, but the close-up footage of the three men showed only concentration. There was even a suggestion, in the way the commander, a twenty-six-year-old lieutenant, suddenly shouted an order, that he had spotted something amiss in the dust beside the highway. It was too late.

The roadside bombs, a collection of anti-tank mines rigged to produce a blast that was powerful enough to rip the guts out of a Bradley tank, detonated simultaneously as the vehicle passed between them.

The film clip of a British Scimitar rising into the air before turning over in flames received considerable airtime across the Muslim world. In the Iraq bazaars, it became a 'must-have' DVD for anyone whose electricity supply was intermittent or whose satellite dish had been pushed out of alignment by coalition bombing. The propaganda coup of a small Iraqi cell taking out a coalition vehicle with home-made bombs was irresistible, particularly as viewers and experts alike claimed to see fear, not concentration, on the faces of the three Western soldiers. It was taken as an indication that morale in the coalition forces was crumbling and that an end to the occupation was near.

With a different set of ethics governing the coverage of war in Britain, news editors decided against screening the close-up footage for fear of generating complaints about insensitivity. Only one of the men had survived, albeit with disfiguring injuries, and in such circumstances even the most hardened broadcasters felt the line between reportage and exploitation was here too thin to be tested.

MINISTRY OF DEFENCE
BRITISH FORCES SURGICAL HOSPITAL, IRAQ

Confidential report

Subject:	Lt Charles Acland 893406
Regiment:	Light Dragoon Guards
	– Royal Armoured Corps
Date of injury:	24 November 2006
Date of admission:	24 November 2006
Date of discharge:	26 November 2006 – 19.30 hours
Onward destination:	South General Hospital,
	Birmingham, UK
Reason for return:	Reconstructive surgery
Current patient status:	Unconscious but stable
	– strapped for immobility
Drug treatment:	See attached chart

To Whom It May Concern

Lt Charles Acland sustained serious head and facial injuries
during an attack on his Scimitar RV. He has fractures of the
left supraorbital, zygomatic and maxilla. His wounds have
been cleaned, all foreign material, dead and burnt tissue
removed and superficial bleeding stopped. Pressure monitor
readings of the patient's brain and arterial flow show nothing
significant, although the severity of the patient's injuries
suggest brain damage is likely. An immediate CAT scan is
recommended. He has an open wound on the left side of his
face – a 2cm wide, 0.5cm deep, 10cm long avulsion – caused

by the splitting and cauterizing effects of hot shrapnel. Muscle and nerve damage is extensive and his left eye is beyond repair. An antibiotic regime was introduced on admission and temporary dressings applied to the open wound to prevent infection.

One

WHEN CHARLES ACLAND regained consciousness, he thought he was dreaming about a visit to the dentist. Certainly, the numbness in his mouth suggested novocaine even if the rest of the fantasy was absurd. He was lying on his back, staring up at a moving ceiling, and a bell was ringing loudly behind him. *An alarm?* He tried to raise his head to see where it was, but a hand descended on his chest and a woman's disembodied face loomed over him. *The dentist?* He watched her lips move, but couldn't make out what she was saying over the insistent clamour of the alarm. He toyed with asking her to turn if off, but doubted that novocaine would allow his words to be understood. She wouldn't be able to hear him anyway.

Somewhere at the back of his mind was a lurking fear that he didn't recognize. For no reason that he understood, the closeness of the woman worried him. He'd been in this position before – flat on his back and unable to move – and there was a strong association in his mind with pain. Fleetingly, another woman, slender, dark-haired and graceful, appeared in his line of vision. There were tears in her eyes, but Acland had no idea who she was. His instinctive reaction was dislike.

His only points of reference were the alarm and the ceiling moving above his head. Neither had any meaning for him. He could have floated forever in morphine-induced detachment if increasing awareness hadn't told him this wasn't a dream. He started to experience sensations. A jolt as the trolley crossed a threshold. The sympathetic tightening of stretcher straps as his body shifted. A low ache at the back of his jaw. A brief stabbing pain that knifed up his neck. A puzzled realization that only one of his eyes was open.

With a sense of dread, he knew he was awake . . . with no idea who he was, where he was or what had happened to him . . .

*

Subsequent awakenings increased his dread. He came to understand that the ringing was inside his head. It grew more bearable with each return to consciousness, but he couldn't hear what was said by the faces that stared down at him. Their mouths opened and closed but nothing reached him. Nor did he know if his own mouth was relaying the signals his brain was sending to it. He tried to speak of his fears, but the lack of response in the faces above him persuaded him his lips weren't moving.

Time was meaningless. He couldn't tell how often he drifted in and out of consciousness or how long his periods of sleep lasted. He convinced himself that days and weeks had passed since he'd been brought to this place, and a slow anger burned inside him as threads of insight began to knit together. Something cataclysmic had happened. He was in hospital. The talking heads were doctors. But they weren't helping him and they couldn't see that he was awake. He had a terrifying anxiety that he was in the hands of enemies – *why?* – or that he was trapped forever in a paralysed state that allowed him to think and reason, but left him unable to communicate.

The dark-haired woman suffocated him. He hated the smell of her and the touch of her hand on his skin. She was always there, weeping soft, round tears down her pale cheeks, but her sadness failed to move Acland. He knew intuitively that the tears were for show, not for him, and he despised her for her lack of sincerity. He felt he should recognize her. Every time he woke and watched her through a half-closed lid, a sense of familiarity swam just below the surface.

He knew his father before he knew her. Recognition of the tired-looking man who hovered at the edges of his vision came like an electric shock. In the next moment, he knew who the woman was and why her touch repulsed him. Other memories flooded back. He recalled his name. Charles Acland. His occupation. Lieutenant, British Army. His last deployment. Iraq.

He had a clear recollection, which he played over and over in his mind because it offered an explanation, of boarding an RAF Hercules on the day he left for the Middle East. He guessed the plane must have crashed on take-off, for his last memory was of buckling himself into his seat.

*

'Charles. Wake up, Charles.' Fingers pinched the skin on his hand. 'There's a good boy. Come on, now. Wake up.'

He opened his eye and looked at the middle-aged nurse who was bending over him. 'I heard you,' he said. The words came out as a long slur but he knew he'd said them.

'You've had an operation and you're now in recovery,' she told him, answering the question she thought he'd asked. *Where am I?* 'If all goes well, you'll be returned to your own bed this afternoon. You're connected to a PCA pump –' she guided his left hand towards a control set – 'otherwise known as patient-controlled analgesia. It allows you to be in charge of your own post-operative care. You shouldn't need any pain relief for a while, but if you begin to feel discomfort press the white button. The morphine will help you sleep.'

He jerked his hand away immediately.

'It's up to you,' she said easily, 'but this way you can manage the pain yourself. The doses are measured and the machine overrides any attempt at self-indulgence.' She smiled cheerfully. 'You won't be on it long enough to become an addict, Charles. Trust me.'

He didn't. He had an instant understanding that he didn't trust any woman, although he had no idea why that should be.

The nurse held up a black plastic egg-shaped object. 'I'm going to put this in your right hand. Tell me if you can feel it.'

'Yes.'

'Good man.' She placed his thumb on a button at the top. 'Push that if you need me. I'll be keeping a close eye on you, but in case of emergencies, holler. You're a lucky fellow. If God hadn't given you a skull like a rhinoceros, you wouldn't have survived.'

She started to move away but Acland used his free hand to catch at her skirt. 'How did it crash?'

'Say again.'

He took the words back into his throat like a ventriloquist and repeated them in slow, guttural fashion. 'Khow . . . di' . . . i' . . . khrash?'

'How did what crash?'

'The plane.' He tried again. 'Khe khlane. I was on a khlane.'

'Don't you remember what happened?'

He shook his head.

'OK. I'll ask someone to explain it to you.' She patted his hand again. 'But don't worry, love. You've got a few wires crossed, that's all. They'll right themselves eventually.'

*

Time passed and nothing happened. The nurse returned at intervals, but her complacent smiles and inane comments annoyed him. Once or twice, he attempted to remind her that he needed explanations but, out of stupidity or bloody-mindedness, she refused to understand what he was saying. A scream was circling around his head and he found himself struggling with anger in a way that he didn't understand. *Everything*, from the curtained cubicle he was lying in to the sounds from outside – muted voices, footsteps, a phone ringing – conspired to ratchet up his irritation.

Even the nurse had lost interest. He counted off the seconds between her visits. Three hundred. Four hundred. When the interval reached five hundred, he put his finger on the buzzer and kept it there. She bustled in with a stupid laugh and attempted to remove the plastic egg from his hand, but he wrestled it away from her and held it against his chest. 'Fuck you.'

She had no trouble understanding that, he thought, watching her smile disappear. 'I can't turn it off if you keep your finger on it,' she said, indicating a bleeping light on a remote receiver clipped to her waistband. 'You'll have everyone in here if you don't let go.'

'Good.'

'I'll disconnect it,' she warned. 'You're not the only patient who's had surgery today.' She held out her palm. 'Come on, Charles. Give me a break, eh? I've made the call. It's not my fault it's taking so long. This is a National Health Service hospital, and there's only one psychiatric consultant on call at the moment. He'll be here before long. You have to trust me on that.'

He tried to say he didn't need a psychiatrist. There was nothing wrong with his brain. He simply wanted to know what had happened. There were other men on the plane. Had they survived? But the concentration needed to speak the words (which were incomprehensible even to his own ears) was so intense that the woman easily deprived him of his buzzer. He swore at her again.

She checked the PCA, saw that he hadn't used it. 'Is it pain that's making you angry?'

'No.'

She didn't believe him. 'No one expects you to be a hero, Charles. Pain-free sleep will do you more good than staying awake and becoming frustrated.' She shook her head. 'You shouldn't be this alert anyway, not after what you've been through.'

*

When the psychiatrist finally arrived, he said much the same thing. 'You look brighter than I was expecting.' He introduced himself as Dr Robert Willis and drew up a chair beside Acland's recovery-room trolley. He was mid-fifties, thin and bespectacled, with a habit of staring into his patients' eyes when he wasn't consulting a computer printout of their notes, which he placed on his knees. He confirmed Acland's name and rank, then asked him what his last memory was.

'Khetting o' kh' khlane.'

'In England?'

Acland stuck a thumb in the air.

Willis smiled. 'Right. I think it might be better if I do the talking. We don't want to make this painful for you . . . or for me. Give me a thumbs-up for yes and a thumbs-down for no. Let's start with a simple question. Do you understand what I'm saying?'

He watched the lieutenant's thumb shoot up.

'Good. Do you know what happened to you?'

Acland jabbed repeatedly towards the floor.

The man nodded. 'Then we'll take this slowly. Do you remember arriving in Iraq? No. Do you remember anything about Iraq?' Repeated downward jabs of the thumb. 'Nothing at all? Your base? Your command? Your squad?'

Acland shook his head.

'Right. Well, I can only go by the medical and regimental reports that came with you, and the newspaper coverage that I've just taken off the net, but I'll tell you as much as I know. If there's anything you want repeated, raise your hand.'

Acland learned that he'd spent eight weeks attached to one of the UK military bases near Basra. He had taken command of a four-Scimitar, twelve-man reconnaissance troop whose task was to search out insurgent crossing points along the Iraq/Iran border. He and his troopers made two recce patrols, each of three weeks' duration, which were described by his CO as 'extremely successful'. Following a few days R&R, his troop was then deployed to recce ahead of a convoy on the Baghdad to Basra highway. As commander, Acland was in the lead Scimitar with his two most experienced troopers, Lance Corporals Barry Williams and Doug Hughes. The vehicle had been attacked by an improvised explosive device buried in a roadside culvert. The two lance corporals had died in the explosion, but Acland had been thrown clear. All three men had been recommended for decoration.

Willis turned a piece of paper towards the young lieutenant.

It was a printout of a newspaper article with a banner headline saying: *Our Heroes*. To the side, under a photograph of him at his passing-out parade, were two portraits of smiling men, posing with their wives and children, over the caption: *devastated families mourn brave dads*. His own caption read: *seriously injured but alive*. 'Do you recognize them, Charles? This –' he touched a face – 'is Barry Williams and this is Doug Hughes.'

Acland stared at the pictures, trying to find something he remembered – a feature, a smile – but he might have been looking at strangers for all the recognition he had of them. He suppressed a surge of panic because he'd shared a Scimitar with these men on two extended recce trips and knew how close he must have grown to them. Or *should* have done. It didn't make sense that he could forget his men so easily. 'No.'

Perhaps Willis noticed his concern, because he told him not to worry about it. 'You took a hell of a knock to the head. It's not surprising you have holes in your memory. It's usually just a question of time before things start to return.'

'Khow khong?'

'How long? It depends how bad your concussion is. A few days, perhaps. You won't remember everything all at once . . . We tend to retrieve memory bit by bit, but—' He broke off as Acland shook his head.

'Khow khong –' he pointed to himself – 'khere?'

'How long have *you* been *here*?'

Acland nodded.

'About thirty hours. You're in a hospital on the outskirts of Birmingham. It's Tuesday, 28 November. The attack happened on Friday and you arrived here early yesterday. You had a CAT scan during the afternoon and an operation this morning to plate the bones in your left cheek and above your left eye.' Willis smiled. 'You're in pretty good shape, all things considered.'

Acland raised his thumb in acknowledgement, but the conversation had done little to allay his fears or his sense of resentment.

How could he forget eight weeks of his life? How could thirty hours have turned into an eternity? Why had the nurse said his wires were crossed?

What was wrong with him?

*

The days that followed were difficult ones. Acland lost count of the number of times he was told he was lucky. Lucky he'd been thrown clear before the vehicle turned over. Lucky the insurgents were too few in number, or too poorly armed, to follow up the attack by shooting him. Lucky the shrapnel hadn't entered his brain. Lucky he still had the sight of one eye. Lucky the blast hadn't destroyed his hearing completely. Lucky he was still alive . . .

For whatever reason, he'd been put in a side room away from other patients. Acland suspected it was his mother's doing – she had a habit of getting her own way – but he didn't complain. If the choice was between being stared at by his parents or being stared at by every Tom, Dick and Harry who entered the ward, he was better able to tolerate his parents. But he found their constant presence draining.

His father was the worst culprit on the 'lucky' front. Unable to understand what his son was saying, or too impatient to work it out, he would take up a stance by the window and keep repeating phrases like 'The gods were smiling on you that day', 'Your mother can't believe how close we came to losing you', 'They told us it was touch and go at the beginning', 'Damnedest thing I've ever come across.'

For the most part Acland pretended to be asleep, because he was bored with playing the 'thumbs-up' game. He didn't feel lucky and he saw no reason why he should pretend that he did. At twenty-six, he had his whole life in front of him, but it didn't look like being the life he'd chosen for himself. He felt a cold knot of fear every time his father mentioned the future.

'The army gives grants for retraining, Charles. What do you think about signing up to an agricultural course for a couple of years? You might as well learn the modern way of doing things at the taxpayers' expense.'

Acland stared at the wall in front of him.

'It was just a thought. Your mother's keen to have you home. She suggested we put you in the annexe so that you have your own space.'

The idea was abhorrent to Acland. He tolerated his mother's presence in his room because he had to, but he was becoming increasingly resistant to her touch. Whenever possible, he crossed his arms to avoid having his hand stroked, wondering what she'd been told about his condition that meant he had to be treated like a child. It wasn't as if she'd caressed him when he *was* a child. Demonstrations of affection never happened in the Acland household.

The only respite he had was when the medical staff took over and his parents were asked to leave. He appreciated the consultant surgeon, Mr Galbraith, who talked him through his injuries and told him what he could expect in the coming months. Galbraith explained that the damage was to the left-hand side of his face, that he'd lost a considerable portion of soft tissue due to the splitting and burning effects of the shrapnel, and that his eye had been damaged beyond repair. Nevertheless, reconstructive surgery had improved immeasurably in the last decade through the use of microvascular techniques and tissue expanders, and the surgical team was confident of a good outcome.

Galbraith warned Acland that to achieve the best results might take months. Operations could last up to fourteen hours; the patient needed recovery time of weeks between ops; and other specialisms, such as neurosurgery and ophthalmology, might have to be brought in for assessment and assistance. The aim of the team would be to keep impaired nerve functioning to a minimum and to source a donor site that wouldn't result in a visible difference between the colour and texture of the grafted skin flaps and the skin of the face, particularly in the reconstruction of the lid and socket tissue to accommodate a glass eye.

The surgeon looked for a reaction, but didn't find one. 'I hope that's gone some way to putting your mind at rest, Charles,' he said. 'I realize it's a lot to take in at one go, but the message is an optimistic one. When you're talking more freely, you can fire as many questions at me as you like.' He offered a hand. 'I look forward to knowing you better.'

Acland grasped the hand and held on to it to keep the man from going. What he wanted to say was, 'Why would I need a neurosurgeon?' but the words were too complicated. Instead, he touched the side of his head with his other hand and asked, 'Is brain OK?'

Galbraith nodded. 'As far as we can tell.'

He released the man's hand. 'Why can't I re – emb – er?'

'Because you were unconscious for three days and amnesia is a common symptom of traumatic head injury. Are you having problems understanding what's said to you?'

'No.'

'You certainly don't look as if you are. Dr Willis described you as extremely alert for someone who'd been out cold for three days. Do you remember talking to him?'

'Yes.'

'Do you remember the details he gave you about the attack?'

'Yes.'

Galbraith smiled. 'Then you've nothing to worry about. It's short-term memory loss that's disabling. Sufferers struggle to understand or retain information . . . They lose skills they once took for granted and have to undergo prolonged therapy to relearn them. Yours is localized or retrograde amnesia, which means you've forgotten events within a defined time period. It's quite normal after concussion . . . but rarely permanent.' He examined Acland's inexpressive face. 'Does that reassure you?'

No . . . But the lieutenant stuck his thumb in the air anyway. He couldn't bear the thought of any more fussing. He'd have no privacy left if anyone knew what was going on inside his head.

Confidential Memo

To:	Dr Robert Willis, Psychiatric Dept
From:	Nursing Station 3
Senior Nursing Officer:	Samantha Gridling
Patient:	Lt Charles Acland 893406
Room:	312
Date:	5 December 2006

Thank you for taking my call and apologies for interrupting your session. Further to the brief outline I gave you over the phone, please find further details below. I've since questioned my staff to see if anyone else has had a run-in with Charles, and several have reported a refusal to answer questions, being sworn at, an almost permanent anger and suspicion about medication and analgesia. There's no question in my mind that he's targeting the female nurses, since none of the male nurses made any complaints.

FYI: One of the auxiliaries – Tracey Fielding – told me he ordered her to 'take her fucking hands' off him this morning when she tried to straighten his bed. Tracey says he spoke quite fluently and she had no trouble understanding him. She decided to treat it as a joke and answered, 'You should be so lucky,' but abandoned the bed-making because Charles was clearly on edge.

The two incidents I mentioned to you over the phone were also directed at women, myself being one, and both involved violence or threats of violence. They are:

1. Yesterday evening, Charles lost his temper with his mother. She told me she was trying to comb his hair when he caught her

by the wrist and forced her arm on to the bed. She said he looked 'absolutely furious' and twisted her hand backwards until she was kneeling on the floor. It was only because her husband came into the room and managed to release her that Charles didn't hurt her badly. Both parents are understandably upset and I suggested they stay away for twenty-four hours. I'd like you to talk to them about going home for good. While no one can condone Charles's behaviour, it's clear to all of us that his mother is driving him mad. She calls him 'her little boy' (!!!) both to his face and in front of others.

2. As soon as Mr and Mrs Acland left, I went to check on Charles. His door was closed, he'd detached himself from his drips and he was standing by the window. I invited him to get back into bed. When he took no notice, I walked towards the buzzer to call for assistance, and he moved in front of me to stop me doing it. Upright and with clenched fists, he's over six feet and very intimidating. I warned him that his behaviour was unacceptable, and he said quite clearly, 'I don't give a shit.' To avoid provoking him further, I left the room. When I returned five minutes later with a male nurse and a security guard, Charles was back in bed and reattached to his drips. Correctly! He was very pale, and I think he gave himself a scare, but he's a damn sight more 'with it' than any of us realized. His recovery speed is extraordinary.

I'd appreciate a visit ASAP after your return from Warwick. Pro tem, I've re-rostered the staff so that Charles has only male attendants, but there aren't enough available to make the rota workable for more than 48 hours. I'm also concerned that his mother won't stay away. FYI: I will be on station till 17.00 but am contactable at home on 821581.

SNO Samantha Gridling, Nursing Station 3

Two

WILLIS DREW UP A CHAIR beside Acland's bed and placed his notes on his knee. If he'd had any doubt that his presence in the room was unwelcome, it was confirmed by the young man's stony indifference as he stared at the wall in front of him. 'I've got some good news and some bad news for you, Charles. The good news is that your parents have decided to go home and the bad news is that Tony Galbraith almost certainly gave you an exaggerated picture of what is achievable through reconstructive surgery.'

At least he had Acland's attention. The lieutenant's good eye flickered briefly in his direction.

'The surgeons will do what they can, but in the end you'll have to decide for yourself how much scarring you're prepared to live with. It's about learning to live with a different face. However good your medical team, however well you manage your own expectations, there will always be a gap between what you hope for and what is possible.'

Acland gave a grunt of what sounded like amusement. 'It must be worse than I thought if a shrink has to break the news.'

Willis avoided remarking on the improvement in his speech. 'It's not pretty,' he agreed frankly. 'The shrapnel burned the flesh down to the bone and took your eyelid and most of your eye. Realistically, you should expect some permanent scarring and problems with the nerve and muscle functions on that side of your face.'

'Message received and understood. Will try to be realistic, sir.'

Willis smiled. 'Robert will do just fine, Charles. I'm not in the

21

army. I'm a civilian psychiatrist who specializes in dealing with trauma.'

'To the head?'

'Not necessarily. Most injured men experience difficulty making the transition from active service to inactive patient. I gather you'd rather be out of bed than in it, for example.'

'There's nothing wrong with my legs.'

'Maybe not, but you were damn lucky to make it successfully in and out of bed yesterday. Forget the condition you arrived in . . . and the drugs you're on . . . and the fact that you had a major operation a week ago . . . your brain hasn't had time to adjust to mono-vision. By rights you should have gone arse over tit the minute you took your first step.'

'Well, I didn't.'

'No. You seem to have the constitution of an ox and the balance of a tightrope walker.' He eyed the young lieutenant curiously. 'How did you manage to catch your mother's wrist so easily? You should have missed by a mile.'

Acland produced a ball of tissue from under his sheet and tossed it from one hand to the other. 'I've been practising.'

'Why don't you want anyone to know?'

A shrug. 'It's like a zoo in here . . . with me as the latest exhibit. People keep prodding me to see how I'm going to react. Most of the time I don't feel like performing.'

'Is that why you shut your door last night?'

'Partly.'

'Why else?'

'To show that I could. I knew someone would barge in eventually to prove they were doing their job properly.'

'The senior nurse found you intimidating.'

'Good.' He spoke with satisfaction.

Willis made a note. 'Don't you like her?'

'Am I supposed to?'

Strange answer, Willis thought, giving one of his dry smiles. 'You're outside my usual remit, Charles. As a rule it takes weeks for patients to become as stroppy as you seem to be. They start by being grateful and compliant and only become irritated when progress isn't as quick as they'd like.' He paused. 'Are you in pain?'

'If I am I can ask for something.'

The psychiatrist consulted his papers again. 'Except you never do. According to what I have here, you didn't use the PCA and you refuse analgesics. Are you really pain-free . . . or is it a macho thing?' He paused for an answer. 'You ought to have a continuous dull ache around the site of your surgery, and acute stabs of pain every time you cough or move. Is that not happening?'

'I can live with it.'

'You don't need to. Your recovery won't happen any faster because you suffer. It might even hinder it.' He studied the young man's impassive face. 'Is your amnesia still worrying you? Are you blaming the opiates for it?'

'How can I remember anything if I turn myself into a zombie?'

'And you think pain's any different? It's just as deadening to the concentration as morphine.' He watched Acland toss the tissue ball again to prove him wrong. 'Well, maybe not in your case,' he said with dry humour. 'What have you remembered so far?'

'Nothing much. I had a flashback where I was being driven along a road that I didn't recognize . . . but now I'm thinking it was a dream.'

'I doubt it. Snippets of memory always feel like dreams at first. You'll know they're real when you can put them in context.' He leaned forward encouragingly. 'Being able to recall your command will take the uncertainty out of it. I imagine doubt about your leadership is what's troubling you the most, isn't it?'

Acland stared rigidly back at him. He had no intention of discussing his fears with anyone, let alone a psychiatrist.

Willis took off his glasses to give himself an excuse to look away. 'There's nothing alarming about your amnesia, Charles,' he murmured, using a corner of Acland's sheet to polish the lenses. 'The brain bruises like any other part of the body when it takes a knock. It just needs time to heal.'

'That's OK, then.'

'You'd be in a lot more trouble if the metal had come at you from a different angle or you hadn't been wearing your helmet when you were thrown from the vehicle. A pierced or shattered skull is a different kettle of fish entirely. The brain doesn't recover easily from that kind of damage.'

'So I was lucky?'

'Certainly . . . if the only choice was between serious brain damage and concussion. Real good fortune would have been that the shrapnel missed you altogether.' He replaced his spectacles. 'I gather you don't like being told you're lucky.'

'What makes you say that?'

'You lost your temper yesterday morning when one of the auxiliaries urged you to cheer up because you're better off than some of the others in here.'

'That's not what she said.'

'What did she say?'

'Invited me to keep my pecker up . . . so I invited *her* to take her fucking hands off me.' He squeezed his fist round the tissues. 'She told me I should be so lucky, then stomped out of the room. I haven't seen her since.'

Willis was nonplussed. 'Are you saying she touched you inappropriately?'

'No, Doc,' Acland answered sarcastically, 'I'm saying she stood on one leg in the corner and danced a fandango. Look, it's no big deal. I don't enjoy being treated like a piece of meat . . . but I'm probably the only man in here who feels that way.'

'Do you want to report her?'

'No chance. She's already given her side of the story. Who's going to believe mine?'

Who indeed? As far as Willis knew there had been no similar complaints against Tracey Fielding. The interesting factor was how similar Acland's and Tracey's accounts were – it took only a small twist to put a sexual slant on the incident – and he wondered if Acland had deliberately read more into 'keep your pecker up' than had been intended. If so, it worried the psychiatrist, although he didn't pursue it.

Instead, he asked Acland if he had any objection to seeing his parents before they left. 'They're downstairs and they'd like to say goodbye.'

'Do you have a mirror? I might be more sympathetic if I know what my mother's been bawling about.'

Willis shook his head. 'There's nothing to see except bandages, Charles.'

The lieutenant pointed to the right-hand side of his face. 'Not on this side.'

'Yes, well, that's not pretty either, and I don't want you taking the wrong messages from it. You've got a black eye, your skin colour ranges from yellow to indigo and your face is still swollen . . . but the damage isn't permanent and you'll recognize yourself with no trouble in a few days.'

'I wouldn't bet on it,' said Acland with more truth than irony. 'Mum keeps referring to a photo in her wallet to remind herself what I used to look like . . . and Dad says my appearance was so altered when I arrived here – he claimed my head had swollen to twice its normal size – that he didn't believe the soldier on the trolley was his son.'

'That's not unusual, Charles. Often the impact of injury is greater on the family than it is on the individual. The patient knows what he has to do – survive and get better – but it requires a huge amount of ego-focused energy to achieve it. If he allows his family to drain that energy away, it becomes much harder. Parents and spouses rarely understand that. They subscribe to the myth that love cures everything and feel rejected if their love isn't wanted.'

Acland stared at his hands. 'I hope you told my folks that. It sounds like a much better reason for attacking my mother than the real one.'

'Which was?'

'Too many bloody questions.'

'I was told she tried to comb your hair.'

'That too.'

'What were the questions about?'

'Nothing of any importance.'

*

Acland watched the little pantomime of his father shepherding his mother protectively into the room to say goodbye and wondered if his lack of guilt was because he'd finally brought her to her knees. He paid lip service to her need to have every unpleasantness swept under the carpet by saying he was sorry and allowing her to kiss him on the cheek, but they both knew it was a charade. There was a little more warmth in the handshake he gave his father, but only because he knew the kind of recriminations the man was going to face for his son's misdemeanour.

*

Over time, as some of his memories began to return, Acland asked Robert Willis why the process was so unpredictable.

'In what way?'

'I remember some things but not others.'

'What sort of things?'

'People . . . briefings . . . a couple of recces that we made . . . the heat . . . the landscape.'

'Do you remember your two lance corporals?'

Acland nodded. 'There's a cleaner here who smiles the way Barry smiled. I get flashbacks every time I see him.'

'Doug, too?'

'Yes. They were good blokes.'

'Do you have any memories from the day of the attack?'

'No. I don't even remember receiving the orders.'

'But you know what they were. I showed you the report. Intelligence had a tip-off that the convoy might be targeted, so your CO sent his best crew to scout ahead. He said he had complete confidence in you and your men.'

'What else could he say?' asked Acland cynically. 'If he'd slagged us off, morale would hit rock bottom. Soldiers would question what the hell they were doing there when even their CO doesn't stick up for them. It's bad enough that the British public thinks we're fighting a rotten war.'

He spent his time watching the twenty-four-hour news channels on the television in his room. Occasionally, Willis took him to task for it, arguing that a concentrated diet of shock-value news gave a distorted view of the world. War was the currency of broadcasters, not of the man in the street. Acland ignored the advice, denying that he felt a personal involvement with the British soldiers in Iraq and Afghanistan, or that he found each new death depressing.

'Your CO spoke very highly of you,' Willis reminded him now, 'described all three of you as men of the highest calibre. Aren't you being decorated for it?'

'Only mentioned in dispatches. If we'd been the best we wouldn't have been taken out so easily.'

Willis eyed him thoughtfully for a moment, then flipped through the papers on his knee. He withdrew a sheet. 'This is a paragraph from the investigators' report. "Lieutenant Acland's Scimitar was attacked by two improvised explosive devices which were buried in freshly dug culverts at the side of the road and detonated simultaneously as the vehicle passed. The culverts were tunnelled by sophisticated moling equipment and the explosives detonated by remote signal."' He ran his finger down a few lines. 'It details evidence taken from the scene and from a video made by the insurgents, and it goes on: "This suggests an expertise in the construction, camouflage, placing and detonation of IEDs that has hitherto only been seen in Northern Ireland. Future training must include this development to avoid further loss of life. It is no longer enough to alert men to the possibility of a single roadside bomb in a burnt-out car or rubbish bin."'

He looked up. 'What they're saying is that there was nothing you could have done. You and your men were the first victims of a new form of attack, and your only mistake was to be in the wrong place at the wrong time.' He read continued cynicism in Acland's expression. 'What makes you think it was your fault?'

'Nothing.'

'Did any of your squad express dissatisfaction with your command?'

'Not that I recall . . . but maybe I've chosen to forget it.'

Willis gave one of his dry smiles. 'You're confusing different types of amnesia, Charles. Yours – which goes by the general term of retrograde amnesia – is usually the result of head injury or disease, and is not governed by choice. Emotional amnesia – which *may* involve an element of choice – follows a traumatic psychological experience. In some cases this is so devastating to an individual's ability to function that he blocks all memory of the incident in order to cope.' He paused. 'Nothing that I've seen suggests your amnesia has an emotional basis . . . but perhaps there's something you haven't told me?'

'Like what?'

'Did anything happen before you left for Iraq?'

Acland stared at him for a moment. 'Nothing important.'

It was his favourite answer, thought Willis. 'Perhaps not,' he murmured, 'but I suspect most people would say that being ditched by their fiancée on the day of their departure was –' he sought for a word – '*upsetting*.'

Anger flared briefly in the younger man's face. 'Who told you that?'

'Your parents. They couldn't understand why you never mentioned Jen or why she hadn't phoned or sent a card . . . so your mother called her. Jen told her she couldn't go through with it and felt it was fairer to let you know before you left. Is that what happened?'

'Pretty much.' Acland produced a tissue ball and tossed it idly from hand to hand. 'It must have pissed my mother off something chronic to hear it was Jen who ditched *me*.'

'Why?'

'She spent months trying to make it happen the other way round.'

'You were supposed to ditch Jen? Didn't your mother like her?'

'Of course not. She hates competition.'

Willis could believe that. He'd admired Mrs Acland's fine-boned looks but he hadn't liked her. He'd seen no more sincerity in her showy displays of grief than her son had done. 'Were you upset by Jen's letter?'

'I never read it.'

'She told your mother she sent it by registered post to your base.'

'I didn't bother to open it . . . just chucked it in the bin.'

Willis tapped the end of his pen against the notes on his lap. 'You must have known what was in it. You had Jen's name deleted from your records as someone to be informed in the event of your death.'

'When?'

'Presumably on your arrival in Iraq.'

'I don't remember.'

'Do you remember feeling any grief? Do you feel grief now?'

'No.'

Willis was sceptical. 'Most of us do when relationships end, Charles. Novelists don't write about broken hearts for no reason. Sometimes the pain can go on for months.'

'I don't feel anything for her at all.'

Willis tried a different tack. 'What did you think of your CO? Would you describe *him* as a good bloke?'

'Sure. He lost his rag from time to time but he never held grudges.'

'What about the job you were doing? You talked about loss of morale earlier. Was morale low while you were out there?'

'Not where I was . . . but we didn't have much contact with the locals. It was the guys on the ground in Basra who took the brunt of the resentment, and they all said that was hard to deal with.'

29

'Were you afraid at any point?'

'Yes.'

'When?'

'Every time a car came towards us with a solitary driver. We held our breath until he passed in case he was a suicide bomber.'

'So you remember some feelings – you liked the people you worked with, you empathized with low morale, and you were afraid – but you've suppressed your feelings for your fiancée. What do you think that means?'

Acland gave an ironic shrug. 'That I had to forget her to function properly?'

'Except you haven't forgotten her, you just don't like her any more.' Willis watched him pump his hands together, monotonously squeezing air from between his palms. 'What emotion do you think you'd have felt if you had read her letter?'

'I didn't read it.'

He was lying, Willis thought. 'Would you have been hurt?'

The lieutenant shook his head. 'I'd have been angry.'

'Then you must have been angry whether you read it or not, since you obviously knew it was a "Dear John" letter.' He took off his glasses and rubbed them on his cuff. 'Why does anger worry you?'

'Who says it does?'

'You implied your amnesia had an emotional basis, and you've been struggling with anger since you arrived here. It's a strong emotion. I'm wondering if you think it caused you to fail your command in some way.'

'How?'

'Lack of concentration.' Willis replaced his glasses and studied the young man. 'I think you're blaming the deaths of your men on the fact that your mind was on Jen . . . and you've convinced yourself that's why you've forgotten the attack. You believe you were guilty of negligence.'

Acland didn't answer.

'I don't pretend to understand every working of the brain,

Charles – it's a complex organ that contains around one hundred billion neurones – but I doubt the two events are related. You might have been distracted during the first week of your deployment but not after two months. I imagine you placed Jen in a box to concentrate on suicide bombers – it's what most of us would do in the same situation – and anger never came into it. It's hardly plausible that you'd box up the bombers to concentrate on her, is it . . . not if you held your breath every time a car went by?'

'No.' The young lieutenant's hands relaxed suddenly. 'But it's odd. She was a damn good fuck. I'd expect to feel *something*.'

DR ROBERT WILLIS

MD, PSYCH

Extracts from notes on Lt Charles Acland
January/February 2007

. . . Charles is suspicious of me. He wants to return to active service, and his reluctance to talk about his anxieties is clearly associated with this ambition. He thinks I'm acting for the army as a 'mental health monitor'. [Query: How worried is he about his state of mind?]

. . . He places too much weight on his mental health assessment and not enough on his physical handicaps. I wonder if the reason for this is that he's adapted well to the loss of his eye but hasn't come to terms with the psychological impacts of sudden inactivity . . . the death of his men . . . feelings of inadequacy . . . guilt, etc. . . .

. . . Personality change It's hard to form an opinion after the event, but his current demeanour – cold restraint broken by occasional bursts of temper – seems to be new. His CO describes him as a 'popular, outgoing officer with excellent leadership ability and good social skills' . . . his parents as 'loving and dependable', a 'nice person with numerous friends'. Both suggest a confident extrovert personality who conformed well to the conventions of the middle class. [Query: Why am I seeing an angry, introspective 'rebel'?]

. . . I'm struck by Charles's intelligence, which appears to be well above average. He is alert and observant – viz. his ability to reattach his own drips correctly – and has learned to compensate for his blind side in record speed. He's also highly motivated and has developed his own fitness regime since being allowed out of bed.

. . . He's reticent about his relationships, blocking questions about his parents by saying he gets on well with them. [NB This is clearly untrue, particularly re his mother.] However, he did describe them on one occasion as 'mutually absorbed' and 'complacent'. When I asked if this meant he felt excluded, he said, 'Not at all. I've always been my own person.'

. . . He claims he had no problems being sent away to boarding school at eight. 'It gave me independence.' [NB Independence seems to matter to him. He refers to the family farm as 'the ball and chain'. 'I'm an only child. I'm expected to marry and have children and inherit the damn thing.']

. . . His indifference towards his fiancée appears to be genuine, although mention of her irritates him. He says she's 'history', therefore talking about her is pointless. He shows a similar indifference to the people who've sent cards. He doesn't write letters or make phone calls, and he's requested no visitors.

. . . Self-imposed isolation He spends hours alone in thought or watching the news channels on television. He avoids, or cuts short, any attempts at communication, often through rudeness. He distrusts and/or is contemptuous of the medical staff and other patients, has difficulty containing his frustration at what he perceives as stupidity or slowness, and transfers his anger and aggression into physical activity, such as pumping his palms together or clenching his fists.

. . . He rejects any idea that disfigurement is a contributory factor, claiming he doesn't care what people think. [NB This is

almost certainly untrue. He shows typical symptoms of a
patient with facial deformity . . . refers to himself as a 'freak
show' . . . dislikes being stared at . . . has difficulty judging
other people's reactions . . . distrusts shows of friendship . . .
talks regularly about being in 'a zoo' . . . turns his chair so that
his uninjured side is towards the door.]

. . . <u>Attitudes to sex</u> Despite describing Jen as 'a damn good
fuck', he blocks every question on the subject and presents as
a sexually repressed individual. He's highly protective of
himself, particularly his genitals. He objects to female nurses
and has accused one of the men of being gay. [Query: Is this
repression or obsession? Query: Sexual orientation? Not clear.]

. . . <u>Traumatic brain injury/subsequent antisocial behaviour</u>
I asked Henry Watson to take another look at the CAT scan for
frontal lobe damage. He remains of the opinion that there is
none but suggested a second scan, using MRI. He confirmed
my assessment that Charles's current symptoms are not typical
of an antisocial disorder but refused to offer a view on whether
a changed personality occurred suddenly or evolved over time.

. . . He expressed some concern about Charles's contempt for
others, which implies arrogance, lack of empathy and an
inability to connect emotionally, but was less troubled by the
shows of aggression – attack on mother, clenched fists, etc. –
which he described as 'hot-blooded'. [NB Typically, sociopaths
show no emotional discharge when they're angry but plan
their violent reprisals in dispassionate 'cold-blooded' ways.]

. . . <u>Reprisal</u> Watson suggested I contact the ex-fiancée to find
out if Charles has made any attempts to communicate with
her . . .

From: Jennifer Morley [jen@morley.freeline.net]
Sent: 21.02.2007 16:56
To: robert.willis@southgeneral.nhs.uk
Subject: Lt Charles Acland

Dear Dr Willis

Thank you for your letter. I hope you don't mind an email in return, but I thought it would be quicker. I'll answer your last question first. No, Charlie hasn't been in contact since before he went to Iraq. In fact I wouldn't have known he'd been injured, or which hospital he was in, if his mother hadn't phoned. I gathered from what she said that Charlie hadn't told her we'd split up. Well, I'm not surprised! As far as I know, he never tells his parents anything.

I was extremely sorry to hear what happened, and I hate the idea that Charlie doesn't want me to know. He must realize I still care about him. We were together for about nine months in total – dating on and off for the first two, an 'item' for the next four, and engaged from July of last year. I've written several times, but I haven't had a reply. I've also phoned the hospital every few days, but the operator won't connect me.

I assumed this meant he was unable to write or talk, but your letter says he's up and about and doing well. His mother said he has amnesia, and from the letters after your name I'm guessing you're a psychiatrist. Am I right? So is amnesia what you're helping him with? I should perhaps mention that my phone's rung a few times recently but when I pick it up there's only silence and the caller's number is always withheld. I was thinking it was a nuisance caller, but now I'm wondering if it's Charlie. If so, can you tell him I'd like to speak to him?

I can't believe he's forgotten me – that wouldn't be possible, would it? I mean, we were <u>so</u> close. I'm not sure how amnesia works, but I'm quite hoping Charlie's forgotten why we split. It was a stupid row about nothing and I feel <u>awful</u> about it now. I get the feeling the person on the other end really wants to talk to me but loses courage when he hears my voice. Do you think it's Charlie?

You say it will help his recovery if you know more about me and the relationship we had together. Which means Charlie hasn't told you anything. Why aren't I surprised?!!! (You're looking at the original zipped mouth. Charlie never talks about anything to do with himself, and it all goes back to his mother. She's the original control freak. You could have knocked me over with a feather when she phoned. I only met her once and she didn't like me one little bit. Too much competition in the 'looks' department, according to Charlie!)

Charlie's a chameleon. He projects different images of himself to different people. With his regiment, he's a man's man. With me, he's a woman's man. With his parents, he clams up and pretends he's not there. I accused him once of lacking the confidence to be himself, but he said there was no point getting into arguments unless he had to. The trouble is, when the arguments finally happen, it's always red-mist stuff. That's why we split. A silly little row turned into a full-scale war.

I'm not what Charlie's parents wanted in a daughter-in-law. He was supposed to marry a home-maker, not an ambitious London-based actress. I've had a few small parts on TV but most of my work's in the theatre, and Mary and Anthony went from approval of the engagement to disapproval in ten seconds flat when I said I wasn't planning to leave London or have babies any time soon. If at all, in fact. Charlie then dropped his bombshell about the farm – that there was no way he would ever take it on – and his parents blamed me for setting him against the place. It caused a huge number of rows between them, which inevitably spilled over into our relationship.

We met at a New Year's Eve party at the end of 2005. Charlie was more smitten than I was at the beginning – he told me it was a *coup de foudre* when he first saw me – but he's the kind of guy who grows on you. He's very persistent, very generous and very difficult to say no to. In some ways, he's every woman's idea of the perfect man – respectful, patient, good-looking, determined, kind – Mr Darcy in fact. But in others, he's a bit of a nightmare, because he keeps his emotions bottled up and only says what he <u>really</u> thinks when he's angry.

Yes, I did send a 'Dear John' letter the day before he went to Iraq. We'd had this huge bust-up (the row) the last time I saw him – the week before – and he hadn't bothered to apologize. I think now that he was stressed out about going to war, but he did and said some things that were unforgivable and I decided the relationship wasn't worth it. I talked it over with a friend and she said there was no excuse for violence. She also said it would be fairer to tell him sooner rather than later.

I regret the letter now because I should have been more understanding. Charlie masks his feelings so much that it's difficult to tell when he's nervous or afraid, and I truly believe he was both before he left for Iraq. He said once that manoeuvres were no real test of ability under fire because soldiers knew they wouldn't die in training. Another time he said that a commander had to be up to the task or he'd be letting his men down. I think those worries may have been preying on his mind and I feel so guilty that I added to them by taking my friend's advice. I shouldn't have listened to her. Perhaps he would have come home in one piece if I hadn't.

There's not much else I can tell you except that I'd love to see him. I did wonder if your letter meant that he feels similarly . . . I'm not saying that we can retrieve what we had immediately, or in precisely the same way – I can't take that level of possessiveness again – but we were very close for a long time and on my side there's still a huge amount of love and affection. Will you tell him that?

Thank you.

With best wishes,

Jen Morley

If you want to know more about Jen Morley, visit
www.jenmorley.co.uk

Three

WILLIS FLICKED THROUGH the notes in his lap. 'Has your fiancée made any attempts to contact you since you've been here, Charles?'

'*Ex*-fiancée,' Acland corrected, squeezing one fist inside the other. He was standing in his favourite position by the window in his room, leaving the doctor to sit in the chair. 'Why do you want to know?'

'Just interested. I thought she might have called to find out how you're getting on.' He studied Acland's unresponsive expression. 'Women have soft hearts. They forgive and forget very quickly when someone they've loved is in trouble.'

'There's nothing for her to forgive – *she's* the one who did the ditching – and there's not much to forget either. We weren't together that long.'

'You can store up quite a few memories in nine months, Charles.'

'Have you been talking to her?'

Willis avoided the question. 'Merely doing my research. It helps me to understand a patient if I know what was happening in the months before his trauma.'

'I'll take that as a yes.' Acland walked to his bedside cabinet and pulled open a drawer to remove a pile of unopened envelopes with his name and address written in the same handwriting. 'All yours,' he said, scattering the pile across the bed before returning to the window.

'Why don't you want to read them?'

'There'd be no point. I'm not planning to write back.' He watched Willis finger one of the envelopes. 'What's she been telling you?'

'I haven't spoken to her. She sent me an email, saying she regrets ending the relationship the way she did and would like to see you.'

'Meaning what?' Acland asked sarcastically. 'That she's blissfully happy and can afford to be generous to a cast-off? Or that she hasn't found anyone else and wants her meal ticket back?'

Again Willis hedged. 'Is that how you think she saw you?'

'It's how I *know* she saw me. All men are meal tickets to Jen.' He paused, inviting Willis to answer. 'It's not sour grapes, Doc. She has a good brain and a good body and she uses both to full advantage. I admired her for it when I liked her.'

'And now you don't?'

'Put it this way, I've no plans to let her take me for another ride.' He nodded to the envelopes. 'It makes me angry that she thinks she can. I wasn't that easy to manipulate even when we were together.'

Privately, Willis questioned the truth of that remark, suspecting the letters remained unread because Acland feared the turmoil that reawakened emotions might produce. He placed the point of his pen against a query he'd made on his notes. *Nuisance calls?* 'Have you thought about phoning her to tell her you're not interested?'

Acland shook his head. 'I've nothing to say that silence won't achieve better.'

Interesting choice of word, thought Willis. 'You mean that *ignoring* her won't achieve better?'

'Right.'

'But isn't that equally manipulative? In the absence of a definite no, silence is usually taken for assent . . . or at least a continuing willingness to listen. Perhaps she thinks you're reading her letters.'

'That's her problem.'

'Maybe so, but she wouldn't keep sending them if she knew

where she stood.' He paused. 'Does it amuse you that she's wasting her time?'

'No. It's up to her if she wants to write drivel . . . There's no law that says I have to look at it.'

'Do you think about revenge?'

'All the time. I've a hell of a score to settle with the Iraqis who killed my crew.'

'I meant against Jen.'

'I know you did and it was a stupid question, Doc. I can't even picture her face these days.' He studied the psychiatrist's thoughtful expression. 'If she sent you an email, you'll have visited her website and seen her photos. Who does she remind you of?'

'Uma Thurman.'

Acland nodded. 'She really works on the image – thinks it'll get her parts – but I have a better memory of Uma Thurman in *Gattaca* than I do of Jen. It was her favourite movie, even though it's ten years old now. We used to watch the DVD whenever she was bored . . . and now the only face I see if I bother to think of Jen at all is Uma's.' He went back to staring out of the window. 'It's a revenge of sorts. At least I get the last laugh.'

If what you're saying is true, Willis thought. 'Was Jen ever mistaken for Uma Thurman?'

'All the time. It was the whole point of the exercise . . . to be noticed.'

'Did that annoy you?'

'Sometimes, when she went too far.'

'How did she do that?'

'Pretended to *be* Uma Thurman . . . talked in an American accent. She only did it with women. It gave her a real buzz to see their mouths fall open.'

'What about men?'

Acland thumped one fist into the other and squeezed down until his knuckles turned white. 'She played herself. Your average bloke doesn't have the nerve to chat up a superstar. With men she

got her buzz out of persuading them she *wasn't* Uma Thurman
. . . just a stunning, but accessible, replica.'

'Were you jealous?'

'I'm sure Jen's told you I was. How long was this email? Did
she say I was so possessive she didn't have room to breathe?'

'Were you?'

He made a noise in his throat that sounded like a laugh. 'The
opposite, Doc. I wasn't possessive enough. Every time she went
through her sad little pantomime, it bored me stiff. I didn't sign
up to be the adoring boyfriend of Uma Thurman's stand-in.'

'What did you sign up for, Charles?'

'Not what I got.' He exhaled a breath on to the pane and
watched the water droplets evaporate almost immediately. 'I fell
for a fantasy.'

'Meaning what? That you wanted Uma Thurman and the
lookalike was a disappointment?'

Acland didn't answer.

'Was that Jen's fault?'

'You tell me.' He turned round, massaging his knuckles. 'I'm
sure it's all in her email.'

Willis gathered his papers together. 'You don't trust me much,
do you, Charles?'

'I don't know, Doc. I haven't come to a decision yet. When
you're not here, I never think about you at all . . . and when you
are, I'm thinking about my answers.'

*

During March, as if prompted by the early spring that had people
congregating in T-shirts in the sunshine, Willis talked about the
dangers of alienation and social withdrawal. He tried various ways
to spark a response from Acland, but a blunt appraisal of how
isolation could lead an individual to obsess about single issues –
usually people or topics that made him angry – was the only one
that worked.

'You're making me nervous, Doc. I get the feeling you're trying to tell me something you know I won't enjoy.'

'You're right,' said Willis. 'I want you to socialize more.'

'Why?'

'You spend too much time on your own and it's not good for you. Society hasn't gone away while you've been recuperating. The pressure to interact remains . . . as do the conventions that govern behaviour . . . and both those imperatives are particularly true of the army.'

They were sitting in the psychiatrist's office and Acland half-turned so that the light from the window struck the injured side of his face. Willis assumed the shift was deliberate, because in that profile it was impossible to believe the other side of the face was untouched. The observer saw only the slack, nerveless flesh, empty eye socket and hideous, discoloured gash that destroyed any beauty the man had ever had.

'Do you want to talk about why you're so reluctant to have visitors or mix with the other patients?' he went on.

'You mean apart from looking like a freak?' Acland turned back so that he could watch the doctor's reaction. 'That's what you're gagging to know, isn't it? Do I see myself as a freak?'

Willis arched an amused eyebrow. '*Do* you?'

'Sure. The two halves of my face don't match . . . and I don't recognize either.'

'Is that what keeps you in your room?'

'No. It's everyone else's injuries I can't take. There's a squaddie on the ward who got barbecued when his petrol tank exploded. If he survives he'll look like a tortoise – move like one, too. *He* knows it, *I* know it. There's nothing I can say to a guy like that.'

Willis watched him for a moment. 'How did you deal with injured men before, Charles? Did you wash your hands of them . . . leave the responsibility to someone else?'

'It's different in the field. All you have to say to a bloke who's down is that a chopper's on its way. He's probably out of it anyway, so he won't even know what's happened to him till he reaches the hospital.'

'Mm. So it's the long-term effects of injury that you have a problem with? Do you think the squaddie would be better off dead?'

Acland spotted a trap. 'I've no idea, Doc,' he answered lightly. 'I've never spoken to him. If he has the guts to see the ops through, then he's strong enough to live. That's the only answer I can give you.'

'And his quality of life?'

'Whatever he can make it.'

'Are you applying the same philosophy to yourself?'

'I'm hardly likely to say no, am I?'

'Why not?'

'You'll give me a black mark for depression.'

Willis sighed. 'I'm not interrogating you, Charles, I'm trying to help you. This isn't an exam . . . you don't get marked for it.' He folded his hands under his chin. 'You seem to have lost your confidence since your injury and I'm trying to find out why.'

'I'd say I was more confident. I used to care what people thought about me and now I don't.'

'I'd be more convinced of that if you tested yourself occasionally. Staying in your room and avoiding contact means you never expose yourself to what other people think.' He paused. 'One of life's nastier ironies is that we all know how important first impressions are because we use them ourselves . . . yet none of us wants to be judged on appearance alone.'

Acland cracked his knuckles. 'At least I wasn't barbecued,' he said impassively.

Willis glanced at his notes and took another tack. 'You've been complaining about headaches again.'

'I didn't complain . . . I merely mentioned I had one.'

'Where do they occur? Temple area? Top of the head? Back of the head?'

Acland gestured towards the left-hand side of his forehead.

'They start behind the dead eye and spread outwards. Mr Galbraith reckons it's phantom pain from losing the eye – the same way amputees get phantom pain in their stumps. He says it's effectively migraine and he's given me some guidelines on how to cope with it.'

'Good. Did he discuss your MRI scan with you?'

'Which one?'

'The most recent one,' said Willis drily.

'He said it was clear. Why did I need it anyway? I keep being told I haven't got brain damage, then someone goes behind my back and orders another scan.'

'Your surgeons need them. MRIs give a more detailed picture – for example, tiny blood clots which might explain the migraines.'

Acland watched him closely for a moment. 'Does an MRI show what a patient's thinking?'

'No.'

'Pity, because we could jack these conversations if it could. You're wasting your time on me. I'm not depressed and I'm not alienated . . . I'm *bored*. I don't want to be here. There's nothing wrong with me that a bit of stitching won't put right. If I talk to my mother on the phone, she goes on and on about people I've never heard of . . . and all my father can think about is which of his sheep has foot rot. I don't *care* about any of that. I don't *care* that the guy in the next room likes Jordan's tits. I just want this whole tedious exercise over so that I can get back to my unit. And, no, I'm not expecting miracles. I'm out of here the minute they've cobbled enough together to make me halfway presentable.'

'That's some speech for a man who doesn't say very much. You certainly don't sound depressed.'

'I'm not.'

'But do you understand my worries about withdrawal, Charles? If you're bored then do something active. You know where the gym is. The physios will work out a fitness regime that complements what you're already doing in your room.'

'I've tried that, and I left more frustrated than I arrived. I burn off more calories doing this –' he pumped his palms – 'than I did following their pathetic exercises.'

'You've tried it once,' Willis said mildly, 'and you left after fifteen minutes when another patient came in. The physios thought it was because you didn't want to be stared at.'

Acland shook his head.

'You called yourself a freak,' Willis reminded him.

'Only to emphasize that the rest of me is fine. I'm not good in this sort of environment, Doc. I used to jog six miles every morning before breakfast, and it does my head in to have some stupid woman whoop and holler if I manage to lift a miserable little dumbbell in one hand. Do you know how patronizing that is? The other patient was an amputee and she applauded like an idiot because he managed to hop a couple of steps. He's a regimental sergeant major, for Christ's sake. He'd have eaten her for breakfast before he had his leg blown off.'

'Nick Hay,' Willis agreed. 'He's stone deaf in one ear, so his balance is shot to pieces, and staying upright on one leg is a major achievement. Did you speak to him?'

'No.'

'Why not?'

'For the same reason I haven't spoken to the squaddie. What would I say? Look on the bright side, mate, you could have lost *both* legs? He knows damn well what his situation is . . . a medical discharge, followed by months of hawking himself around civvie street looking for a job.'

'Are you worried the same thing's going to happen to you?'

'No. The CO says he'll support me if I want to return to the regiment.' He frowned suspiciously as Willis glanced at his notes. 'Unless you've been told something different?'

'Only the usual. That you'll have to prove your fitness to the medical board.'

'That won't be a problem.'

'I hope you're right,' said Willis with what sounded like sincerity.

*

Sometimes Acland woke in the middle of the night, certain that maggots were devouring the raw flesh of his wounds. As a child, he'd seen a sheep die of blow-fly strike after larvae had eaten into the animal's living flesh, and the image still haunted him. His subconscious told him that the eyes were the entry point to his brain and he jerked out of sleep in a frenzy, kneading his empty socket to stop the blinding spasms of another migraine. But he kept such episodes to himself for fear of being diagnosed as paranoid.

*

Because he interpreted Willis's comments on withdrawal as a warning, he forced himself to socialize and phone his parents on a regular basis. He gained little from doing it except nods of approval from the psychiatrist, because his interest in other people's affairs was zero. It was a test of his endurance to sit through vacuous conversations about wives and children who meant nothing to him, or fake a response to a joke by lifting a thumb or making a grunt of acknowledgement in the back of his throat.

It helped that no one expected him to smile. He even found it curious that a lively expression could fade abruptly when the person he was speaking to remembered his disability. Once or twice, in the privacy of his room, he tested the elasticity of his reconstructed flesh in an attempt at a smile, but the ugly, lopsided grimace in the mirror looked more like an arrogant sneer than an expression of warmth.

His surgeons expressed pleasure at the progress he was making, but Acland wasn't impressed. After four months, the same number of operations and two lengthy recuperation periods outside hospital – which he chose to spend in a Birmingham hotel rather than return to his parents – his dead eye socket and tapered scar looked as livid and inelastic as they had ever done.

He found it easier to show no emotion at all, which was a truer reflection of how he felt, for without the means to demonstrate joy or empathy, the sensations themselves seemed to have withered and died.

Four

DESPITE WHAT HE'D TOLD Robert Willis, Acland hadn't forgotten Jen. In the same way that an orderly's smile reminded him of one of his dead soldiers, the turn of a woman's head sometimes reminded him of her. Such recognitions left him with none of the grief that memories of his crew evoked, but he hated the brief sensations of shock they gave him. It was one of the reasons why he preferred male nurses.

When the tap came at his open door on a Friday afternoon in April, he assumed it was a cleaner. He was standing at his window, watching a woman push a double amputee in a wheelchair along a tarmac path. They were of an age, so Acland guessed they were partners, but as neither could see the other's face their expressions said exactly what they were feeling. Both looked unhappy and frustrated, and it seemed to Acland that whatever relationship they'd had was over.

'Charlie?'

He recognized her voice immediately, and his reaction was so extreme that he had to put a hand against the window to steady himself. He thought he was experiencing shock again until adrenalin kicked in and he knew the emotion he felt was fear. He continued to stare out of the window. 'What are you doing here?'

'I came to see you.'

'Why?'

She put a husk into her voice. 'Do I need a reason, Charlie? I'd have come straight away if the hospital hadn't kept telling me you didn't want visitors.'

He ran his tongue round his mouth to produce some saliva. 'Whose idea was this? Dr Willis's?'

She avoided the question. 'I hoped you'd be pleased to see me.'

'Well, I'm not. The block on visitors hasn't changed. They shouldn't have told you where I was. Are you going to leave of your own accord or do you want me to call someone to throw you out?'

'At least let me say sorry before I go.'

'What for?'

'The way it ended.'

'I'm not interested. If I had been, I'd have read your letters.'

'Did you get them?' she asked with a catch in her voice. 'When you didn't answer, I thought perhaps the hospital was keeping them from you until your memory came back.'

'Well, now you know.'

'*Please*, Charlie.' He heard her step into the room. 'Couldn't we order a pot of tea or something? I came by train and it took me ages to get here . . . and the taxi from the station was like an oven.'

'Don't do this, Jen.'

She sighed. 'It wouldn't have happened if you hadn't kept going away.'

Acland told himself grimly not to be drawn into one of her blame games. 'Not interested,' he repeated.

There was a short silence and when she spoke again her tone had an edge to it. 'I could have reported you. Maybe I should have done. You wouldn't have been sent to Iraq if I had. I did think about it, you know.'

He watched the amputee put the brakes on his wheelchair to prevent his partner pushing him any further. 'I knew you weren't that stupid. Even a brain-dead zombie knows what mutually assured destruction is.'

She gave a small laugh. 'But I didn't have a regiment to be drummed out of. You might at least thank me for that.'

He didn't say anything.

She reverted to cajoling. 'I know you felt bad about it, darling,' she said in her soft voice, 'but if I'm willing to let bygones be bygones, can't we just forget all about it?'

God! It wasn't fear he was feeling, it was anger. *Incredible anger.* It ripped through his body like a tide, urging him to put his hands round her slender neck and squeeze the life out of her. 'You need to leave,' he said, struggling for composure. 'I stopped caring months ago and nothing you do or say will change that.'

'You know that's not true.'

He half-turned to show his uninjured side. She was dressed demurely in navy blue from her neck to below her knees, with her hair twisted up behind her head. He felt goose bumps on the back of his neck as another spurt of adrenalin drenched his system. His first instinct was to look at her hands.

'I wore it for you,' she said, reaching up to take the clip from the back of her head. 'Remember *Gattaca*? You always said you preferred Uma in uniform.' She smiled as her blonde hair fell to her shoulders. 'Does it bring back good memories?'

He didn't answer.

She pulled a face. 'You're such a bear. I thought you'd approve for once. It's when I showed too much that you used to complain.' She took another step forward and dropped her shoulder bag on to his chair, eyeing him from under her lids. 'It's just a look, Charlie. Image is everything these days. Will Dr Willis like it? You know he's been writing to me.'

Acland took a breath through his nose to calm himself. 'He's a psychiatrist . . . He doesn't judge people on appearance.'

Her face lit with amusement. 'Everyone does, Charlie. It's how the world works.' She tilted her head to one side to examine him. 'So what's wrong with you anyway? You look fine to me.'

'I want you to go, Jen.'

She ignored him. 'I can't, not yet. You haven't let me tell you how sorry I am.' She put the husk back into her voice. 'It was your fault, you know. You never tried to understand how unhappy

I was about you going away. I hardly recognized you when you came back from your desert training in Oman.'

'The feeling was mutual.'

'It was good at the beginning.'

Was it? All he could remember now were the fights. 'I don't want to do this, Jen.'

'Please, Charlie,' she cajoled again. 'This is really important to me, darling.'

He avoided the trap of asking why. 'I don't care.'

'I don't believe you.'

'No,' he agreed harshly, 'but you never did understand the difference between what was real and what wasn't. *This* is real.' He slammed one fist into the other. 'You come one step closer . . . or try that "darling" crap on me again . . . and I'll take your head off.'

Her eyes flashed briefly, but whether in annoyance or alarm he couldn't tell. 'Why are you being so cruel?'

Acland pressed a finger against his dead socket, where a pain was starting. 'I'm not. I'm being honest . . . which isn't a word you'd understand.' He watched her mouth thin to an unattractive line. 'Have you run out of money? Is that why I've been picked for the treatment again? Maybe you think I'm going to be paid thousands in compensation.'

A line of tears appeared along her lashes and she looked baffled suddenly, as if the visit wasn't going the way she'd expected. 'I thought you wanted to see me. Someone keeps phoning and hanging up. I hoped it was you.'

'No chance. I don't even call the people I'm fond of.'

'You never used to be like this.'

'Like what? *Bored?* He paused. 'I was always bored. Somewhere along the line I hoped I'd find a real person behind the pathetic pretence, but I never did. Not one I wanted to spend time with at any rate.'

'*Cold,*' she said. 'You were never cold, Charlie. You might have been easier to live with if you had been.'

'Don't delude yourself. Adulation's the only thing you ever wanted. You were halfway bearable as long as men admired you.'

'You shouldn't have been so jealous. They were always going to look . . . You knew that from the moment we met.'

Acland shook his head. 'Don't do this,' he warned.

'Why not? You were crazy about me. I've been worried sick it's my fault that you ended up in here. Were you thinking about me when your Scimitar got hit?'

He watched her take another step towards him. 'I swear to God, I *will* hurt you if you come any closer, Jen. Do you understand that? I don't give a shit what kind of fantasy you're in at the moment, but it doesn't include me.' He paused. 'It never did. The woman I liked never really existed.'

She couldn't or wouldn't believe him and the teardrops fattened along her lashes in beautiful sorrow. 'Don't be unkind to me, Charlie. I'm so unhappy. Can't we be friends at least?'

She lifted a hand towards his face as if she believed that touch alone could reignite the feelings he'd had for her. His response was so rapid that he caught her wrist and bent it away from him before it even reached shoulder height. 'Not any more,' he said icily. 'I've already told you, I'm not going down this route again.'

'You're hurting me.'

'I doubt it.' He stared at her for a moment, then slowly slid his grip from her wrist to her palm and crushed the bones inside his fist. 'How about that?'

This time the tears were a genuine expression of pain. 'God!' she snapped. 'You're breaking my fucking fingers.'

'That sounds more like the Jen I know.'

She tried to reach her bag with her free hand and he jerked her away from it. 'Bastard!' she hissed. 'I'll get you for this.'

'Better and better. I'd hate to think I'd been wrong about you.' He applied more pressure to her palm. 'Why did you come?'

She relaxed suddenly. 'Dr Willis suggested it.'

He could smell the shampoo on her hair. 'Don't lie.'

'It's the truth, Charlie. He thought it would help you if we could talk through what happened. He says you still have un-resolved issues about the relationship.'

Unresolved issues . . . ? Would Willis use a term like that? Acland stared at Jen for a moment, then manoeuvred her backwards towards the door. 'Then you'd better tell him he's wrong. There are no unresolved issues at my end. He might believe it if it comes from you.'

She made another grab for her bag. 'I need my stuff, Charlie.'

'I know you do.'

He jerked her away from it a second time and heard her hiss of anger as she made a furious writhing movement to pull herself free, punching at his arm with her other fist. Acland managed to keep his hold because he'd been ready for her, but he'd forgotten how strong she was. He caught her flailing fist at the first attempt and, without thinking, jerked her towards him in order to exert the same crushing force on both palms. In doing so, he exposed the injured side of his face.

Of course she screamed. It was a dramatic moment. If either of her hands had been free she would have clapped it across her mouth in the clichéd, angst-ridden gesture of Hollywood actresses. There was no banality that Jen wouldn't use in search of attention. She gave a thready wail in mimicry of a panic attack – 'Oh-oh-oh' – which slowly swelled in volume as she took in the full extent of his injuries.

Impassively, he forced her wrists together so that he could clasp both in one hand, then raised the other to circle her neck with his fingers. As the tips dug into her skin, the scream petered out and she stared at him in alarm. 'What are you doing?'

'Shutting you up.'

She started to struggle again. 'I can't breathe, Charlie! I can't fucking *breathe*!'

There was a flurry of movement in the doorway and a man's voice demanded, 'What the hell's going on? Jesus Christ!' Acland felt himself being grabbed from behind in a bear hug. 'Let her go, Charles. *Now!* You're killing her.'

Acland released his grip and pushed Jen away. 'It would take more than that to kill her,' he said, allowing himself to be manhandled to the other side of his bed. He watched cynically as she sank to the floor in a sobbing heap. 'You'd need to drive a stake through her heart to do it properly.'

The man, one of the male nurses, pushed him roughly into the corner and told him to stay put. 'You've got real problems, mate,' he said disgustedly, reaching for the emergency bell.

*

Robert Willis arrived fifteen minutes later. He nodded to the security officer who was guarding the door and, without speaking to Acland, retrieved Jen's bag from the chair and handed it to a nurse. He told the officer he wanted to speak with his patient privately, then shut the door and sat down. He was content to let a silence develop and, for the first time, Acland appreciated the calmness of Willis's nature and the economy of his movements. The tic of his own furiously pumping fists began to relax under their influence.

He was standing in the corner where the male nurse had pushed him. 'What's she told you?' he asked at last.

'That you tried to strangle her,' Willis said unemotionally. 'There's a lot I didn't understand. She's fairly distraught. Are you going to sit down?'

'No. I like it better when I know what's behind me.' Acland stepped back and propped his left shoulder against the wall. 'She said you told her to come.'

'I didn't. I advised her to stay away.'

'That's not what she said.'

Willis gave a small shrug. 'Then you'll have to choose which of us you want to believe.'

The lieutenant stared at him for a moment. 'Does she know I'm going to London tomorrow?'

'Not unless she's heard it from you. I've only communicated with her twice . . . once to make contact and the second time to acknowledge her email and say you weren't interested in seeing her. The visit to London wasn't on the cards at that stage.'

'What about this woman I'm staying with?'

'Dr Campbell? As far as I'm aware, she doesn't even know Jen Morley exists. She certainly wouldn't have her contact details.' Willis leaned back and crossed one leg over the other. 'Is that why you think Jen came? Because I wanted you to re-establish your friendship before the trip?'

'It crossed my mind.'

'I'm not that devious or that stupid, Charles. Why would I want to compromise your first attempt at normality? More particularly, why would I want to compromise Susan Campbell's safety by sending her a volatile patient who doesn't trust me?'

'I don't know.'

'Well, I suggest you start thinking about it because I shall have to inform Susan of today's episode . . . and she may refuse to take you. Was Jen telling the truth when she said you tried to strangle her . . . or was that another invention?'

'Not exactly. I did put my hand on her throat.' He looked away. 'Have you called the police?'

Willis shook his head. 'Not yet. Jen said it was partly her fault – you told her to leave and she refused – but in any case she doesn't want you prosecuted.' He tapped his fingertips together. 'That's not to say it won't happen. Our head of security might decide to report you in the best interests of staff safety, although I persuaded him to wait until you'd given me your side of the story. So . . . do you want to tell me what happened?'

'Not particularly.'

The psychiatrist clasped his fists and levelled his forefingers at Acland's heart. 'It wasn't an invitation, Charles, it was an instruction . . . and don't test me because I'm not in the mood. You've gone out of your way to make enemies here. You're aggressive and rude and the consensus view is that you have a problem with women. Do you think an attempt to throttle your ex-fiancée is going to do anything to mitigate that opinion?'

'I don't care.'

'Well, you should. Friendless people get pushed to the margins . . . and that's a lonely place to be. Did Jen give any other reason for coming, apart from saying it was my suggestion?'

'No.'

'Did she offer an explanation for why I might have invited her?'

'To talk through unresolved issues about the relationship.'

'That's not the kind of language I use,' said Willis mildly. 'I try to avoid the more obvious clichés.' He paused. 'But let's say I had suggested such a conversation, do you think I'd have left the pair of you to go it alone? How would that help me understand anything?'

'You could have drooled over Jen for half an hour while she gave you a blow-by-blow account.'

Interesting choice of language. 'Why would I want to do that?'

'No idea, Doc . . . but she's dressed up like a dog's dinner to impress someone.'

'You, presumably. Part of her distress seems to be that she was hoping to mend fences and was upset when you said you weren't interested.'

'She knew that before she came. We were dead in the water long before I went to Iraq.'

Willis eyed him thoughtfully. 'What went wrong?'

'It didn't work out.'

'Why not?'

Acland stared at the floor as if the answer lay there. 'It just didn't. Has she said any different in her letters to me?'

'No. They're bland and anodyne, and only evoke memories of happy times.'

'She likes war movies. Soldiers get wounded and nurses read to them. She'd never write anything to her detriment.'

Willis frowned. 'You seem to know her better than she knows you. She doesn't give the impression of a woman who believed the relationship was –' he echoed Acland's phrase – 'dead in the water.'

Acland raised his head and there was a sardonic gleam in his eye. 'You're about to make a liar out of me, Doc.'

'How?'

'I told Jen you didn't go by appearances.' He paused. 'You'll be putty in her hands if you forget what her profession is. She can produce any emotion you like –' he snapped his fingers – 'just like that. None of it's real.'

'Her distress seems real. Why would you want to strangle her, Charles?'

Acland shrugged. 'Ask *her*. She'll be a lot less distressed by the time you get back . . . as long as she's got her bag.' He held the man's gaze for a moment. 'What's she already told you?'

'That she tried to touch your cheek and you went berserk. She said you crushed her hands.' He left out the end of Jen's sentence, where she'd claimed in hysterical tones that he'd enjoyed hurting her.

'She didn't know what was wrong with me till I turned to face her. That's when she started on the screaming routine.'

'So you decided to strangle her to shut her up?' murmured Willis ironically.

Acland shifted his position against the wall. 'I never came close to strangling her. I wanted to give her a fright . . . persuade her to back off and leave me alone. Do you think I couldn't have snapped her neck if I'd wanted to?'

'That's hardly the issue, Charles. You shouldn't have put your hands on her at all.'

The lieutenant cracked his finger joints one by one. 'But it's OK for her to put her hand on me? Is that what you're saying?'

'Not if it was inappropriate.'

'It was. I told her at least twice not to come any closer . . . even warned her I'd hurt her if she didn't back off.'

'Did you want to hurt her?'

'Yes.'

'Did you enjoy it?'

The knuckle-cracking tic worked harder and faster. 'No.'

Willis didn't believe him. 'Are you going to tell me why having Jen too close worries you?'

'You don't know her the way I do.'

'Then tell me about her. Describe your relationship.'

'There's no point. She's history. I'm not planning to see her again.'

'Are you sure? You seem to have strong feelings for her still.'

Acland dropped his hands to his sides abruptly, as if he realized how much they were revealing about him. 'Only anger,' he said with apparent calm. 'First, that she came at all . . . second, that she took no notice when I asked her to leave . . . and third, that she thought she could change my mind if she stayed long enough.'

'Has she behaved like that before? Is that why you described her as manipulative?'

'Yes.'

'What were the other occasions?' He sighed at the lieutenant's expression. 'I'm not trying to catch you out, Charles. I'm trying to work out if you're safe to send to London. At the moment I'm deeply confused about the relationship you had with Jen. On the one hand, you describe her rather crudely as "a damn good fuck" . . . On the other, you react violently the minute she tries to touch you. Was your pride hurt when she ended the engagement? Is that what we're dealing with here?'

Silence.

'Why pretend indifference when you clearly don't feel it?'

Acland leaned more heavily into the wall, as if his legs weren't strong enough to support him. 'It's not a pretence. I *am* indifferent. If she'd left when I asked we wouldn't be having this conversation.'

'Why do you think she didn't?'

'She won't accept "no". It isn't a word she hears very often. I'll put money on you giving her permission to sit in your office so that you can go back and pat her hand. Everyone falls for the act.'

'You're right about the office, but not about the hand-patting,' said Willis mildly. 'Therapists tend to avoid physical contact for fear their actions will be misconstrued.'

'You'd better be careful, then. She'll probably sit in your lap if she thinks she can persuade you to repeat what I've said.'

'Why would I do that?'

'You've repeated what *she's* been saying.'

'But she isn't my patient, Charles, and I have no duty of confidentiality towards her. She's a virtual stranger who was brought to my office in tears, claiming she'd left her bag in your room and was too frightened to ask for it back. Without her train ticket and money for taxi fares she can't get home. What did you expect me to do? Throw her out on her ear and tell her it was her fault for coming without an invitation?'

The sardonic gleam reappeared in Acland's eye. 'You really *do* need to be careful, Doc. If you've already bought into the fear and the vulnerability, the next thing you know you'll be driving her home like a proper little gentleman.'

'Is that what happened to you the first time you met?'

Acland nodded.

'And you wouldn't recommend it?'

'It depends how willing you are to be exploited.'

*

Willis cursed fluently under his breath as he returned to his office. He'd had to work hard to persuade Charles to accept a room with Susan Campbell between operations and he was extremely reluctant to see the arrangement fall apart. To date, the lieutenant's two recuperation periods had been spent in a hotel in Birmingham, where he'd appeared to neglect himself. On both occasions, he'd returned to the hospital showing signs of early malnourishment, but any suggestion that he stay with his parents was met with a brick wall.

As an old friend and psychiatric colleague who ran a bed and breakfast in London, Susan had offered an alternative, but whether she'd be willing to take Charles now was anyone's guess. With little difficulty, Willis transferred his irritation to Jen. Rather than tell a lie, Charles would avoid a question or say nothing, signalling his unwillingness through a variety of physical tics, but Willis had no such faith in Jen's honesty.

She said you told her to come . . .

Five

WILLIS FOUND THE HOSPITAL'S head of security, Gareth Blades, waiting in the corridor outside his office. The man, a burly ex-policeman, took him by the arm and led him away from the door. 'Ms Morley's inside with your secretary. I thought I'd catch you before you went in. What's been going on between these two, Bob?'

'It seems to be a case of who you want to believe. Has Ms Morley changed her mind about reporting it to the police?'

'No. She's worried about making things worse for the lieutenant . . . Says she'll retract what she's already told us if we take it any further.' He gave a sour smile. 'I don't think there's any doubt he attacked her. She's holding herself together at the moment, but she was shaking like a leaf at the beginning.'

'Does she have any bruising?'

'Not that I can see. I asked her to let a nurse check her neck for marks, but Ms Morley refused. She's wearing a buttoned-up collar and there's nothing visible above it. I'm betting there's plenty underneath, though. She's very slender . . . It wouldn't take much to bruise her.'

'What about her hands and wrists? The lieutenant said he caught them to stop her touching him.'

'I didn't notice anything, but she's wearing long sleeves. Maybe you could take a look when you go back in.'

'If she doesn't want to report him, we can't force her, Gareth.'

'I know, but I'm not happy about it. There's other people's safety to consider.'

'He's going to London tomorrow for a couple of weeks. Does that solve your problem?'

'Not if he's coming back. The nurse who brought Ms Morley's bag said Acland had a go at his mother shortly after he arrived here. Is that true?'

'It was a different scenario. He was in a lot of pain and she wouldn't stop fussing over him. He grabbed her hand to stop her stroking his hair.'

'The same nurse said he's been rude to most of the staff. He sounds like a ticking time bomb, this fellow. Did he explain why he assaulted Ms Morley?'

'He asked her to leave several times and she wouldn't go. She also ignored his warnings about standing too close. It became a physical confrontation when she tried to touch his face.'

'Why didn't he press his bell?'

Willis shrugged. 'He wouldn't have been able to reach it if Ms Morley was between him and the bed . . . not without revealing the injured side of his face.' He fell silent for a moment. 'He's very conscious of his scars. As I understand it, she started screaming when she finally got a view of them. That may have caused him to react the way he did.'

'He should have backed off.'

'As should she,' Willis pointed out mildly. 'It takes two to tango, Gareth. She's the one who came looking for *him*, don't forget . . . not the other way round. The lieutenant's done all he can to distance himself from her.' He paused. 'Has she said why she came?'

'As a friend. They were engaged, apparently, and she wanted him to know she was still there for him even though the relation- ship hadn't worked out.' He gave another sour smile. 'It looks as though she's well out of it. The male nurse who rescued her said Lieutenant Acland had his hand round her throat and was bearing down like a man possessed. Do you know if he's been violent towards her before?'

'Have you asked her?'

'Won't say . . . but she's obviously wary of him. Have you any objections if I talk to him myself? Is he mentally fit to be interviewed?'

Willis nodded. 'You won't get many answers. I suspect he'll allow you to believe Ms Morley's version of events. He seems to have no interest at all in correcting people's bad opinion of him.'

'Why not?'

'I wish I knew,' said Willis honestly. 'At the moment I don't know whether I'm dealing with post-traumatic guilt over the death of two troopers . . . or something far deeper.'

'Like what?'

'The prolonged destruction of a personality.'

*

In the flesh, Jen Morley looked less like Uma Thurman than in her website photograph, but there was no denying the similarity. She had the same wide-set eyes in an oval face and the same look of childish innocence. She greeted Dr Willis with charm and composure, rising gracefully from her seat and placing her slender hand in his. 'I'm so sorry to be a nuisance, Doctor, but everyone's been incredibly kind –' she flashed a smile at his secretary – 'particularly Ruth.'

He glanced at her wrist as he released her hand, but it was covered by a cuff. 'How are you feeling?' he asked, gesturing for her to sit down again and moving round the desk to his own seat. 'You're certainly looking better.'

'A little shocked still,' she confided, turning sideways on her chair and crossing her ankles neatly beneath her. 'But what about Charlie? I'm more worried about him. Is he all right? I feel awful about what happened.'

Willis made a conscious effort to view her through neutral eyes, but his first impression was that she reminded him of Charles's mother. Different hair colouring and a very different kind of beauty, but she had the same instinct to display herself to good advantage, in the elegant way she sat and in what she said. Mrs

Acland had invariably started with a question about Charles's welfare, only to steer the conversation towards herself, and Willis wondered if Jen would do the same.

He nodded to his secretary, who was signalling a desire to leave. He watched her say goodbye to Jen, then pause in the doorway to send him a telephone sign with her thumb and little finger against the side of her face. 'One thing before you go,' he called after her. 'I'm expecting a call from Henry Watson in the next few minutes. You can ask anyone else to call back later, but I need you to put Henry through. Do you mind telling him to keep it brief?'

'No problem,' said Ruth, closing the door behind her.

Willis took off his glasses and polished them vigorously on his handkerchief, peering short-sightedly across his desk. The intended effect was to diminish him, take away his authority, and he saw the tension ease from Jen's shoulders. 'Charles is also a little shocked, Ms Morley, but with less reason perhaps. I gather he wasn't expecting you.'

'I wrote to tell him I was coming.'

Willis allowed the lie to go. Charles had solemnly handed every new communication to the psychiatrist and the last one had been two weeks previously. There had been no mention of a visit, merely a repeat of what she'd written in her earlier letters: *I've missed you . . . Do you remember the time . . . ? I'm lonely without you . . .* None made any reference to what had caused the split, and Willis wondered if she seriously believed what she'd put in her email, that amnesia might have wiped the incident from Charles's memory.

He chose to flatter her ego. 'You and Charles must have made a handsome couple, Ms Morley. You're a very beautiful woman . . . But I'm sure you've been told that a hundred times.'

She took the compliment in her stride. 'Thank you . . . and, yes, we were a handsome couple. Charlie, too. Is that part of his problem? He wouldn't turn round when I entered his room. Is he embarrassed by his face?'

Willis answered generally. 'Most people find it difficult to come to terms with disfigurement. Other people's reactions are often hurtful.'

'I screamed,' she admitted, 'and I'm so annoyed with myself. I can't *believe* I did anything so stupid.'

'I'm sure he understands.'

'Do you think so? The last thing I wanted to do was upset him . . . I just wanted to be friends again.' She gazed rather wistfully at the psychiatrist. 'I did it all wrong, didn't I?'

'It would have helped if you'd told me you were coming.'

'I should have done,' she agreed. 'You did warn me he wasn't interested.' She gave a small sigh. 'The trouble was, I didn't believe you. Charlie gets silly ideas in his head when he thinks the world's against him, but I can usually persuade him out of them.'

Willis nodded. 'I'm sure that's true. You're very—' He broke off to reach for the telephone. 'Will you excuse me for just a moment? This shouldn't take long.' He placed the receiver against his ear. 'Hello, Henry.'

Ruth's voice spoke quietly at the other end. 'Before you go gooey at the knees, she's not as innocent as she looks. I think she went through your jacket earlier. I left her alone for a couple of minutes and she moved damn fast to get away from it when I came back.'

'Don't worry on that score. There's nothing important there. Anything else?'

'She was ratty as hell before her bag arrived, then she asked to go to the Ladies. When she came out again she was sweetness and light. Gareth fell for it . . . but I didn't –' Willis sensed her smile down the line – 'probably because I've never been as pretty as that.'

Willis chuckled. 'OK. Thanks, Henry. That's very helpful.' He replaced the handset and smiled absent-mindedly at Jen. 'Where were we? Oh, yes . . . Charles.' He eyed her with a puzzled expression. 'He seems to think I told you to come, Ms Morley. Did he get that idea from you?'

She shook her head. 'It wouldn't have been true.' She thought for a moment. 'He's quite jealous, Dr Willis. If he knows you and I have been writing to each other that might have made him suspicious.'

'He does,' Willis agreed. 'I mentioned I'd written to you and that you'd replied.'

'Did he ask what I'd said?'

'Not that I recall.' He smiled apologetically, as if it were his fault that his patient was so uninterested. 'Was jealousy a problem in the relationship? You didn't mention that in your email.'

'You'd have thought me arrogant.'

'Not at all,' said Willis in surprise. 'I can easily imagine you being the focus of a man's jealousy. You must attract a great deal of attention every time you go out. Was that hard for Charles?'

'Hasn't he told you?'

Willis shook his head. 'He's been very reticent about everything. All I know is what you put in the email. I remember you mentioned a violent argument. Was that prompted by jealousy?'

Fleetingly, a look of wariness crossed her face, as if she feared that his unassuming manner and constant fussy cleaning of his glasses were a front.

'You don't have to tell me if you don't want to,' he assured her. 'I'm not of the school of thought that says anything useful can be raked from dead ashes. Charles has told me he has no feelings for you any more and I've no reason to disbelieve him. He certainly didn't want to see you today.'

She didn't like that. 'He wouldn't have been so angry if he didn't love me still.' She fiddled with the clasp of her bag. 'He was crazy about me. A friend of mine used to call him my personal guard dog . . . panting to lie in my lap one minute . . . and showing his teeth the next if anyone came too close.'

It wasn't an analogy that sat easily with Willis. The Charles he knew was too self-contained to display his feelings so obviously. *Nevertheless* . . . 'That suggests possessiveness. Is that how you'd describe him? As a controlling lover?'

'Totally. I couldn't breathe without Charlie's permission. Another friend – the one who persuaded me to break off the engagement – said he had me locked in a cage like an exotic bird, and if I didn't break out I'd have no freedom left.'

Willis took note of the mixed metaphors. There was a world of difference between a caged parakeet and a siren who handed titbits to a Rottweiler. *Nevertheless* . . . 'Your friend was right,' he agreed. 'It sounds like an extremely unhealthy relationship.'

But Jen didn't like that either. Perhaps she felt the criticism applied equally to her. 'Not from Charlie's point of view. He had everything he wanted. He turned *up* when it suited him . . . snapped his *fingers* when it suited him . . . and showed me off like a *trophy* when it suited him.'

'So why didn't he welcome you with open arms today? You said it was you who ended the engagement?' He put an upward inflection at the end of the sentence.

'That's right.'

He smiled. 'Men are very simple creatures, Ms Morley. Most of us hanker after an easy life and take a reprieve when it's offered.' He breathed on one of his lenses. 'If you were everything Charles wanted, why didn't he grasp your olive branch?'

There was a slight narrowing of the huge eyes, but whether in irritation or confusion the doctor couldn't tell. 'His pride won't let him. He's still very hurt.'

It was a reasonable answer and Willis acknowledged it with another thoughtful nod. 'Even so, I'm not clear why you want to rekindle the ashes, Ms Morley. You implied the relationship was stifling.'

'I miss him,' she said simply. 'I hoped the fact that he hadn't told his parents about the split meant he felt the same.' She produced a crumpled tissue from her sleeve and held it to her nose. 'You can't explain love, Dr Willis. It's chemistry. It happens.'

'Mm. I'd say that's a better description of infatuation. Chemistry has a nasty habit of producing volatile mixtures that end in an explosion.'

She shrugged impatiently. 'We were good together.'

'In what way?'

'Every way . . . in bed . . . talking . . . having fun . . . when we were out. It *worked*.' She smiled slightly. 'I asked him once if he ever thought about being with another woman and he said only Uma Thurman . . . but I think he was joking.'

'I imagine a lot of men fantasize about Uma Thurman. Do you replicate the image to encourage them to transfer their fantasies to you?'

Another tiny shrug. 'It's not something I can help. God made me this way.'

Willis eyed her with amusement. 'I don't *do* God, Ms Morley. I'm of the existentialist view . . . that each individual chooses, and takes responsibility for, the path he or she follows in life.' He replaced his spectacles on his nose, tucking the arms behind his ears. 'And, with respect, I'm not convinced that a passing resemblance to a successful actress is a good enough reason to hitch a free ride on her reputation. Rightly or wrongly, it suggests to me that you lack the confidence to be yourself.'

She half-lowered her lids to hide her expression. 'Is that something Charlie said?'

'No. I was reflecting on your comments in your email about chameleons lacking confidence. It's a description that seems to fit you rather better than it fits Charles.'

'You don't know him the way I do.'

Willis smiled. 'I'd be a millionaire by now if I'd been given a pound every time someone said that.' He clasped his hands in front of him. 'He doesn't seem to share your enthusiasm for Uma Thurman.'

'That's not true.'

'A couple of minutes ago you said he referred to her as a joke.'

'Not *her*. Him being with her. He knows it'll never happen.' She touched the tissue to her eyes. 'Me dressing up was the next best thing. Why do you think my friend described me as an exotic bird? I had to deck myself out like Irene Cassini in *Gattaca* – the

Uma Thurman character Charlie most fancies . . . like *this* –' she gestured towards her suit – 'otherwise he couldn't do it.'

'What?'

'Sex.'

Willis let the word hang in the air while he thought about the monkish young man upstairs who avoided all contact with female nurses. *Was Jen telling the truth?* It would explain a few things if she was, he reflected, not least Charles's refusal to go anywhere near the subject of sex. 'I'm not sure I understand. Are you saying he couldn't achieve an erection without the Uma Thurman stimulus?'

She smiled unhappily. 'Not at the beginning. It was just a game at the beginning.'

Willis made what he could of this. 'And then the game took over. Charles preferred the fantasy woman to the real one. Is that what happened?'

'It made him angry if I refused.'

Willis thought of the conversations he'd had with Charles about Jen's resemblance to Uma Thurman. The lieutenant had certainly talked about a 'fantasy', but not in the kind of terms that suggested arousal. 'Then I wonder why he didn't respond more positively towards you today,' he said slowly. 'You seem to have done everything you could to evoke positive memories.'

'He wouldn't look at me. He stood by the window with his face turned away.'

'Not all the time. He wouldn't have been able to catch your hands otherwise.'

'It was too late by then. He'd already lost his temper.'

'With Jen Morley or Uma Thurman?'

'What difference does it make?'

'It seems quite crucial to me. If he lost his temper with Jen Morley why would he want to throttle Uma Thurman? You seem to have irritated him in both roles.' He folded his hands under his chin. 'Are you sure this isn't *your* sexual fantasy, Ms Morley?'

Dampness welled in her eyes. 'Why are you being cruel to me?'

Willis showed surprise again. 'It was a fair question. I assumed you wouldn't have come dressed like that if you hadn't been looking for intimacy with Charles. It suggests the fantasy was a mutual one . . . in your mind anyway.'

'That's disgusting,' she said with a sudden show of anger.

'Then I'm mystified, Ms Morley. What was the point of today's exercise? What were you trying to achieve?'

The question seemed to worry her because she checked the contents of her bag while she worked out an answer. 'What you said before . . . I was trying to remind him of the good times. He liked the attention I got when we were out and people mistook me for Uma.'

Willis frowned. 'I thought you said he was jealous. The parallel you used was a guard dog who snapped at anyone who came too close.'

She stared at him with growing irritation. 'But it gave him a hell of a buzz at the same time. He loved the idea that other men envied him.'

'I'm sure he did,' he said easily. 'It's a common duality of emotion. Did you feel the same way? He was a good-looking man before his injury.'

'Are you asking do *I* get jealous? Then, no, I've never needed to be,' she said dismissively. 'Men are more afraid of losing me than I am of losing them, Dr Willis. That may sound boastful, but it's true.'

'Not in the least. You've obviously had far more relationships than Charles.'

'So?'

'They don't seem to last very long. Is it always you who ends them?'

'It's hardly going to be the man, is it?'

Willis smiled. 'I don't know, Ms Morley,' he said honestly. 'I'm having trouble understanding why Charles is so unwilling to mend fences if it was you who broke the engagement. In my experience, it's the partner who doesn't want the affair to end who tries to resurrect it . . . and the one who makes the decision to split who moves on.'

'Charlie hasn't moved on. He'd be taking visits and phone calls if he had.'

This time Willis's nod was a genuine recognition that she was right. Whatever bonds had held these two together were still strong. *Nevertheless* . . . 'He won't talk about you . . . won't read your letters . . . indeed, shows every determination to draw a line under the relationship. Why would he do that unless he's made up his mind to confine you to history?'

He'd finally goaded her into showing her anger openly. 'Because he's *ashamed*,' she said through gritted teeth. 'And if you want to know *why* . . . which you probably *don't*, since you're on his side . . . it's because he *raped* me. And it wasn't just *any* old rape. He pushed me against a wall and *buggered* me. I bet *that* little fact hasn't come out in your cosy conversations with him.'

'No,' Willis agreed matter-of-factly, 'but I guessed something of the sort from your email. You said he was violent towards you.' He might have added that Charles's demeanour, whenever the subject of Jen came up, also suggested shame.

'He behaved like a brute,' she said with a pronounced shudder. 'I've never been so frightened.'

'I'm not surprised. Rape is a terrifying ordeal under any circumstance.' Willis let a beat of silence pass. 'Shouldn't you have thought more seriously about coming to see him alone today?'

She delayed answering by blowing her nose. Too forcefully. When she took the tissue away there was a smear of blood on her upper lip. 'He hasn't tried to strangle me before . . . or looked as if he was getting a thrill out of hurting me.' Her eyes narrowed. 'And before you ask whether he got a *thrill* out of the rape,' she went on belligerently, 'the answer is I don't know because I couldn't see his face. When he'd finished, he pushed me to the ground and left.'

'And that was the last time you saw him before today?'

'Yes.' She rushed to pre-empt him again. 'And the reason I

wasn't afraid about coming alone was because this is a *hospital*, Dr Willis.' She gave an angry laugh. 'I thought it would be a safe place to talk to him. I expected him to be on a ward . . . or at least that there'd be a few doctors and nurses around.'

'Mm.' Willis set to with his spectacles again, breathing on the lenses and using his handkerchief to wipe them clean. 'Which makes it more surprising that you chose to play up to his Uma Thurman fantasy . . . and didn't leave when he asked you to.'

The glasses routine was getting on her nerves. 'I could have had him booted out of his regiment if I'd reported him . . . still could, probably. The army doesn't condone rape any more than the rest of society does. How do you think the police will react if I say he had another go at me today?'

'At a guess, question your motives in coming here . . . ask why you didn't report the rape at the time . . . or why you began by telling hospital security that you didn't want the authorities involved this time.' He shook his head at her expression. 'You're on a slippery slope to real delusion if you think you can act the victim in this, Jen. The police will work out, as quickly as I've done, that it's you who's been using sex to manipulate this relationship, and that's a poor basis for a rape allegation . . . particularly when there's only your word that it happened.'

Her eyes hardened. 'You'd better hope I don't report you to whatever association you belong to. I bet there's nothing in the psychiatric code that says it's OK to condone violence against women just because the rapist's your patient.'

'I'm sure you're right,' Willis agreed lightly, 'but it's a big leap from my pointing out the flaws in your story to you accusing me of condoning violence against women. I'd find your allegation more believable if you'd said you'd made a crude attempt to seduce Charles. He's a fastidious man – I suspect he'd regard any such attempt as exploitative and demeaning – and I can imagine him turning on you in those circumstances. Rather as he did today, in fact.'

'You weren't there. You don't know anything about it.'

Willis replaced his spectacles. 'Except you obviously came dressed like that for a purpose – to trigger some pleasurable memories, perhaps – and it appears to have provoked the opposite response. Charles has only negative associations with your Uma Thurman look. Do you want to tell me why?'

'No.' She stood up abruptly, clasping her bag to her chest. 'It's late. I have to go.'

'Then I'll take you to the taxi rank in the visitors' car park. There's a short cut through the staff entrance.'

'I don't need an escort,' she said. 'I want the Ladies. I'll leave by the main entrance.'

Willis shook his head as he rose to his feet. 'I can't let you go alone, I'm afraid. If you insist on a lavatory stop, I'll have to call a female security officer to accompany you.'

Jen looked murderous. 'Why?'

The psychiatrist gave an apologetic shrug. 'Hospital policy. We don't allow drug abuse on the premises. What you do outside is a matter between you and your conscience . . . but I'd show some restraint if I were you.'

She took a swipe at him with her bag and staggered slightly when she missed by a mile.

He eyed her with amusement. 'I'm just the messenger, Ms Morley. Don't shoot me because you don't like what I say.'

'Fuck *you*!' she said out of the mouth of an otherworldly angel.

Southwark Echo, *Thursday, 12 April 2007*

Third murder victim 'beaten to death'

FOLLOWING THE DEATH of Kevin Atkins, a 58-yr-old builder from south London, police have a confirmed a possible link with the murders of Harry Peel, 57, and Martin Britton, 71. Mr Atkins sustained fatal head injuries in what police have described as a 'frenzied attack'. His cleaner discovered his body on Wednesday morning but post-mortem tests showed he'd been dead for at least four days.

Det Supt Brian Jones, who has been leading the inquiries into the murders of Harry Peel and Martin Britton, said there were similarities between the cases. 'All three men lived alone and were found in their beds,' he said. 'The attacks were violent but there were no signs of forced entry and we believe the victims knew their assailant.'

He refused to comment on the men's army records. Harry Peel spent five years in an infantry regiment from the age of 18. Martin Britton, a high-ranking civil servant at the Ministry of Defence, was conscripted into the Royal Army Pay Corps as part of his National Service. Kevin Atkins served 15 years in the army, most notably as a corporal in 2 Para during the 1982 Falklands War. He was decommissioned in 1983.

Det Supt Brian Jones denied rumours that Harry Peel and Kevin Atkins had been forced out of the army because of homosexual activity. He also refused to comment on whether a male prostitute is being sought in connection with the murders. 'We are keeping an open mind.' He urged anyone with information to come forward. 'Whoever is doing this is extremely dangerous.'

Police have welcomed the help of the gay community in drawing attention to the danger of casual sex with strangers. 'Most of us think of our homes as safe,' said a spokesman, 'but they're not. They're the place where we let down our guard and make ourselves vulnerable.'

DR ROBERT WILLIS

MD, PSYCH

Extracts from notes on Lt Charles Acland
April 2007

. . . Contradictory reports about Charles's time in London.
Susan Campbell says he disappeared on Saturday evening
after one of her other guests, a young woman, tried to be
friendly with him. Thereafter, he avoided the girl and
withdrew into his shell. Susan's conclusion is that he becomes
anxious when people get too close. Touching and invasion of
personal space appear to be real issues for him.

. . . Charles made no mention of the young woman but
describes the stay as 'difficult' because of Susan's attempts at
friendship. Her kindness [he calls it 'mothering' and 'bossy
interference'] was 'overpowering' and he kept out of her way
as much as possible. They both agree he went running every
night, sometimes for hours on end.

. . . I asked Charles what he plans to do if the army rejects his
request to return to active service. He said it won't happen
and has made no plans for an alternative. He has blocked all
discussion on the subject since I suggested that a return to his
parents' farm might be his only choice if things don't work out
as he hopes.

. . . Susan believes his worries about his future are as
debilitating to his confidence as his disfigurement is. Perhaps
more so. She suggests Charles has defined himself for so long
as a soldier – through a declared ambition at school and then

in reality through his regiment – that he's unable to define himself in any other way. Susan's view – a pessimistic one – is that Charles will impose even more isolation on himself if the army rejects him.

. . . She feels he's struggling with profound issues that aren't easily explained by his injuries or concerns about his career. [Query: Sexual orientation? Susan's query also.]

. . . Every attempt to talk about Jen angers him. He says he wants to forget her completely and can't do that if I keep reminding him of her existence. When I mentioned the rape allegation, he said, 'There's a cast of thousands for the part of Jen's rapist. She doesn't exist if men don't lust after her . . .'

METROPOLITAN
POLICE

INTERNAL MEMO

To: ACC Clifford Golding
From: Det Supt Brian Jones
Date: 13 April 2007
Subject: Kevin Atkins inquiry

Sir,

In answer to your question re the likelihood of a single perpetrator, the relevant SOCO preliminary findings from Kevin Atkins's apartment are as follows. In brief:

1. No forced entry.
2. Victim found on his side, dressed in a bathrobe.
3. Bathrobe pulled up to expose the buttocks.
4. 'Foreign object' bruising/lacerations to rectum.
5. No evidence of sexual intercourse.
6. Opened, half-consumed bottle of wine in the living room – two cleaned glasses on the draining board in the kitchen.
7. No useful fingerprints – some accounted for, some unknown.
8. Frenzied attack to the head – similar weapon used (round-headed blunt instrument).
9. Subsequent damage to walls and property with same weapon.

10. No apparent resistance from the victim.
11. No indication of how the victim was immobilized.
12. Wallet emptied of cash – no credit cards taken.
13. Mobile telephone stolen.

Despite 7 April being the probable date of death, FSS have
yet to deliver a full report on Atkins. I am also waiting on
an update to the psychological profile from Britton's murder.
Meanwhile, the focus of the inquiry team continues to
concentrate on the army connection, male prostitutes,
methods of contact, stranger sightings in the area and
people known to the victims.

I will, of course, keep you updated as information comes in.

With kind regards,

Brian

Detective Superintendent Brian Jones

Six

ACLAND'S DECISION TO abandon further surgery in favour of a quick return to the army came as no surprise to Robert Willis. The lieutenant's fuse had become shorter by the day since his return from London, made worse when a small operation, designed to begin the process of creating a pouch for a glass eye, showed minimal results.

He was left with an empty, misshapen eye socket, irregular migraines, persistent low-level tinnitus and a blade-shaped scar up his cheek, but as no one could guarantee that further operations would produce a significantly better result in an acceptable time-frame, he opted to live with the face he had. He was warned by Mr Galbraith that in an image-conscious world he could expect adverse reactions, but he rejected the surgeon's advice and chose instead to confront the prejudices of the image-conscious by drawing attention to his disfigurement.

On the day of his departure, at the fag end of April, he buzz-cut his hair to half an inch, donned a black eyepatch and went in search of Robert Willis for a verdict. He found the psychiatrist in his office, deep in concentration in front of his computer.

Willis's startled expression at the tap on his open door was as much to do with the fact that he hadn't known anyone was there as with his lack of immediate recognition of the man in his doorway, but the response pleased Acland. Surprise and alarm were preferable to sympathy and disgust. 'Am I disturbing you, Doc?'

'Do you mean am I busy . . . or do I find your appearance disturbing?'

'Both. Either.'

'You certainly made me jump.' Willis gestured towards a chair on the other side of the desk. 'Take a pew while I finish this sentence.' He shifted his gaze to his monitor and typed a few words before clicking on save. 'So what are you hoping for?' he asked. 'Shock and awe? Or just shock?'

'It's better than pity.'

Willis stared at the lean, expressionless face that was staring back at him. Part of him could see that the image Acland had created for himself was magnificent – hard, tough and old beyond his years – but the other part saw only a tragic death of youthful innocence. There was no reconciling this implacable man with the boyish, good-looking one in photographs from before his injury.

'You've nothing to fear from pity, Charles, although I can't say the same for loneliness. You won't make many friends looking like that . . . but I presume that's the intention.'

Acland shrugged. 'A glass eye won't help me see any better . . . and the surgery will just delay my return to the army.'

'You're placing a lot of faith in this return.'

'My CO's supporting me.'

'That's good.'

Acland came close to smiling. 'You might as well say it, Doc. I know you pretty well by now. The medical board won't be as easily persuaded as my CO.'

'No,' said Willis with a sigh. 'I'm afraid they'll view your blind side as a liability and offer you a desk job instead. But that's not what you want, is it?'

'So I'll have to prove the board wrong. Other people have done it. Nelson's the greatest admiral this country ever had and he was one-eyed. If it didn't stop him, it won't stop me.'

'Everything was a lot slower in Nelson's day, Charles . . . including the ships. He had time to make decisions which isn't given to commanders in today's armed forces.'

'What about Moshe Dayan? He made it to general in the Israeli army.'

Willis avoided another negative reply. 'True . . . and a lot more contemporary. Are you hoping the eyepatch will prompt some positive memories from the board?'

'What if I am? Will it work?'

'I don't know,' Willis answered honestly, 'but I suspect you'll find the decision is made by computer. You'll be asked a series of questions and your responses will trigger answers to another block of questions that you won't be asked.'

'Like what?'

'Can you see to your left without turning your head? No? Then the computer will answer every other question relating to vision with a negative. For example, "Are you able to monitor a radar screen?" You'll say yes – you might even be able to persuade an army doctor to put a tick in that box – but the program will give you an automatic no because you've already indicated that you have a blind side.'

'You don't need two eyes to watch a screen.'

'You do if you're in the middle of action and giving coordinates to a gunner. A fully sighted man can watch two things at the same time, a one-eyed man can only watch one. You won't know if the gunner's received the instruction unless you look away from the screen.'

'I won't need to. He'll confirm over his radio.'

'A doctor might agree with you,' said Willis gently, 'but a computer won't. Written into the software will be an acknowledgement that accidents happen. The intercom might fail . . . the gunner might mishear the coordinates . . . *you* might mishear his confirmation. But in any case, you won't be able to stop yourself turning away from the screen. It's human nature to double-check. Every soldier – right down to the lowliest private – needs visual confirmation that the man next to him knows what he's doing. It's a necessary impulse when your life depends on it.'

Acland stared at his hands. 'Did you design this program, Doc? You seem to know a lot about it.'

Willis shook his head. 'I don't even know if it exists, I'm just making an educated guess. The government uses a similar system to assess disability claimants, because doctors are seen to be more sympathetic than computers. The decision-makers work on the principle that if you take the human element out of the equation, it's harder for a cheat to get benefit.'

'What if I lie and say yes to the original question?'

'You can't. You're not the one who feeds in the answers. It's a doctor who does that and he'll have your medical notes in front of him. Even without the evidence of the eyepatch, he'll know that you're unsighted on one side.'

Acland turned towards the window, deliberately presenting his blind side to Willis. 'So what you're saying is that I haven't a hope in hell's chance of getting back into a Scimitar.' It was a statement rather than a question, as if he were confirming something he already knew.

'Not necessarily,' the psychiatrist answered as lightly as he could. 'I'm saying it's a possibility.' He watched the young man flick a tear from his good eye with the back of a finger. 'But you'll be better able to argue your case if you understand what you're up against. No decision's final . . . and your CO's support will carry weight at any appeal.'

There was a lengthy silence before Acland spoke again. 'What about yours, Doc? Will your support carry weight?'

'I hope so. I've given you a positive assessment.'

'Have you mentioned Jen in it?'

'No.'

'My parents?'

'No.'

'I should be OK, then.'

'Except it's not your mental health the board will be assessing, Charles. It's the physical handicaps of semi-blindness, persistent tinnitus and chronic migraines. *Those* are what you have to min-imize.' He gave one of his dry smiles. 'No one on the board is going to be interested in disappointing relationships.'

'Thanks, Doc.'

'For what?'

Acland swung back with a twisted smile on his face. 'Keeping it real . . . managing expectation. At least I won't make a fool of myself. It doesn't do to blub in front of retired colonels.' The smile died abruptly. 'Still . . . I'm never going to get my sight back so I might as well give it my best shot now. If they chuck me out, I'll learn to live with it.' His tone hardened. 'That's the *one* thing I am getting good at . . . learning to live with things.'

Willis opened a drawer and took out a business card. 'There are two things you can do with this, Charles,' he said, pushing it across the desk. 'Bin it or keep it. The number will put you through to an agency who can reach me any time, day or night. I don't expect to hear from you for several months . . . if at all . . . but I'll return your call immediately.'

'What if I phone next week?'

'I'll be surprised,' the psychiatrist said frankly. 'Whether you stay in the army or not, I'm afraid you're about to shed friends quicker than you make them. You'll walk away, closing doors behind you, rather than try to sustain relationships that you think are meaningless.'

Not for the first time, Willis wondered if a female psychiatrist would have been a better choice for this lad. With none of the formal baggage that came between men – the instinctive reluctance to show affection, the necessary distance demanded by alpha males – she could have adopted a softer approach which might have allowed the lieutenant to weep for the person he'd been.

METROPOLITAN
POLICE

INTERNAL MEMO

To: ACC Clifford Golding
From: Det Supt Brian Jones
Date: 1 May 2007
Subject: Peel/Britton/Atkins inquiry

Sir,

Progress to date

As I reported yesterday, there's been little movement in the
P/B/A inquiry since the initial flurry of interest last month
when we made public that we believed the murders were
linked. The team has interviewed some 2,500 people –
friends, relatives, neighbours, employees, taxi drivers,
regulars at the different gay clubs and bars – but there are
no consistent factors between the three men apart from
varying lengths of army service and homosexual leanings.

The wives of the two younger men, Peel and Atkins,
describe their husbands as bisexual. Mrs Peel says the
estrangement was never supposed to be permanent. 'We
were going through a bad patch and Harry picked up a
bloke in his taxi one night. They had sex and it confused
Harry. He'd had a couple of encounters when he was in the
army which he never forgot. He told me he wanted to try

the 'gay' scene for a while. We agreed he should rent a bedsit so that he could have his own space, but he used to drop by almost every day. He talked about moving back the last time I saw him.'

For the six months of the estrangement, Peel was a regular on the gay scene. He visited the bars and clubs – either as a punter or in his role as cab driver. He preferred working nights and most of the bouncers knew how to contact him if customers wanted a taxi. In support of his wife's claim that he was talking about 'moving back', several of his friends say he missed her. They had been married for 24 years.

Mrs Atkins cites her own affair as the reason for her divorce. 'Kevin was very discreet about his gay encounters because he didn't want to embarrass me or the kids. They started about five years into the marriage. As far as I know they were always one-night stands, so I think he probably did use male prostitutes. It was like an addiction, something he had to do every so often, but he always said it was me he loved. I suppose you can't help your feelings. I couldn't help mine when I fell in love with Roger. Kevin blamed himself when I asked for a divorce. He said he'd promise never to go with a man again if I'd stay with him, but it was too late by then.'

Atkins was also known to attend the bars and clubs, although not to the same extent as Peel. We have found one 'partner' that he took home for a single night – a 28-yr-old marine who admits to being paid – but Atkins preferred using dating agencies on the net. Most of his encounters seem to have been with soldiers. His wife said he loved his 15 years in the Parachute regiment. 'He wasn't a predator. He was only interested in consensual sex.'

Friends of Martin Britton describe him as homosexual. He lived in a committed relationship for 20+ years until 2005, when his partner, John Prentice, died of cancer. There are some indications that Britton had casual relationships afterwards – his brother, Hugh, speaks of seeing younger men at the house from time to time – but he can't remember their names and gives only vague descriptions. Despite considerable help from the gay community, we have been unable to locate anyone who admits to going to Britton's house in the last two years other than his established friends.

Britton's photograph was not recognized by any of the staff or regulars at the bars and clubs in the area, and his friends say he wasn't the type to trawl for sex. In addition, none of them support his brother's claims to have seen younger men in the Greenham Road house. The descriptions neighbours have given of his visitors match his friends – older men and women – but everyone agrees that he rarely entertained.

His next-door neighbour, Mrs Rahman, said, 'When John was alive, he and Martin used to go to the theatre and opera on a regular basis. They both loved classical music and anything to do with the stage. Martin said it wasn't the same when there was no one to share the experience with, and he stopped going after John died. Most evenings he sat at home and listened to his CD collection alone. It was sad. I think Martin was shy and, without John to keep pushing him to do things, he simply withdrew into himself. I can't imagine him inviting strangers back for sex. He just wasn't like that.'

This would suggest that his brother's evidence is unreliable. However, Hugh Britton was Martin's only regular visitor. He used to call in once a week to make sure 'everything was all right'. He said further, 'There were often people in the house when John was alive, so I didn't think anything about it. I remember Martin introducing one of the young men as a colleague of John's. I didn't stay very long because I was pleased Martin had someone else to talk to. I certainly didn't get the impression the other man was there for sex.'

John Prentice was employed as PR for a Chinese silk fashion chain, but we can find no work colleague who a) fits the description – male, blond and 30-ish; or b) irrespective of description, paid a visit to Martin Britton when his brother dropped in. Only three say they ever went to Greenham Road, even when John was alive, and they are all women in their late 50s.

Only two of the victims, Martin Britton and Kevin Atkins, had computers. Both hard drives have been examined. Atkins had irregular contact with two gay 'dating' sites and rather more frequent visits to gay and straight 'soft porn' sites. A list of emails shows how he selected and confirmed prospective partners for one-night stands and all the men interviewed have solid alibis for the night of his murder. There are no overlaps between the partners Harry Peel found at the clubs and the partners Kevin Atkins found via the internet. Martin Britton's hard drive is 'clean' of pornography or 'dating' sites, and we can find no emails relating to casual sex.

Cross-referencing army and regimental data has produced nothing. We can find no consistent features or persons between the men, except that Martin Britton, as an MOD employee, had access to Peel's and Atkins's archived records. NB We place no significance on that.

Correspondence, diaries, itemized landline bills show no common names, addresses or phone numbers between the three victims. Similarly, itemized mobile accounts for Peel and Atkins. (Britton used a 'pay as you go', for which there are no records.) Several numbers (all different) on the Peel and Atkins accounts have been disconnected. No success yet in tracing the previous 'owners' of the numbers. NB We have requested Atkins's server to keep his mobile 'live' on the off-chance it's still active and we can track its movements. Nothing to date.

It remains unclear how any of the victims made contact with their killer or how they 'found' the same person.

Conclusion

While there are some similarities in the lives and backgrounds of Peel and Atkins – bisexuality, marriage, known to engage in casual gay sex but reluctant to commit to permanent gay relationships – there is nothing similar in Martin Britton's background.

At the moment, there's no evidence that the men Hugh Britton saw with his brother were sexual partners, nor any indication of how Britton 'found' them if they were.

Psychological profile

As requested, I attach a full copy of James Steele's reworked psychological profile. We commissioned it after the Britton murder, but he has refined it to include information from the Atkins crime scene. In brief, Steele's opinions are as follows:

1. The murders carry the same signature – method of killing (skull fractures suggest a round-headed club or similarly shaped heavy object, wielded with considerable force), no sexual intercourse, damage to the rectum, the turning of the bodies to expose both buttocks, rage taken out on property . . . etc. (Steele suggests that the handle of the 'club' may have caused the rectal injuries. From gel evidence inside the anus, FSS believe the 'instrument' was covered by a condom before insertion, probably to assist its introduction.)

2. A signature is also apparent in the half-drunk bottle of wine in the living room and rinsed glasses in the kitchen. Steele suggests the initial approach was 'social' rather than 'sexual'. (This sits well with Britton, who is regularly described as 'fastidious'.)

3. We are looking for <u>one</u> individual. Steele believes both Britton and Atkins would have been suspicious if a 'visitor' had turned up with a companion. (Steele does not preclude the possibility that a companion waited outside but points to the fact that none of the neighbours or passers-by saw anything suspicious on the night of the murders.)

4. The discrepancy between the lack of 'forced entry' evidence and the frenzied nature of the attack suggests a manipulative and convincing individual who is easily roused to anger.

5. Steele posits the theory that the perpetrator was naked or semi-naked during the attack. (No sightings of any individual in bloodstained clothing afterwards.)

6. Because fingernail scrapings show no evidence of skin contact, and none of the victims has defence wounds, Steele believes all three were immobilized before they were attacked. In the absence of anything specific from the post-mortems and toxicology reports, he suggests a stun gun to the neck or head. (FSS have re-examined Kevin Atkins to this purpose but say there's too much bruising in both areas to corroborate Steele's theory.)

7. Steele cites the lack of evidence at the crime scenes as an indication that we are looking for a 'high-IQ, forensically aware' killer. He also suggests that we keep an open mind about the damage to the rectum and the exposure of the buttocks. The illusion of 'gay sex' may have been done for amusement and/or as a blind – or double blind – to create confusion about the perpetrator's sexual orientation.

8. Steele further advises that we avoid labelling the victims 'gay', despite Britton's declared single-sex status, as it may influence our decisions.

9. He points to the difference between Britton's lifestyle and that of the other two victims. He describes Britton as 'old-fashioned' and 'intellectual', and suggests he may have invited his killer in for 'companionship'.

10. Steele believes an army connection may be the means by which the killer wins credibility with his victims and/or gains access to their premises.

11. He draws particular attention to the victims' habit of keeping cash on their premises. As a taxi driver,

Harry Peel dealt only in cash; Martin Britton shopped 'locally' using cash; as a builder, Kevin Atkins kept cash in a roll to pay casual workers. This habit may have been known to the killer.

Steele's Recommendations

The perpetrator is likely to be male, aged 18–25. He may be a prostitute/escort and/or current army or ex-army. Drug addiction may be what drives the prostitution and leads to the sudden outbursts of anger. The individual may be known to other men who have employed his services. The most likely motive was money.

The paucity of forensic evidence suggests an average or above-average IQ and a premeditated willingness on the part of the perpetrator to commit a crime. In support of this, Steele cites the fact that weapons must have been brought to the properties by the killer.

In the absence of any real overlaps between the three victims, Steele proposes we go back to the drawing board. He believes the killer knows the area well, probably lives within a three-mile radius of the crime scenes, and is happy to go 'freelance' when a suitable punter/victim presents. If so, he will be using the direct approach and arranging the meetings away from the bars and clubs. Steele warns that if we concentrate all our energy on the 'gay scene' and/or recognized 'dating' agencies we may overlook the obvious – that our killer is free to kill because no one else knows of the arrangement.

He adds, 'There may be something distinctive about this individual that encourages a sympathetic response. Martin

Britton, in particular, would have needed a powerful stimulus to overcome his natural reserve and invite the killer back to his house.'

Steele advises that we concentrate the inquiry on a search for clients who have experienced anger or violence at the hands of a male prostitute but have managed to avoid the fates of Peel, Britton and Atkins. He also advises that we reinterview Mrs Peel, Mrs Atkins and Hugh Britton in an attempt to identify behavioural characteristics that might trigger the killer's rage at an early stage of the encounter.

With kind regards,

Brian

Detective Superintendent Brian Jones

Southwark Echo, *Friday, 4 May 2007*

72-yr-old attacked for mobile telephone

ABIMBOLA OSHODI, 72, was recovering in hospital last night after being kicked and punched by two assailants when she refused to hand over her mobile telephone. The assault is the latest in a spate of similar violent muggings in the south London area in the last few months.

Police are warning everyone to be aware of the danger of displaying mobiles too obviously. A spokesman said, 'Carrying a cell phone in your hand is a green light to anyone intent on theft.'

Abimbola's assailants are described as a young white male, slim, approximately 5' 10" tall, with blond or ginger hair, and a young white female, approximately 5' 4" tall, with dark hair. Both wore hoodies and Doc Martens-style boots.

Eight weeks later

Seven

DR WILLIS HAD BEEN a good reader of minds. When Acland's request to return to active service was finally denied at the end of June, the last person he wanted to confide in was the psychiatrist. He was convinced, on little justification, that Willis's first words would be 'I told you so'. Certainly, most of Willis's predictions had come true, leaving Acland to brood over his own naivety in believing there was a place for a disabled officer in a modern fighting force.

The medical board's findings were crushingly negative. Recognition was given to Lieutenant Charles D. B. Acland's clear desire to return to duty, but his ambition was at odds with the severity of his disabilities. His blind side would make him a liability in action, and his tinnitus and increasingly frequent migraines would reduce his competence to make decisions. As the first duty of the board was to consider the safety of all service personnel, it was the opinion of the members that Lieutenant Acland would pose a risk to others if he were allowed to resume his command in the field.

Even in his own mind, Acland drew a veil over his departure from his regiment. He handled his disappointment badly, rejecting any suggestion of a desk job and freezing out anyone who tried to help him. He persuaded himself he'd become an embarrassment – a hanger-on to a group rather than a member of it – and, when he packed his bags on the day of his departure, he knew he'd never see any of his colleagues again. He exited the barrack gates without ceremony or farewell, a lonely and embittered man with deep-set fears about himself and his future.

After the comments he'd made to Robert Willis about his stay with Susan Campbell – 'too many people . . . and they all gape like idiots . . .' – Acland's choice to live in London might have seemed a strange one. Yet, despite his distinctive appearance, he knew he could be anonymous in the capital city. Passers-by might stare but he wouldn't attract the same attention as he would in a smaller community. The gossiping curiosity in his parents' village would have driven him mad. He craved obscurity. The chance to rethink his life without interference or pressure from outside.

With no dependants, an unspent salary while he'd been in hospital and a deposit account swollen by compensation from the MOD for injuries sustained on the battlefield, Acland had no incentive to find a job. Instead, he took a six-month lease on a ground-floor flat in the Waterloo area and lived like a pauper, eating frugally and only spending money on the rare times he stopped at a pub for a lager.

He spent his days running, telling anyone who tried to strike up a conversation with him that he was in training for the London marathon to raise money for wounded ex-servicemen. He even believed at times that the point of the exercise was a charitable one instead of a way to shut down his brain and keep him apart from the rest of humanity. He became increasingly reluctant to make eye contact, preferring wary retreat to well-meaning interest about who he was and what he was doing.

He developed a physical revulsion against anyone wearing Arab or Muslim dress. Willis hadn't prepared him for the hatred he'd feel. Or the fear. His body was shocked with a surge of adrenalin every time he saw a bearded face above a white dishdash, and he crossed roads or turned down side streets to avoid contact. His dislike grew to encompass anyone who wasn't white. Part of him recognized that this response was irrational, but he made no attempt to control it. He felt better when he could shift the blame for what had happened on to people he didn't understand, and didn't want to understand.

Willis had warned him that some of his reactions might surprise him. The psychiatrist had talked in general terms about the consequences of trauma, and how grief, particularly for oneself, could skew perspective. He encouraged Acland not to dwell on the aspects of the tragedy that had been outside his control. Guilt was a powerful and confusing emotion, made worse when all memory of the incident was lost. As ever, Acland had steered him away from discussing the deaths of his men.

'It's not guilt I feel,' he'd said.

'What do you feel?'

'Anger. They shouldn't be dead. They had wives and children.'

'Are you saying you should have died instead?'

'No. I'm saying the Iraqis should have died.'

'I think we should discuss that, Charles.'

'No need, Doc. You asked for an answer and I gave you one. I'm not planning to wage war on Muslims in the UK just because I wish we'd got to the ragheads before they got to us.'

But he wanted to wage war on someone. He had dreams of pressing a pistol barrel to the side of a head and watching the white cotton keffiah bloom with blood. And other dreams about turning his Minimi LMG on an ululating crowd of women in burkhas and mowing them down at the rate of eight hundred rounds per minute. He would burst out of sleep, drenched in sweat, believing he'd done it, and his heart would pound uncontrollably. But whether from guilt or exultation, he couldn't tell.

He knew he was in trouble – his migraines grew worse as his dreams grew darker – but, in a perverse way, he welcomed the pain as a form of punishment. It was natural justice that *someone* should pay. And that *someone* might as well be him.

*

Acland's precarious equilibrium flipped spectacularly five weeks after he moved to London. He was minding his own business over a quiet pint at the bar of a Bermondsey pub when a group of sharp-suited City brokers pushed in beside him. They were hyped up about the money they'd made that day, and their voices became louder and more intrusive as the drink started flowing. Two or three times Acland was buffeted by those on the fringes, but he wouldn't have reacted if one of them hadn't spoken to him. The man, who could only see Acland's right profile, tapped him on the shoulder when he didn't receive an answer.

'Are you deaf?' he asked, waving a glass of orange juice under Acland's nose and jerking his chin towards the empty stool on Acland's blind side. 'I asked you if you'd consider moving to give the rest of us some room.'

The accent was singsong, unmistakably Pakistani, and Acland's reply was immediate and involuntary. He hooked his right arm round the back of the man's neck and punched him squarely in the face with his left fist. The broker went down with a howl of anguish, knocking against his friends, blood spurting from his nose.

The rest of the group turned alarmed faces towards Acland. 'Jesus!' said one. 'What the hell's going on?'

'I don't like murderers,' Acland told them, returning to his lager.

There was a second or two of surprised silence before someone bent over to help the man to his feet. He took a serviette from a dispenser on the bar and held it to his nose, staring angrily at his assailant. Whatever his religion or nationality, he was dressed like a westerner in a dark suit, shirt and tie. Only his fringed beard and choice of drink suggested Islam. 'You cannot behave like that in this country.'

'I was *born* here. I can behave any way I want.'

'I, too, was born here.'

'That doesn't make you English.'

'Did you hear that?' the Pakistani demanded excitedly of his friends. 'This man attacked me on racial grounds. You're my witnesses.' He was stockier and heavier than Acland and he fancied his chances with his colleagues to back him up. He wagged his finger in admonishment. 'You're a maniac. You should not be allowed out.'

'Wrong,' said Acland in a deceptively mild tone. 'I'm an *angry* maniac. Even an ignorant Paki should be able to work that out.'

It was like waving a red rag at a bull. Enraged by the insult, the man lowered his head and charged. Had he come at Acland from the left, he'd have stood a better chance but, from the right, it was a no-brainer. He couldn't compete in strength, speed or fitness – a broker's life is a sedentary one – and the only way he knew how to fight was to flail his fists in the hope of landing a blow. He wasn't expecting Acland to move off his stool as fast as he did, nor that Acland would exploit the forward motion of his run to slam him headfirst into the side of the bar before kicking his feet from under him.

Acland could have left it at that, but he didn't. He was aware of urgency behind the bar and shouts from the Pakistani's friends, but the suppressed hatred of months had been looking for a target and this loud-mouthed broker had volunteered himself. 'You should have kept your mouth shut,' he murmured, dropping to one knee and clamping both hands under the man's chin, preparing to snap his head back and crush his spinal cord between two vertebrae.

Only the shock of a bucket of melting ice pouring over the back of his neck from the other side of the bar made Acland hesitate.

'Cut it OUT!' barked a woman's voice as a dozen hands hauled him off and tossed him aside. 'I SAID . . . cut it OUT!' she roared as one of the brokers launched a toecap at Acland's ribs. 'No one MOVES till the police get here!' She gave a piercing whistle. 'JACKSON! HERE, mate! PRONTO!'

Her words fell on deaf ears. Acland absorbed an onslaught of kicks from the other brokers while uninvolved customers scattered hastily to avoid the fight zone. The Pakistani added to the confusion by staggering to his feet and grabbing at anyone or anything that might keep him upright. As he threatened to overturn a table, a huge woman with cropped and streaked dark hair emerged from behind the bar. 'Easy now,' she said in a deep, melodious voice that betrayed no excitement at all. 'You're bleeding like a stuck pig, my friend. Let's have you out of harm's way.'

With a grunt of effort, she hoisted Acland's victim in her arms and dumped him unceremoniously on the counter. 'All yours, lover,' she said, before weighing into the fray. 'You heard the lady,' she said, smacking two of the Pakistani's friends on the back of their heads with meaty hands. 'Cut it out. This is an orderly house. All breakages have to be paid for.' She elbowed her way past two more to look down at Acland. 'You all right?' she asked him.

He squinted up at her. From the floor she looked like a mountain of white muscle, with calves, thighs, shoulders and neck bulging out of her biker boots, black cycling shorts and sleeveless T-shirt like inflated bladders. He flinched in alarm as one of her booted feet came down like a piledriver. 'The lady said, don't move,' she rumbled in her deep bass, as her heel ground into a soft leather shoe. 'That includes kicking.'

'Jesus Christ, Jackson!' the offender yelped. 'You're fucking well hurting me!'

'I'll hurt you some more if you don't back off.' She tilted her heel to release him. 'Anyone else want to mess with a three-hundred-pound weightlifter? I eat steak for breakfast, so a few cream puffs won't faze me.' When no one offered themselves, she proffered a hand to Acland and pulled him to his feet. 'Over there,' she ordered, nodding to a bench seat against the wall. 'And you lot to that table,' she told the brokers. 'We're going to sit nice and quiet till the cops come.' She smiled broadly. 'And afterwards you can twiddle your thumbs in the nick for several hours until you're invited to make statements.'

They stared at her mutinously. 'Give us a break, Jackson,' said one. 'We've all got homes to go to.'

'Is that my problem?'

'We're good customers, and it wasn't us who started it.'

'So? This is *my* home. I don't have the luxury of calling a taxi and leaving the mess behind.' She spread her huge legs and folded her arms across her chest, daring them to challenge her. 'Daisy and I don't come to your houses and behave like spoilt children. What gives you the right to do it in ours?'

'We didn't. It was that racist bastard over there. For no reason at all, he punched Rashid in the face and called him an ignorant Paki.'

Jackson shifted her gaze to Acland. 'Is that right?'

Acland ran a finger under his eyepatch and massaged the damaged nerves in his empty socket. 'Near enough.'

'How near?'

'I had a reason.'

She waited for him to go on and, when he didn't, she said, 'I hope it was a good one, my friend, because you're lucky you can still see. If Rashid Mansoor was any kind of fighter, he'd have glassed your other eye and you'd be blind.'

The arrival of the police put an end to the exchange. Still enraged, and mopping his bloody nose, Mansoor gave his name and accused Acland of calling him racist names and trying to kill him. Acland merely gave his name. A migraine was thudding in his head and Jackson wasn't alone in noticing how pale he was. An officer asked if either man needed medical treatment, but both said no. Mansoor was too intent on holding the floor and Acland too drained to move.

Excitable anger raised the Pakistani's voice to a high-pitched squeak which was difficult to understand, so the officer in charge cut him short and turned to Jackson for an explanation. She described accurately what she'd seen when she came out but couldn't say who'd started it because she'd been in the kitchen at the time. Her partner, Daisy, a shapely blonde with a deep cleavage, was no better informed. She'd been serving a customer at the other end of the bar and only realized a fight had broken out when the shouting began. The brokers, glancing surreptitiously at their watches, said the first they knew about it was their friend hitting the floor with blood on his face and Acland saying he didn't like murderers.

The officer in charge shifted his attention back to the two men. 'All right, gentlemen, what was this about? Which of you spoke first?'

Acland stared at the floor.

'*I* did,' Mansoor said defensively, 'but I was perfectly courteous. I asked this person if he'd mind moving to the empty stool next to him to make room for the rest of us. He didn't even bother to answer, just grabbed me round the neck and punched me.'

'And that's all you said?'

The Pakistani hesitated. 'I had to repeat it. He failed to hear me the first time, so I tapped him on the shoulder and asked him again.' He remembered the words he'd used. *Are you deaf?* 'I could only see one side of his face,' he finished lamely.

The officer frowned. 'What difference does that make?'

'I wouldn't have spoken to him if I'd realized he was –' Mansoor gave an awkward shrug as he sought for an appropriate expression – 'well, that he'd been in an accident . . . had surgery . . . whatever. *You* know.'

'Not really. You're talking gobbledygook as far as I'm concerned. What were these racist names he called you?'

'He said I was a murderer and an ignorant Paki.'

'And what did you call him?'

'A maniac.'

The policeman turned to Acland. 'Is there anything you want to say?'

'No.'

The man eyed him for a moment, then looked enquiringly at Jackson. 'Either this one's had too much to drink or he needs a doctor. He's green to the gills.'

'He took a kicking from Rashid's friends . . . so unless Rashid sees it differently I'd say they're about even in the assault stakes.'

The policeman looked at the Pakistani and nodded when he shook his head. 'What about you, Jackson? It's your property. Do you want me to arrest the whole lot for criminal damage and take them back to the station –' there was a glint of amusement in his eye, as if they'd been down this road before – 'or give them a warning and throw them out? I can't make an exception of Captain Kidd here.'

'What kind of choice is that?' she said sourly. 'I'll lose my business if word gets out that I handed a sick man to you lot . . . even worse if the punters have to clamber over him to reach the front door.'

The officer grinned. 'I'm guessing he'll look a lot grimmer if you make me drag him down to the station . . . and it'll make your job harder.'

'Mm.' She took the empty ice bucket from the bar and placed it on the brokers' table. 'Five quid each for the aggro you've given me, and I'll let you go . . . but it's fifty quid to you two jerks,' she said, aiming her index fingers at Acland and Mansoor. 'I'm damned if Daisy and me are going to wipe up after you, so you either pay for an agency cleaner or get down on your knees and scrub up the blood yourselves.'

The brokers produced fivers with indecent haste and made a beeline for the exit before anyone could rewrite the rules. 'That's my kind of justice,' said Jackson, passing the ice bucket to Daisy and winking at the policeman. 'Instant compensation for the victims and no official time wasted on paperwork.' She rubbed her thumb and forefinger under Mansoor's nose. 'OK, my little Muslim friend, it's your turn. Ante up.'

Mansoor took out his wallet with bad grace. 'What about *him*?'

'Oh, he'll pay, don't you worry about that.' She took the Pakistani's money. 'But, first, I'm going to do you a favour and keep him alive, otherwise you'll be down at the police station answering questions about murder.' She stooped over Acland. 'Where are you hurting?'

He continued to stare at the floor. 'Head,' he muttered through clenched teeth, holding back the bile that rose in his throat with every eye movement. 'Migraine.'

'Have you had a migraine before? Do you recognize the symptoms?'

'Yes.'

'What did your surgeon say was causing them?'

'Phantom pain.'

'From losing your eye?'

'Yes.'

'Do you have pain anywhere else? Ribs? Back? Did any of the kicks do any damage?'

'No.'

'Can you stand up?'

Acland made an effort to comply, but the movement sent bile shooting into his mouth. He clamped both palms over his mouth and retched convulsively.

'Great!' said Jackson sourly. 'Chuck us a towel, Daisy.' She caught the cloth and handed it to Acland. 'Use that,' she said, hauling him upright and hoisting him over her shoulder in a fireman's lift, 'and don't mess up my clothes or it'll cost you another fifty.' She paused briefly in front of the two police-men. 'I'll knock him flat if he's a nutter and goes berserk,' she warned, 'so don't try pinning GBH on me if he complains to you afterwards.'

'You're all heart, Jackson.'

'That's the truth of it,' she agreed, carrying the weight of a grown man on her back as easily as she would a child.

*

Acland remembered her lowering him on to a bed and telling him to use the bowl that she placed beside his pillow. Shortly after-wards she came back with a briefcase and asked him about the injuries to his face. Where had the surgery been done? Was he on any drugs? When was the last time he'd seen a doctor? How often did he have migraines? How did he manage them? Were they getting worse? Was nausea always involved? What remedies did he use?

He answered as well as he could, mostly in monosyllables, but when the retching continued unabated, she offered him an injection of an anti-emetic to help him take on fluids and keep a painkiller down. Worn out, he agreed. He fell asleep soon after the sedative properties of the analgesic took effect, but not before he had revealed rather more about himself than he'd ever told Willis.

*

Sunshine filtered through a gap in the curtains when Acland woke the next morning and he could hear the clatter of crockery in the kitchen downstairs. There was no confusion about where he was or what had happened. He remembered every event of the previous evening – or thought he did – right up to the question he'd put to Jackson shortly before she gave him the anti-emetic. 'Are you a doctor?' But he couldn't recall if she'd answered.

He was lying on his left side, facing the window, and he noticed his shoes and socks on a chair beside it. He was naked except for his underpants but had no idea when his clothes had been removed or who had done it. He levered himself into a sitting position to look around the rest of the room. It was small and utilitarian with a pinewood wardrobe in one corner and a pedestal basin and mirror on the wall opposite the window. The vomit bowl, emptied and washed, stood with his wallet, watch and eyepatch on the bedside cabinet, and a hand towel lay folded next to his pillow. There was no sign of his jacket, shirt or trousers.

He strapped on his eyepatch, then checked the time by his watch. Almost nine o'clock. Wary of squeaking floorboards, which would tell whoever was in the kitchen that he was awake, he slid out from under the duvet and tiptoed to the wardrobe. At the very least he was hoping for a dressing gown, but all he found were five empty coat hangers. Feeling foolish, he put on his socks and shoes, tucked his wallet into the waistband of his underpants, then stripped the pink floral cover from the duvet and wrapped it round his middle.

He eased open the door to the landing and poked out his head, looking for a bathroom, but all the adjoining rooms were firmly closed. To his left was a staircase, and the sounds from the kitchen carried clearly up the well. Aromas, too. Someone was grilling bacon and the smell shot pangs of hunger through his empty stomach. He couldn't tell if he was in a private part of the building or if the nearby rooms were to let, so with an increasing sense of awkwardness he edged quietly along the landing, looking for anything that might indicate a lavatory.

It was sod's law that when he finally plucked up the courage to try a handle he'd find Jackson inside. She was sitting astride a bench press, facing the door, with her arms stretched out at shoulder height and a dumbbell in each huge fist. She gave a throaty chuckle at Acland's appearance as she bent her elbows to bring the dumbbells back on to her chest. 'Nice skirt,' she said. 'If you're looking for the bathroom it's the room opposite yours. You can borrow the robe on the back of the door, but don't go using my razor. I'll be through in five minutes.'

A flush stained the lieutenant's neck and cheeks as he backed out with a muttered apology, and Jackson wondered if he was younger than the thirty-something she'd estimated last night. It was difficult to age him with his buzz-cut hair and damaged face, but she'd certainly thought him older than Mansoor and his friends. As she straightened her arms to raise the dumbbells again, she revisited some of the answers he'd given her about his medical history.

What caused your injuries? *A piece of metal.* In a car accident? *If you like.* What does that mean? *Nothing . . . it was an accident.* Did you have migraines before? *No.* What do you take for the pain? *I don't. I put up with it.* Why? *It helps me function.* Most people function better without pain. *I do OK.* Sure you do. You look like shit and attack the first person who annoys you. What kind of functioning is that? *I'm alive, aren't I . . . ?*

The answers he'd given after the retching ceased but before the painkiller took effect were even more interesting. Who died? *Two of my men.* Are you in the army? *Not any more.* Why not? *I'm not good enough.* How did Rashid Mansoor upset you? *I've been trying to avoid them.* Pakistanis? *Murderers.* Will anyone be worrying about you? *Only me . . .*

*

Acland was sitting on his bed with his door wide open when Jackson emerged at the end of her exercise session. He was wearing her navy-blue bathrobe and he greeted her with more confidence than he'd shown five minutes earlier. 'Are you a doctor?'

She folded her beefy arms across her chest and subjected him to a close scrutiny. She looked to be in her mid-forties and was as tall as he was, over six feet, but her muscular jaw, short spiked hair and sloping shoulders made her look more like a man than a woman. She was dressed in similar singlet and shorts to the ones she'd been wearing the previous evening, showing off thigh muscles that were so developed she had to stand with her feet apart. 'You keep asking me that . . . and I keep telling you I am . . . but I can't seem to convince you. Don't I look like a doctor?'

He contemplated the inflated biceps and disproportionately flat chest. 'Not one that I've ever seen. You called yourself a three-hundred-pound weightlifter yesterday.'

'I exaggerated. I'm more like two-fifty, but it doesn't have the same scare factor as three hundred. Have you never met a doctor who does weight training before?'

Not a female one that looked like you, he thought. 'I don't think so. I've never met a doctor who runs a pub either.'

She watched him struggle to hold her gaze. 'It's Daisy who runs it, I just have an interest in the property. I used to be a full-time GP, now I'm employed through the local primary care trust to cover out-of-hours services and the drunks and drug addicts in the police cells. It means I'm on call at weekends and two or three nights a week. It was my evening off yesterday, so I should have been sitting with my feet up instead of playing nursemaid to you.'

He couldn't tell if she was annoyed or being ironic. 'I'm sorry.'

'No need to be. You went out like a light once you agreed to let me give you something.' She saw his suspicion. 'The injection was a metoclopramide anti-emetic to stop you dehydrating and the painkiller was codeine combined with paracetamol. Nothing more sinister than that. What did you think I was giving you? Heroin?'

Acland found her difficult to read. Her intense stare was unnerving and he decided it was easier to look at his hands. 'I don't take drugs.'

'So you told me last night. You said you function better without them.' She paused, as if expecting him to answer. 'How are you feeling this morning?'

'OK.'

'Hungry?'

'Yes.'

'Good. Daisy's cooked enough bacon and eggs to feed the five thousand, and I'm damned if I'm going to eat it on my own. I've too much respect for my cholesterol levels. Your clothes are in the laundry room, so you can come down in the robe . . . and don't forget your wallet. You owe me a hundred quid from last night – fifty for Rashid's blood and fifty for vomiting down my back – plus an extra fiver to Daisy for the breakfast.'

He followed her on to the landing. 'What about paying for the bed?'

'You get one night free, but if you make a habit of falling sick on the premises it'll cost you thirty quid every time you use it. No cheques.' She set off down the stairs.

It was on the tip of Acland's tongue to say he had no intention of ever returning to her pub. 'It was a one-off,' he told her instead. 'It won't happen again.'

'We'll see. You haven't tried Daisy's breakfast yet.'

*

Daisy was the complete antithesis to Jackson – a warm, friendly, curvaceous blonde who looked ten years younger than her partner. She was also quite uninterested in money. When Acland tried to pay for his food, she laughed and told him not to be so silly. 'If you hadn't eaten it, Jackson would. She's the resident dustbin.'

Jackson had no such qualms. 'Where's my hundred?' she asked, washing down a mouthful of fried bread with a huge swallow of tea. 'Daisy's a pinko liberal. She thinks profit's a dirty word and all criminals come from broken homes.' She held out her palm. 'I expect people to pay their dues.'

'You gave me a choice,' Acland reminded her mildly. 'Pay up or clean.'

'Too late. Daisy did the business last night. Blood and puke stains are the devil to get out once they've soaked in.' Her partner frowned, as if she were about to contradict, but Jackson spoke again before she had the chance. 'You're lucky I'm not charging you for a new vest. It'll need ten washes at least to get rid of the lager you spewed down my back.'

Acland counted off five twenties and handed them over with the fiver that Daisy had refused. Jackson took the lot and twisted in her chair to put it in the drawer of a unit behind her. He had a brief glimpse of a smaller stack, topped by a ten-pound note, before she closed the drawer again. 'Mansoor's contribution,' she said, catching his eye as she turned back. 'Not a bad night, all in all.'

He felt a sudden dislike for her, or perhaps he'd disliked her all along and it was distrust that now set his teeth on edge. She was an ugly woman – gross and greedy – and she clearly enjoyed bullying anyone who was at a disadvantage. He wondered briefly about Daisy's role in the relationship. Was she Jackson's obedient slave? A piece of eye-candy to be discarded when someone prettier came along? Was she there out of love? Necessity? Was it an equal partnership? He watched her butter some toast for Jackson and realized he didn't care. Revulsion against the whole set-up had him scraping his chair legs across the floor and standing up.

'I need my clothes,' he said brusquely. 'If you point me in the right direction, I'll get them myself.'

Surprised by his tone, Daisy gave a doubtful smile. 'Are you all right?'

'I'm fine . . . but I need to go now. I'm late.'

'OK.' She pointed to a door behind her. 'Through there, first room on the right and you'll find your stuff on the ironing board. When you've changed, continue down the corridor and you'll find an exit on to Murray Street at the end. Can you find your way from there?'

Acland nodded.

'Just make sure you leave my bathrobe behind,' said Jackson, taking another piece of toast and sticking a buttery knife into the marmalade. 'It cost me a fortune.'

He took a deep breath and addressed Daisy. 'Thank you.'

'For what?'

'Clearing up after me . . . breakfast . . . washing my clothes.'

Daisy smiled slightly. 'You shouldn't believe everything Jackson says, you know. She bends the truth to suit herself.'

The non sequitur confused him. 'I don't understand.'

Jackson jumped in again before the other woman could answer. 'The robe cost two quid from an Oxfam shop,' she told him, 'but that doesn't mean you can take it.'

'I wasn't going to,' Acland said stiffly, untying the belt and shrugging out of it. 'Here.' He draped it over the back of his chair. 'I wouldn't want you accusing me of theft after I've gone.'

Her gaze travelled with amusement from his underpants to his socks and shoes. 'You jump to too many conclusions, my friend, and none of them reflect well on you. Being one-eyed doesn't make a man blind or stupid – or *shouldn't* – although in your case I'm beginning to wonder. You can come back when you've learned some tolerance . . . but not before.'

'It won't happen,' he said, heading for the door. 'I can't bloody well afford it.'

'Of course you can,' she said comfortably. 'Daisy offers a ten per cent discount to anyone who stays the week.'

Eight

DEPRIVED OF MOST of his cash by Jackson, Acland stopped at an ATM on the way to the tube station. He pulled his wallet from his back pocket and flipped it open to retrieve his Switch, but as soon as he thumbed the plastic from its slot, he noticed that Robert Willis's business card was in the wrong place. It should have been tucked behind the American Express but now it was where the Switch had been.

He had a mental picture of Jackson going through his wallet, looking for someone to phone, and he knew she'd have found a psychiatrist irresistible. What had Willis told her? What had *she* told Willis? 'Your patient's showing psychopathic tendencies, Doctor.' 'Did you warn him that injuries to the head can inhibit moral sense?' 'Did you know he was dysfunctional when you gave him the all clear?'

Acland wondered why he'd kept Willis's card, except that it was a link, however tenuous, with a time when he was still in the army. Perhaps, too, he had hoped to leave an upbeat message one day that everything had worked out fine, as if somewhere in his subconscious the psychiatrist's good opinion mattered to him. Instead, Willis now knew that every gloomy prediction he'd made had come true. Acland was a loner. He was suspicious to the point of paranoia. And the recurring pains in his head were making him unstable.

Someone shifted impatiently in the rapidly building queue behind him and he went through the process of inserting the card and tapping in his PIN. He pictured Willis phoning his parents, or giving their number to Jackson, and a sweat of humiliation broke out in the small of his back. Did they know their son had run amok in a London pub? *Christ!*

He felt a prod in his back. 'Are you planning on taking that money, son, or are you just gonna look at it?'

Acland drew in a breath through his nose and resisted the impulse to round on the man and punch him in the face. With a muttered apology, he tugged the wad of twenties out of the ATM's metal grip, stuffed them into his wallet and turned away.

Another prod. 'You've forgotten your card.'

It might have evolved into a rerun of the previous evening if the creaky voice hadn't so clearly belonged to an old man. Nevertheless, Acland swung round and grabbed an arthritic finger before it could jab him again. 'Don't do that,' he grated, staring into a pair of rheumy eyes.

Indignantly, the eighty-something wrestled himself free. 'I was trying to do you a favour, mate, but go ahead . . . leave the card. Do you think I care if you're robbed of all your savings?'

'I don't like people touching me.'

The pensioner wasn't easily intimidated. 'Then stick a sign on your back. There's not many of us gonna realize you're a bad-tempered bastard if we're standing behind you. A man's gotta see your face for that.'

*

Acland took up a position across the road in the shadow of a plane tree. He was prepared for a long wait – even welcomed a period of calm in the hope his anger might dissipate – but, in the event, he abandoned his stake-out after fifteen minutes. The old man had been right. His temper was evil. When the attack happened there was no sympathy in his heart, just an increase of frustrated fury. Now what? he thought in unfeeling calculation. *Now* what?

*

Back in his flat, the lower one of two in a converted Victorian terraced house, he tore up Willis's card and, for good measure, burned the pieces in an ashtray. He followed that by going into the pint-sized garden that came with the apartment and lighting a ceremonial bonfire of anything that connected him to the army – commission papers, regimental documents, pay slips, medical board reports. He would have tossed his old fatigues on to the flames as well if the woman above him hadn't shouted out of her window that what he was doing was illegal.

Taking breaths to compose himself, Acland raised his head to look at her, shielding his eye with one hand. He'd avoided her as far as possible, put off by her excessive show of friendliness on the day he took over the lease, and the way she reminded him of Jen. He could have tolerated any other tenant, but not a woman who demanded attention.

She'd arrived at his door with a bottle of wine, entered without invitation, shortened his name to Charlie and insisted that he call her by her nickname, Kitten. In short order, he learned that she was a thirty-five-year-old divorcee with two children, that her ex was a two-timing bastard, that she was lonely, that she thought Charlie's eyepatch was 'cute' and that she was always up for a night out as long as somebody else paid.

After an hour of making an effort to be polite – he was about to spend six months with this woman as a neighbour – Acland's responses became increasingly monosyllabic. There was nothing about her that attracted him. She even looked like Jen. Blonde, vacuously pretty with large mascaraed eyes, and a body like a beanpole, clad in tight jeans and a cropped top. She drank most of the bottle, but couldn't hold the alcohol and veered between vicious remarks about her ex's new wife and clumsy, slurred attempts to tell Charlie she found him attractive. When she asked him coyly if she was outstaying her welcome, he delivered a curt yes and her mask slipped abruptly.

Playful flirting gave way to hissing antagonism. She was only trying to be friendly. What sort of woman did he think she was? Acland listened to her without comment, wondering what she'd expected from him. Sex? Admiration? Whichever, he turned from being 'cute' to 'sick' in the time it took her to stumble to his door.

Her subsequent spite took the form of petty nuisances – intrusive noise from upstairs, litter thrown into the garden or in front of his door, watching to see when he left and when he came in. On the outside, he presented a frigid indifference; on the inside her behaviour ate away at the fragile respect he still had for her sex. The whole experience was a dangerously negative one for a man as alienated as Acland. In the end, her only achievement was to reinforce his distrust of women.

He saw a movement in the upstairs window of the next-door house and shifted his gaze from Kitten to their elderly neighbour. It was hard to tell from the man's disapproving expression whether his grievance was with the bonfire or with Kitten's colourful language about Acland's criminal behaviour.

'You're a fucking moron!' Kitten finished angrily. 'I'll call the police if you don't put that bloody thing out now.'

Behind her, Acland caught a glimpse of a child's anxious face. 'Go ahead,' he said. 'It's not illegal, it's just not encouraged in case people like you complain. The police have better things to do than explain to a screeching harridan that she's got her facts wrong.' He saw the child pluck at her sleeve, then jump away to avoid a vicious jab from her elbow.

'It's the summer, for Christ's sake,' she hissed. 'Do you know what the temperature is? We'll all go up if a spark hits the fence. Can't you *see* that? Or are you blind in both fucking eyes?'

Acland looked at the fire. 'It's under control,' he murmured, using his foot to nudge the remains of a cardboard folder towards the dying flames.

'No, it's not. My baby's choking on the smoke. Do you want me to sue you when he gets asthma? You're so damn selfish. Don't they teach you about climate change in the army?'

'There'd be no point. You don't count pollutants when an oil well blows up, you just count the corpses. Have you ever seen a body burned to the bone while it's still alive? The stink's so bad you can't go within ten yards without breathing apparatus. All you can do is watch the poor bastard die . . . and that's not pretty.'

'Keep your voice down,' she said angrily. 'I don't want my kids having nightmares.'

'Then don't pretend one little fire in London does more damage than what's going on in Iraq and Afghanistan. Every time a Tornado takes off the ozone layer takes another hit.' He watched his army medical card melt and curl. 'War destroys everything. Better your children understand that now. It'll give them a chance to enjoy their lives before the world goes up in flames.'

But she wasn't interested in philosophy. 'Don't you tell me how to raise my kids. At least they don't run around the streets half-naked and shout their heads off in the middle of the fucking night. You're a headcase. It wouldn't surprise me if you're the gay killer. You're psycho enough for it.'

Acland hadn't realized that his terrifying awakenings from nightmares were loud enough to carry to the floor above. He squinted up at her again. 'What gay killer?'

'Don't pretend you don't know.'

He eyed her for a moment, then trod out the ashes with his shoe. 'You should see a psychiatrist,' he said. 'Someone ought to tell you that the reason men don't want to have sex with you isn't because they're gay. It's because you're a complete turn-off. Your husband proved that by leaving.'

'Bastard!' She threw something at him – a china ornament – but it missed and fell with a thud into some weeds by the fence. 'You don't know anything about me.'

Acland's fingers itched to retrieve the missile and launch it back again – there was no way *he* would miss – but he held himself in check. 'I know enough not to want to know any more,' he said with sudden resolve, heading towards his french windows. 'I'm out of here as soon as I've packed my stuff.'

*

He rued his spur-of-the-moment decision as soon as he was back inside. With five months of his tenancy left he would be paying rent on an empty space until the agents could be bothered to advertise for another occupant. But there was no going back on it. The bitch upstairs would have a field day if he changed his mind.

In any case, he knew he couldn't go on like this. Something had to change. At times the pains in his head were unbearable.

He resisted any impulse to take up Jackson's offer of a bed. If he thought Kitten would gloat over a change of mind, he could just imagine what Jackson would say if he crawled back in under twenty-four hours with his tail between his legs. He was more inclined to listen to Robert Willis's voice inside his head, even if burning the card had been an attempt to cut his ties with the man.

'We can all walk out, Charles – it's the fashionable thing to do these days – it's asking to be let back *in* that takes courage.'

On another spur-of-the-moment decision, he called a cab and gave the driver the name of the road that Willis's colleague, Susan Campbell, lived in. 'Which number, mate?'

'I can't remember. Just go slowly when we get there. I'll recognize the front door when I see it.'

'You're the boss.'

Twenty minutes later, and after three passes up and down the street, the cabbie drew into a parking space and turned round. His expression was wary, as if he'd begun to suspect that his passenger's disfigured face was a reflection of something warped inside. 'We can do this all afternoon, mate, but the meter's ticking and I need some proof that you can pay. I reckon you're looking for somewhere to doss . . . but that somewhere ain't gonna be this cab.'

With a sigh, Acland took out his wallet. 'I know which house it is. I just don't know if I want to go in,' he said, sorting the fare.

The driver grew more amenable at the sight of cash. 'I feel the same every time I visit the ex's place to take my kids out.'

Acland handed over a twenty-pound note. 'I don't suppose you know of a cheap hotel somewhere? I don't care which part of London it's in.'

'How cheap?'

'Thirty quid a night.'

The cabbie laughed. 'You've gotta be joking. It's the height of the tourist season. You could get lucky on a last-minute deal somewhere, but it'll cost you an arm and a leg to drive around looking for it. If you've a laptop, you might find something on the internet, but I wouldn't bet on it. London's expensive.'

'What about a pub?'

'Same problem.' The man handed over the change. 'I'd stick it out here for a night if I were you and have a rethink in the morning. Cheers.' He pocketed the tip Acland gave him and eyed him sympathetically. 'Why don't want you want to go in? What's waiting on the other side?'

'Questions,' said Acland wryly, opening the door and backing out with his kitbag.

'And you won't have an answer for any of them, eh? Or not ones that you want to give. Mother?'

'Close enough.'

'That's the difference between the sexes, mate. Blokes are happy to hold up their hands and take a caning . . . women insist on examining the bloody entrails. If you don't believe me, talk to my ex-missus. She rips my guts out every time I see her.' He drew away from the kerb with a hand raised in farewell.

Acland slung the kitbag over his shoulder and walked the fifty yards to Susan Campbell's house. 'You said come back any time,' he reminded her when she opened the door. 'Did you mean it?'

She looked more like a charlady than a psychiatrist. Her grey hair was piled on top of her head with large red clip and a cigarette dangled from the side of her mouth. It was a poor indication of what she was really like. Acland knew from his previous stay that the untidy, garrulous image she projected hid a genuine toughness underneath.

'Are you safe to let in?'

'As safe as I was before.'

'Mm. Except you seem to make a habit of attacking people just before you come to me.' She assessed him briefly, then pulled the door wide. 'I've been talking about you on the phone.'

'I thought you might have been.' He followed her into the corridor. 'News seems to travel faster round the National Health Service than it does round the army. What did the doc say?'

Susan led him past her sitting room, where a couple of paying guests were watching television, and showed him into the kitchen. She stubbed out her butt in an over-full ashtray on the table. 'That you punched an inoffensive, overweight Muslim who's never lifted anything heavier than a pen all his life.'

'I damn nearly killed him.'

'Is that why you came? Are you worried you're going to do it again?'

'Maybe.'

Susan pulled out a chair and pointed to it. 'Sit down. I'll make you a cup of tea.' She busied herself with a kettle. 'What other reasons brought you here?'

Acland lowered himself on to the seat. 'I had to leave my flat and I couldn't think of anywhere else to go. It'll only be for one night. I'll look for a new place tomorrow.'

'What happened at the flat?'

'Nothing. I just don't like the woman upstairs.'

Susan poured boiling water on to a tea bag and poked it with a spoon. 'Did you have a fight with her?'

'Only a verbal one. She takes it personally if a man doesn't want to sleep with her.'

Susan took what she could from this answer. 'It's difficult when people won't take no for an answer.'

'Right.' He thanked her for the mug of tea she handed him, but placed it on the table as if he wasn't interested in it. 'What else did the doc say?'

'That you're dangerously underweight for your height.'

'How would he know? I haven't seen him for weeks.' Acland watched her for a moment. 'You should tell him not to believe everything Jackson told him. The woman's the size of whale. She probably thinks everyone's dangerously underweight compared with her.'

Susan tucked a stray strand of hair behind her ear and went on as if she hadn't heard. 'That you're under-employed and have too much time on your hands . . . that you think too much and your thoughts are misdirected . . . that someone should give you a kick up the arse and remind you that you're a functioning individual.' She opened her fridge and peered at the contents. 'I'm a bit short on food at the moment but I can rustle up a cheese sandwich. How does that sound?'

'Bloody awful,' he said rudely. 'Which doc have you been talking to?'

'Both of them.'

'What about patient confidentiality?'

'Quite unbreached. All three of us have treated you at one time or another.' She took a slab of Cheddar off the shelf and retrieved some bread from an earthenware crock. 'You can't run without eating, Charles. It's elementary mechanics. You'll end up badly malnourished if you do. How much weight have you lost since you left hospital?'

'I don't know. There weren't any scales in the flat.'

She took a knife from a drawer and cut into the bread. 'Vehicles don't function too well when their engines overheat either, so why aren't you trying to manage your migraines instead of allowing them to control you?'

'They don't control me. I've worked out a way to live with them.'

'So what went wrong last night?'

'It wasn't a migraine that caused the fight . . . it was a stupid loud-mouthed bastard poking me in the shoulder. And it's not just Muslims either. An old white guy kept sticking his finger into me this morning when I was trying to get some money out of the bank and I damn near clocked him one as well. I don't like people touching me.'

'So I gathered the last time you were here.' She smiled slightly. 'But I didn't ask you what made you lose your temper, Charles, I asked you what went wrong with your method of coping with pain. It's one thing to say you *live* with migraine, quite another to suffer such a debilitating episode in public that a doctor has to intervene with medication.'

'It was a one-off.7 If I'd been allowed to drink my pint in peace I'd have been OK.'

'I doubt it. Alcohol on an empty stomach is one of the primary triggers . . . as is intense exercise without regular fluid intake . . . prolonged guilt-ridden stress . . . sleep patterns disrupted by nightmares . . . a refusal to take medication. Do you want me to go on?'

'No.' He watched in silence as she prepared the sandwiches for him. 'I've had enough lectures to last a lifetime,' he said with sudden irritation. 'Everyone I meet has an opinion . . . even the cabbies.'

Susan chuckled. 'And what were you expecting from me? A *hug*? You'd have turned catatonic if I'd even tried.' She wagged a butter knife at him. 'You knew perfectly well what you were going to get . . . you told Robert I was bossy and interfering. You wouldn't be here if you hadn't wanted a lecture.'

Acland cracked his finger joints. 'Go on, then,' he said with grudging amusement. 'I'm ready. Give me your best bollocking.'

'Nn-nn.' She shook her head as she pushed the plate of sandwiches towards him. 'I'm just the middleman. You need medical attention, Charles. When you've eaten those, I'll call a taxi and take you to a doctor.'

He eyed her suspiciously. 'I'd rather stay with you.'

'It's a Friday night in August, Charles. All my beds are taken for the weekend.'

'Which doctor?'

'How many do you know in London?'

Nine

'WHAT IF I HADN'T shown up at your place?' Acland asked Susan in the cab. 'You all seem so interested in my affairs, what would you have done then?'

'There's nothing we could have done. None of us knew where you lived. Jackson thought you might contact Robert when you realized she'd put his card in a different slot, but Robert was less optimistic. He said you'd see that as loss of face.'

'Did either of them phone my parents?'

Susan shrugged. 'I've no idea. The only information I have is that Jackson spoke to Robert at about eleven o'clock last night and he phoned me this morning to give me her number. You'd already left by the time I called her.' She watched him withdraw into the corner of the seat. 'We didn't gossip about you, Charles. Jackson told me what had happened and asked me to reiterate her offer if I saw you. That's all.'

'You said she told you I needed a kick up the arse.'

'I didn't say she didn't have a sense of humour. Would you rather she'd used a more PC expression like "Charles needs to refocus and learn motivational skills"? She strikes me as a very down-to-earth woman – a straight speaker who dislikes touchy-feely waffle as much as you do. Or have Robert and I misread you on that?'

'No.'

'Then what's the problem?'

'You're making my decisions for me. The only reason Jackson's happy to have me back is because she'll make a profit on my room, but that doesn't mean I'm happy to go along with it.'

'So stop the cab and get out,' Susan said reasonably. 'You're a free agent. Go back to your flat.'

He ignored the invitation and slumped deeper in his seat. 'All I wanted was a bed for the night.'

'You wanted help,' she contradicted mildly, 'and that's exactly what I'm giving you. You attacked a man yesterday evening . . . and, from what you told me, came close to doing it again at the bank this morning . . . not to mention the neighbour who pro-voked you. You've given yourself a series of frights. That's what brought you to my house.'

'Then why are you taking me to Jackson? If I'd wanted *her* help I'd have gone straight to the Bell.'

'Would you? That's not the impression you gave her. She said she couldn't see wild horses dragging you back unless I came with you.' Susan smiled at his mutinous expression. 'I'm doing what you want me to do, Charles. If I wasn't –' she nodded towards the driver – 'you'd tell him to stop.'

Acland stared out of the window. 'If you say that again, I might just do it.'

'To spite me, or to spite yourself?'

He turned back with a sigh. 'Have you ever met Jackson?'

'No.'

'Well, she's pretty damn scary.' He stretched out his arms. 'Over six feet . . . *this* wide and looks like Arnold Schwarzenegger. She makes her girlfriend do all the work, eats like a hog and sits on piles of cash that she screws out of her customers after she's bullied them into submission. Why would I rather be with her than with you?'

Susan made a pretence of thinking about it. She had put a similar question to Robert that morning. 'Why are you so keen for Charles to go to this Dr Jackson? Shouldn't I try to enrol him in one of my programmes . . . or, even better, persuade him back to Birmingham so that he can re-enter yours? What do you know about her?'

'Henry Watson knows her from when he was at the Middlesex.

She was working as a GP in one of the poorer parts of the East End and she gave him some comprehensive data on the incidence of adolescent depression in her practice for his research paper. He was very impressed by her. She devised an early-warning system for kids at risk and persuaded the local schools to use it. The stats in her area showed a marked improvement afterwards.'

'But Charles doesn't trust women further than he can throw them. Does Dr Jackson know that?'

'She seems to know more about him than we do, Susan. He talked incessantly for half an hour, apparently, although she says he probably won't remember doing it.' He paused. 'I've always thought he might respond better to a woman . . . It's one of the reasons I asked you to take him in when he was in London.'

'And it didn't work,' Susan reminded him. 'He was very suspicious of me.'

'I know.' Another pause. 'Henry calls Dr Jackson "Jackson". He says she doesn't have a Christian name – or if she does, she doesn't own to it – and looks as if she could have taken on Mike Tyson in his prime and won. He also says she's incapable of mollycoddling anyone, tells it how it is, refuses to tiptoe around prissy sensibilities, and gains respect as a result . . . particularly from adolescent boys. Henry thinks she's the bee's knees.'

'But Charles isn't an adolescent, Bob.'

'He's showing all the hallmarks . . . alienation . . . rejection . . . distrust . . . reacting violently when he's annoyed.'

'All the more reason to put him into a programme. Supposing he turns on Dr Jackson?'

Willis hesitated. 'I've given her as much information as I'm able to. There's not much else I can do as he's not my patient any more. *Or* yours. The only influence either of us will have is if he contacts us . . . and I'm inclined to suggest he takes up Jackson's offer.'

'What if I disagree?'

'Just don't make up your mind until you've spoken to her.' Susan thought she could hear him removing his glasses for the inevitable polishing. 'She's says Charles is so undernourished he wouldn't stand a chance against her, but she's confident he'll only reappear if he's willing to accept her terms.'

Acland rephrased his question when Susan didn't answer immediately. 'What makes you think I'd rather be with Jackson?'

'Off the cuff, because you'll feel safer with her. She's big enough and tough enough to keep you in line . . . you'll do her less damage if you lose your temper . . . she'll have no compunction about restraining you or calling the police if you take a swipe at her.' She flicked him a mocking smile. 'Plus, she's uninterested in you as a sexual partner, isn't the motherly type, cures migraines, sits with her patients, wipes up after them . . . even washes and irons their clothes. What more would you want?'

'It's Daisy who does all that.'

'How do you know?'

'Jackson said she did . . . but it's obvious, anyway. You only have to look at them. I can't see Jackson wielding a mop. The only thing she's interested in is weightlifting.'

'So Daisy's a kept femme?'

'What's a femme?'

'A lipstick lesbian . . . a beautiful gay girl who's attractive to both sexes. Heterosexual men find them confusing. When they're not fantasizing about them, they demote them to the role of wife and confer womanly attributes on them such as a willingness to clean. It's the opposite with butch lesbians. A butch looks like a bloke –' she flicked him another teasing smile – 'so she's assumed to be the husband, with masculine attributes such as complete ignorance about where the cleaning equipment is stored.'

Acland didn't say anything.

'As I understand it, Daisy runs the pub and Jackson works as an out-of-hours locum. They've been together ten years and pooled their resources five years ago to buy the Bell. Daisy's responsibilities are located front of house, in the bar areas and restaurant, and Jackson's, because of her locum work, are concentrated back of house, in the private accommodation. They have staff, so they don't do it all themselves, but I doubt Daisy had any involvement with you last night. If she was working the evening shift she wouldn't have had time.'

'Then why did Jackson pretend she did? It's not as though I made any disparaging remarks about lesbians. I was careful not to. The only thing I said was that Jackson didn't look like a doctor . . . and she doesn't. She wears Lycra shorts and a vest, and bloody great boots on her feet.'

'What were you expecting? A white coat?' Susan laughed. 'God help you if a baker ever offers to medicate you.'

'I wasn't expecting a muscle-bound mountain who looks as if she injects testosterone twenty-five times a day,' Acland retorted irritably. 'How many female doctors do you know who look like Arnold Schwarzenegger?'

'None,' said Susan honestly, 'so I'm guessing Jackson's unique. It sounds to me as if she took exception to your prejudices and gave you some rope to hang yourself. You ought to know better than to judge a person on appearance alone, Charles. You're deeply offended when it happens to you.'

'I didn't show her any prejudice. If she thinks I did, then she's the one with the chip on her shoulder . . . not me.'

Susan shook her head. 'You attacked one of her customers because he looked like a Muslim. You can't show more prejudice than that.'

*

The cabbie drew over as two police cars roared down the middle of the road, sirens blaring. Shortly afterwards, they joined the back of a long tail of stationary cars, with flashing blue lights indicating a blockade about four hundred yards ahead. 'It looks like an accident,' he said through the gap in the security window. 'Do you want to walk from here? The traffic'll be just as bad if I try the side streets. Both lanes are blocked, so it could take hours to shift.'

'How far away are we?' Susan asked.

'Half a mile max. About the same distance again after the

accident. Just go straight ahead. The Bell's on the corner of Murray Street.'

They opted to walk. Acland paid the fare and watched the cabbie perform a U-turn after another police car had passed. 'I can't seem to set foot in the place without the police being called,' he said wryly as he slung his kitbag over his shoulder.

'Perhaps it's a meaningful coincidence. You seem to have had one or two in the last twenty-four hours.'

They set off up the pavement, Acland matching his long stride to Susan's shorter one. 'Like what?'

'Falling sick in a pub where one of the landladies is a doctor . . . finding yourself homeless on the same morning you were offered a bed . . . knocking on my door after I'd spoken to Jackson on the phone.'

'The first two might have been coincidences, but the last one wasn't. You're the only person I know well enough in London to ask for a bed . . . and you're a friend of Doc Willis. It was odds on he'd have put you in touch with Jackson.'

'Have you heard of Jung's theory of synchronicity?' she asked, stepping off the pavement to avoid people coming the other way.

'No.' He joined her to walk beside the stationary cars.

'It proposes the idea of *meaningful* coincidences, as when you come across a word for the first time, then meet it again a couple of hours later. Why have you never noticed it before if you come across it twice in two hours? And why do you meet it again a week later?'

'Because your eye passes over it until you discover what it means. Once you understand it, it becomes part of your vocabulary.'

'That's the logical explanation. There's a mystical element to synchronicity that talks about people, places and things being attracted to a person's soul and acquiring significance as a result.'

Acland was immediately suspicious. 'I'm *not* attracted to Jackson.'

The rubber-necking crowd around the accident was getting

thicker, and Susan slowed to search for a cigarette pack in her bag. 'Not on a conscious level, perhaps, but subconsciously you're immensely attracted to her.' She opened the pack and popped a cigarette between her lips. 'I could be wrong,' she said, flicking her lighter, 'but I'd say she's earned more respect from you in one night than you've felt for anyone since you were injured. You may not *like* her, Charles . . . you may find her ugly and grotesque . . . but you do *admire* her. She had the balls to wade into a fight and there aren't many women with the courage to do that.'

'What if I do? Where does synchronicity fit in?'

They came to a halt. 'It depends how you interpret meaningful coincidence. You gave me a thoroughly logical explanation for the chances of the same word recurring twice in two hours – a cause-and-effect explanation – which argues that an individual has some influence over what happens to him. But synchronicity argues the other way – from effect to cause – and says if a person looks for meaning in a coincidence, he'll probably find it.'

Acland was looking over the heads of the crowd towards the flashing blue lights, trying to spot the accident. 'It sounds like a pile of pants. Are you telling me Jackson's my soul mate?'

'No, just that the coincidence of rowing with your neighbour might mean you were destined to take up Jackson's offer.'

'Is that why you refused me a bed . . . because you believe in stuff like that?'

'Not necessarily. Shall I give you a more logical explanation for why we're here?'

'Sure.'

'Consciously or subconsciously, you picked a fight with the woman upstairs to give yourself an excuse to leave your flat, then came to me on the pretence of wanting a bed for the night because you knew I'd be able to put you back in touch with Jackson.'

'I wouldn't need help with that. I know where she lives.'

'But this way you don't lose face. Having me along puts the arrangement on a professional footing.'

Acland glanced down at her. There was a small curve at the

side of his mouth, which was the closest she'd seen to a smile. 'Why couldn't it just be that shit happened, and you were the only person I could think of to take me in?'

'You're too resourceful,' she told him. 'You'd have slept in a shop doorway if it had suited you better.'

'Not a doorway,' he said. 'Anyone's easy meat in a doorway. I saw an old fellow being kicked by a gang of drunken teenagers not so long ago. It was about two o'clock in the morning and they all had a go at him. One of the boys urinated on him.'

'What did you do?' she asked curiously.

'Walked him to the twenty-four-hour Gents in Covent Garden so that he could clean up a bit. He wasn't too keen to go on his own in case they came after him. Then he asked me to take him to a bar in Caroline Street. He said there was a hot-air vent at the back which would help him dry off. I gave him a leg-up over the railings at the side of the building.'

Susan's curiosity deepened. Such a show of friendship seemed very out of character for Charles. 'Who was he?'

'No one.' Acland shrugged abruptly. 'OK, he was *someone* . . . an old soldier, I think – he kept saluting and calling me sir – but I didn't have much choice. He was drunk as a skunk himself, stank to high heaven and wouldn't let go of me.'

'What did you do to the yobs?'

'Gave them a scare,' he said shortly.

'How?' She studied his unresponsive face, then changed the subject when she realized he wasn't going to answer. 'So why have we stopped? What's happening?'

'The road's taped off, but I don't think it's a car accident. I can't see any wrecks.'

'I heard they found bomb-making equipment in one of the flats,' said a woman beside Susan. 'They've cleared the road in case it goes off.'

Acland shook his head. 'We're too close. They'd have pushed us back five hundred yards.' He jerked his chin at the surrounding houses and offices. 'There are people at all the windows. The police would have evacuated the buildings if they were worried about an explosion. Imploding glass causes more damage than shrapnel.'

'It's a crime scene,' said a young black guy who was leaning on the roof of his BMW. 'I've seen this shit on TV. The cops wear white overalls when they're collecting evidence. I'm betting there's been a murder.'

'How do we get through?'

'I don't know, mate,' he said amiably, 'but you're better off than me. At least you're on foot. I'm stuck with the motor.' He pointed across the road. 'You can hang a right just before the tape . . . but you'll have to push a way through. This gig's drawn a bigger crowd than the Live 8 concert in Hyde Park.'

'Cheers.'

'*De nada*. If you see some cops, do me a favour and tell 'em to pull their fingers out. I've got a lady waiting for me and she'll smack me around if I'm late again.'

'Do you want to give her a call?' Susan asked as Acland steered her between the BMW and the car in front. 'I've a mobile you can borrow.'

'Already done it.' The man opened his palm to show his own cell phone. 'She called me a mother –' he broke off to grin at Susan – '*liar*,' he amended. 'Not too trusting, my lady. I'm hoping this thing's big enough to make it on to the news.'

Susan waited until she and Acland reached the other side of the road before she laughed. 'He's living in cloud-cuckoo-land if he thinks his lady will accept the news as an excuse. She'll say he heard it on his radio and smack him around even more.'

Acland paused at the kerbside. 'You think that's funny?' he asked curiously.

Susan dropped her half-smoked cigarette into the gutter and ground it out with her heel. 'I suspect the cheeky grin meant he was joking.'

'Not necessarily. Five of the drunks who were kicking the old soldier were girls . . . and they were bloody vicious. The most the boy did was piss on the poor old sod, and he only did that because the girls told him to. It was sick.'

'How did you scare them off?' Susan asked again.

'They didn't like the look of my face when I took off my eyepatch,' he said, surveying the crowded pavement. 'You'd better hang on to the back of my jacket. That guy wasn't joking about the need to push.'

**>>>Reuters wire service to UK broadcasting stations
>>>BREAKING NEWS>>>BREAKING NEWS>>>BREAKING NEWS
>>> Friday 10 August 17:17**

Bermondsey man viciously attacked

Elderly London pensioner Walter Tutting, 82, sustained life-threatening head injuries from a vicious attack in broad daylight today. He was taken to intensive care at St Thomas's Hospital after collapsing inside the doorway of an empty shop in Gainsborough Road, Bermondsey.

Hospital authorities describe Mr Tutting's condition as 'critical'. It is not known whether he was able to give details about his assailant.

Shop renovators Jim Adams, 53, and Barry Fielder, 36, found Mr Tutting when they returned from a lunch break. 'He was in a bad way,' said Jim Adams. 'We were shocked that no one helped him. Passers-by must have thought he was drunk.'

Police have called for witnesses. A spokesman said, 'As this incident happened around lunchtime, there must have been people who saw it. We believe Mr Tutting crossed Gainsborough Road before collapsing in the shop doorway. Passing drivers may have seen him.'

He refused to comment on whether police are linking this attack to the recent murders of three men in the SE1 area. Harry Peel, Martin Britton and Kevin Atkins all died from serious head injuries.

Traffic was brought to a standstill when part of

Gainsborough Road was sealed off for a fingertip search. Witnesses say police discovered bloodstain evidence in an alleyway opposite the empty shop where Mr Tutting was found. The alley leads to Mr Tutting's house, which has been sealed off pending examination.

Mr Tutting is a widower with three children and seven grandchildren. His daughter Amy, 53, is at his bedside.

Ten

ACLAND AND SUSAN'S ROUTE brought them to the other end of Murray Street. As they walked down it towards Gainsborough Road, they saw a throng of people standing outside the Bell with glasses in their hands. Disasters were good for business, it seemed.

Susan's pace slowed. 'We've picked a bad night to come here,' she said. 'I can't see Jackson finding time to talk to us with all of this going on.'

Acland shared her reluctance. He thought he recognized one of the brokers in a group at the edge of the pavement. 'Maybe we should leave it till tomorrow.'

Susan shook her head. 'They know we're coming. I spoke to Daisy before we left.' She fished out her mobile and scrolled for numbers that she knew weren't there. 'It's such a nuisance. I used the landline both times. We'll have to push our way in and hope for the best.'

'We could go somewhere else and wait till the police clear the road,' Acland suggested. 'It can't last forever.' His reluctance to be there was growing by leaps and bounds.

Perhaps Susan understood this because she placed a hand on his arm, keeping it deliberately light to avoid the immediate withdrawal that was his normal reaction to being touched. 'Don't worry. It'll be OK. Nothing's ever as bad as you think it's going to be.'

But as things turned out, she couldn't have been more wrong. Four plain-clothes policemen moved in on Acland the minute he entered the pub, removing his kitbag from his hand and pinioning his arms. Taken by surprise, he offered no resistance, but, as one of the officers handcuffed him and advised him he was under arrest, he watched Daisy, who was standing in front of him, give a small nod of acknowledgement to Susan Campbell.

*

The capture was so rapid and so professional that few of the pub's customers realized what was happening. In under thirty seconds from the time Acland had followed Susan inside, he was in the back of a car being driven to Southwark East police station. The only explanation he was given by the two detectives accompanying him was that he was wanted for questioning in connection with an assault. Once inside the station, he was given a police tracksuit and asked to remove his clothes and boots, before being taken to a secure interview room, where he was left to brood for an hour.

If the aim was to unsettle him, it didn't work. Acland was used to being alone with his thoughts. Yet the truth was he didn't think about anything much, not even to speculate on why he was there. Perhaps it was Susan's cheese sandwiches, or the warm, stuffy air of the room, but he kept drifting into a light sleep. Somewhere along the line his energy levels had hit rock bottom. Like a driver at the wheel of a moving car who is too bone-weary to consider the fatal consequences of exhaustion.

In a nearby room, Detective Superintendent Brian Jones removed his jacket and draped it over the back of a chair while he watched Acland on a television monitor. He'd come straight from the incident room, a thick-set, no-nonsense man in his early fifties, who was seen as a bully by some of his team. He pulled up a chair and sat down.

'Has he been like this since you brought him in?' he asked.

'Pretty much,' said an officer who'd been in the car with Acland. 'He nods off for a couple of minutes, then jerks his head up and stares at the ceiling for a while. Like that. If he's on anything, it's not obvious. Dr Campbell, the woman he came with, says he's been with her since four o'clock, and she's convinced he hasn't taken anything in that time. He didn't have any paraphernalia when we searched him.'

'What kind of doctor?'

'Psychiatrist.'

'Have you asked her if she thinks he's fit to be questioned?'

'Yes. She says he suffers from migraines, but doesn't believe he has one at the moment. He was talking to her quite freely in the taxi coming over.'

'Have you told her why he's here?'

'Not in detail. All I said was that he answered the description of a man wanted in connection with an assault.'

'And?'

'She assumed it related to the incident at the pub last night.'

'Good. That may be what our friend in there is thinking as well.' Brian Jones removed some photographs from a folder and selected a snapshot of an elderly man looking straight into the camera. 'I'd rather do this without a solicitor, so, in the first instance, we'll treat him as a witness. You two –' he pointed to the man he'd been speaking to and a detective inspector – 'show him this and let's see what his reaction is. If he insists on a solicitor, we may need to do the interview under caution . . . but keep pressing the fact he's just a witness. The rest of us will watch on the monitor.'

*

Acland regarded the two officers in silence when they entered the interview room. He acknowledged their introductions with a small nod – Detective Inspector Beale and Detective Constable Khan – but otherwise remained impassive, his hands clasped loosely on the table in front of him.

'He's very controlled,' said the detective superintendent, watching the screen. 'Most people show some indication of nerves after an hour in an interview room.'

They heard Beale apologize for keeping Acland waiting as he and Khan took seats on the other side of the table, then go on to explain that witnesses were being sought in connection with an incident earlier in the day. 'We're interviewing anyone who might have seen something,' he said, leaning forward to place the snapshot in front of Acland. 'Do you recognize this man, sir?'

Acland lowered his gaze to the picture but otherwise didn't move. 'Yes.'

'Can you tell me how you know him?'

'We had a run-in at the bank this morning. He was in the queue behind me and kept poking me in the back. I told him I didn't like being touched and he got shirty with me.'

'Did you hit him?'

'No. I caught him by the wrist to stop him, then let him go when he pulled away. Is he saying I hit him?'

Beale avoided an answer. 'What happened after you released him?'

'Nothing. I left.'

'Where did you go?'

'Home.'

'Where's home?' Khan asked.

Acland gave the address of his flat.

'Did you make a detour . . . go anywhere else before returning to Waterloo?'

'No,' said Acland, glancing at the photograph again. 'I went straight there.'

'What time did you arrive?'

'Eleven . . . twelve. I can't really remember.'

'Did anyone see you?'

Acland nodded. 'The woman upstairs and a next-door neighbour.'

'Do you know their telephone numbers?'

'No.'

'Names?'

'Not the neighbour's, but the woman in the flat above calls herself Kitten. Her mail was addressed to Sharon Carter, so I presume that's her real name.' He watched Khan write it down. 'What am I supposed to have witnessed?'

Beale eyed him for a moment. 'Mr Tutting was taken to hospital at about one-fifteen this afternoon.'

'Who's Mr Tutting?'

'This gentleman –' Detective Inspector Beale tapped the snapshot – 'the one you had a run-in with at the bank.'

'What's wrong with him?'

Beale hedged. 'He collapsed in the street.'

'I'm sorry.' Acland looked at the photograph again. 'He had more guts than most people of his age . . . He told me to stick a sign on my back saying I was a bad-tempered bastard.'

Brian Jones signalled to another member of his team. 'Hop in there and pull Beale and Khan out . . . but make sure the photo remains on the table. We'll leave Acland to stew for ten minutes. I want to see what he does. And get Khan on to this Kitten female. We need to verify some times.'

*

Left alone, Acland showed no interest at all in the photograph. After a minute or two of staring ahead, he stood up, placed his hands on the floor and performed a perfect gymnastic handstand against the wall. He held his position for a full minute before embarking on a series of vertical press-ups, lowering his forehead to within an inch of the floor before pumping his arms straight again.

'He's a strong lad,' said Jones, 'but I can't think that's doing much for his migraines.'

Detective Inspector Beale, a tall, fair-haired man in his mid-thirties and Jones's number two on the inquiry team, watched the monitor over the superintendent's shoulder. 'Does he know he's being filmed?'

'What if he does?'

'That kind of press-up's damned hard to do. It probably helps that he's thin as a rake – less weight to shift – but . . . even so. Perhaps he's telling us something.'

'What?'

'That he's strong enough to wait us out. The only time I tried a vertical press-up, I got stuck in the down position.'

'What did you make of him?'

'Honestly?' Beale collected his thoughts. 'I'll be surprised if he's our man. He's too straight. He wasn't fazed by Walter Tutting's picture and I didn't notice any hesitations before he answered my questions. If he'd beaten the poor old boy's head in, I don't believe he'd have given me the spiel about Walter calling him a bad-tempered bastard.'

'I wouldn't bet on it. Look at his control . . . it's like watching a metronome.' Jones swung his chair towards the inspector. 'OK, let's say you're right. Why did Walter tell the paramedics that it was "the bloke at the bank with the eyepatch" who did it? Are you suggesting there were two men with eyepatches at the bank today and Walter had a run-in with both?'

'No, but Walter lost consciousness again very quickly and his daughter says he forgets where he lives sometimes . . . so he might have confused the two incidents. Maybe he never saw his attacker and just assumed it was the same man.' He jerked his chin at the monitor. 'The only reason this lad's in the frame is because the uniformed guys recognized his description from last night. We wouldn't have known where to start otherwise.'

Thoughtfully, the superintendent tapped his forefingers together. 'He's the sort of person we're looking for . . . ex-army . . . volatile temper . . . a fight last night . . . a run-in this morning with an eighty-two-year-old . . . knows how to damage people . . . doesn't like being touched. Why does he have a psychiatrist in tow? What's that all about?'

'According to Dr Campbell, she's just a friend.'

'Why did she accompany him to the Bell?'

'For moral support. He felt he'd made a fool of himself last night and didn't want to face the landlady alone.'

'The landlady being another doctor.' It was a statement rather than a question.

'Yes. She's quite a character, apparently. Goes by the name of

Jackson and operates as an out-of-hours locum. I've left a message with her call service asking her to come in ASAP.' He paused. 'It's another reason why I don't fancy Lieutenant Acland for the attack on Walter. According to Susan Campbell, Dr Jackson offered him a room at the pub and he decided to take it because he doesn't like where he's living at the moment. But why would he come back so soon after beating an old guy half to death? He must have known the place would be crawling with police.'

'He didn't expect Walter to be in any condition to give a description.'

'But he couldn't rely on other witnesses staying quiet. It was broad daylight and the eyepatch makes him distinctive. Someone was bound to have seen him . . . if only in Gainsborough Road.'

Jones shrugged. 'History's littered with perverts who return to the scenes of their crimes. It gives them a thrill to see how important they've become.' He glanced at the screen again. 'I'm more interested in why female doctors seem to be falling over themselves to offer support. Why does he need it? What's wrong with him?' He stood up. 'Did you say Dr Campbell's still here?'

'Yes.'

'Then let's have another chat with her.'

*

But Susan couldn't, or wouldn't, answer questions about Acland's psychiatric or medical conditions. 'He's not my patient. I'm just a friend.'

The superintendent nodded. 'I appreciate that, Dr Campbell, but all we need to know is whether, in your judgement as a friend, he's competent to answer questions. It's not in his interests or ours to compromise the information he gives us.'

She shrugged. 'All right . . . I'd say he's perfectly competent.'

'You told my sergeant he has migraines.'

'On and off. He had a bad one last night, so I doubt he'll have another in the short term. You'll know to back off if he does. He goes white as a sheet and starts vomiting.'

'Was it a migraine that prompted the assault last night?'

'I've no idea. I wasn't there and I haven't asked him about it.'

'Does Dr Jackson know? Is that why she offered him a bed . . . to stop him attacking people when he has migraines?'

Susan gave a surprised laugh. 'Good Lord! That's an outrageous conclusion to draw, Superintendent. For the record, I know of no occasion when Charles has lashed out *during* a migraine. If you ask him – or indeed Dr Jackson, who witnessed the episode last night – I'm sure they'll both say he's too incapacitated to move when the pain's bad enough to make him retch.'

'What about the lead-up to a migraine? How many times has he lashed out then?'

'From personal experience, never. Charles has always behaved entirely appropriately in my company.'

'But you know about the incident last night.'

'Only that it happened. I've no idea what caused it. Have you asked the other man? It usually takes two to make a fight.'

Jones subjected her to a long scrutiny. 'Why are you so protective of Lieutenant Acland? Do you see yourself as a mother figure in his life?'

'What makes you think I'm protecting him?'

'Because you're still here, Dr Campbell. Aren't you confident that he can look after himself?'

'Perfectly confident . . . but I've never had a friend arrested in front of me before. I expect it happens to you all the time –' her eyes gleamed ironically – 'but I'm entirely ignorant of the etiquette in these circumstances. I fear it wouldn't be good form to leave without saying goodbye.'

'Would you like Inspector Beale to ask Charles if he wants you to stay?'

She shook her head. 'It'll be a waste of time. He'll certainly say no.'

'And you wouldn't leave anyway?'

'No.'

'Then I'm curious, Dr Campbell. He's not your patient . . .

you're not related to him . . . there's a considerable age gap between the two of you . . . you don't regard yourself as a mother figure . . . he doesn't need your protection . . . yet you refuse to leave. What's the basis of this friendship?'

Susan allowed her amusement to show. 'Are you wondering if Charles and I have an *intimate* relationship, Superintendent?'

'The possibility did occur to me.'

'I'm flattered that you think he might be interested,' she said in a lightly mocking tone, 'but I have enough trouble showing enthusiasm for sex with men of my own age. I couldn't possibly cope with an active twenty-six-year-old. If you must make leaps of imagination, try admiration instead. Do *you* have a son?'

'Yes.'

'How old?'

'Twenty-two.'

'So just four years younger than Charles, who's trying to come to terms with the death of his crew, the loss of his career, partial blindness, low-level tinnitus, migraines and disfigurement . . . and all in the service of his country. How well would *you* have dealt with that at twenty-six? How well will your *son* if a similar tragedy happens to him?'

*

'He'd expect me to keep him in idleness, and his mother to wait on him hand and foot, the same as he's doing now,' said Jones acidly as he and Inspector Beale returned to the viewing room. 'He's got a degree in business studies – paid for by yours truly – and he sits on his bloody arse all day playing computer games. I threatened to throw him out if he doesn't get a job, and the wife started bleating about unconditional love. What's that supposed to mean, eh?'

'It's American for putting up with crap from your children,' said Nick Beale with a smile. 'We have to embrace them whatever they do because it's our fault they've gone off the rails. We haven't given them enough love.'

'Too much, more likely.' He lifted an enquiring eyebrow at Ahmed Khan. 'Any joy?'

The detective constable nodded. 'According to Sharon Carter, Charles Acland had returned to his flat by eleven-thirty. She was watching *This Morning* on the television and they had a row because he lit a bonfire in the garden. She said her window was open and she noticed the smoke while the fashion segment was on . . . and that's always after eleven-thirty apparently. I'll double-check with the TV company, but Sharon's confident about the time.'

'What was he burning?'

'Old files. Sharon said the ashes are still out there, with charred pieces of paper and cardboard. Lieutenant Acland trod on the fire when she threatened to call the police.'

'Does she know when he left again?'

Khan gave another nod. 'She watched him get into a cab at three-thirty. He put his kitbag in first, then she said he gave her two fingers behind his back before climbing in after it. She knows it was three-thirty because the *Ricki Lake Show* was just starting on ITV2.'

'Could he have gone out between either of those times without her seeing him?'

Khan looked amused. 'I doubt it. I had chapter and verse of everything he's done in the last month. This is one *very* bored woman, sir. She seems to keep one eye on Acland and the other on her television set.'

'Does she fancy him?'

'Not any more. She said he was rude to her when she tried to be neighbourly, but she's carrying one heck of a grudge over it. I suspect she made a pass at him and was comprehensively rejected. She referred to him several times as a closet gay.' He paused. 'I'm not sure we should place too much reliance on this, but she also told me she thought he was the gay killer. She said he's a complete weirdo. He goes running most days and shouts in his sleep at night.'

Jones glanced at the monitor, which showed Acland back in his chair and staring fixedly at the wall in front of him. 'Perhaps we're barking up the wrong tree,' he said slowly. 'Perhaps the attack on Walter isn't part of the series.'

Eleven

DESPITE KITTEN'S BAD-TEMPERED support for his story, the police were in no hurry to release Acland. It would be several more hours before his clothes, boots and kitbag were returned to him. During that time, most of which he spent in silent contemplation of his hands, he gave minimal details of his army service, refused the offer of a solicitor and granted permission for a search of his property.

His clothes were meticulously examined for bloodstains, his flat was turned upside down, and the bonfire ashes retrieved from the garden to sift for anything other than paper and cardboard. Sharon 'Kitten' Carter was reinterviewed in person and repeated her vitriol about Acland's 'weirdness', while the elderly next-door neighbour corroborated her timings before offering some vitriol of his own against her.

There was a brief flurry of excitement when a call came through from the Forensic Science Service to report that washed-out blood splatters had been detected on the right sleeve of Acland's jacket, the right cuff of his shirt and the knee areas of his trousers, but it was quickly dashed by Nick Beale, who'd had a five-minute interview with Jackson.

He placed a rough sketch of a man on the table, with written descriptions of his clothes – *brown leather jacket, grey cotton trousers, white cotton shirt, Caterpillar bruiser roll boots* – and arrows pointing to the jacket sleeve, the shirt cuff and the trouser knees with *Rashid Mansoor's blood* beside them.

'The descriptions match what the lieutenant was wearing when we brought him in,' Beale told Jones, 'and Dr Jackson advised us not to waste time on the marked areas. She said both she and Acland were splashed during the fight in the pub because this Mansoor had a nosebleed. She washed the lieutenant's shirt and trousers, and sponged down the jacket, but these are the places where the stains were visible.'

'Damn!'

'Do you want FSS to run a DNA match with Tutting?'

'There's no point if it isn't his blood,' said the superintendent morosely. 'This inquiry's already cost a fortune. I'd be hard pressed to justify an expensive DNA procedure for no good reason, particularly if we have to trawl around looking for this Rashid Mansoor character in order to eliminate him.'

'Except, if Acland did strike Walter, it's possible the blood splatters might have replicated the fight last night.'

'And pigs might fly, Nick,' said Jones with sudden weariness. 'FSS describe the stains as "washed-out", but there's no washing machine or dryer in Acland's flat and he wouldn't have had time to do them by hand. The place is as basic as they come.' He blew a despairing whoosh of air from his mouth. 'The guy's a monk. He seems to live a completely spartan existence.'

'So why are we hanging on to him?'

'He fits the profile . . . and if Tutting isn't part of the series, Acland might still have been responsible for the first three.'

Beale shook his head. 'The timeline doesn't work. According to Dr Campbell, he's been out of circulation for months. First in Iraq . . . then in a hospital in Birmingham.'

Jones shook his head. 'I had another word with her. She said he had a fiancée who lived somewhere in this area and he used to visit her regularly . . . possibly around the time Peel and Britton were killed. Dr Campbell also said Acland was staying with her at the time Kevin Atkins was found. She remembers discussing the murders with him.'

*

In a parallel operation, Walter Tutting's small terraced house had become a major crime scene. Unlike the previous murders, the attack had taken place in the hallway. On a first reading of the evidence, a scenes of crime officer phoned to advise Detective Superintendent Jones that it looked as if Walter had put up a fight as soon as the assailant entered.

'I know it's early days, Brian, but there's nothing to suggest this bastard got much beyond the front door. Something must have spooked Walter because we think he took a walking stick from a stand in the hall and tried to defend himself. We found one lying on the carpet near a pool of blood.'

'Walter's blood?'

'Yes . . . probably from a cut on his head.'

'Is there blood on the stick?'

'Not that we could detect . . . I sent it for analysis about three hours ago. If we're lucky, Walter landed a blow on something useful and we'll get some DNA off it. The best scenario would be that the old boy hit hard enough to mark his attacker . . . which might be a detail worth releasing to the press. If someone already has suspicions about a partner or colleague, an unexplained bruise might just persuade them to call us.'

'Are you sure the stick wasn't used *against* Walter?'

'As sure as I can be. I checked with his consultant at St Thomas's and she's confident that the defence wounds on his arm and shoulders were made by something heavier and more compact . . . like a hammer or a baseball bat.'

'What about the indentation in the wall?'

'It's certainly similar to what we found in the other properties – semicircular and fairly deep into the plaster – but I'm guessing it was a first attempt that missed rather than an angry thrashing around afterwards . . . which may be why Walter had time to arm himself with the walking stick. There are no blood or skin traces in it, as there were in the others . . . and, if it was a baseball bat, it was covered in some kind of fabric. We think we've found fibres.'

Jones frowned into the receiver. 'There were no fibres in the plaster indentations in the other houses.'

There was a short pause while the SOCO broke off to speak to someone in the room. 'I need to go, Brian. Look, I'll have more tomorrow, but at the moment I'm thinking on the hoof. Assuming this is the same guy, then a possible scenario is that he carries the weapon in a bag and only takes it out when he's ready to use it. In Walter's case, it never got that far. Our man lashed out – bag and all – as soon as he realized the old boy was spooked.'

'Are there enough fibres to tell us what kind of bag?'

'I don't know, but you might be interested in the consultant's idea. When I described the indentation to her, she suggested a glass paperweight in a sock.'

'Is that likely?'

'A paperweight would certainly be easier to carry around London undetected, but I can't see it doing the sort of damage we've seen on the previous victims. You made the point yourself, we haven't found fibres anywhere else . . . and, out of the sock and without a handle, there wouldn't be any leverage. All the force would have to come from the speed of the attacker's arm.'

'But it's possible.'

'Not in my opinion. Most of us would drop a lump of glass as soon as we broke into a sweat . . . but if you come up with a fit, strong guy with dry palms and a grip like steel, I suppose it might be . . .'

*

Acland fitted the bill nicely, thought Jones, as he introduced himself and shook the young man's hand. No sweat and fingers like grappling irons. 'I'm sorry you've had to wait so long,' he went on, pulling out the other chair and sitting down. 'Has anyone explained to you why?'

'Not really.'

The detective superintendent clicked his tongue in apparent condemnation of his team. 'My fault. I should have given clearer instructions . . . or reached here sooner. Can I offer you a cup of tea or something to eat?'

'No thank you.'

Jones pulled off his jacket and slung it over the chair behind him. 'Which do you prefer? Charles or Lieutenant Acland?'

'Whatever you like. *You're* the policeman.'

The superintendent smiled. 'I don't blame you for being angry, Charles. The custody officer tells me you've been in this room for over five hours. By rights, you should be climbing the walls and demanding to know what's going on.'

Acland regarded him warily. For whatever reason – perhaps because they didn't fit the man's Rottweiler appearance – he was suspicious of Jones's attempts at pleasantry. 'Would it have done me any good?'

'It wouldn't have done any harm. We're fairly used to irritation in interview rooms . . . particularly from the innocent.' He held the younger man's gaze for a moment. 'A man with infinite patience is rare. It makes me wonder if you have a better idea what this is all about than you've been letting on. Are you willing to say how much you know . . . or how much you've guessed?'

Acland leaned forward to place a finger on Walter Tutting's photograph. 'This man was taken to hospital earlier in the day after collapsing in the street. I'm guessing that whatever caused his collapse wasn't natural because your men stopped the traffic to search the road.' He took a breath. 'You've made up your minds I had something to do with Mr Tutting's collapse, either because I was seen arguing with him at the bank this morning or because I was involved in a fight last night at the Bell . . . probably both. With the help of Jackson, Daisy and Susan Camp-bell, you arrested me when I returned to the pub and brought me here in handcuffs to answer questions.'

'Go on.'

'That's it . . . a combination of what I've been told and what I've guessed.'

'If you thought we were investigating you, why didn't you ask for a solicitor?'

'You'd have been even more suspicious.'

'It doesn't work like that, Charles.'

'Yes, it does. That's why I gave you free rein of my property and possessions to prove I have nothing to answer for.'

Jones wasn't surprised that Susan Campbell had declared Acland fit to answer questions. He certainly fitted the profile of a 'forensically aware' killer. 'I admire your confidence.'

'In myself or in the police?'

'Both.'

Acland shook his head. 'I have no confidence in the police. The inspector said I was here as a witness . . . but he was lying. I was arrested and brought here as a suspect and I don't even know what crime I'm supposed to have committed.'

Jones folded his hands on the table. 'Do you want to make a complaint?'

'Not unless you tell me you've found something incriminating in my kitbag or at my flat. We'll both know how it got there if you do.'

'Are you suggesting I or one of my team would plant evidence?'

'Judging by the way I've been treated so far . . . yes.'

Jones smiled slightly. 'You're very alert for a man who had such a serious migraine incident last night that a doctor had to attend to you. Do vertical press-ups clear your brain, Charles?'

'If they do, that's my business . . . and I don't like being filmed. This is a free country, not a police state.'

'I'm sorry you have such a dim view of us. We make more enemies than friends in our line of business, but someone has to do it . . . Rather like soldiering, wouldn't you say?'

Acland ignored the jibe. 'I have a dim view of the whole of society. You're just one face of it.'

'Have you ever been arrested before?'

'No.'

'You take a dim view of Muslims as well, I hear . . . *and* elderly men.' Jones reached for Walter Tutting's photograph when Acland didn't answer. 'What did Mr Tutting do to annoy you? Did he think you were gay and make a pass?'

Acland looked faintly outraged. 'That's ridiculous.'

'Why? Which part of the idea offends you? That an elderly man might be gay or that he might think *you're* gay?'

'Neither. I'm just not as obsessed with sex as you seem to be.'

The superintendent steepled his hands in front of his mouth and studied the young man curiously. 'You're quite a puritan.'

Acland stared back at him with a frown of incomprehension. 'What do any of my views have to do with Mr Tutting? He poked me in the back, that's all.'

'I'm interested in why you seem to have taken against society. Have you been treated badly since you came home?'

'Not particularly.'

'So what's changed?'

'Me. I feel as if I'm living in a world that's obsessed with trivial things . . . and I can't see that any of them matter much.' He sounded uncomfortable, as though voicing his beliefs was alien to him.

'And what *does* matter, Charles?'

'I'm still trying to find out. I've been reading about a Danish philosopher called Søren Kierkegaard. He said, "Life is not a problem to be solved, but a reality to be experienced." That's about as much understanding as I have at the moment.'

'Reality can be pretty grim.'

'It depends what you make of it.'

Jones nodded. 'What about love? Where does that fit in?'

No answer.

'Weren't you in love with your fiancée, Charles? I gather she lives in this area and you visited her regularly last year. We need her name and address.'

Shock flared briefly in the younger man's eye. 'Who told you?'

'Dr Campbell.' Jones raised a questioning eyebrow. 'Did she make a mistake? Was the information supposed to be confidential?'

Acland hunched forward and pumped his fists beneath the table. 'Jen has nothing to do with this. I haven't seen her in months.'

'Nothing to do with what, Charles?'

Silence.

'If she lives nowhere near Mr Tutting we won't bother her . . . but if she *does* –' Jones allowed a beat of silence to pass – 'we might need to look at whether you've had a run-in with him before.'

'She wouldn't know one way or the other.'

'Will your parents be able to give me her name and address? Your regiment?'

A flash of real dislike sparked in Acland's eye. 'Her name's Jen Morley and she's in Flat 1, Peabody House, Harris Walk . . . and if that's anywhere near Mr Tutting then it's a coincidence.' He unclenched his fists and pressed his palms on the table as if he was about to stand up. 'Why are you doing this? Don't I have any rights over who you're allowed to discuss my private business with?'

The superintendent spread his hands in a gesture of apology. 'Not if I need an independent witness to confirm what you tell me.' He paused. 'If you're worried that Ms Morley's going to say something detrimental about you, then it might be in your interest to consult a solicitor.'

Acland tilted his head back to stare at the ceiling. He took several deep breaths through his nose.

'We can take a break any time, Charles. Perhaps you'd like to change your mind about that cup of tea?'

'It won't make any difference.'

True, thought Jones. 'Did Mr Tutting's poking finger annoy you enough to follow him home?'

'Not unless he lives in the tube station and was fast enough to sprint ahead of me after I left the bank. Your inspector said he collapsed in the street. Was that another lie?'

Jones ignored the question. 'Our forensic staff have found bloodstains on your jacket, shirt and trousers. Do you want to explain how they got there?'

Acland's dislike flared up again, but this time his anger was palpable. It throbbed in the air between them. 'I *knew* you'd plant something on me,' he snarled. 'You're more corrupt than the ragheads we were ordered to protect. They'll stab anyone in the back if it gives them an edge, but at least they're open about it.'

There was a short, thoughtful silence while Jones rubbed the side of his jaw with the back of one hand. 'Let me understand you correctly. Are you saying there's no way blood could be found on your clothes unless the police put it there?'

'Yes.'

'Then why did Dr Jackson tell us it came from Rashid Mansoor's nose? Was she lying?' He watched the knuckles on Acland's fists turn white with suppressed frustration. 'It makes me suspicious when I'm accused of corruption, Charles. I ask myself what the other person's trying to hide.'

'Nothing,' said Acland through gritted teeth, 'but at least you know how it feels to be accused of something you haven't done.'

'Do you own a baseball bat?'

'No.'

'What about a glass paperweight?'

'Everything I have is in my kitbag.'

'Which holds how much? Not a lot. For most men of your age, their laptops and stereos would take up several kit bags. Where's the rest of your stuff?'

'If you mean the things I don't use any more, they're at my parents' house in Dorset. The stereo's defunct, the computer's so old it works by clockwork and I've grown out of reading the *Beano* or playing with model aeroplanes.'

'Do you have a storage container somewhere?'

'No.'

'What about friends? Is anyone looking after anything for you?'

'No.'

'I've seen what's in your kitbag, Charles. Are you telling me that's all you own in the world?'

'Yes.'

'No one travels that light.'

'*I* do.' The young man gave an indifferent shrug. 'You should try it one day. It's easier to keep going when you're not weighed down by possessions.'

'So we're back to a world obsessed by trivia?'

'If you like.'

'And to a man who needs to be on the move all the time. Are you afraid your past is going to catch up with you, Charles? Are you happier leaving everyone behind?'

Acland's lips twisted fractionally. 'I wouldn't want to be in the rut you're in. You look about as pleased with your life as my father does, and he's been grinding along the bottom of a furrow for years, carrying the debts of a farm on his back.'

'Perhaps he feels it's the responsible thing to do. We can't all scrounge off others. Someone has to create the wealth.'

'That's the general view.'

Jones's smile was sarcastic, prompted as much by the memory of his own debts as by a political view on individual responsibility. 'But you disagree?'

Acland stared past him as if searching for a distant horizon. 'I wouldn't put my life on the line for it. Chasing wealth is no more ethically justified than turning your back on it.'

'Which makes you what? A monk?'

'An idiot,' Acland said slowly, shifting his attention back to the superintendent. 'I went to war for people like you and ended up with this.' He touched his patch. 'Pretty stupid, eh?'

*

Jen Morley reacted angrily when DI Beale and DC Khan rang her doorbell at ten-thirty at night. She delivered a few choice expletives via the intercom, said they'd woken her up and refused to let them in. 'How do I know you're the police?' she hissed in an undertone. 'You could be anyone.'

Beale leaned into the speaker beside the glass-panelled entrance to the block. 'I can see your front door from here, Ms Morley. If you open it, I'll give you a number to call. Ask for a description of Detective Inspector Beale and check it against the person you see.'

'I can't, I'm naked.'

'I'm happy to wait while you put something on.'

There was the sound of a man speaking in the background and Jen raised her voice to answer him. 'No, it's just some yobs mucking around. I'll be back in a minute.' She dropped into a whisper again. 'Look, do me a favour and fuck off,' she snapped. 'I'm busy, OK. I'll talk to you tomorrow.'

Beale placed a hand over the intercom and nodded to Khan. 'Check the window,' he whispered, nodding towards a lighted, curtained pane to the right. He lowered his hand again. 'We only need five minutes, Ms Morley. I appreciate it's late at night but it *is* important. Do you have a dressing gown? You can talk to us outside your flat if you'd rather.' He replaced his hand over the speaker as Khan slipped back beside him.

'There's a half-clothed Jap with her,' the other man breathed. 'He's tapping his watch and hanging on to his wallet for dear life.'

'Five minutes, Ms Morley,' Beale said again. 'That's all we need.'

'Jesus!' she said angrily. 'OK, wait there.' The handset at her end rattled furiously onto its rest.

They watched her emerge from her door and shut it carefully behind her, before clutching her robe about her middle and making her way across the communal hall. From twenty yards away, she had a willowy elegance that fleetingly reminded both men of someone they knew; close to, the impression faded. There was nothing elegant about the bloodshot eyes, the smudged make-up or the swollen bottom lip that suggested someone had been chewing on it.

She opened the door a couple of feet and inserted herself in the opening to prevent them entering. 'You'd better have something more than that if you're expecting to come in,' she hissed when Beale tried to introduce himself and show his card. 'A search warrant at least.'

Beale wondered how often she'd been served with a warrant and made a mental note to check the records. 'We just want to ask you some questions, Ms Morley. We understand you were engaged to a man called Charles Acland until a few months ago? Is that correct?'

'What if I was? What's he been saying about me?' She touched the sleeve of her gown to the end of her nose. 'It'll be lies whatever it is.'

It wasn't the answer Beale had been expecting. As a delaying tactic, he took out his notebook and flicked through it. 'You remind me of someone,' he said in a conversational tone. 'Have we met before?'

'Uma Thurman,' she retorted impatiently, as if it should have been obvious. 'Everyone thinks I'm Uma Thurman.'

Beale nodded, wondering if she realized how rough she looked. 'I can see the resemblance now.'

'Whatever. Just get a move on. I'm freezing to death here.' She rubbed her arms to prove the point. 'Charlie always lies. I could have had him done for rape . . . *and* he knows it.'

Beale nodded again, as if he had this information already. 'When did that happen?'

'The last time I saw him . . . before he went to Iraq. Then he tried to strangle me in the hospital after he came back.' Her hand strayed to her neck. 'I bet he hasn't told you *that*.'

'No.'

'Did he tell you about the rape?'

Beale shook his head.

'There you are, then. You can't believe anything he says. If you want my opinion, his brain's more damaged than his face. Ask his psychiatrist if you don't believe me. He knows what happened. He was there when Charlie tried to kill me.'

He . . . ? 'What's this psychiatrist's name?'

Jen looked on the point of answering, then changed her mind. 'I can't remember. I left as fast as I could in case Charlie had another go.' She was becoming restless. 'Look, it's water under the bridge. I haven't seen Charlie for months and that's the way I want it to stay. Are we done now?'

'Not quite, Ms Morley. It's the time when you were together that we're interested in. How often did Charlie come here?'

'Whenever he could. He was crazy about me.'

'Every weekend?'

'Sure . . . when he wasn't driving his tank over Salisbury Plain . . . or going to bloody Oman on manoeuvres.'

'Over what time period? When did you first get together?'

She glanced over her shoulder, as if she could hear something from her flat. 'Most of last year. We met at the beginning and split just before he went Iraq.'

Beale checked his notebook. 'Do you remember if he was in London the weekends of the 9th/10th or 23rd/24th of September?'

'Is this a joke? I don't even remember what I was doing last week.'

Both policemen could believe that. 'Have you any way of checking?' Beale asked.

'No.' She frowned at him. 'What's this about? What's Charlie done?'

When Beale hesitated, DC Khan stepped in. 'Do you mind telling us what caused the split?' he asked. 'Was there a specific reason?'

She looked at him with an expression of contempt. 'I didn't much like being raped.'

'I understand that,' he agreed, 'but you said Charlie was crazy about you . . . and rape suggests an unacceptable level of violence within the relationship.'

She started to close the door. 'He's not good at controlling his anger.'

Khan placed his hand on one of the glass panels to prevent her. 'What did you do to make him angry?'

'Nothing,' she said coldly, 'except refuse to give him what he wanted.'

'Which was?'

'Use your imagination. What do men usually want?'

Khan smiled slightly. 'It depends on the terms and conditions. Most men expect to get it free from their fiancées.'

Her eyes narrowed to slits.

'Did he catch you with a client, Ms Morley? Is that what made him angry?'

'*Fuck* off!' With a sudden surge of fury, she used both hands to slam the door, glaring at them briefly through the glass before turning on her heel.

Beale watched her re-enter her flat. 'Great!' he said sarcastically. 'I play up to her movie-star image and you call her a prostitute. How did you think she was going to react?'

'I don't know,' said Khan thoughtfully, 'but she's pretty aggressive. What do you reckon she's on?'

Twelve

IN EXCHANGE FOR HIS possessions, Acland was asked to sign a receipt, confirming that every item had been returned. He unpacked his kitbag and checked the contents in front of DI Beale and the custody officer. The inspector felt oddly embarrassed as the young lieutenant withdrew his meagre tally of belongings. Apart from the clothes, which represented a tiny proportion of what Beale had in his own wardrobe, there was a small radio, a wind-up alarm clock, a toilet bag, a pair of trainers, some leather flip-flops, a mess tin and metal cup, a thermos flask, a spoon, knife and fork, a notebook, a couple of pencils and a paperback entitled *An Introduction to Philosophy.*

The super was right, thought Beale. Either there was a storage container somewhere or this lad was a monk, and the question that intrigued them all was, how had a monk ever become engaged to a woman like Jen Morley? Susan Campbell had refused, or been unable, to shed any light on it.

'I've never met her and I've never discussed her with Charles,' she said firmly.

Brian Jones had invited her into the side room where Acland was still being screened on the monitor. 'Would you be willing to speculate?' he asked. 'This lad strikes us as being abstemious to the point of obsession, while DC Khan and DI Beale here describe Ms Morley as an aggressive, foul-mouthed call girl. What might the attraction have been?'

'Sex.'

Jones gave a grunt of amusement. 'As simple as that?' He

glanced at the screen. 'He's handsome enough on his right-hand side. He must have been quite a catch before the injury. I find it hard to believe he'd tie himself to a prostitute just for sex. Why didn't he pay her for it?'

'She's not your run-of-the-mill Tom,' said Beale. 'More of a high-class hostess for visiting businessmen. She has a good speaking voice and probably scrubs up well . . . even if she was looking pretty rough this evening.'

'She's funding a habit,' said Khan confidently. 'She just about held it together while we were talking to her, but it was a close shave. If we'd waited outside her flat, we'd have seen her head for her dealer the minute her client left.'

Jones switched his attention back to Susan. 'Could Charles have been hoping to save her? I wouldn't have thought he was that naive or stupid, but he's certainly a puritan . . . and puritans have a nasty habit of believing they can cure other people's behaviour.'

'You're asking me questions I can't answer,' she said. 'I don't know what Charles was like when he was engaged to Jen . . . I don't know what *she* was like. All personalities develop over time – we tend to mould ourselves to the people we live and work with – but prolonged drug abuse is often associated with the biggest changes. If this gentleman here –' she indicated Khan – 'is correct, then it's possible the Jen he saw tonight is not the one Charles became engaged to.'

'What about *him*? He's had a pretty serious bang to the head. Can that affect the personality?'

'Of course. But in numerous different ways. How long do we have? My lecture on short-term memory loss usually takes an hour.'

Jones tapped an impatient finger on the table. 'It's a simple question, Dr Campbell.'

'But the answer isn't, Superintendent. There are too many variables.'

'Give me one.'

'Depending on the severity of the injury, it's possible that a bang on the head may lead to impaired mental function – such as difficulty remembering, confusion and loss of communication skills. As this often gives rise to irritability and frustration, then, yes, a bang on the head can be said to affect the personality.'

Jones closed his eyes and took a deep breath. 'Is the Charles we've met tonight the one who was visiting Ms Morley on a regular basis last year?' he asked grimly.

'I've no idea. I didn't meet him until after they split.'

'All I want is an opinion, Dr Campbell. It's hardly a breach of confidentiality if Charles wasn't your patient at the time and isn't your patient now. I need persuading that he has nothing to do with this inquiry . . . and your refusal to offer any guidance isn't helping with that decision.'

Susan frowned. 'Which inquiry? The inspector said his alibi stood up for the assault on Mr Tutting.'

'Any information that supports his story will be helpful.'

'I don't have any information.' She held his gaze for a moment. 'Look, it may come as a shock to you, but you probably know him better than I do. The longest conversation I've ever had with Charles was in the taxi coming here.'

'What did you talk about?'

'I was trying to disabuse him of the idea that pretty lesbians are kept women, and butch lesbians don't know how to operate washing machines.' Humour crept into her voice. 'Would you like me to do the same for you, Superintendent? I imagine your understanding of lesbian relationships is no more profound or more sophisticated than Charles's.'

'If he's that ignorant, why does he want to live with a couple of them? Does he think he can *cure* them?'

Susan wasn't amused. 'It's irrelevant what their sexual orientation is; he's choosing to live with Jackson and Daisy.'

'Why?'

Susan shrugged. 'At a guess, he knows he has to start trusting people again, and he believes he's found someone dependable in Jackson. She won more respect from him in a single night than anyone else has done since his injury.' Her glance rested on the screen for a moment. 'It won't surprise me if he's changed his mind, though. Trust is a fragile thing at the best of times.'

*

DI Beale and his uniformed colleague shook their heads when Acland pointed to some items of clothing that he hadn't repacked in his kitbag and asked if either of them objected to him taking off his shirt in order to add some layers underneath. But Beale was shocked by how thin Acland was. The ribs of his back showed all too clearly, giving unhealthy credence to the idea of a self-denying ascetic; where he found the strength to do vertical press-ups was a mystery.

Beale watched the lieutenant pull three T-shirts over his head before replacing his shirt. 'You look as if you're planning to head for the Antarctic,' he said in a friendly tone.

Acland ignored him to examine his boots and jacket, which were in a separate pile. He used his sleeve to rub the toe of a boot. 'What did they use on these?'

'Blood detectors . . . probably luminol or fluorescein.'

Acland pulled a second pair of socks over his feet and laced up his boots. 'Do I get compensated if the leather goes rotten two weeks down the line . . . or is that the price I pay for being a witness?'

'It shouldn't.'

'Right,' said Acland without emphasis, as he shrugged into his jacket, 'like an armful of injections shouldn't give you Gulf War Syndrome.' He picked up his wallet and checked it before tucking it into his kitbag and drawing the strings tight. 'Is that it?'

The custody sergeant passed him a receipt and a pen. 'We just need your signature, sir . . . also the address where we can contact you and a mobile phone number if you have one.'

'You know I don't. You've searched everything I have.' Acland signed his name, hesitated briefly, then wrote, 'The Bell, Gains-borough Road' beneath it. 'What happens if I decide to move on from the Bell?'

'You're at liberty to do that, Lieutenant, as long as you or Dr Jackson notify us of your new address. There are no police bail conditions attached to your release, but that status could well be revised if you fail to inform us of your whereabouts.'

'My car's out back,' said Beale. 'I'll drive you down myself. Dr Campbell phoned Daisy Wheeler ten minutes ago. She's expecting us.'

Acland busied himself with the straps of his kitbag. 'Why would Dr Campbell make the phone call?'

'She offered to do it when I told her we were releasing you. She's been in the waiting room all the time you've been here.'

Clearly surprised, Acland raised his head. 'Have you been questioning her?'

'Only to establish your alibi.'

'Then what's she still doing here? Why hasn't she gone home?'

'For support, I imagine,' Beale answered matter-of-factly. 'She says she's your friend. I promised to drive you both to the Bell when your interview was over.'

There was a flicker of indecision on the lieutenant's face before he gave a small nod. 'I hadn't realized . . . I thought she'd be long gone.' He hoisted the strap over his head so that the bag lay diagonally across his back. 'I appreciate the lift . . . thanks . . . but do you mind if I wait outside while you fetch Susan? I could really do with some fresh air.'

'Sure.' Beale opened the door and pointed to the right. 'Down here, hang a left at the end and the exit to the car park is straight ahead. Mine's the silver Toyota nearest the building.'

'Cheers.'

Beale wondered about that look of indecision as he watched the younger man walk away. He wondered, too, about the extra layers of clothing. He raised his voice. 'You're not planning to abscond are you, Lieutenant?'

Acland paused briefly, turning to look at him. 'If I did, I'd be letting Susan down,' he said, 'and I've never let a friend down yet.'

*

Susan lit a much-needed cigarette as she and Beale exited the police station to find a deserted car park. She propped her bottom against the Toyota bonnet and puffed smoke into the air while she watched the inspector scout around the exit to see if Acland was in the road. 'What did you expect?' she asked him. 'I warned you he might change his mind.'

'He said he wouldn't let a friend down,' protested Beale impatiently, 'and as it was in reference to you, I assumed he meant it.' He eyed her accusingly, as if it were her fault. 'He gave me his word.'

'Obviously not, if he doesn't view me as a friend,' said Susan thoughtfully. 'You should have let me speak to him in the interview room.'

Beale flicked the remote on his key fob and opened the passenger door for her. 'He can't have gone far. We'll drive around and see if we can spot him.' He pointed to the 'No Smoking' sign on his dashboard. 'Sorry. Rigid rule, I'm afraid. You'll have to put the fag out before you get in.'

Obligingly, Susan obeyed before lowering herself into the seat. 'I think we should go straight to the Bell. It'll be a waste of time looking for him. He won't come with us even if we do find him.'

'Wouldn't you rather go home?'

'No,' she said firmly, attaching her seat belt. 'I need to talk to Jackson. She said she'd be back at the pub by twelve-thirty.'

Beale climbed in the other side. 'I suspect Charles is planning to spend the night in the open – he added another layer of clothes before he left – so I'll have him picked up in the morning.' He put the key in the ignition and started the engine. 'Let's just pray no one gets murdered between now and then,' he said with feeling, 'because I'm not sure who'll be for the higher jump . . . him or me.'

Susan smiled unsympathetically. 'You need your head examining if you seriously believe that Charles Acland would pass himself off as a male prostitute in order to prey on lonely old men.'

Beale fired the engine, engaged the gears, then looked over his shoulder to reverse out of the parking space. 'What made you come up with that comment?'

'Your superintendent mentioned the gay murders . . . wanted to know if Charles had been in London when the last one happened.'

'He wouldn't have told you that posing as a male prostitute is the murderer's MO. We don't know how he gets in.'

'I read the newspapers.'

Beale turned on to the main road. 'The press is guessing . . . we're *all* guessing.' He glanced at her. 'But let's say you're right, why should that exclude Charles?'

'Because the whole idea of sex alarms him at the moment. He's an intensely private person who won't let anyone get too close. Your boss described him as abstemious. I'd describe him as self-protective and fastidious. Do you think that state of mind is conducive to sexual activity?'

'There's nothing to indicate that intercourse took place. The murders may have been the reaction to a proposition of gay sex.'

Susan shook her head. 'Charles would never have got as far as the bedroom,' she said confidently. 'He won't even enter a front door without coaxing. He's uptight about his facial disfigurement, does everything he can to keep people out of his private space and won't intrude on anyone else's. There's no way he'd get beyond the hall in a stranger's house –' she arched an ironic eyebrow – 'particularly if he thought sex was behind the invitation.'

The inspector glanced at her. 'So why didn't you give that opinion to the superintendent? He'd have released Charles three hours ago if you had.'

With a sigh of irritation, she lit another cigarette without asking his permission. 'No, he wouldn't. He'd have done what you just did . . . jump at any half-arsed theory that might associate Charles with the attacks. I don't even know why he came under suspicion in the first place.'

Beale lowered her window a couple of inches to draw the smoke away from him. 'The man who was attacked today effectively named Charles as his assailant.'

'How? Your boss told me he was unconscious.'

'He came round briefly when the paramedics arrived. When they asked him who'd done it, he said it was a man with an eyepatch, and Charles admits that he had a row with Mr Tutting earlier in the day.'

'He told me about that. He said some old chap kept jabbing him in the back. Was that Mr Tutting?'

'Yes.'

'Then why have you allowed Charles to go?'

'His alibi stood up,' said Beale, drawing to a halt at some traffic lights. 'We think Mr Tutting confused the two incidents because Charles was back at his flat by the time the attack happened –' he cast an ironic glance at Susan – 'having yet *another* row. This time with his upstairs neighbour.'

She sighed again. 'He told me about that, too. As I understand it, the woman's lonely and she took against Charles when he rejected her advances.' She paused. 'You must think he's in fights all the time, but I don't think that's true. I agree he's had a bad twenty-four hours, but the fact that he came to me suggests he's aware of it and doesn't want it to happen again.'

'What makes you think the super wouldn't have understood that?'

'Too many negative associations. Fights . . . rows . . . aversion to sex with a woman . . . seeking help from a psychiatrist. In your boss's shoes, I'd have leapt for the more obvious conclusions. At least this way he seems to have found out for himself that Charles is so opposed to anything to do with the flesh that he's slowly killing himself from starvation.'

Beale recalled the protruding ribs. 'Is he doing it deliberately?'

Susan flicked her cigarette out of the car window. 'I don't know, but if you want to pray about anything, then pray it's not Charles's body that's found tomorrow morning.'

The traffic lights turned green but Beale ignored them. 'Are you serious?'

'It depends how many reserves he has.'

Beale moved off in response to a car's flashing lights behind him, but drew into the kerb once he was through the junction. 'I can't ignore information like that, Dr Campbell,' he said, turning to her. 'If your concerns are valid and he's as vulnerable as you suggest, then I'm duty-bound to organize a search for him.'

'That's why we're going to the Bell,' she said. 'He'll avoid policemen like the plague ... but I think he might talk to Jackson.'

The inspector shook his head as he reached into his jacket pocket for his mobile. 'How's she going to find him? He could have walked a mile in any direction by now.'

Susan laid a restraining hand on his arm. 'I have an idea where he might be,' she said, 'but if I'm wrong, it won't do any harm to delay for half an hour. At least give Jackson a chance.'

'You're placing a lot of faith in this woman, Dr Campbell.'

'Not half as much as I'm placing in Charles,' she murmured cryptically.

Thirteen

JACKSON PARKED HER CAR at the top of Caroline Street, alongside the rear of Drury Lane Theatre, took a torch from her dashboard pocket and walked down towards the Aldwych. She knew the two pubs on the right-hand side, the Henry Fielding and the Pepys Tavern, but both were attached to the buildings beside them. Not a railing in sight, she thought grimly, convinced she was on a wild-goose chase. Susan's directions had been hopelessly vague – *a bar in Caroline Street with a fenced-off gap at the side* – and Jackson seriously doubted that any such gap existed in a part of the city that priced square yards in tens of thousands of pounds.

At one o'clock in the morning, this part of Covent Garden was deserted, although a regular flow of traffic passed along the Aldwych, heading from the Strand towards Fleet Street. The theatre, pubs and handful of restaurants had long since closed and Jackson had the road to herself. Making her way down the pavement, she flicked her torch at every vertical shadow thrown against the buildings by the street lighting, but each property was firmly attached to the one beside it. With a sigh of frustration, she crossed to the other side and walked back up, repeating the exercise. Nothing.

Nor was there anything Jackson would class as a bar, apart from the two pubs. One of the restaurants had its windows obscured by discreet net curtaining, but the name – Bon Appetit – hardly suggested a drinking establishment. She leaned on her car roof and studied an empty unit across the road which was undergoing renovation. There was no gap between it and the building to the right of it, but it stood on the corner of Caroline Street and Russell Street and the weathered fascia board above its white-washed windows showed some barely discernible letters which looked like 'Giovanni's Bar & Grill'.

More in hope than expectation, Jackson made her way into Russell Street and walked along the side elevation of the unit, where more whitewashed panes reflected the beam of her torch. The gap, when she came to it, was just a yard wide and appeared to serve no purpose at all, apart from offering a glimmer of day-light to the few upper-storey windows in the adjoining property. The metal railings, seven feet high, six inches wide and without a crosspiece in the middle to offer a foothold, were merely prevent-ing access to a narrow, twenty-yard-long passageway with a brick wall at the end. There were no doors opening off it and no sign that it was ever used, except as a receptacle for cigarette butts, which lay in filthy piles around the entrance.

Jackson moved to the left and lined up her torch to shine at a diagonal down the alley. The beam wasn't strong enough to do more than produce a pinpoint of light on the bricks at the end, but she was able to steer it a fair way to the right before it jumped forward to the side wall of the passage. For whatever reason, this wasted space in the heart of London made a ninety-degree turn, and it didn't take a genius to work out that it was heading back towards Giovanni's redundant kitchen.

Nor did it take a genius to work out why the railings were necessary. During the previous three centuries, when Covent Garden had been a working flower and vegetable market and labour was cheap, the Garden never slept. Fresh produce came in during the hours of darkness to be sold by the stall holders the following day, chop shops and brothels stayed open round the clock, and theatregoers and opera lovers flocked in for afternoon matinées and evening performances. Intruders down any passage-way would have been met and challenged.

Now, with the market gone and the area converted to a day-time tourist attraction, only a fool would leave a recessed back door vulnerable to a burglar's jemmy at night, and his insurance premiums would be prohibitive if he did. With another sigh of frustration, Jackson studied the bars and wondered how Acland had got over them without a lift. Assuming he was even in there.

She raised her voice. 'Charles! Are you there? It's Jackson. Susan sent me. Can I talk to you, please?' No response. 'Is *anyone* there?' she called next. 'I'm not the police. I'm just trying to find a friend.' She pointed her torch towards the right angle, looking for movement, and thought she saw the flash of something white. A face?

'I'm hoping a friend of mine's in there,' she shouted. 'Will you help me? He's a young guy with an eyepatch.'

'Who are you?' The voice was cracked and gritty from smoke and alcohol.

'My name's Jackson. Is he with you?'

'Maybe.'

'Will you ask him to talk to me?'

'I'll ask but it doesn't mean he'll say yes.' There was a long pause. 'He says he's not coming out. You'll have to come in.'

'Great!' She ran her torch over the bars, which were held upright by two crosspieces at the top and bottom cemented into the brickwork on either side. 'How do I get over this without help? Is there a knack to it?'

She heard a snicker of laughter. 'It helps to be skinny, girl . . . and from the way you're blocking most of the entrance, that ain't the case. There's ties holding the outer bars. If you can get a toe on to any of 'em it makes it easier . . . but you'd better put a coat over the spikes at the top. With your size, you'll come down on 'em like a ton of bricks if you're not careful.'

Jackson swore under her breath as she examined the inch-wide rivets that secured the framework into the buildings. Even in bare feet, she'd have trouble securing a toehold and she certainly didn't fancy the ornamental spearheads that capped the upper crosspiece. Nevertheless she stooped to unlace her boots. 'Will you do me a favour?' she called. 'Come and hold the torch so that I can see what I'm doing?'

'As long as you don't blame me when you go arse over tit.'

'I won't.' She reached up to place her boots upside down on the two middle spikes, then shrugged out of her jacket and rolled it into a tight pad to cover the remaining spikes on the left-hand side. A figure approached down the passageway and she played torchlight briefly over a bearded face before handing the gadget through the bars. 'Cheers.'

The light turned on her. 'Gawd struth, you're a big lass. You sure you want to do this?'

'It depends how drunk you are.' She reached through the bars again to guide the beam towards the rivets on the left. 'Let's see if you can keep your hand steady.'

'Steady as a rock when I'm drunk,' the man confided on a gale of alcoholic breath. 'Only get the shakes when I'm sober. How's that?'

'It'll do.' She placed her hands on either side of her boots on the top crosspiece, inserted her left toe on the highest rivet she could reach, took a deep breath, hoisted herself off the ground and locked her arms. 'Where next?'

'That's why it helps to be skinny. If you take it easy, there's room for your arse and your prick between the spikes. You have to squeeze down carefully, mind.' Another snicker. 'I'm not saying it doesn't sting occasionally.'

'You're a great help,' said Jackson sarcastically, transferring her weight to her right hand and using her left to rearrange her jacket over her boots to make an improvised saddle. 'Here.' She retrieved her mobile from her trouser pocket. 'Catch this.' She tossed it down to him before clamping her right hand over the crosspiece again. 'If I get skewered on this sodding thing, call an ambulance before I bleed to death. And *don't* move the torch!'

'Bossy, ain't you?' he said. 'Just like my old woman.' But he'd caught the mobile cleanly and the beam remained focused on the rivets.

'With a husband like you, I don't blame her,' said Jackson, supporting her weight on her hands and working her left foot up the wall. 'Did she ever get to spend money on the kids, or did you drink it first?'

'Wasn't around long enough for nippers.'

Jackson's toe locked on to another rivet. 'I'm aiming to straddle this thing, so get ready to move in case I lose my balance.' With a grunt, she straightened her left leg, swung the other one over the saddle and, in a surprisingly graceful movement, like a female gymnast on the asymmetric bars, reversed her grip and twisted over the spikes. 'Never even touched it,' she said with satisfaction as she lowered herself to the ground.

The wino nodded approval. 'Not bad for a big girl,' he agreed. 'You've got some muscles on you, that's for sure . . . assuming you *are* a girl.' He ran the torch up and down her body. 'You're not one of those guys who want to be women, are you?'

'No,' said Jackson without offence. 'I've always had a fanny.'

She reached down her jacket and boots and stepped away from the cigarette butts, wiping detritus off her socks with the back of her hand before relacing the boots. She held her breath while she did it to avoid taking in the man's aroma. Susan had told her the story of the urinating yobs to explain why she thought Charles might be in Caroline Street, and Jackson concluded that not only was this the vagrant in question but, judging by his powerful smell, he hadn't washed his clothes since the episode. Either that or he had prostate problems.

She stood up and opened her palm. 'Mobile?' she asked pleasantly. He gave it to her but wasn't so keen to give up the torch. She gestured down the passageway. 'You lead,' she said. 'I'll follow.'

But he had quaint ideas about escorting women and insisted on walking beside her, shepherding her carefully with one hand behind her back and lighting the ground in front of her with the other. It made for close communion in the narrow confines of the alley and Jackson wasn't entirely sure that he wasn't touching her up. He was a couple of inches shorter than she was, but his shoulders looked powerful and, despite the grey streaks in his beard, she suspected he was younger than he looked.

'There's three of us,' he told her, 'me, a young lad who's out cold and your bloke.'

'What kind of "out cold"? Drugs?'

'Never seen him with any . . . but I can't swear to it. He turned up in a right state about half an hour ago, saying he felt sick and his belly hurt. He passed out shortly afterwards.' They rounded the corner and he directed the beam towards a couple of seated figures in front of a darkened doorway, one leaning against the other. 'It's not much,' he said apologetically, as if Jackson had made a request to join them, 'but it's safer than the Strand. You get some real nutters down there.'

'What name do you go by?' Jackson asked him.

'Chalky.' He played the torchlight over some bags against the wall as if to satisfy himself they were still there, then handed the torch back to Jackson. 'The lootenant –' he pronounced it the American way for reasons best known to himself – 'was planning to go for help till you turned up. He says you're a doctor.'

'True.'

'So will you look at the lad? My guess is he'll be dead if no one does anything.'

'Sure. What's his name?'

'Ben. I dunno his last name.'

She walked forward and flashed the light into Acland's face. 'You might have given me a hand over the railings,' she admonished mildly, kneeling beside the other figure. 'What good would I have been with a spike up my arse?' She shone the torch over the grey, unconscious face of his companion.

'I didn't think you'd come in if I climbed out.'

'Why not?' she asked, rolling the youngster's lids back with the ball of her thumb and shining the light into his unresponsive eyes.

'I don't know what your agenda is. You told me you worked for the police the first time I met you.'

'Only in a medical capacity. I don't round up witnesses for them.' Jackson leaned forward to sniff the unconscious boy's mouth. 'How long's his breath been smelling of nail polish remover?'

'Since he got here. It was even stronger when he was awake.'

'Have you tried speaking to him? Calling his name? Any response?'

'No. He's been like this from the moment he passed out.'

She turned the torch on the youngster's neck, where patches of inflamed skin stood out against his ashen pallor. 'How long have you known him, Chalky?'

'A month or so. He's a pretty lad, so the shirt-lifters came after him. I took him under my wing cos I don't hold with that kind of malarkey. The fact a little lad's run away shouldn't make him easy meat for the first predatory pervert that passes by.'

'I agree. Has he been complaining of thirst?'

'Haven't seen him for a while.'

'Does he pee a lot?'

'Anywhere he fancies.'

'How old is he?'

'Said he was eighteen . . . but I reckon fifteen's nearer the mark. What's wrong with him?'

'His symptoms suggest diabetic coma brought on by a build-up of chemical poisons in his blood.' She took out her mobile, scrolled down her menu and punched in a number. 'Yes . . . Trevor Monaghan, please . . . Dr Jackson . . . It's an emergency. Cheers.' She glanced up at Chalky. 'Go back to the railings and holler when you see an ambulance, and *you* –' she said to Acland, fishing her car keys out of her back pocket – 'hop round to my car and get my medical bag out of the boot. It's a black BMW and it's parked on the corner of Caroline Street opposite this bar.' She pressed the keys into his hand. 'Trevor? Are you on call? I need you to meet me in A&E. I've one sick kid for you, mate . . . Deep diabetic coma . . . initial diagnosis, ketoacidosis shock from untreated type one. Can you organize the ambulance from your end? Yes . . . absolute priority . . . the corner of Caroline Street and Russell Street in Covent Garden . . . And we need a fire crew . . . there's no way out of here without ladders . . .'

*

'Is he going to die?' asked Chalky twenty minutes later as the paramedics loaded the stretcher into the ambulance. He'd been impressed by the speed of the operation. Seconds after shouting down to Jackson that the ambulance had arrived, he'd called again to say that a fire crew were erecting a ladder gantry over the railings. 'You'd have to be pretty ill to have this many people turn out for you.'

Jackson was using Acland's back to write a note to the consultant. 'He's very ill, Chalky. Juvenile diabetes is a serious condition, and living on the streets won't have helped any.' She signed her name and tucked the piece of paper into an envelope which she took from her medical bag. 'If it's any comfort, I'm sending him to an expert.' She slapped the envelope into Chalky's hand. 'Make yourself useful . . . Give this to the driver, then grab your stuff and follow me down to my car. I'll give you a ride to the hospital.' She levelled a finger at Acland. 'You, too . . . and bring everything of Ben's. There might be some personal information in it.'

Acland shook his head and retreated against the nearest wall, where his, Ben's and Chalky's bags were stacked. Because of the narrow confines of the passageway, they'd been ordered to remove themselves and their possessions before the stretcher was brought in. 'It's nothing to do with me. I don't know the boy.'

'Me neither,' said Jackson, kneeling to close her bag, 'but it didn't stop you involving me in his problems.'

'It was your choice to come here.'

'True.' She stood up. 'So what's the deal?'

'There isn't one. You're not responsible for me. You go your way . . . I'll go mine.'

She eyed him curiously for a moment, then gave a small shrug of disappointment. 'You're not the person I thought you were,' she said.

'Ditto,' Acland murmured.

'Then we've both wasted our time.' She offered a small nod of farewell and headed towards the ambulance, where she had a brief word with the paramedics and Chalky before continuing on to her car.

Chalky came back. 'Shift your arse,' he ordered. 'Your lady friend wants to follow the meat wagon so that we can see the lad safely delivered.' He retrieved all the bags from the pavement, including Acland's kitbag, and set off after Jackson.

Acland stalked angrily behind him. 'Did she tell you to do that?'

'What?'

'Take my kitbag.'

'Just doing you a favour, mate.'

'Not interested. I want my stuff.'

'Then show the lady some gratitude first.' Chalky crossed Caroline Street and dumped all the bags into Jackson's open boot before slamming it shut. 'Grow up, son,' he said scathingly. 'Do you think anyone's ever cared enough to come looking for *me*?'

*

Jackson made no comment when Acland slid into the seat behind Chalky and pulled the door closed. She merely lowered the windows to dispel some of the older man's aroma then headed down towards the Aldwych. Amused by Chalky's cheerful announcement that it was the first time he'd been in a car since he'd walked out on his old woman, she encouraged him to talk about himself. How old was he?

'Last time anyone took notice, thirty-three . . . but I gave up counting after that. I went for a drink with some mates . . . had a few too many jars . . . and found the wife waiting for me when I got home. She had a bad temper, that woman. Didn't want to celebrate my birthday herself but got steaming mad because *I* did. Is that fair or is that fair?'

Jackson smiled. 'How long ago was that?'

'Now you're asking.' He thought for a moment. 'Twenty-two years, give or take a year or two. I was born in '51 . . . joined the army in '69 . . . spent three years in Germany . . . did a couple of stints in Northern Ireland . . . married in '78 . . . fought in the Falklands in '82 . . . cashed in my chips a year later . . . then took to the road when I couldn't stand the missus any longer. She blamed me for the lack of nippers. That's what got her riled.'

'Did you think about getting help for it?'

'Nah. Waste of time. Reckoned the best thing I could do was bugger off and let her have a bash with someone else.' He sounded quite cheerful about it. 'It wasn't much of a marriage. She only liked me when I wasn't around – sent letters and such – then, soon as I came home, the knives came out.' He pulled a face. 'The drink might have had something to do with it. Couldn't face her without a few jars under my belt . . . Kept asking myself why I'd tied myself to a roly-poly pudding – no offence – when I should have gone for something I could have got my arms round.'

'What did you do after you left the army?'

'Couldn't settle to anything. The world seemed pretty flat after the Falklands.' Chalky sighed. 'I should have stayed a soldier. I got a buzz out of going to war.'

Jackson glanced at Acland's face in the rear-view mirror, but if he had any fellow-feeling with Chalky's views, he wasn't showing it. 'What rank were you?'

'Made it to corporal just before we left for the South Atlantic. Best year of my bloody life that was . . . been downhill ever since.'

This time Acland did show some interest. 'Which regiment?' he asked.

'Two Para.'

'Which company?'

'B Company.'

'So you were in the attack on Goose Green?'

Chalky lifted a grimy thumb in the air. 'Certainly was. It was us took Boca Hill. I lost a good mate there.' He shook his head in sudden wistful nostalgia. 'We joined up together and I can hardly remember what he looked like now . . . Makes you think, doesn't it?'

Acland stared out of the window as Jackson turned on to Waterloo Bridge. The river was only beautiful at night, when the lights along its banks gleamed like diamonds on black velvet, and the Palace of Westminster, lit by arc lamps, looked more like a fairy castle than the seat of government. In daylight hours, with the embankments and bridges thronged with people and cars, he could see no beauty in it at all. 'So how come a corporal from 2 Para ends up drinking meths in the gutter?' he asked harshly.

Surprisingly, Chalky didn't take offence. 'I never drink the *dyed* meths,' he said, as if such abstinence were a matter for pride, 'though I still go for the white stuff when I can get it. It's not so bad – rots your brain and rots your liver – but it's cheap and it keeps the boredom at bay for a few hours.' He scratched the beard at the side of his face. 'I prefer cider.'

'That's not an answer. You wouldn't have made corporal if you hadn't had something going for you. What happened to that person?'

Chalky shrugged. 'Who knows, son? Maybe he just got lost on the Falklands.'

Fourteen

THE AMBULANCE HAD ALREADY arrived by the time Jackson turned off Lambeth Palace Road into St Thomas's A&E entrance. With every emergency parking space taken, she glanced at Acland in the mirror and asked him if he had a valid driving licence.

He nodded. 'No one's asked for it back yet.'

She pulled over and opened her door. 'There's a staff car park round the side. Find the main entrance and follow the signs. I just need a couple of minutes to check through the kid's things . . . see if I can find out who he is. If you're challenged, show this – ' she pointed to a medical priority sticker on her dashboard – 'and ask them to page Trevor Monaghan or phone me on this number.' She took a card from her pocket and passed it back to him.

'Don't go looking through anything of mine,' said Chalky firmly. 'The black rucksack belongs to the lad . . . everything else belongs to me . . . and it's private.'

Jackson eased out from behind the wheel. 'You're safe on that score,' she said sarcastically. 'I'm not in the habit of rifling through plastic carrier bags full of rubbish.'

She opened Acland's door and handed him the keys. 'You're very trusting,' he said, climbing out.

'Why shouldn't I be? You're not planning to steal a BMW, are you?'

He watched while she opened the boot and made a quick search of Ben's rucksack. 'I haven't driven since I lost my eye.'

'So? You can see well enough to climb railings.' She removed a label from the inside flap with a name, Mr B. Russell, and an address in Wolverhampton. 'I'll take this for the moment, but can you go through his things with a fine-tooth comb after you've parked? We need home address, surname and next of kin.'

'Shouldn't the hospital do it?'

'It'll be quicker this way.' She took out her medical case and slammed the boot shut again. 'Bring the bag to reception when you've finished and ask them to page me or Dr Monaghan –' she eyed him for a moment – 'and don't leave Chalky alone in my car. I'd prefer the contents to be intact when I come back.'

Acland wanted to tell her that he knew what she was doing – tying him to a responsibility he hadn't asked for – but she was gone before he could say it. In any case, part of him rose to the occasion, even if he recognized, and resented, how easily Jackson manipulated him.

'You sure you can drive this thing?' asked Chalky suspiciously as Acland climbed in beside him and turned his head to focus his good eye on the gearbox. 'I notice no one asked me what I thought about it.'

Acland saw with relief that the car was an automatic. 'If you want to make yourself useful, help me get out of here. Shout if I get too close to anything on my left.'

In the event, it was more by luck than good judgement that Acland made it safely to the car park. Chalky was about as much use as a maiden aunt who'd never been in a car in her life. He peered religiously out of his window but, with a complete lack of spatial awareness, he failed to mention a single hazard until after it had passed.

'You damn near hit a bollard back there,' he said helpfully as Acland killed the engine.

'Thanks for warning me.'

'Didn't need to. You were doing OK on your own.' He pulled a baccy tin out of his coat pocket and started to shred wisps of tobacco on to a Rizla. 'So what's the plan?'

'We both get out so you don't pollute the doctor's car any further.'

'She's some woman,' said Chalky, rolling the paper in his fingers. 'Seems pretty interested in you.'

'She's a lesbian.'

The older man gave a snort of amusement. 'The meths hasn't totally rotted my brain, lad. I've a few dyke friends down in Docklands – they tend to hang together for safety – but I share a cider with them from time to time. They look after each other . . . There's a couple of schizos in the group that the others take care of.' He paused to run his tongue along the paper. 'The doc's doing the same for you.'

Acland got out and walked round to open Chalky's door. 'She wants me to check the boy's rucksack to see if she missed anything.'

The older man studied him thoughtfully. 'You'd better let me do that, son. The kid doesn't like strangers poking through his stuff any more than I do. Think I didn't notice you eyeing up the bags in the alleyway?'

Acland ignored him. 'I'll only be looking for next-of-kin details. You can watch while I do it if it'll make you happier.'

But Chalky was more interested in creature comforts. 'I'll take a quiet smoke and a drink in here where it's warm. You can show me what you've found afterwards . . . and I'll tell you what's important and what isn't.'

'No chance.' Acland put his hand under the other man's elbow and heaved him upright. 'You can do your smoking and drinking on that wall over there.'

'I'm not taking orders from you, lad.'

'I outrank you.'

Chalky shook him off. 'Not in my world, you don't,' he said with sudden belligerence. 'In my world, anyone who's been at this game longer than you takes precedence . . . and that includes young Ben in there.'

Acland kept an eye on his fists. 'You don't want to take me on, Corporal. I've been a mean bugger since the ragheads destroyed my face.'

'You look it,' Chalky agreed. 'Seen guys like you before . . . fucked on the outside and fucked on the inside. What the hell? The wall's as good as anywhere.' He removed a half-bottle of vodka from another pocket. 'I got lucky,' he said by way of explanation as he wandered off. 'A lass gave me a tenner this morning . . . said I reminded her of her grandpa.'

*

If Acland had ever thought about leaving, he abandoned the idea as he watched Chalky perch on the low wall bordering the car park and unscrew the vodka with shaking hands. Perhaps it was the desperate way the corporal sucked at the alcohol, or the fact he looked older than the fifty-six he was claiming, but the scene – Dickensian in its harsh reality – burned into Acland's brain. He couldn't imagine this man as a soldier with the fortitude to march and fight for two days on the desolate ridges of the Falkland Islands.

He retrieved Jackson's torch from the dashboard pocket, then opened the boot and upended Ben's rucksack in the front corner. The ceiling light was strong enough to show objects, but Acland propped the torch on his kitbag to help him decipher anything written. He experienced a similar embarrassment to DI Beale as he surveyed the adolescent's pathetic haul. There were more gadgets than Acland possessed – a couple of mobile telephones, a digital camera, a BlackBerry and four iPods – but fewer clothes. Acland guessed the gadgets were stolen – certainly none of them had functioning batteries – but he separated out the mobiles and the BlackBerry in case there was anything relevant on them.

There were several envelopes, all addressed to Ben Russell c/o a drop-in centre in Whitechapel. Inside were handwritten letters from someone called Hannah. Acland skimmed through them. *I miss you so much . . . Dad's been over the moon since you left . . . He's such a knobhead . . . keeps saying out of sight, out of mind . . . I feel sorry for your mum . . . I saw her in town and she looked really sad . . .* At the top of each letter, by way of Hannah's address, was *The Hell Hole*, but the frank marks on the envelopes suggested they'd been posted in Wolverhampton.

In one of the rucksack pockets, Acland found a photograph of a simpering girl with straight blonde hair, heavily made-up eyes and pale pink lips. A flourishing dedication had been scrawled in felt-tip pen across the bottom – *Love you, babe – don't forget to write –* and on the back in pencil was written *25 Melbury Gardens, WV6 0AA.* It didn't take Einstein to work out that this was the address for Ben's return letters, although Acland doubted it was where Hannah lived. The 'knobhead' father wouldn't ignore letters from London.

He repacked the rucksack, placing the phones, BlackBerry, envelopes and snapshot in the front pocket, then dropped it to the ground at his feet. He took another look at the array of bags that Chalky claimed were his, then stepped away from the car and raised his voice. 'Are you sure nothing else in here belongs to Ben? I remember him bringing more than just the rucksack into the passageway.'

'You're talking through your arse.'

Acland studied him for a moment. 'If you keep claiming to be a soldier,' he said coldly, 'I'll slit your bloody throat. Nothing you've ever done in your whole miserable life allows you to range yourself with the guys I've led.'

'I don't take that kind of talk off jumped-up lootenants.' There was noticeably more aggression in Chalky's tone, as if vodka had released the fighter in him. 'If you're looking for his cash, he wears it in a belt . . . same as I do. The nurses will have pocketed it by now.'

'Nurses don't steal off kids, Chalky, and neither do I. Which of these bags is his? I'll go through the lot if necessary.'

'Jesus *Christ!*' The corporal heaved himself off the wall and came towards him. 'I'll have your guts if you've touched anything of mine.' He loomed menacingly at Acland's shoulder. 'It's the Londis bag . . . the one with the baccy and the booze. They're no good to him here. He won't be able to smoke and drink in a sodding hospital, will he?'

Acland pulled the Londis carrier forward and untied the polythene handles that were holding the contents together. Two hundred Benson & Hedges and a bottle of whisky. 'How did he get them? You said he was fifteen.'

'Nicked 'em.'

'You can't nick spirits and cartons of cigarettes off the shelf.'

'OK, he paid for 'em . . . probably in a Paki shop. Pakis don't care who buys the stuff as long as cash changes hands.'

'Where would he get the money?'

'Snaffled a rich bitch's handbag, I expect. They're thick as pig shit, those women.' His tone was contemptuous now. 'They yackety-yack with their friends outside cafes, and they don't even know their bag's gone till they come to pay. All you need's a diversion – a mate pretending to beg – and the bitches all look at him while you do the business behind them.'

'You're a real hero, Corporal.'

Chalky shouldered the lieutenant aside. 'It's an ugly world, son, and stripes and pips don't mean a fucking thing outside the army. The sooner you get wise to that the better.' He took the carrier out of Acland's hands, retied the handles and shoved it to the back of the boot. 'There's nothing in there that'll do a sick kid any good.'

'Did he have a duffel bag with him?'

Chalky coughed smoker's phlegm into his throat and spat it on the ground. 'Not that I saw.'

'Are you sure?'

Something in the lieutenant's tone irritated him. 'You calling me a liar? Just take the rucksack.' He closed the lid. 'I'll wait in the car till you're done.'

Acland clicked the remote on the key fob to lock the doors. 'You'll wait on the wall,' he said without hostility. 'I'd prefer my kitbag to be here when I get back.'

*

It was twenty minutes before Jackson came to find him in the A&E waiting room. He opened the front pocket of the rucksack and showed her the electrical gadgets. 'How's he doing?'

'He'll live but he'll have to stay in for a few days.' She took the chair beside Acland. 'We've found a phone number for the address in Wolverhampton, but no one's answering. Did you come up with anything else?'

Acland removed the photograph. 'I think she's his girlfriend.' He turned it over to show the address, explaining why he thought it was a friend's house rather than her own. 'If it was a commercial poste restante there'd be a PO Box number, so whoever lives there must know her, and probably Ben as well.'

'I'll try it. What about the mobiles? Anything on them?'

'Dead. The BlackBerry, too.' He paused. 'There's a digital camera and four iPods as well. I'd say it's a good bet they're all stolen.'

Jackson viewed him with amusement. 'A dead cert more like. I hope that means you haven't given Chalky free rein of my car. He'll have the seats out of it before you can blink . . . not to mention the CD player and the radio.'

'He's sitting on a wall. Vodka and him don't mix. He's spoiling for a fight.'

'That's alcohol for you. I expect he uses it to self-medicate for depression . . . It's what most of them do. Sometimes it'll send them to sleep . . . other times it'll gee them up for a confrontation. Where did he get the vodka from?'

'Stole it, I should think . . . or got Ben to do it for him. He's appropriated a bag of booze and fags that the lad brought in with him.'

'Payment in kind for a secure pitch for the night,' said Jackson matter-of-factly. 'It's a dog-eat-dog world on the streets. How much did he take you for?'

'Nothing.'

Jackson looked amused. 'Chalky's a pro. You'd probably have woken up tomorrow morning to find most of your cash missing.'

She lifted the phones out of the rucksack pocket and selected a Nokia, removing the back and the battery to check if the SIM card was there. 'I keep a Cellboost in my bag. How's your conscience when it comes to the Data Protection Act? Shall we give it a whirl?'

'Won't it be locked?'

'We won't know till we try.'

*

Following in Jackson's wake, Acland was interested in how many negative reactions she seemed to inspire. He was used to attracting suspicious looks himself, but it was a new experience to see someone else draw the flak. Even in the early hours, St Thomas's A&E was busy, and he saw the faces people pulled as she passed and the way they turned to watch her retreating back. From behind, her bootleg trousers and black leather jacket, topped by her thick neck and short hair, made her look more masculine than ever, and he wondered how many of the reactions were caused by confusion over her gender.

She spoke on her mobile as she walked along, apparently oblivious to the interest she was causing. 'I've another address for you . . . 25 Melbury Gardens, WV6 0AA . . . No name, I'm afraid . . . Not sure, but I doubt it's a relation . . . Possibly someone who knows his girlfriend . . . That's right . . . no surname . . . just Hannah. If I leave his rucksack in the PCT office, will you make sure he gets it? Cheers.' She redialled. 'Anything new for Dr Jackson? Dr Patel covered it . . . ? Thank him for me. No, I'm still at the hospital . . . almost finished . . . ten minutes max but I can be out of here in two if something comes up. Cheers.'

She stopped outside an office and punched a code into an electronic lock before ushering Acland inside. She passed him a piece of paper and a pen from the desk. 'Print "Ben Russell" on that in block caps and leave it with the rucksack in the corner,' she told him, taking her case from behind the door and propping it on her knee to open it. 'OK, let's see what we can find.'

Acland watched her unwrap the Cellboost. 'Why don't you put the SIM card in your own Nokia and read it that way?'

'I'm on call.' She connected the booster to the phone and hoisted a meaty thigh on the edge of the desk while she waited. 'There's usually a lull about this time. The busy periods are in the lead-up to midnight and after three o'clock in the morning.'

'Why?'

'Human nature and blood-sugar levels. Parents check on children before they go to bed themselves . . . Adults tend to worry in the hours before dawn when they're at their lowest ebb. It's a common time for people to die.'

Acland finished writing Ben's name and moved the rucksack into the corner. 'I wouldn't like that.'

'What?'

'Finding someone dead in bed.'

'Then don't take a job in a hospital or a nursing home or you'll come across them on a regular basis.' Jackson cupped a hand round the mobile to see the battery level. 'Hardly anyone dies at home these days, yet most of us would rather fall asleep in our own beds than attached to drips in a sterile environment full of strangers.'

'Maybe doctors shouldn't strive so assiduously to keep people alive.' He spoke the words grimly.

Jackson eyed him for a moment. '*All* people? Are you saying we should have left Ben to die in an alleyway because life-long insulin is going to cost the rest of us a fortune?'

'No.'

'Who, then? *You?*' She removed the Cellboost from the mobile and fired it up. 'If you're looking for someone to blame because you're still alive, then blame your men. They could have abandoned you in the desert and saved the medics the time and trouble of putting you back together again. Not to mention the decent dinner I might have had if you and Chalky hadn't insisted on saving the lad upstairs.'

'Sorry.'

'Accepted . . . and you're right, it's locked.' She gave him the pen again. 'The IMEI number should be under the SIM card.' She prised the casing open and removed the piece of plastic, reading aloud a series of digits. 'Got that?'

Acland nodded. 'How do you know how to do this?'

'A policeman taught me.' She moved round to the chair and switched on the computer. 'OK, what I'm about to do next is highly illegal so if you don't want to be involved you'd better wait outside the door.'

'Involved in what?'

'Me asserting that I'm the owner of this phone in order to access the master code.' She tapped in a website address, then held out her hand for the IMEI number.

'I'll read it to you.'

'Then bear in mind that everything I'm doing is being recorded on the hard drive. You're aiding and abetting a fraudulent use of someone else's data.'

Acland shrugged indifferently and read out the number. 'Why would a policeman teach you to do something illegal?'

'Daisy forgets security codes . . . including the burglar alarm.' Jackson clicked the mouse, then leaned back while the screen worked out permutations. 'The woman has a PhD in First World War poetry . . . can recite most of Rupert Brooke . . . but can't hold a four-digit PIN in her head. I've had to learn the tricks of the trade for all the security devices in the pub. If she puts in the wrong code, nothing works.'

'Why doesn't she use the same code for everything?'

'Because she's a dipstick where mobiles are concerned. She's had more lost or stolen than you've had hot dinners. If she used the same four numbers on her phone as we do on the alarm, the pub would have been stripped bare months ago. Any Tom, Dick or Harry can do this.' She nodded at the monitor. 'There you go. A usable master code.' She reached for the Nokia and punched in the numbers. 'Bingo. Let's start with ICE.'

Acland watched over her shoulder as she went into the address book. 'What's ICE?'

'In Case of Emergency. It's the recognized site for next-of-kin details so police and paramedics don't have to call every name in the address book.' She read the name that appeared. 'Belinda Atkins. That doesn't sound very hopeful . . . it's a London phone number.' She put in 'Russell', but the only names that appeared under 'R' were 'Randall', 'Reeve', 'Roddy' and 'Rush'.

'Try "Atkins"?' Acland suggested.

There were five of them: Belinda Atkins, Gerald Atkins, Kevin Atkins, Sarah Atkins, Tom Atkins. 'So whose phone is it?' Jackson asked. 'It's obviously not Belinda's, if she's the next of kin.'

'Kevin's,' said Acland. 'He's the only one without a landline. All the others have two contact numbers. It's a good way of remembering your own mobile number.'

'Give it a go,' she said, offering him her own phone and reading out the digits.

'As long as you do the talking if anyone answers. *I* wouldn't want to be woken at this time of night to be told about a stolen mobile.' He pressed the 'call' button and the handset in Jackson's hand started playing 'The Ride of the Valkyries'.

Jackson killed it. 'I know the name Kevin Atkins,' she said slowly, 'but I can't think why. Where would I have heard it before?'

'A patient?'

She shook her head. 'Somewhere else. I'm sure I've seen it fairly recently, too.' She lapsed into a brief silence. 'Damn! It's really bugging me.'

Acland nodded to the lit screen. 'Try Google,' he said.

*

Neither was prepared for the information that came up.

<u>BBC NEWS / England / London / Third murder victim beaten to
death . . .</u>
The body of **Kevin Atkins** . . .

<u>Guardian Unlimited / Special reports / Murder of **Kevin Atkins** part
of a series . . .</u>
Detective Superintendent Jones, who is leading the murder inquiry, said . . .

<u>The Sun Online – News: Male prostitute sought for gay killings . . .</u>
Police warn gay community to be vigilant following the murder of **Kevin
Atkins** . . .

Jackson's response was disbelief. 'There's no way that kid could
beat anyone to death. He's skin and bones. His sugar levels would
have gone haywire the minute he started pumping adrenalin.'

Acland's response was extreme agitation. 'You shouldn't have
done this. I'm going to be crucified.'

Jackson clicked on the BBC news report and scanned down it.
'The story's four months old. More to the point is why hasn't the
server disconnected the phone?'

Acland turned away, pumping his fists violently. 'Who cares?'

'*You* might if the police come bursting through the door,' she
said. 'They're obviously still tracking it . . . and *we've* just given
them its location.'

'Shit!'

'Calm down,' Jackson said sharply. 'It's Ben who's going to be
in the firing line . . . not you and me. The first question they'll ask
him is how did a murdered man's mobile get in his rucksack?'

'He'll say I put it there.'

'Why would he do that?'

'Because I'm the obvious fall guy. I was in the alleyway with
him . . . and Jones already thinks I'm involved in these murders.'

Jackson eyed him thoughtfully. 'The kid won't know that
unless you told him.'

Acland ignored her. 'I can't even prove the damn thing was in his rucksack. Chalky was sitting on a wall when I found it.' He started pacing the floor. 'Shit! Fucking *shit*!'

'You were searched at the police station,' Jackson reminded him, 'and you didn't have the mobile on you then.'

He swung round in fury. 'I've *never* had it on me,' he snapped, 'but it won't stop the bastards accusing me. There's no way they'll believe this was chance. They'll say Ben was stashing stuff for me . . . and our meeting was prearranged.'

Jackson allowed a pulse of silence to pass. '*Was* it?' she asked dispassionately.

Acland came close to stamping his foot. 'I only found out what his name was when Chalky told you.'

'Does he know yours?'

Acland shook his head angrily, as if the question was irrelevant.

'What about Chalky? Does he know you as anything other than lootenant?'

'No.'

'Then Ben will have a tough time implicating you in whatever he's been up to,' she said calmly. 'If he was sick enough to go into a coma, I doubt he'll even remember you were there . . . let alone be able to describe you.' She closed down Windows and turned off the computer. 'However suspicious you are of the police, they don't usually manufacture evidence out of thin air . . . and a prearranged meeting requires some foreknowledge of the other person, such as a name or a recognizable description . . . not to mention a means of communication.'

Rather than allay Acland's anger, this reasoned approach seemed to stoke it up. 'Don't patronize me,' he warned.

'Then use your brain,' Jackson murmured, reaching for her medical case and lifting it on to the desk. 'No one's going to be interested in you. It's the wretched kid who'll be put through the mill . . . just as soon as he's well enough to answer questions. Me, too, if I've wiped anything important off Atkins's SIM card.'

'You shouldn't have interfered.'

'Maybe not, but the guy who owned that phone was murdered, so on balance I'd say I did a good thing.'

'You might feel differently if you'd been held for six hours.'

'I doubt it,' she said coolly. 'I don't panic as easily as you seem to do.'

Acland slammed his palms on to the desk. 'I *told* you . . . *don't* patronize me.'

Jackson shrugged. 'You're not giving me much choice. If you want respect, you'd better find a way of dealing with fear that doesn't involve throwing a tantrum.'

He thrust his face into hers. 'I *knew* I shouldn't have got in your car. Every time I trust a woman, I get fucking *shafted* . . . and I'm sick to death of it.'

She stared back at him, unmoved. 'If you carry on like this, I'll start to question your actions myself. Are you going to back off . . . or do we play this charade to the end? I'm not remotely interested in bolstering your self-esteem by allowing you to intimidate me.'

Reluctantly, Acland straightened and stepped away. 'For all I know you've set this up. Your lady friend did a fucking neat job of getting me arrested last time.'

Jackson rose to her feet. 'Daisy couldn't organize a piss-up in brewery. It was me who told the police you were coming . . . and before your hackles go up again, we were only asked about the fight in the pub and whether we knew how to contact you. I had no idea you had a connection with Walter Tutting until they took you in for questioning . . . and neither did Daisy.'

'She made the arrest possible. She pointed me out to the police as soon as I came through the door.'

'She had no choice. You assaulted one of her customers and she has a licence to protect.' Jackson shook her head at Acland's sullen expression. 'What did you expect her to do? Jeopardize everything she's worked for to avoid you feeling hard done by? If so, you've some strange ideas about other people's priorities.'

'I sure as hell don't understand yours,' he retorted angrily.

'Why come looking for me? I'd be long gone if you'd kept your nose out of my business. The kid's no concern of mine. Once I'd called the ambulance, I'd have left.'

'The phone would still have existed and it would still have belonged to Kevin Atkins,' she pointed out, 'and you'd have looked a lot guiltier if you'd vanished at that point. Do you think Chalky wouldn't have said that a lieutenant with an eyepatch was the third person in the alleyway?'

'The police wouldn't have been involved. It's only because you're a control freak that we're in this mess. If you'd left well alone, the mobile would have remained untouched in the rucksack and the server wouldn't have been able to track it.'

'And you'd prefer it that way?'

'Yes.'

'All right,' she said abruptly. 'Then you and Chalky had better disappear. I can't imagine he'll be any keener than you to assist in a murder inquiry.' She tucked her own mobile into her pocket, opened her medical case, put the stolen mobile and the spent Cellboost into an envelope, then closed the lid. 'You'll have the time it takes me to drive from here to Southwark East police station to put distance between yourselves and this hospital. I won't mention either of you unless I'm asked directly if you were here.'

Acland squared up to her. 'What good's that if the paramedics saw us?'

Jackson shouldered past him to pick up the rucksack. 'The police won't bother with paramedics when they have Kevin Atkins's phone,' she said bitingly. 'The only person they'll be interested in is the sick boy upstairs. Or is that too complicated for you to understand?'

Fifteen

BY THE SIMPLE EXPEDIENT of making another series of calls, Jackson stymied all Acland's attempts to speak to her as they returned to the car, but he couldn't tell whether she was blanking him deliberately or whether the calls were necessary. One was a request for an update on Ben's condition with a warning that the police would almost certainly want to interview him, another the information that she had taken responsibility for the rucksack herself, and the last an apology to her agency that she would be out of commission for another hour at Southwark East police station.

She was ahead of Acland as they entered the car park and took the full brunt of Chalky's alcoholic ill-humour. 'About bloody time,' he growled. 'Did you think I'd give up and go away if you held out long enough? Fancy my stuff, do you?'

Jackson ignored him to flick the locks on the BMW. She put her case and Ben's rucksack on the back seat. 'I'm sorry if we've inconvenienced you,' she said pleasantly enough. 'The boot's open, Lieutenant. Do you want to give Chalky his bags and take your own?'

The corporal moved quickly to prevent Acland removing anything. 'I'll do my own, thanks.' He tossed out the kitbag, then looped his fingers into the remaining assortment of carriers and tatty holdalls. 'What's up?' he asked Jackson suspiciously, stepping away from the car.

'I'll leave the lieutenant to explain it to you.'

'Where are you taking the lad's rucksack?'

'Southwark East nick.'

'Like hell you are. Anything he has in there he came by fair and square.'

'Then there's nothing to worry about,' said Jackson, watching Acland close the boot after emptying it. 'You can come with me if you like . . . kill two birds with one stone. Sign for the rucksack's contents, so that nothing goes astray if everything's kosher, and vouch for the kid's honesty in front of the cops. Interested?'

'Depends what you've found.'

'A mobile that doesn't belong to him.'

Chalky gave a grunt of disgust. 'You can't shop him for that. There's dodgy phones all over London. Easiest bloody things to pinch. That's no reason to give the lad grief.'

'It's not just any stolen mobile, Chalky. The man who owned it was murdered.'

He stared at her out of bloodshot eyes. 'How do you know?'

'I got it working,' she said. 'It's still connected to the server. I think the police kept it alive in case anyone tried to use it.'

'The lad won't know anything about a murder . . . probably doesn't even know who he stole it from. No need to say where you found it.'

Jackson shook her head. 'I'm afraid I'll have to.' She opened the door. 'The lieutenant's making his own way from here. Do you want to do the same . . . or come with me? You'll lessen the grief for Ben if there's anything you know that might help him.'

Chalky shook his head. 'There's nothing 'cept what I've already told you. Him and me hardly know each other. Showed him a safe place to sleep and that's about it. He came maybe five or six times.'

'What did you talk about?'

'Me . . . nothing. Him . . . music and some girl he was keen on. Never really listened . . . just let him rabbit on till he nodded off.'

'You said you met him a month ago. Have you any idea how long he'd been in London before that?'

'No. '

'You also said gays were interested in him. Do you know if he ever went with any of them? Would he have sold himself if he needed money?'

Disgustedly, Chalky spat on the ground, as if to demonstrate his feelings about anal sex. 'Didn't ask. Can't stand the buggers. Just showed him a safe place to kip.'

'What would your guess be?'

'Depends what he's on. Cider comes cheap . . . heroin comes expensive. Most of 'em do it if they're on the drugs.' He made to move away, but a strong emotion suddenly burst out of him. 'It ain't *right*!' he said loudly. 'It's not just the lads these bastards are after, it's the lasses as well. If you're going to tell the cops anything, tell 'em that.'

'Sure,' said Jackson easily, 'but which bastards are we talking about? Punters or dealers?'

'*All* of 'em! They treat runaways like garbage. When they're not emptying themselves into the poor little sods, they're getting 'em hooked on heroin. It shouldn't be allowed.' He launched another globule of spit on to the tarmac. 'You can't blame the kid for turning vicious. It's the only way any of 'em know how to survive.' He nodded. 'I'll see you around some time.'

Jackson watched him walk away. 'Are you coming?' she asked Acland.

He stared after Chalky for a moment, then opened the back door and put his kitbag inside. 'Yes.'

*

If either had expected a sense of urgency to greet their arrival at the police station, they were disappointed. The team who'd interviewed Acland earlier had clocked off shortly after his release and the detective constable who was assigned to deal with them appeared to know less about Walter Tutting and Kevin Atkins than they did. Stressed about her work schedule, Jackson quickly became irritated when he cut short her attempt at an explanation to pull out a form and ask for their names and addresses.

'I don't have time for this,' she said curtly. 'I'm on call. We need to talk to Detective Superintendent Jones or DI Beale as a matter of urgency –' her eyes narrowed – 'and you know perfectly well who I am. The WPC on reception gave you my name over the phone.'

The man looked at her with the same half-amused expression that had been on the faces of the people in A&E. 'I still need your details, Ms Jackson.'

'It's *Dr* Jackson and *Lieutenant* Acland,' she told him. 'The Bell, Gainsborough Road. I guarantee the superintendent will not object to being woken if you inform him that we have Kevin Atkins's mobile. It was on a homeless lad who's been taken to St Thomas's. Walter Tutting's in the same hospital.'

He filled in their names and address. 'Telephone number?'

'Oh, for God's sake,' she snapped, losing her patience. 'Just call the superintendent.'

'When I've satisfied myself that it's necessary.'

'Then try DI Beale.'

'Same answer.'

Jackson eyed him for a moment. 'What time does the superintendent usually come in in the morning?'

The man shrugged. 'I wouldn't know. It depends on his shifts.'

'Where can I leave a message for him?'

'With me.'

She leaned forward. 'Then put this: "Can't get past the arrogant dickhead on night duty who has a problem with dykes. Urgent you contact Jackson ASAP at the Bell re gay murders. She has evidence linking a homeless man to Kevin Atkins." Add the time and tell your boss we've taken the evidence with us because we don't trust you to look after it properly.' She handed the rucksack to Acland and stood up.

'I'm merely following standard procedure, Dr Jackson,' said

the constable. 'If I phoned the superintendent every time someone claimed to have important evidence, he'd be dead of exhaustion by now. Do I take it you're terminating this interview because you no longer wish to report a crime?'

'No. I'm terminating it because I haven't the time to play up to your image of yourself. You can add that at the bottom of the message.'

'What about you, sir?' he asked Acland. 'Have you anything to add?'

'Only that, in your shoes, I'd consult with someone else before Dr Jackson and I leave.' He paused. 'I was signed off by a custody sergeant called Laver or Lavery. If he's still on duty, you might do yourself a favour by talking to him.'

*

'You should have let Jones eat him for breakfast,' said Jackson after the door closed behind the constable. 'Why so helpful suddenly? What's a middle-aged Gruppenführer to you?'

Acland shrugged. 'He's out of his depth. It's obviously a big deal to wake the boss in the middle of the night.'

'He's a small-minded bully with a power complex.'

'You're not much better. You only took him on because he was an easy target. I didn't notice you lamming into any of the patients in A&E for sneering at you.'

She leaned against the wall and crossed her arms. 'It's bad business practice to attack customers. Policemen are in a different category altogether. They have professional standards to uphold, which don't include treating members of the public like a sub-species.'

Acland allowed a silence to develop. He still couldn't decide what he thought about this woman. There was so much about her that repelled him – the forcefulness of her character, her outspokenness, her need to dominate every situation – and little to earn his sympathy other than admiration for her as a doctor and a nagging resentment at the negative reactions she seemed to attract from strangers. He looked up to find her staring at him.

'What?' he asked.

'Is it me you have a problem with or women in general?'

Acland gave another shrug. 'You enjoy intimidating people. Maybe the guy did know your name . . . and maybe he is a small-minded bigot . . . but he wasn't going to think any better of you for being called an "arrogant dickhead".'

Jackson refrained from pointing out that this wasn't an answer to her question. Instead, she said, 'Why should it matter what he thinks of me?'

'It doesn't.'

'He'd have cocked his leg even higher if I'd been wearing a skirt and make-up,' she responded lightly. 'Most people take me for a bloke in drag . . . or a male transsexual going through gender reassignment. I receive fewer sniggers dressed like this –' she uncrossed her arms and gestured towards her masculine attire – 'than if I wear women's clothes. A butch dyke in trousers and workman's boots is less alarming than a muscular transvestite weightlifter in pastel pink.'

Briefly, humour creased the undamaged side of Acland's face. 'You wouldn't wear pink in a million years. Not threatening enough. I bet you get a real buzz from seeing people move out of your way.'

Jackson watched him for a moment. 'Is that what the scars and the pirate-patch do for you? Who moves aside faster? Men or women?'

He didn't answer.

'You want to be careful how you exploit that, Lieutenant. Some men get a taste for seeing fear in women's eyes.'

*

The speed of events moved up a pace as soon as the superintendent arrived. He ignored the detective constable's explanations about how he couldn't guarantee the mobile was Kevin Atkins's because he hadn't been allowed to see it and addressed his remarks to Jackson and Acland. 'Where is it?'

'Here.' Jackson flipped the locks on her medical case and handed him the envelope. 'The battery was dead but I used a Cellboost to fire it up because I thought it belonged to a homeless kid who's in a diabetic coma in St Thomas's. I was looking for next-of-kin details. It's still switched on.'

Jones slipped the gadget on to the table. 'Where did you find it?'

'In this.' She lifted the rucksack to show him. 'It belongs to the boy – we think his name's Ben Russell – although we haven't been able to confirm that yet.' She watched Jones touch the end of a pencil to one of the buttons to light up the LCD. 'I went into ICE, which gave me Belinda Atkins, and then into Atkins. The number recorded under Kevin is the number of that phone. I recognized the name.'

'His daughter's name's Belinda.' Jones used the pencil to scroll down the screen. 'Geoff and Tom are the sons, and Sarah's his ex-wife . . . still recorded under Atkins. It's definitely his.' He looked up with a frown. 'How did you unlock it? Or do we have Lieutenant Acland to thank for that?'

Jackson shook her head. 'It was me.' She described how she did it. 'I'm not so au fait with other makes of phone, otherwise I might have had an attempt at the other one as well.'

'Which other one?'

She nodded to the rucksack. 'In here. Also a BlackBerry and some iPods.'

'Quite a haul.' He glanced from her to Acland. 'Where does the lieutenant fit in?'

'He's staying with me.'

'Meaning what? That you returned to the Bell to pick him up before you came here?'

Acland stirred when Jackson hesitated. 'She came looking for me,' he said. 'I was with the boy and another man when she found me. We were sleeping rough in an alleyway. The kid went into a coma and Dr Jackson had him admitted to St Thomas's when she realized how serious it was.'

Jones nodded. 'Inspector Beale phoned to say you'd gone in the opposite direction. How well do you know this boy?'

'I don't know him at all,' said Acland.

The superintendent gave a sceptical smile. 'You expect me to believe that? You come into contact with two complete strangers in under twenty-four hours . . . Walter Tutting and this kid . . . *both* apparently connected with the same murder inquiry . . . and you claim you didn't know either of them previously. That kind of coincidence doesn't happen, Charles.'

'Obviously it does or it wouldn't have just happened to me.'

'No one's that unlucky.'

Acland pressed his palm over his eyepatch, grinding the heel into the throbbing nerve ends. 'If I am, it's working in your favour,' he pointed out. 'You wouldn't have the phone if Jackson hadn't followed me and the boy hadn't fallen sick. A different doctor or a healthy kid, and the stuff would still be untouched in the rucksack.'

'Assuming it was there in the first place. How long were you alone with the lad before Dr Jackson arrived?'

'Never. The older guy was already in the alleyway when I got there.'

'So there was no opportunity to switch items from the lad's bag to yours, or vice versa, without anyone seeing you do it?'

'No.'

'And no opportunity to conveniently *lose* –' he smiled again as he put emphasis on the word – 'anything he was carrying for you?'

'No . . . but that's not what he was doing.'

'Why should I believe that?'

Acland put out a hand to steady himself against the edge of the table. 'I don't know,' he said harshly, 'unless the boy tells you the same . . . except you won't believe him either.'

'You look ill,' said Jones unemotionally. 'I suggest you sit down before you fall over.'

'No thank you. I'd rather stand.' The lieutenant stepped away from the table and squared his shoulders.

Jones gestured peremptorily at Jackson. 'He needs attention, Doctor . . . looks as if he's about to faint. Will you see to him, please?'

She shook her head. 'Only if he asks for my help . . . not otherwise. It's well outside my remit to wrestle unwilling patients to the floor. I'll leave the rough stuff to you and the constable here –' she watched the superintendent push his chair back – 'although I wouldn't advise any unnecessary use of it,' she finished mildly.

'Oh, for God's sake!' Jones rose impatiently to his feet and walked round the table. 'Sit down, man,' he said, gripping Acland's arm and pushing him towards a chair. 'This isn't Guantanamo Bay.'

He barely had time to finish the sentence before Acland seized his wrist and spun him round in a classic half nelson, using one hand to force Jones's chin on to his chest and the other to put torque on the bones of the forearm. 'You shouldn't have done that,' he murmured into the man's ear. 'I wasn't bothering you . . . I wasn't threatening you . . . and I've made it clear several times that I don't like being touched.'

Jones made no attempt to resist. 'You've made your point, Charles. Now let me go before you find yourself in serious trouble.'

Jackson took a step backwards to block the detective constable. 'You heard the man, Lieutenant. You can put him down now. It's not a fair fight, anyway. He's twice your age and three times as flabby . . . and our friend here wants to arrest you.'

Acland stared at her for a moment, then released his hold and pushed the superintendent away. 'What's a middle-aged Gruppen-führer to you?' he asked. 'I thought you didn't like bullies.'

'I don't, but that doesn't mean I want them to die of apoplexy.' She jerked her chin towards the corner of the room. 'You look as if you're on the brink of throwing up, so do us all a favour and sit on the floor over there with your head between your knees.' She watched him retreat, then shifted her attention to the constable. 'If you're willing to take the other corner, I'll see to your boss . . . If you're not, I'll hold the line here to prevent another clash. You're a little too pumped up for my liking.'

'Sir?'

'I'm all right,' said Jones, resuming his seat and loosening his collar. 'No harm done.' He took a couple of breaths and addressed his next remark to Jackson. 'You think me unreasonable to ask tough questions of the lieutenant? We've been on this inquiry for months . . . tonight is the first time we've had any meaningful leads . . . and they've both involved this young man.'

Jackson shrugged. 'The first one didn't. It might have seemed that way for a while, but you proved to your own satisfaction that he wasn't responsible for the attack on Mr Tutting. You might just as well argue that I've been involved in both leads – you'd still be searching for the lieutenant if I hadn't delivered him to you – so why aren't you asking tough questions of me?' She smiled slightly. 'And why isn't the recorder on?'

'It's a good thing it isn't, otherwise the assault would have been caught on tape and your friend would face charges.' Thoughtfully, he rubbed his wrist as he studied Acland's bent head. 'You're not dying on me, are you, Charles?'

'No.'

'I didn't think so. That's one hell of a grip you have.' He took another deep breath. 'I'll string your guts for garters if you try to sue me. This inquiry's already strapped for cash . . . and I'm damned if I'll approve compensation because a witness has issues about his personal space.'

'You weren't overly keen on yours being invaded.'

'True . . . but I'm a police officer, and the law protects me in a way that it doesn't protect you. How far would you have gone if Dr Jackson hadn't been here?'

'If you're asking whether I'd have beaten you to death, then the answer's no,' said Acland. 'That particular method of killing isn't encouraged in the army. It takes too long. If I'd wanted you dead, I'd have crushed your spinal cord.'

'Why mention beatings?'

'That's how Kevin Atkins was killed.'

'How do you know?'

'The doctor Googled his name on the hospital computer.'

Jones glanced at Jackson and she nodded. 'It's common enough knowledge,' he agreed. 'Have you been following the cases in the newspapers, Charles?'

'No.'

'But you were in London when Kevin Atkins was murdered. You discussed the case with Dr Campbell.'

Carefully, Acland raised his head and stared hard at the superintendent. 'If I did, I don't remember. I only remember staying in my room most of the time to stop her discussing *anything* with me. She talked for talking's sake, and I don't recall that much of what she said was worth listening to.'

Having been on the receiving end of Susan Campbell's homily on short-term memory loss, Jones had some sympathy with him. 'So who was this other man in the alley?'

'Ask Jackson. She spoke to him more than I did.'

'Doctor?'

'He called himself Chalky, claimed to be mid-fifties, and said he was a corporal during the Falklands War. Five-foot-tennish . . . dark, greying hair and beard . . . brown overcoat . . . stank to high heaven and looks older than he is. He refused to come with us, but I imagine he's fairly well known on the streets. From what he told us, he's been homeless for twenty years.'

The Falklands War ignited Jones's interest. 'Had you met him before?' he asked Acland.

'Once. I saw off a group of drunken teenagers who were bullying him, then helped him climb the railings into the alleyway. That's how I knew it was there.'

'What were the teenagers doing?'

'Kicking him.'

'Was the sick lad one of them?'

Acland hesitated. 'I don't know. There was a boy urinating on Chalky . . . but I never saw his face. He was wearing a hoodie. The rest were girls.'

'I don't think Chalky would have helped him tonight if he'd taken a thrashing off him,' said Jackson drily. 'He told me he's been trying to protect Ben from shirt-lifters. He wanted me to pass on to you that the streets aren't safe for boys or girls. The dealers get them hooked and the kerb crawlers take immediate advantage.'

'Tell me something I don't know,' Jones said equally drily. 'Are you saying this Chalky's homophobic?'

Jackson was ahead of him. 'Along with a goodly percentage of the population, Superintendent. I don't think it means he's a killer.'

Jones turned back to Acland. 'Will he vouch for the fact that you never tampered with the rucksack?'

'I doubt it.'

'The man's a chronic alcoholic and not the type to volunteer information,' said Jackson in answer to the superintendent's frown. 'He'll have a convenient loss of memory . . . assuming you can find him.'

'Where did you last see him?'

'Outside St Thomas's. He'll be gone by now.'

'Then let's hear what you have to say. To your knowledge, was the lieutenant ever alone with the boy's things?'

Jackson glanced at Acland, as if seeking permission to answer.

'Yes,' she admitted. 'There was a period when he and Chalky stayed with the car and I was in the hospital.' She explained how she'd left Acland to drive the BMW while she followed the paramedics into A&E. 'I asked the lieutenant to search the ruck-sack for anything that might help us locate the next of kin . . . and he brought it to me about twenty minutes later.'

'And showed you the mobile?'

'Yes.'

'Why didn't you tell me this earlier?'

'You were only interested in what happened in the alleyway.' Jackson broke off briefly to marshal her thoughts. 'Look, I'm obviously missing something, because I can't see why you keep harping on about this. What would Charles have to gain by putting Kevin Atkins's phone in the boy's rucksack? It makes no sense at all . . . particularly as he could have ditched anything compromising down the first grating between the staff car park and the A&E entrance.'

'He wasn't to know you'd bypass the PIN.'

Jackson frowned, trying to follow his logic. 'What difference does that make? He knew we were trying to identify the kid, so the chances were high that Atkins's mobile would be examined eventually. Why gamble on something so unpredictable when he could have got rid of the evidence altogether?'

'It depends what the gamble was. Supposing the lad had died? The case would take on a very different complexion in those circumstances. A dead rent boy, who wasn't too happy about selling himself, would make a compelling candidate as a gay killer.' Jones spread his hands in a damping gesture at Jackson's immediate show of irritation. 'Don't be naive about people's motives, Doctor. If you sit in court for a day you'll hear many more unlikely stories than that.'

'There was no suggestion that Ben was going to die. The paramedics started hydration treatment in the ambulance and the endocrinology unit was ready to go into action as soon as he reached the hospital. Both the lieutenant and Chalky knew that his chances of survival were excellent even before we left Covent Garden.'

'You're wasting your breath,' Acland said, pushing himself off the floor and leaning his shoulder against the wall. 'I told you this would happen.'

'At least I'm fighting your corner,' said Jackson coldly, 'which is more than you ever seem to do. You have two speeds. Red mist and pained martyrdom . . . and the pained martyrdom is getting on my nerves.' She eyed him with disfavour. 'We went through the silent treatment yesterday after you attacked Rashid in the pub . . . and it didn't impress me then. Guilt isn't a negotiable commodity, Lieutenant. You can't trade it like an indulgence.'

His return stare was hostile. 'Don't patronize me.'

'Then stop behaving like a jerk and live with the sins you *have* committed. Signing up for someone else's isn't going to put the clock back . . . any more than refusing to take painkillers has . . .'

METROPOLITAN
POLICE

INTERNAL MEMO

To: ACC Clifford Golding
From: Det Supt Brian Jones
Date: 13 August 2007
Subject: Assault on Walter Tutting
12.00–13.00, 10.08.07

Sir,

We continue to believe the assault on Walter Tutting was part of the series. Update as follows:

- **Lt Charles Acland** Resident at the Bell, Gainsborough Road. Now on police bail and still being treated as a material witness. Known contacts with Walter Tutting and Ben Russell. Was in possession of Kevin Atkins's mobile for a brief period before handing it in.
- **Ben Russell** Currently a patient at St Thomas's Hospital. Believed to have had Atkins's mobile in his possession for some weeks (see below).
- **'Chalky'** Name unknown. Current whereabouts unknown. According to what he told Dr Jackson and Lt Acland, he has had intermittent contact with Ben Russell over the last four weeks. He may also be in possession of a canvas duffel-style bag that Lt Acland believes Russell brought into the alleyway and which

Chalky may have hidden inside one of his own. These facts are contradicted by Russell (see below). NB As 'Chalky' is a common nickname for the surname 'White' army records have been searched for a Corporal White on active service during the Falklands War. Two were found, but neither has any involvement with the inquiry.

Walter Tutting

Despite dissimilarities at the crime scene, we remain of the opinion that the attack on Mr Tutting is connected to the earlier murders. This view is cautiously endorsed by John Webb, senior SOCO at the victim's house. I am sending his preliminary report under separate cover. We have been unable to interview Mr Tutting, who remains under heavy sedation in St Thomas's Hospital. His doctors have expressed optimism about a return to consciousness in the next few days.

Kevin Atkins – mobile telephone

This is the most promising lead we've had so far. We are currently working on a printout of the address book in cooperation with the Atkins family. I expect further information in the next two days re previously unidentified numbers, accessed websites, texts, photographs, etc. FYI: The only fingerprints retrieved from the casing have been identified as Ben Russell's, Lt Charles Acland's and Dr Jackson's. We found no Unknowns and none belonging to Atkins, which suggests the casing was cleaned after the murder. There's a possibility of a DNA reading from saliva inside the mouthpiece, although FSS is predicting Atkins as the most likely donor.

BlackBerry/second mobile/iPods

Interviews with Ben Russell, and initial searches of the memories, suggest the BlackBerry and second mobile are unconnected with the inquiry. We have yet to confirm ownership, but interviews with relevant parties are being arranged. Meanwhile, I have requested continued searches of the memories. The iPods contain variously Garage, Rap, Brit Pop and Indie, but again appear to have no connection with the inquiry. FYI: A variety of fingerprints were recovered from the different casings, but we were only able to identify Russell's and Acland's. FSS confirms there was no obvious attempt to clean these items before or after their thefts.

Ben Russell

Russell has been interviewed on three occasions in St Thomas's Hospital in the presence of his mother and a solicitor. Due to his age and medical condition, he has been treated throughout as a 'vulnerable' witness. His full details are attached, including cautions and an ASBO issued in Wolverhampton, but the essential points are:

- Benjamin Jacob Russell
- 16 yrs old
- Brought up in Wolverhampton
- Poor education record
- Cautioned twice for drunk and disorderly

- Served with ASBO following complaints from neighbours
- Left home last year after row with stepfather over theft of money
- Claims to have lived in a squat in Birmingham for first 6 months (vague on detail)
- Claims to have been sleeping rough in London for approx. 3–4 months
- Still has contact with girlfriend, Hannah, 13 – resident in Wolverhampton
- Admits to a sexual relationship with Hannah
- No record of arrests/cautions in the metropolitan area
- Admits living from theft and begging but denies prostitution
- Recently diagnosed type one diabetic

Russell has no memory of going to the alleyway on the night of Friday, 10 August, but agrees he has been sleeping there from time to time since 'Chalky' introduced him to it. He calls 'Chalky' Grandpa, but knows nothing about him except that he's a 'decent bloke'. He denies owning a canvas duffel bag or seeing one in Chalky's possession. He also denies knowing a man with a black eyepatch or anyone going by the names of 'lieutenant'/'lootenant' or Charles Acland.

Russell freely admits to the thefts of the mobiles, BlackBerry and iPods, although he is vague about when, where and how he stole them. In 3–4 months, he estimates he's stolen approx. 15–20 mobiles and says the methods are 'pretty similar' so the incidents become 'blurred'. During the interviews the mobiles were referred to as 'the Nokia' and 'the Samsung'. He says he lifted one of them (he thinks it was the Samsung) from a woman's open bag while she was paying for a newspaper. He saw her from behind, so the description is of no value – 'tallish'. He claims he found the other (Atkins's Nokia) in a small holdall that he stole off a bench seat in Hyde Park while the owner was 'watching a couple snogging'. Again no useful description except that it was a man – 'dark hair and dressed in black'. Possibly a suit.

Russell describes the holdall as black and similar to the one cycle couriers use – approx. 40 x 30cm. He 'ditched' it in bushes near the Diana Memorial Fountain as soon as he'd searched it and can't remember what else was in it apart from the mobile, a bottle of aspirin and a pack of sandwiches – all of which he took. His best recollection on the rest is 'a newspaper, maybe a brown envelope and some keys'. FYI: A search of the area produced nothing, nor has a bag of that description been handed in by the public or the park ground staff.

Russell is unable to pinpoint when either of these thefts took place, although his best guess is 2–4 weeks ago. His usual MO is to 'collect' a handful of items and sell them to a fence in the Canning Town area (he has so far refused to give us a name or address on this), but he denies selling anything during the last month because he's been feeling too ill to make the trip. He remembers calling his girlfriend on one of the phones (he thinks the Samsung) because it was active when he stole it, but the other was 'dead'.

Conclusion

I can see no point in diverting resources on a wild-goose chase after a 'tallish' woman or a dark-haired man, nor in factoring these descriptions into the inquiry. Russell is an unreliable witness and is quick to agree that it may have been the BlackBerry or one of the iPods that he stole from the handbag and/or the holdall. His descriptions of his other victims are equally vague – he thinks two of the iPod owners were 'a black guy' and 'a kid'.

Through his solicitor, Russell was made aware of the seriousness of the inquiry. Although nervous of being interviewed, Russell maintained an even demeanour throughout the three sessions. Neither DI Nick Beale nor I detected any difference in his reactions when it came to questions about the Nokia. We are of the opinion, therefore, that it is more likely he stole the mobile from Atkins's killer than from Atkins himself or from Atkins's house.

I have asked James Steele to consider the implications of this re the psychological profile. Our assumption has been that the mobiles were stolen as trophies and/or because they were the means of communication between killer and victim. In either event, I am unclear why the killer was carrying at least one of them in public. To what end?

Our two most positive lines of inquiry at the moment are Kevin Atkins's mobile and the attack on Walter Tutting, and I have instructed all efforts to be concentrated in those two areas.

With kind regards,

Brian

Detective Superintendent Brian Jones

Sixteen

BEN RUSSELL'S MOTHER looked tired and depressed, as if the strain of the last three days had taken their toll. A small, grey-haired woman, she sat at her son's bedside, interminably lacing her fingers and pretending not to care that he was only interested in what was playing through the headphones attached to a TV and radio console beside him. In daylight, and conscious, his unsmiling mouth and permanent scowl identified him clearly as the alienated youth he was, and Jackson doubted any joy would come of this mother-and-son reunion.

He was in a side room on his own, segregated from the other patients because of the continued police interest in him, but Jackson had a good look through his open door as she and Trevor Monaghan passed. They came to a halt ten yards down the corridor. 'How old is the mother?'

'Sixty-seven,' murmured Monaghan. 'Thought she was through the menopause at fifty-two, slept with her old man for the first time in twelve months and ended up pregnant. Poor woman. The husband was dead of lung cancer a year later.'

'Any other children?'

'Four . . . all much older than he is. There's a brother of thirty-eight who has a couple of teenagers of his own. The kid was brought up as an only child – spoilt rotten, as far as I can make out – but wasn't a particular problem until husband mark two came on the scene. Now the wretched woman's blaming herself for marrying again. Ben's been in constant trouble ever since.'

Jackson pulled a wry expression. 'How many times have I heard that before? It's the history of every runaway.'

'Mm. Mrs Sykes wants me to say it was diabetes that sent Ben off the rails.'

'Instead of what? The stepfather?'

Monaghan shrugged. 'Take your pick. She blames everything from over-compensation for his father's death . . . changing her name when she remarried . . . to having to share her time between the son and the new husband. The only thing she's not prepared to accept is that Ben behaves the way he does because he wants to. She keeps telling me he's a good boy underneath.'

'Is he?'

'Not that I've seen. He's a rude little bugger. Are you sure you want to talk to him?'

Jackson nodded. 'Preferably alone. Any chance of prising the mother away?'

'What's the quid pro quo?'

'A bottle of Scotch if I get an uninterrupted half-hour with the door closed. I want to know what he's told the police.'

*

'Rude little bugger' was about right, thought Jackson, after the door closed and she was left alone with Ben. He studiously ignored her until she swung the Patientline TV console to one side, switched off the power and plucked the headphones from his ears.

'Good morning, Ben,' she said pleasantly. 'My name's Dr Jackson. We've met before but you probably don't remember me. I was the doctor who attended you before the ambulance arrived.'

The scowl deepened as he assessed her. 'Are you a dyke?'

'Last time I looked I was.' She prevented him retrieving the headphones by unplugging them and dropping them out of reach on the floor behind her. 'Life's a bitch, eh?'

'You shouldn't have done that.'

'Why not? They're not yours and you aren't paying for them.

It's either me, the taxpayer, who's funding your TV habit . . . or your poor long-suffering mother.' She took the chair that Mrs Sykes had been sitting in.

'It's the law. You put your hands on me. I could have you done for assault.'

'Then you'd better report me to Superintendent Jones the next time he questions you about the contents of your rucksack. That was some stash you had hidden away inside it. Where did it all come from?'

'None of your fucking business. I don't answer questions unless Mum and the solicitor are here.' He clasped his hands together and extended his two forefingers to point in her direction. 'I've got rights.'

'What kind of rights?'

'I don't have to talk to you.'

'Suits me. I'll do the talking for both of us.' She settled herself deeper in the chair and crossed her legs. 'You have a condition that means you'll be subject to monitoring for the foreseeable future. The quicker you learn to take an active role in your treatment – particularly in the adjustment of insulin, food intake and exercise – the shorter your dependency time . . . but it's only the brightest and most cooperative teenagers who succeed in managing their disease without the help of a parent. The chances—'

'I know all this,' Ben broke in impatiently, 'and I'm sick of hearing it. I didn't ask to be born with fucking diabetes, did I?'

Jackson ignored the interruption. '—of an ungrateful little toe-rag who wants his own rights respected but doesn't give a toss about anyone else's . . . as long as he's free to steal to his heart's content . . . and make his mother's life a living hell—'

'You don't know the first thing about it!' the boy snarled, levelling his fingers at Jackson's eyes. 'What about what *she's* done to me?'

'Ah, well, that's a different issue altogether,' said Jackson mildly. 'Children can behave as they like, but mothers get lumbered with whatever rotten hand fate deals them. I can't imagine yours is taking any pleasure from having a retard for a son. I expect she's sitting in the canteen right now, wishing she'd made your father wear a condom.'

'I'm not a retard.'

'You could have fooled me. Why didn't you go for help when you first started feeling unwell?'

'It's my life. Maybe I wanted to die.'

'You wouldn't have gone looking for Chalky if that was the case. It must have taken some effort to climb those railings in the state you were in. You became comatose within ten minutes of arriving.'

'What if Chalky hadn't been there? I'd have died then.'

'You gave yourself a better chance than if you'd folded up in a shop doorway. You're a vagrant. Passers-by would have thought you were asleep.' She lapsed into a brief silence, watching him. 'But you don't do doorways, do you? Chalky said you have a thing about being propositioned by gays.'

'I hate the fuckers.'

'Have you ever gone with one?'

He swivelled his pistol fingers towards her again with a look of pure hatred on his face. 'No,' he snarled. 'I'd rather die.'

Jackson didn't believe him. Such intense homophobia suggested the opposite – an abusive long-term relationship or self-disgust that he'd sold himself for money when he needed it. 'What's your step-father like?'

'He's a creep,' he said dismissively.

'What kind of creep?'

'Thought he owned the house just because he married Mum.'

She watched his mouth work in a kind of impotent fury. 'Are we talking rules and discipline . . . or something else?'

'I hardly knew the bastard and he started behaving like my dad. All we ever did was row.' He stared resentfully at Jackson. 'Everything was fine till he came. I wouldn't have left if it hadn't been for him.'

'Is that what you told your mother?'

'What if I did? It's true.'

Jackson shook her head. 'Your stepfather altered the dynamics of your relationship with your mother. From the look of her, I'd guess you've been ruling the roost for years. You were a little god in your own universe . . . and you had your nose put out of joint when someone arrived to challenge you.'

'Whatever. You weren't there and you don't know me,' he muttered, falling back on the clichés of inarticulate youth.

'If everything had been fine from your mother's perspective, she wouldn't have brought your stepfather in,' Jackson pointed out reasonably. 'I expect she was lonely. Did you think about that when you decided to go into battle to get rid of him?'

'Shut up!'

Jackson shrugged. 'Problems don't disappear just because you refuse to talk about them. At some stage you'll have to resolve the issue of where you'll go when you leave here . . . and the streets aren't an option . . . not for someone who's insulin dependent.' She waited through a brief silence. 'I could be wrong, but I get the feeling you've been forced to do things to survive that you'd never have done if you'd stayed at home.'

'It's none of your business.'

'It is if it affects your health,' she said dispassionately. 'It won't help your diabetes if you have an undiagnosed STD. Have you told anyone about your sexual history?'

'No . . . and I'm not going to either.'

'It's a simple test and you're in the right place for it,' Jackson said calmly. 'It may even have been done as routine when you were admitted. Do you want me to ask Dr Monaghan to talk to you about this? He won't discuss it with your mother, if that's what's worrying you.'

He flicked her an assessing glance, as if to see how trustworthy she was. 'What about you?'

'I won't repeat anything you say . . . unless you give me permission.'

'You'd better not,' he said aggressively.

'I've given my word.'

He watched her out of the corner of his eye. 'I'll slit my bloody wrists if anyone finds out. It makes me sick every time I think about it.'

'What happened?'

'I only did it once. This bastard said he'd give me thirty quid if I went to a hotel with him. It was a fucking set-up. There were five of them and they made me do it for nothing. They thought it was funny . . . told me to go to the cops if I reckoned I'd been cheated.' He pointed his fingers at the wall, took aim and performed a mock recoil. 'I wanted to kill them . . . still do.'

'I don't blame you,' said Jackson. 'I'd feel the same.'

'I only did it for the fucking money.'

'When did it happen? How long ago?'

'A few months back,' he said vaguely, 'around the time I met Chalky.'

Months . . . ? 'Is that why he took you under his wing? Did you tell him about it?'

'Some . . . not much. I didn't want him going round saying I was a fucking gay, did I?'

Jackson smiled. 'I suspect you're safe on that score. I imagine Chalky has too many secrets of his own to gab about anyone else's.'

Another assessing glance. 'Do you know him?'

'He was in the alleyway the night you went into a coma. I think he may have taken a canvas bag that belonged to you.'

Ben's answer was immediate. *Too immediate* . . . ? 'Nah,' he said firmly. 'The only thing I had was the rucksack.'

'What about the carrier bag of booze and fags? Chalky said that was yours.'

'He's an alky. He talks out of his arse most of the time.'

'He did his best to help you. I had to ask him questions to find out when your symptoms first started.' She watched his eyes widen in alarm. 'He didn't know much . . . said he'd only known you a month . . . maybe seen you five or six times.'

Ben stared at his hands.

'So who's right? You or Chalky? When did this gang rape actually happen?'

'A month ago.'

Jackson doubted that. With type one diabetes, fissures or sores wouldn't have healed in four weeks. But she let it go. 'Do you know if the men were wearing condoms?'

The boy's shoulders squirmed with embarrassment. 'I never saw – they made me lie face down on a bed while they took it in turns – but I reckon they did. One of them thought I had Aids because I was skinny . . . and the bloke I went with told him to double up on the skins.' He squeezed his eyes shut to block off tears. 'I really hate the fuckers.'

'With reason,' she agreed easily. 'Bastards like that should have their tackle ripped off and nailed to their front doors. Would you recognize them if you saw them again?'

'No. Is it them gave me diabetes?'

Jackson shook her head. 'It's not a sexually transmitted disease. You've probably been developing it over the last few weeks, but Dr Monaghan can set your mind at rest about Aids and STDs with a few simple tests.'

'Why can't you do them?'

'Because one of the tests involves a quick look up your bum . . . and it'll be less embarrassing for you if a bloke does that.'

'Shit!'

She smiled again. 'Yup! There'll definitely be some of that, but don't worry . . . yours won't smell any different from anyone else's. Trust me, I'm a doctor.'

Ben gave a grudging lift of his lips in return. 'You don't look like one.'

'I'm a bodybuilder in my spare time.' She saw a gleam of interest flicker in his eyes. 'Once you're eating properly and your insulin's adjusted, you'll put on muscle in no time. I'll give you a workout if you're willing to take instruction from a woman.'

'OK.'

'You'll have to take it seriously,' she warned. 'I'm not interested in time-wasters.'

'OK.'

'What do I get in exchange?'

Ben cast her another wary glance, as if fearing she was looking for a physical display of gratitude and affection. 'What do you want?' he asked suspiciously.

'Information. Upfront ... now ... without the police, your mother or the solicitor listening.'

He became even more suspicious. 'What kind of information?'

'Let's start with how you came by the Nokia mobile.'

*

The request seemed to faze him, although to Jackson's mind he seemed more perplexed than alarmed. She listened patiently while he delivered the same account that he'd given the police and showed only sympathy when he described how unwell he'd felt on the day of the theft. 'The really good thing about stealing the guy's bag was that there were some sandwiches in it. I was fucking hungry.'

'It's a classic symptom of diabetes. Your cells weren't convert-ing glucose to energy, so your brain was telling you to eat ... meanwhile, your system was expelling sugar through your urine and you were losing weight.'

'I was pretty weak. That's why I don't remember the details too well.'

Jackson nodded gravely and encouraged him to describe his other symptoms. He produced quite a litany. Tiredness. Intense thirst. Pains in his abdomen. Frequent urination. Vomiting. Gid-diness. Tremors.

'You were a sick boy,' she agreed.

'Too right. I reckon I fainted a couple of times.'

'No wonder you're confused.'

He nodded.

'Perhaps you hit your head when you fell. That's often a cause of amnesia.'

'Yeah,' he agreed readily. 'I'm pretty sure that happened after I left the park. I remember a lady helping me off the pavement and asking if I was all right.'

'And when did you say this happened?'

'Last month some time. I don't know exactly.'

'Interesting,' Jackson murmured. 'With symptoms as severe as that, I'm amazed you didn't go into a coma immediately.'

The wariness came back into his eyes. 'I've been feeling sick for ages.'

'Mm.' She arched an amused eyebrow. 'Hasn't Dr Monaghan explained that type one diabetes tends to come on suddenly? The usual time-frame is a period of days – not a period of several *weeks*. Fatigue, thirst and frequent urination are typical of onset, but pains in the abdomen and vomiting indicate ketoacidosis, which is what caused your collapse four days ago. I find it hard to believe you've had ketones poisoning your blood for weeks . . . but managed to neutralize them successfully without intervention.'

He ran the tip of his tongue across his lips. 'I guess I'm lucky.'

'Or very odd.' She cocked her forefinger at him, mimicking his pistol hand. 'You can tell me the truth now. There's no one else here, so you can be honest.'

'I have been honest.'

'Nn-nn. If you were falling over and vomiting, then you must have stolen the phone in the twenty-four hours before you col- lapsed. If you stole it four *weeks* ago –' she put ironic emphasis on the word – 'thirst and constant peeing shouldn't have affected your memory. Unless you have a drink or drug addiction that you've been keeping from Dr Monaghan.'

The writhing tic set Ben's mouth going again. 'It's just a *mobile*,' he burst out. 'I know a guy who steals them all the time. He swipes 'em out of bitches' hands while they're texting their mates.' He upended his palm in front of his chest and danced his thumb around while make mincing gestures with his shoulders. 'They don't even *think* someone's gonna walk by and rob 'em . . . and they're usually too scared of being knifed to do anything about it.'

Jackson folded her arms across her chest and stared him down. 'How old are these "bitches"? Twelve-year-old schoolgirls? That's some brave friend you have. Or are you talking about yourself? Does demonizing a little kid as a "bitch" excuse what you do to her?'

'It's just a word,' he muttered. 'Everyone uses it.'

'Not in my presence they don't. In my presence men show some respect for women.'

'Yeah, well—' He trailed off. 'All I was saying was that mobiles get stolen every day and no one takes a blind bit of notice.' He watched her out of the corner of his eye. 'What's so important about the Nokia?'

Jackson took this for cunning rather than ignorance. 'If you don't know the answer to that, you should fire your solicitor. At the very least he should have established why you were being questioned.'

'He did . . . sort of. The cops said one of the things in my rucksack belonged to a bloke who was part of a murder inquiry. It scared the shit out of me because they wouldn't say what it was. But it has to be the Nokia, right? You wouldn't be asking about it otherwise.'

She nodded.

'I knew it . . . I fucking *knew* it!' He stared at her with wide, frightened eyes. 'You're going to tell, aren't you?'

Jackson wondered who he was more afraid of. *His mother . . . the police . . . someone on the street*? 'That you lied about the man in Hyde Park? Probably,' she agreed, 'unless you decide to do it first. It'll look better if it comes from you.'

'You promised you wouldn't,' he said with a spurt of anger.

'I promised I wouldn't repeat information about your health and sexual history,' she reminded him. 'Did the five men have something to do with the mobile?'

He stared at her with a look of indecision on his face, but if his intention had been to unburden himself he was thwarted by the return of his mother. He spotted her face at the glass panel in the door and clammed up immediately, muttering that she'd want to know why the door was closed. Jackson stood up to open it, greeting the woman with a firm handshake and explaining her presence by saying she was the doctor who'd first treated Ben.

'I dropped in to see how he was doing,' she said.

Mrs Sykes's response was as limp as her handshake. 'That's nice.' She stooped to retrieve the headphones from the floor, as if her job in life was to clear up after people. 'He likes his music,' she murmured, plugging them into the console and handing them back to her son.

Jackson watched her resume her seat while the boy clamped the headphones over his ears again. Neither showed any interest in continuing their conversations with her, nor in talking to each other, and Jackson had a feeling that she and Trevor Monaghan might have misunderstood the relationship between them. Perhaps it wasn't the son who was blanking the mother, but the mother who'd developed devices to distance herself from the demands of a child she'd never wanted.

*

Before she left, Jackson sought out Trevor Monaghan again to ask if Ben had been routinely tested for STDs. He nodded. 'It's pretty much standard when we don't know anything about a patient. We couldn't find any needle marks on him but you can never be too careful with HIV and hepatitis.'

'And?'

'Clean as a whistle. Is he worried he's got an infection?'

Jackson gave a neutral shrug. 'Did you do a rectal examination?'

He studied her curiously. 'What's he been telling you?'

'Answer my question first,' she urged. 'I thought that in view of his age, and the fact he's a runaway, you might have checked. He doesn't appear to know about it if you did.'

'He wouldn't. I asked Anna Pelotski to take a look while he was still comatose. She didn't find anything to suggest penetration . . . no old scarring . . . no fissures.' Monaghan paused. 'Has he told you differently?'

'Yes.'

Monaghan shrugged. 'He accused his stepfather to one of the nurses, said Mr Sykes buggered him whenever he was in the mood, which is why he doesn't want to go back if the man remains in the house. I can't say categorically that it never happened – we'd be talking about something that happened a year ago, and he may not have suffered any physical damage from it – but I suspect it's a ruse to get his mother to himself again.'

'He told me he was gang-raped by five men last month.'

'Then he's having you on. In his condition, Anna would have found open sores, and he'd still be hurting.'

'What about longer ago . . . say, three or four months?'

Monaghan was doubtful. 'Five men . . . one after the other . . . all hyped up . . . and no obvious scarring? Can't see it, Jacks.'

She nodded. 'So why invent a story like that? What does he hope to achieve by it?'

'Confusion,' said Monaghan with a touch of irony. 'He's adept at manipulation, that kid.'

Seventeen

FOR NO REASON THAT he felt it necessary to explain, Acland had taken to accompanying Jackson whenever she went out. Released by Jones (this time on police bail) under condition that he reside at the Bell and keep himself available for questioning, he seemed to have an inbuilt radar that told him precisely what the doctor's movements were. While she was in the pub, front or back, he kept to his room, but every time she went to her car, day or night, she found him standing beside it. If the sortie involved a house call to a patient, he remained on the pavement outside; if it was appropriate to walk with her, he did.

Daisy, who had begun to find his attentions to her partner difficult to cope with, said he was acting as if he'd made Jackson responsible for his bail conditions. 'It's not your job to ensure he behaves himself,' she said crossly. 'Tell him to get a life and leave you alone.'

'I quite enjoy having him along,' said Jackson unwarily. 'He's no bother.'

But Daisy liked that even less. 'I might as well not exist for all the attention either of you shows *me*,' she said bitterly.

*

Acland, who was well aware of the tensions he was creating, pushed himself away from the side of the BMW as Jackson rounded the corner. She was doing her usual trick of fiddling with her mobile as she walked along, but he was beginning to understand that she only did it to avoid eye contact with the people she passed.

The cynical side of him said that she had choices about the way she looked. Yes, she was tall, but there was no law that obliged her to model herself on Arnold Schwarzenegger or the Muscles from Brussels, Jean-Claude Van Damme.

On one of the few occasions when he'd found himself alone with Daisy – something he tried to avoid – he'd asked her if Jackson ever competed on the female bodybuilding circuit.

Daisy's response had been withering. 'Don't be an idiot! Have you ever looked at their photographs on the web? She'd have to prance around in a bikini and a fake tan, and stuff her breasts with silicone to give herself some boobs. Can you see Jackson doing any of that?'

He couldn't. Jackson was too individual to conform to a crowd-pleasing image.

As she approached him now, he tried to picture her in a bikini with melon-sized breasts and an orange glow, but it wasn't an image that leapt easily to the imagination. 'Any luck?' he asked.

'Not really. He half admitted he's told the police a pack of lies, but only because I pointed out some flaws in his story. I could have done with another half-hour. His mother came back just as I was getting somewhere.'

'What flaws?'

'Timings. If he was as ill as he says he was when he acquired the mobile, it must have happened recently, but he's told the police he stole it from a dark-haired man between two to four weeks ago.' She smiled slightly. 'Or a tallish woman. He's using his diabetes as an excuse for confusion.'

'Did he mention me?'

'No.' Jackson was surprised to see his shoulders relax slightly. 'Were you expecting him to?'

'He might have remembered me from the alleyway.'

'He's not in the business of remembering,' she said cynically. 'The worse his memory the fewer questions he has to answer.'

'What are you going to tell the superintendent?'

'I don't know. I'm in a bit of a catch twenty-two. I made a

promise that I don't particularly want to break . . . even though I think he was lying through his teeth.' She pulled a wry face. 'I was trying to persuade him to come clean of his own volition, but I can't see him doing that . . . not while his mother's around anyway.'

'Couldn't you tell Jones that it might be worth interviewing him again? That's not a breach of confidentiality, is it?'

'No,' Jackson agreed, tucking her phone back into her pocket, 'but it'll be a waste of time if Mrs Sykes sits in on the interview. Ben will just stick to his original story or make up a new one. He's pretty fast on his feet.'

'Did he say if he had a duffel bag with him?'

'No . . . denied all knowledge of one . . . along with the Londis carrier. The only thing he's laying claim to is the rucksack.' She shook her head. 'I'd say it's odds-on there was a duffel bag, and that Chalky took it because he knew what was in it. I'm sure he's known Ben a lot longer than he admitted to us.'

Acland looked past her towards the river. 'I wonder what *was* in it.'

Jackson studied the stiff set of his jaw. 'Who knows?' She paused. 'Ben won't have told the police if that's what's worrying you . . . he can't, not if he's telling them he knows nothing about it.'

He met her gaze briefly. 'Why would I worry about that? The bag's nothing to do with me.'

She shrugged as she opened the driver's door. 'Good. Then how do you feel about looking for Chalky? He seems to be avoiding the cops, but he might talk to us, and we've a couple of hours to kill. There's a homeless drop-in centre in Docklands. The people there might be able to tell us where these dyke friends of his hang out.'

'Sure,' Acland said easily, opening the passenger door. 'I don't have a problem with that.'

So why don't I believe you? Jackson wondered, watching his fists pump furiously as he settled into the seat beside her.

*

One of the drop-in centre volunteers not only knew where the women were located but also knew Chalky. She shook her head when Jackson asked if she'd seen him recently. 'We've had the police in here asking the same question,' she said, 'but he hasn't been in for weeks. He only ever shows up occasionally.'

'Do you know anything about him? His real name? Where he hangs out?'

The woman shook her head again. 'Sorry. He was in the Falklands War, that's all I know about him. I'm told he has a bad temper when he's drunk – some of our other clients are extremely wary of him – but we operate a strict no-alcohol policy so I've never seen him in that state.'

She gave them directions on how to find the squat where the group of women lived. 'I'm afraid it'll be a waste of time,' she warned. 'The police have already spoken to them and they haven't seen him either.' She allowed her curiosity to show. 'What's made Chalky so popular suddenly?'

'He helped a boy who went into a diabetic coma,' said Jackson disingenuously. 'We thought he might like to know the lad's on the mend. They seem to have known each other for quite a while.'

The woman nodded. 'It's only the youngsters who talk to him in here. They don't seem as frightened of him as the older men.'

Acland raised his head. 'What do the youngsters want from him?'

She looked surprised, as if the question was couched in terms she didn't recognize. 'I assume they find his stories about the Falklands interesting.'

Acland looked sceptical but didn't continue.

Jackson picked up the woman's response. 'Is that what they talk about?'

'It's all he's ever spoken about to me,' she said with a shrug, 'but we only listen in to clients' private conversations if we're invited, and I don't recall Chalky ever doing that.' She smiled slightly. 'I'm afraid he's rather suspicious of us, which is why we only see him rarely.'

'What does he think you're going to do?' asked Jackson.

'Press-gang him into the God squad,' said the woman with a deprecating smile. 'Tie his hands behind his back to stop him drinking . . . shackle him into a bath for two hours and forcibly shave him. Most of the older ones think we have a hidden agenda to sober them up and send them out for job interviews.'

Jackson looked amused. 'And you don't?'

The woman's smiled widened. 'We dream from time to time.'

*

The squat where the group of women was living was an abandoned house in a back street scheduled for redevelopment. It was part of an ugly 1960s terrace, the middle one of nine, all with boarded-up windows and paint-blistered doors. On his own, Acland would never have gained entry, but Jackson easily passed muster, not least because she had the foresight to hold her 'doctor on call' card in front of her during the inspection she was given through a cracked, diamond-shaped pane in the front door.

The door opened six inches. 'Who are you? What do you want?' asked a thin-faced woman with crinkled grey hair, who could have been any age between forty and sixty.

'I'm Dr Jackson and my friend here is Charles Acland. We're looking for a man who goes by the name of Chalky.'

'The police have already been. We haven't seen him since we took over this place, which was a couple of months back.'

'So I heard,' said Jackson, 'but we could still do with any information you have. Are you and the others willing to give us ten minutes . . . tell us what you know about him . . . the kind of places he might be? We need to talk to him about a friend of his who's in hospital.'

'Chalky doesn't have any friends,' the woman said dismissively. 'Everyone gives up on him in the end. He's a vicious bastard when he's in drink.'

'This one's a young lad called Ben Russell.'

'What's wrong with him?'

'He went into a diabetic coma a few days ago,' said Jackson, 'but he's on the mend now. Maybe you know him? Ginger hair, sixteen years old, thin as a rake.'

'No.'

'We think Chalky may have something that belongs to him.'

'Wouldn't surprise me. He always lifts booze when he hangs around with us.' She seemed to think this contradicted her previous assertion that Chalky was friendless. 'We're all in the same boat and he's done us the odd favour from time to time . . . sees off guys who think we're an easy target. Are you a real doctor?'

Jackson nodded.

A flicker of interest showed in the thin face. 'Will you take a look at my partner? She's had pains in her chest for days. It's scaring the shit out of me, but she won't do anything about it. I'll get her to give you the low-down on Chalky in exchange. She knows him better than I do.'

'Sure,' said Jackson pleasantly, gesturing towards Acland, 'but my friend will have to come in with me. Is that a problem?'

The woman glanced in his direction. 'As long as he isn't scared by noisy dykes. There's a couple of mad ones in here who shout their heads off when they see a guy. They won't worry about a butch stud like you, but they'll probably go ape shit at the sight of the pirate.'

'He's a soldier,' said Jackson matter-of-factly. 'He's dealt with a lot worse in Iraq.' She took her keys from her pocket. 'What's your name?'

'Avril.'

'And your partner's name?'

'Mags.'

'OK, Avril. Well, my car's parked in the next road. I'll need five minutes to collect my case.'

Avril pulled the door wide. 'Let your friend do it,' she invited. 'I'll get one of the others to let him in when he comes back. You can talk to Mags about Chalky while he's gone.'

Jackson's eyes creased with amusement. 'No chance. He

doesn't know which drugs to remove . . . and if he's on his own, he might be persuaded to hand the case to one of your mad girlfriends and stay outside.'

Avril bridled immediately. 'We're none of us thieves.'

'Good, because the strongest medication I'll have in my possession when I return is aspirin, and the lieutenant here will be watching my back. Do you still say your partner's suffering chest pains?'

'Are you calling me a liar?'

'Just checking,' said Jackson lightly.

*

Avril's protestations of honesty appeared highly dubious when Jackson and Acland entered the house. From the glimpses they had into the downstairs rooms, the women had hijacked an IKEA lorry. They seemed to have a passion for rattan chairs, straw matting and russet-coloured throws, and it might have been a regular house but for the hurricane lamps and candles that compensated for the disconnected electricity and boarded-up windows.

'Everything's made in China,' said Avril, pre-empting any questions, 'so it's all dirt cheap. A mate got it for us.' She was carrying a torch and directed it towards a staircase. 'My partner's up here but I told the other three to stay in the kitchen. The two schizophrenics are probably more scared of doctors than they are of guys.' She led the way to the next floor and opened a bedroom door. 'Mags won't want a bloke ogling her,' she told Jackson, jerking her head at Acland. 'He'll have to wait outside.'

Over Avril's head, Acland caught a glimpse of an overweight woman with bloated calves sitting in a low chair. Even by candlelight her face was the colour of lard, and the wide-eyed, anxious gaze she turned towards them suggested she knew she was going to be told something she didn't want to hear. To Acland's untutored eyes, death had already come knocking and he withdrew instinctively, taking up a position against the wall in the corridor.

'Call if you need me,' he told Jackson. 'I'll be right here.'

She nodded and went into the room. As the door closed behind her, the corridor was plunged into darkness, with only a faint glimmer of candlelight shining up the stairwell from below. For the first minute or so, Acland could only hear the murmur of conversation in the room behind him, but as his eye adjusted to the darkness his ears adjusted similarly to the low-level noise in the rest of the house. The hum of women's voices was audible from the kitchen – one louder and more petulant in tone than the rest – but he couldn't make out what any of them was saying. Less expected was the muted rasp of a throat being inadequately cleared in the room directly opposite him across the small rectangular landing.

Wondering if it was a trick of tinnitus, he turned his head to listen with his good ear. This time the sound was quite distinct. Whoever was in there was trying to contain a smoker's cough by holding on to phlegm for as long as possible until the need to expel it produced an involuntary spasm. There was nothing to indicate gender – the rasp was a toneless guttural – but, as no light was escaping from under the door and Acland could think of no reason for a woman to sit in total darkness for fear of drawing attention to herself, his instinct said it was a man.

He crossed his arms in front of him and continued to wait.

*

Jackson shook her head in annoyance as they returned to the car. 'Mags couldn't tell me anything about Chalky and didn't like it when I said she needs to exercise and lose weight. Her heart's as strong as an ox. The only thing wrong with her is that she's fat, forty and flatulent, and Avril wants to keep her that way.'

'She looked pretty sick to me.'

'So would you if you never saw the daylight and your partner kept stuffing your face with burgers and chips,' Jackson retorted grimly. 'That is one *very* unhealthy relationship. It suits Avril to keep the silly woman dependent on her.'

'Why?'

'God knows. Companionship . . . self-esteem . . . a misplaced maternal instinct. The best thing Mags could do is walk out now and return to wherever she came from.' Irritably, Jackson snapped the locks on the BMW. 'Avril's a classic controller. She manipulates people by giving them what they want. Like Ben's mother. That's the way *she* operates.'

'You didn't take to Avril, then?'

Jackson gave a grunt of amusement as she opened the boot and put her case into it. 'I wouldn't trust her further than I could throw her. Would you?'

'No,' said Acland with a hint of irony as he opened the driver's door for her and stood back, gesturing for her to climb in, 'but I don't know the first damn thing about women.'

Jackson arched a sardonic eyebrow. 'You don't know much about this one. Do I look as if I can't open a car door for myself?'

He stepped back immediately. 'Sorry. Force of habit.'

'The last man who insisted on treating me like a piece of Dresden china was my grandfather,' she said idly, taking off her jacket and tossing it on to the back seat. 'I was sixteen years old and taller than he was, but he decided I should find out just once in my life how it felt to be treated like a lady. He made a big deal of helping me into his clapped-out Peugeot.'

'Sorry.'

She put her foot on the sill and rested an arm along the top of the door. 'He told me lesbians lead miserable existences, particularly the masculine-looking ones. People snigger at them behind their backs.'

Acland stared doggedly over her shoulder, wondering where this was leading. 'Is he eating his words now?' he asked cautiously.

'I wish he was. He died a couple of years later. It's one of the reasons I went into medicine. He had a perfectly treatable disease that went undiagnosed because his GP was a moron and the waiting lists were so long. Colon cancer,' she explained. 'By the time the poor old boy was referred to a specialist, it was too late.'

'Sorry.'

'Yes,' she agreed, lowering herself on to the seat. 'He was definitely one of the good guys.' She fired the ignition and gestured towards the passenger side. 'Are you getting in?'

Acland shook his head. 'I'll make my own way back.'

Jackson studied him for a moment. 'Any particular reason why you don't want to drive with me suddenly?'

'I could do with the exercise.'

She smiled slightly. 'You shouldn't make eye contact when you tell a fib, Lieutenant. That stare of yours is a lot more expressive than you think.' But she didn't try to persuade him out of whatever he was planning to do. With a brief nod, she slammed the door and engaged her gears.

As she drove away, she watched in her rear-view mirror as he crossed to the opposite pavement and set off back towards the squat.

Eighteen

THE NEWS, LATE ON Wednesday afternoon, that Walter Tutting had emerged from his coma was greeted with relief by the inquiry team. Progress on Kevin Atkins's mobile had been painfully slow. The last incoming call, prior to Jackson's, was from a pay phone at Waterloo station, and a half-hearted hope that the booth might produce results so many weeks later was quickly shattered when information came through that it was cleaned daily. Jones refused to authorize a forensic examination. 'We might as well dig a hole and pour money into it,' he said grimly.

Over sixty entries in the address book had been followed up without success. The majority of contacts were friends, family or business acquaintances, most of whom had been interviewed and dismissed at the time of Atkins's murder. Of the remainder, fifteen, including three male prostitutes, all ex-army, had since accounted for themselves.

Four names remained to be checked but in each case the user's mobile number had been disconnected. They were logged under the single-word tags of 'Mickey', 'Cass', 'Sam' and 'Zoe', but with no ideas of possible surnames from the Atkins family, the team was waiting on a data-search of the server's files, with a warning that results could take days if multiple servers were involved. Even then, there was a good chance the numbers had been registered to companies, which would involve further time-consuming interviews.

The small hope the police had had that the phone had been used with a different SIM card after it was taken from Atkins's house also came to nothing. As did the saliva DNA from the mouthpiece, which proved to be the victim's. In answer to Detective Superintendent Jones's question, 'Why would the killer carry Atkins's mobile around in public?' the psychological profiler shook his head and said it didn't make any sense to him.

'Is that the best you can do?'

'For the moment. Off the top of my head, I can't think of a single convicted serial killer who carried his trophies with him. The usual MO is to secrete anything incriminating inside an area he controls . . . usually his home. You'll have to give me a day or two to research it.'

Jones leaned forward. 'Supposing the boy made a mistake? Supposing he stole the phone from the woman? Would that make a difference?'

'In what way?'

'Women are very protective of their bags. If my wife wanted to hide something, particularly something small, she'd drop it to the bottom of her bag and carry it around with her.'

The psychologist shrugged. 'How sure are you that the lad who stole the phone was telling the truth?'

'Not at all.'

'Then I'd talk to him again before you hare off in a different direction. The most obvious reason for a person to be walking around with trophies is because there was nowhere else to put them.'

'Meaning what?'

'Your killer might be part of the homeless community.'

Arranging another interview with Ben Russell had taken twenty-four hours, and Jones was out of patience by the time the boy's solicitor agreed to make himself available at five o'clock on Wednesday.

'Criminals have too many bloody rights in this country,' he grumbled to Beale as they drove to the hospital. 'We'd have the story out of the kid in half a second flat if he didn't have guard dogs to protect him.'

'We'd have *something* out of him,' Beale agreed, 'but I

wouldn't bet on it being any more truthful than what he's told us already.' He broke off as a call came through for the superintendent, smiling when the man punched the air. 'What's up?'

'Tutting's regained consciousness.' He tapped in his secretary's number. 'Lizzie? Change of plan. I need you to get hold of Ben Russell's solicitor and tell him we'll be running late on the boy's interview. Yeah . . . yeah . . . I know he's a pain in the arse . . . so tell him I don't give a damn whether he's there or not. The kid's lying through his teeth and we both know it.'

*

Jackson gave a startled jump when Acland disengaged himself from a shadowy recess between two buildings halfway down Murray Street as she approached her car.

She hadn't seen him since driving away from the squat the previous day and, by his unshaven appearance and crumpled shirt, he looked as if he'd slept rough overnight. He certainly hadn't returned to the pub.

'What on earth do you think you're doing?' she demanded angrily.

He was dangling his jacket over his shoulder in a 1930s-style affectation that didn't suit him. 'Hitching a ride,' he said.

'Where have you been? What have you been up to?'

'Just walking.'

'For thirty bloody *hours*?' she said scathingly. 'Give me a break! Daisy and I have been worried sick. You're damn lucky the police didn't decide to question you. You're supposed to stay put at the pub.'

'Sorry.' He walked round the BMW to open the door for her while she put her case in the boot. 'If I'd realized it was going to upset you that much, I wouldn't have done it.'

'I'm not upset, I'm angry.'

'Whichever.' He pulled the door wide. 'It was your night off. I thought you and Daisy could do with some time to yourselves. She makes it pretty clear she doesn't want me around.'

'So now it's Daisy's fault?' said Jackson grimly, stalking after him. She wrestled the door out of his hand. 'Get in,' she snapped, 'and stop behaving like Little Lord Fauntleroy. As far as I'm concerned, he was a nasty little brown-noser in a silly suit with a deeply insipid mother . . . and I'm not that easily sidetracked.'

But she was. It certainly didn't occur to her to question why he chose to open the door behind her and toss his jacket across the back seat.

Nor did she pursue the issue of what he'd been doing, although it wasn't clear to her afterwards whether it was her choice or Acland's to steer the conversation towards his mother. She had tried for the last few days to encourage him to talk about his family and his sudden willingness to describe his relationship with his parents took her by surprise.

'If it takes an insipid mother to produce Little Lord Fauntleroy, then you're confusing me with someone else,' he said idly, attaching his seat belt. 'There's no way you could describe *mine* as insipid. In any case, courtesy was drummed into me at school and Sandhurst. Manners maketh man . . . and all that crap . . . but I've never understood why women are allowed to be as rude as they fucking well like.'

Of course Jackson was intrigued, not least because she'd come to recognize that the lieutenant was a puritan. He rarely used vulgar language unless he was angry. 'You think I was rude?'

'Yes.'

'I come from the wrong side of the tracks. You're looking at the last of a long line of working-class grafters who talked in glottal stops and never had an even break in their lives.' She flicked him a mocking glance. 'There wasn't much cause for my ancestors to say thank you to anyone. They had it programmed into their genes to bow and scrape to privileged types like you.'

'You haven't done badly out of it,' he said curtly. 'At least your grafters sound genuine. I don't even know what privilege is except that you get sent away to school at eight so that your parents can claim some cachet from it. Appearance is everything in my family.

As long as the surface passes muster, it doesn't matter how much dirt is being churned up underneath.'

'What kind of dirt?'

'Anything that lets the side down. My father's father was a chronic alcoholic – he was drunk twenty-four seven – but my mother told everyone he had Parkinson's disease. I was scared shitless of him when he was in a rage. He kicked one of our dogs to death in front of me when I was ten. I was too frightened to say anything . . . but I really hated him for it.'

'Did he hit your grandmother?'

'Probably. She left him after my father was born. I never met her – I don't think Dad did either.'

'What about your mother's parents?'

Acland shook his head. 'I've never met them. As far as I know, there was a massive falling out around the time she married my father. They emigrated to Canada . . . but I don't know which came first, the falling out or the emigration. Mum used to fly off the handle every time they were mentioned . . . so no one speaks about them now.' He leaned forward to massage his temples. 'She's likely to—' He broke off abruptly.

'What?'

'Nothing.'

'Do you get on with her?'

He didn't answer.

'Should I take that as a no?'

'She likes her own way. I sometimes wonder if that's what caused the row with her parents. If they disapproved of Dad, they might have tried to stop the wedding.'

'What's to disapprove of?'

'Maybe they thought he'd turn out like his father.'

'Did he?'

Acland shook his head. 'The opposite. He's spent his whole life trying to make up for my grandfather's failings.'

'In what way?'

'Mortgaged the house and the farm up to the hilt to pay off the old man's debts and try to make a go of it. He had a dairy herd until the milk prices dropped and he found it was costing more to produce the stuff than he was being paid for it. I tried to persuade him to sell up at that stage, but—' He broke off on a shrug.

'What?' asked Jackson.

'The silly old fool went into sheep instead. There's too much debt hanging over the place. The best he could afford after the mortgages were cleared would be a cheap brick box on an estate somewhere.'

'What's wrong with that?'

'Mother wouldn't like it.'

Jackson smiled slightly. 'Not grand enough?'

'Something along those lines. It wouldn't be worth it anyway. She'd be at war with the neighbours in seconds.' He stared out of the windscreen. 'Dad earns just enough out of the flock to allow them to stay there, but it's all very precarious.'

'Does your mother know that?'

'I doubt it. She'd make my father's life hell if she did.'

*

Jackson thought of the conversation she'd had with Robert Willis that morning when she'd phoned to say Charles hadn't returned. 'Would he have gone to his parents?' she'd asked.

'I can't see it. He and his mother don't get on, although I'm not so sure about his relationship with his father. He talks more sympathetically about Mr Acland . . . usually to do with the farm and the amount of work the man has to put in.' Willis's dry smile travelled down the wire. 'Mrs Acland seems to be a lady of leisure . . . and I think that offends Charles.'

'What about the girlfriend? I know you said there was no love lost between them, but would she take him in for old time's sake?'

'Jen? Can't see that either, I'm afraid. *She* might go along with it, but I can't see Charles even asking. Does she know he's staying with you?'

'Not that I'm aware of. There've been no phone calls for him . . . and he keeps to his room when he's not out at night with me.'

'Even when he's not sleeping?'

'Yes.' Jackson sighed. 'He seems to have a problem with Daisy and it's making life rather difficult. He cuts her dead if he bumps into her by accident and it's upsetting her.'

Willis hesitated. 'What sort of personality is she? Friendly? Affectionate?'

'Very. I've been wondering if he fancies her.'

'I wouldn't think so. I'd say it's more likely he's afraid she fancies him. He has real difficulty interpreting women's motives.'

'Because of the girlfriend?'

'Because of the relationship, certainly. He talked about signing up to a fantasy. I interpreted that as meaning that he expected to settle down with Jen and live happily ever after . . . but it didn't work out that way.'

'Why not?'

'He never told me,' Willis said, 'but I can make an educated guess. For a number of reasons – principally because Jen allowed her true character to emerge, I suspect – Charles became disillusioned with her.' He paused. 'She tried to persuade me it was her choice to end the relationship, but I don't think that's true. I'm ninety per cent sure it was Charles who pulled out when he realized how angry she was making him.'

'You said he put his hands round her throat in the hospital. Had he ever done anything like that before?'

'I'm guessing the abuse escalated during the latter part of the engagement. Jen has issues of her own which may have provoked it.'

'What kind of abuse?'

Another hesitation. 'I only know of one other episode. Jen

described a particularly vicious rape to me and I'm confident that it did in fact happen. Charles is clearly ashamed of something in the relationship and rape seems to me the most likely cause. I'm guessing Jen used sexual favours to manipulate him – offering them or withdrawing them at whim – which is why he finds women difficult to read.'

Jackson allowed a brief silence to develop before she spoke again. This was information she hadn't been given before. 'So let me get this straight,' she murmured with a touch of irony. 'If Charles wasn't given sex at the time that he wanted it, he took it by force? *Then* . . . not liking the person he was becoming, he ditched his fiancée and is now too ashamed to talk about it? Is that what you're saying?'

'Not exactly. I think you're embellishing what Jen told me. She spoke about *one* rape. I believe it happened as I indicated earlier . . . an escalation of abuse, culminating in a single episode of forced sex. After which, Charles cut all ties with her.'

'Bully for him!'

'Maybe so, but don't assume that Jen's blameless. As a couple they're completely incompatible – in *every* way – and it's my opinion that Charles tried to extricate himself as soon as he understood that.'

'You're making a lot of assumptions in his favour,' said Jackson acidly. 'Why didn't you tell me this before?'

'Because there's no evidence to support Jen's allegation. Charles hasn't admitted anything.'

Jackson wasn't impressed. 'It's one thing to wish a rapist on to *me* – he'd have a job working up the energy – but quite another to put Daisy in his way. What if he mistakes a show of friendship for a sexual advance?'

'That may be why he's avoiding her,' Willis said matter-of-factly. 'He doesn't want to be drawn into another relationship based on flirting.' He amended the sentence immediately. 'I'm not suggesting that your partner seeks anything other than friendship – nor, indeed, that Charles does – but he's intensely suspicious of women who use physical contact to demonstrate empathy.'

'That's hardly an answer to my question.'

'I realize that.' He broke off to order his ideas. 'I can't be a hundred per cent certain, of course, but I'd be very surprised if Daisy was in any danger from Charles. The only two women he's shown any real animosity towards are his mother and Jen . . . and both of them display narcissistic personality traits. In fact, his experience of his mother may well have been why he was attracted to Jen in the first place.' Willis fell into another thoughtful silence.

'Go on,' prompted Jackson.

'Her personality was familiar to him and he mistook that familiarity for love. I doubt he even knows how narcissism shows itself in the early stages of a relationship. He certainly wouldn't expect charm.'

*

Jackson drew up behind a long line of cars waiting to turn right. 'What sort of relationship do your parents have?' she asked Acland.

'They've been married thirty years.'

She gave a grunt of laughter. 'What does that mean? That they're blissfully happy together . . . or that they grit their teeth and get on with it because no one better has ever come along?'

Acland shrugged. 'I haven't asked.'

Jackson glanced at him. 'Isn't it obvious when a relationship's successful?'

'Not to me it isn't.'

'Why not?'

'It depends how you define success.'

'I usually go by how well a couple communicates. If they find each other interesting, then talking comes naturally. They swap information . . . share a sense of humour . . . want their partner to enjoy what they enjoy. I see a lot of troubled relationships in my job, and they're often characterized by mutual avoidance and silence.'

'That's better than constant arguments.'

'Not necessarily,' Jackson demurred. 'For some people, arguing is a form of communication. It also suggests a level playing field within the relationship. It makes me suspicious when I meet a couple where one partner is afraid to challenge the other. I've seen too many situations where the dominant personality is abusive.'

Acland didn't say anything.

'Do your parents argue?'

'Only in private. I used to hear them going at it hammer and tongs when I was a kid.'

'So you don't want arguments in your own relationships?'

'No.'

'Do you believe that's achievable?' she asked. 'Women have come a long way in thirty years. There aren't many these days who won't fight their corner when they disagree with something.' She spun the steering wheel to take the turn before the lights changed. 'You don't seriously expect your view to prevail every time, do you?'

'No.'

'Then you're bound to have arguments,' she said matter-of-factly. 'Daisy and I agree on most things but we've had some ding-dong battles along the way . . . and I don't regret them. It's taught me what really matters to her.'

'Do you lose your temper with each other?'

Jackson shook her head. 'Not really. We raise our voices and storm out in a huff occasionally, but not to the extent that we see a red mist.'

'Who wins?'

She flicked him an amused glance. 'Who do you think?'

He was about to say 'you', but changed his mind. 'Daisy.'

'Every time,' she agreed. 'I don't have her stamina. She'll keep an issue alive for a month if it suits her. Is your mother the same?'

Acland was unprepared for the question. 'It never goes that far,' he said, surprised into answering honestly. 'Dad gave up provoking her a long time ago.'

Jackson found his vocabulary interesting. 'I thought you said they were always arguing.'

'When I was a kid . . . not any more.'

'So you weren't joking when you said they went at it hammer and tongs? These were physical confrontations you were listening to?' She paused for a moment, but went on when he didn't answer. 'Who was doing the hitting?' Silence. 'I assume from the words you used that your mother has more of a temper than your father.'

'You could say that.'

'Have you inherited it?'

He turned to look at her for a moment. 'I'm nothing like my mother,' he said flatly.

Jackson shrugged. 'So you take after your father and avoid confrontation?'

'Yes,' he said harshly.

'You didn't back off with Rashid Mansoor during your fight in the pub,' she pointed out. 'You went at *him* hammer and tongs.'

'He should have left me alone.'

'The same way your father now leaves your mother alone?'

No answer.

'Are you sure you've got your facts the right way round?' Jackson needled him lightly. 'Are you sure it wasn't your mother who did the provoking and your father who lashed out in temper? If he avoids confrontation now it's almost certainly because he's learned to manage his anger.'

Acland leaned forward to press his thumb and forefinger against the bridge of his nose. 'He's too spineless to be angry about anything,' he said contemptuously. 'He had to drive himself to Casualty once with blood pouring out of his arm after she took a knife to him. When he came back, he told me he'd cut himself on some barbed wire. It was pathetic. He was always making excuses for her.'

'Perhaps he was trying to protect you.'

'He made sure everything happened behind closed doors after that . . . then packed me off to school. We played musical chairs around Mother so that she could have everything her own way.'

'And you despise him for that?'

'Yes.' He opened and closed his fists till the knuckles cracked.

Privately, Jackson sympathized with him. It would explain a lot about his character, she thought, if he had no respect for the gentler of the parental role models. She even wondered if his problems with his mother stemmed from a confused admiration for her strength. 'Except it's hard to break cycles of abuse, Charles. If your dad grew up with an alcoholic wife-beater for a father, it must have taken extraordinary control to put up with similar treatment from your mother . . . then reach a point where it doesn't happen any more. Most people would commend him for that.'

'Not me. He wouldn't have married her unless he enjoys being a doormat.'

'He might not have known . . . unless her parents tried to warn him –' Jackson gave a small shrug – 'which may be the reason why she fell out with them. But even if they did, he wouldn't have believed the warning. The relationship she had with them would have been very different from the one she had with your father.'

Acland shook his head stubbornly. 'He lived with his own father long enough. If he'd ever found the guts to stand up to him, he might have done the same with my mother.'

'Is that how you tried to run your relationship with Jen?'

The question, unanswered, hung in the air between them.

'You can't seem to decide which of your parents to emulate,' Jackson went on. 'Whether it's more important to prove who's boss . . . or to walk away when the abuse gets out of hand. Did you get a buzz from hurting Jen?'

Acland stared at her for a moment. 'Not as big a buzz as I got from hurting my mother,' he said before turning away to look out of the passenger window.

Nineteen

LEACHED OF COLOUR, and attached to drips and monitors, Walter more closely resembled a marble effigy than a conscious human being. He lay with closed eyes, and only the minute rise and fall of the sheet across his chest suggested life. Taking his cue from the attendant nurse, who whispered to him to speak clearly, Jones leaned forward. 'Can you hear me, Mr Tutting? I'm a police officer. My name's Detective Superintendent Brian Jones.'

'You don't need to shout. I'm not deaf.' The old man half-opened his eyes. 'Can't see too well, though. Who's the other one?'

'Detective Inspector Nick Beale . . . Metropolitan Police. We're investigating the assault on you.'

'About bloody time. I've been wondering what I pay my taxes for.'

Jones smiled. 'Do you remember what happened?'

'Bastard tried to rob me.'

'Do you know who it was?'

The old man's lips chewed against each other as if thinking was a physical process. 'Fucker with the eyepatch,' he muttered suddenly. 'Never stood a chance . . . came up behind me as I was looking for my key.'

'The man you spoke to at the bank?'

'That's the one.'

Jones looked questioningly towards Beale. 'Do you know this for a fact, sir?' the inspector asked. 'Did you get a good look at your attacker?'

The old man's blue-veined lids closed again. 'Clear as daylight . . . followed me home because he knew I had cash on me . . . nasty piece of work.'

'Are you certain about that, sir? You said you couldn't see too well.'

Walter's mouth started writhing again and he mumbled something they didn't catch. 'Chased him off with my stick after he took a swipe at my head.'

Beale hesitated. 'Was that inside or outside your house, Mr Tutting? Did you let him in?'

The question seemed to worry the old man. He chattered to himself under his breath and Beale thought he caught *silly old fool . . . mustn't tell Amy.* 'Outside.'

'Are you certain about that, Mr Tutting? According to our witnesses, you didn't have a walking stick with you at the bank.'

His mouth worked frantically. 'Can't remember.'

'Has your daughter told you to be careful who you let in?'

'Wouldn't do it . . . always known what's what.'

'You were found collapsed in a shop doorway on Gainsborough Road, on the other side from your house. What persuaded you to cross over? Did no one offer help on your own side?'

'Bit of distance.'

It was Beale's turn to send a puzzled glance towards his boss. 'Between you and the attacker?'

'That's it.'

'Why didn't you dial 999 from your house?'

'Wasn't going to open the door . . . bloody stupid thing to do.'

Beale was about to point out that what he was saying didn't accord with the facts, but Jones butted in. 'You showed a lot of courage, Mr Tutting. There aren't many pensioners who would take on a man younger and bigger than himself. Did you see the weapon he used to hit you? Do you recall what it was?'

'Something heavy.'

'Do you remember doing anything that might have made this person angry?'

'Refused to pay up.'

'He wanted money?'

Walter's eyes snapped open and both men thought they saw fear in his expression. 'She right, then?'

'I don't know, sir. It depends who she is and what she says.'

He made an obvious effort to concentrate. 'Amy . . . been a silly old fool.'

Jones shook his head. 'We believe you're the fourth person this individual has attacked, sir, and the three previous victims are dead. It's only because you fought back that you're still alive.' He paused. 'If you're worried that we're going to repeat what you tell us to your daughter, will you accept my personal guarantee that that won't happen? You're the only witness we have. Your information is vital to us.'

There were too many facts for the old man to absorb. 'It's nothing I did . . . no one opens their doors any more.'

Stifling a sigh, Jones tried again. 'Did you manage to land a blow? Do you recall making contact with any particular part of his body?'

Walter's mouth set to squirming again. 'Skin and bones . . . no better than a stick insect . . . used to watch 'em at school in science lessons . . . never liked 'em.' The look of fear flared in his eyes again. 'Don't tell Amy.'

*

'How much of that was dementia and how much the after-effects of sedation?' Jones asked the nurse, a sister, outside the unit. 'Will he be any less confused tomorrow?'

The woman shrugged. 'Difficult to say. We've been bringing him out gradually and he's been fully awake for three or four hours now . . . so, in theory, the effects should have worn off already.'

'Best guess?'

She pulled a wry face. 'You've seen him at his best. He was a great deal more alert when he was talking to you than when he first came round.' She paused. 'For what it's worth, the first thing he said to me was "Don't tell Amy" and he's been repeating it on and off ever since.'

'Do you know what it is he doesn't want her to know?'

'Not for certain, but his daughter's a dragon – she's been on our backs from the moment he was brought in – and I'm assuming she's the same with him. I can take another guess if you like –' she smiled – 'as long as you don't blame me for being wrong.'

'Go on.'

'The other things he keeps repeating are "Mustn't open the door" and "Been a silly old fool", and I'm sure the three ideas are connected. He more or less told you as much. I suspect his daughter's been drumming into him that he's not to let strangers into the house and now he's trapped in a loop of anxiety because he disobeyed her. Mustn't open the door . . . don't tell Amy . . . been a silly old fool.'

'And it's his attacker he's talking about?'

'I don't know. It depends how long he's been inviting people in. It may be a loop that's been going on for months.'

'What if the daughter can persuade him she's not angry? Will that help?'

'In terms of admitting that he opens his door? I don't know. You'll have to ask a geriatric psychiatrist.'

'Best guess?' Jones prompted again.

'Probably not if his daughter's the one he's scared of. I'd say you'd have better luck with an expert therapist.' She paused again. 'Does it matter? Walter wasn't confused about who did it. He gave you a good description.'

'Assuming he was telling the truth. He lied about where the attack took place.'

'Only because he's afraid of Amy.'

Thoughtfully, Jones rubbed the side of his jaw. 'Is that common in dementia? That a person can shift from truth to lie with no difficulty? Don't you need joined-up thinking for that?'

Beale stirred. 'He seemed fairly switched on at the beginning,' he pointed out. 'Made a joke about paying taxes.'

The sister looked uncomfortable, as if she felt she was being encouraged to stray into areas that were outside her remit. 'You need to talk to a specialist,' she told them. 'Everything I know about dementia could be written on the back of a fag packet.'

'Which is a lot more than we know,' said Jones lightly. 'Do you mind telling us why you think some of what Walter said was true, but not the rest?'

'I'm not sure—' She broke off to collect her thoughts. 'Look, I'll answer your first question. You wanted to know if dementia sufferers can tell deliberate lies . . . and, yes, of course they can. It depends how advanced the condition is and whether, like Walter, they have something to hide. It's the three ages of man thing – the vulnerable elderly lie in the same way that children do when they're afraid they're going to be given a bollocking.'

'So why wouldn't Walter be lying about the man with the eyepatch?'

'Because he didn't need to. His daughter isn't going to be angry with him for describing his attacker. The anxiety loop is about letting the man inside, not about who he was.' She studied their expressionless faces. 'I'm not saying I'm right.'

Jones nodded. 'In fact we've already established that our friend with the eyepatch couldn't have done it. Walter's lying about him as well.' He watched irritation thin the woman's lips. 'I'm sorry. I wasn't trying to trip you up, I was just interested in why you found that part of Walter's evidence convincing.'

'He didn't seem anxious about it.'

'Until the superintendent asked him if he'd said or done anything to provoke the attack,' Beale cut in. 'He started talking about stick insects shortly afterwards. What was that all about?'

The sister shook her head. 'I'm not the person you should be asking. I'll call one of the consultants. They'll be able to tell you far more than I can.' She made to walk past them but Jones blocked her path.

'One last question . . . and don't worry,' he said, raising a placating hand, 'it's a personal opinion I'm after, not a medical one. You described Walter's daughter as a dragon. What kind of attacker would make her so angry with her father that he'd rather pretend it was someone else?'

She checked her watch. 'If you hang on for a few minutes, you can ask her direct. When I phoned to say Walter had regained consciousness, she said she'd be in around six.'

'I'd still like your opinion.'

Unexpectedly, the woman laughed. 'Young, female and pretty,' she said flippantly, 'but I can't see the dragon admitting to it . . . unless you tell her you're looking for a girl in a miniskirt . . .'

*

Jones took out his notebook, turned to a blank page and jotted down some sentences. 'How old is your mother?' he asked Beale.

'Fifty-nine.'

'Happy with her life?'

'Not particularly.'

'What about your kids? How old are they?'

'Seven and five.'

The superintendent eyed him with amusement. 'Good answers, Nick. I'd say that makes you the expert on depressed fifty-somethings and me the expert on bolshie teenagers.' He tore the page out of the notebook and handed it to Beale. 'I'll take Ben, you take Ms Tutting. If you can persuade her to answer these questions, we might get somewhere, but you'll probably have to talk around the subject first.'

Beale read what Jones had written. *Does Walter use prostitutes? Where does he find them? How long's he been doing it? Does he have a regular?* 'Cheers,' he said acidly. 'Do you want to give me some hints on how I'm supposed to discuss an eighty-two-year-old's sexual habits with his daughter? It's not something I've done on a regular basis.'

'Use your imagination.' Jones clapped his number two on the back. 'Just make sure you speak to her before she gets to her father. We won't get a sniff at prostitutes if she thinks she can blame the assault on Charles Acland.'

*

Beale parked himself on a chair in the corridor and phoned through to one of his colleagues to find out what Amy Tutting had been asked in previous interviews. Not very much was the answer. 'She was fairly distraught, so we didn't press too hard.' Most of the questions had related to Walter's regular daily habits, how often she visited him, what she knew of his movements on the day, a check of a police inventory of the contents of his house, and a list of his friends and acquaintances.

She had spoken of her father's increasing forgetfulness but hadn't mentioned putting pressure on him to keep his door closed. Beale's colleague described her as 'a bit uptight', but only because she burst into tears and let rip at her brothers for refusing to help with Walter's care. 'She works full-time as a PA and said it was tiring trying to cope on her own.'

Beale rose to his feet as a smartly dressed, middle-aged woman came through the swing doors. 'Ms Tutting?' He offered his hand when she nodded. 'Detective Inspector Nick Beale. I know you're keen to see your father, but may I borrow you for five minutes before you do? Sister's lent me a small office at the other end of the corridor.' He smiled apologetically. 'It *is* important, ma'am, otherwise I wouldn't ask.'

She was pleasant-looking in a conventional way, with well-groomed dark hair and light make-up, but there were deep grooves at the side of her mouth that suggested it turned down more often than it turned up. She wasn't smiling now. 'How do I know you are who you say you are? You could be anyone.'

Beale produced his warrant card. 'There's a phone in the sister's office. You can double-check my credentials from there.'

Uninterested, she returned the card. 'I've already told your people everything I know. What good will another five minutes do?'

'I'd rather discuss that in private, Ms Tutting. Some of the issues your father's raised are quite sensitive.'

She frowned unhappily but allowed herself to be shepherded down the corridor. 'You shouldn't believe everything he says, you know. He forgot my mother's name a couple of weeks ago . . . kept insisting it was Ella . . . but that's the name of one of my sisters-in-law. He remembered Mum the next day, but there was no arguing with him at the time. He doesn't like being told he's wrong.'

Beale closed the office door and pulled out a chair for her. 'Had Ella been to visit him that day?'

'Hardly. She and my brother live in Australia.'

Beale favoured her with a sympathetic smile as he took the other chair. 'What about your other brother? Is he any closer?'

'Manchester . . . but it might as well be Australia. Dad hasn't seen him in twelve months. He made a flying visit on Sunday because he wanted to know what was happening with the house . . . but he wasn't prepared to sit with Dad.' She fiddled with the clasp of her handbag. 'He said he didn't have time because he had to be back in Manchester by seven.'

'Leaving you to shoulder the responsibility as usual?'

The woman nodded.

'That can't be easy, not when you're working a forty-hour week and trying to have a life of your own. Do your brothers know how hard it is to keep track of what your father's doing?'

Amy Tutting was no pushover. She raised suspicious eyes to Beale's. 'What's Dad been saying?'

Beale hesitated. 'It's more what he hasn't said, Ms Tutting. He seems to be in a continuous loop of anxiety which involves a repetition of three phrases . . . "Mustn't open the door" . . .

"Don't tell Amy" . . . "Been a silly old fool".' He folded his hands on the table and stared at the woman. 'We think the person he's afraid of is you.'

Her mouth turned down immediately. 'Only because I told him I was going to have him certified and put in a nursing home. I'm fed up with it. He's in arrears on his council tax . . . sitting on fuel bills that haven't been paid since the last quarter.' She took a rattling breath through her nose. 'He expects me to cover them, but I don't see why I should.'

Beale agreed with her. 'Is he living on a state pension?'

'Plus what he gets from his contributory pension, but he won't tell me how much that is. He worked as a printer for forty years, so it won't be peanuts.' She looked understandably angry. 'He keeps all his papers locked away to stop me finding out . . . but there's never enough to pay the bills. I've been trying to persuade him to grant me power of attorney and all he says is—' She came to an abrupt halt.

Beale let the silence drift, gambling that her own irritation was motive enough to keep speaking.

'It's ridiculous. The only other way for me to manage his affairs is to put him into receivership through the court of protection, but I need a medical certificate declaring him incompetent for that, and his doctor won't give me one. He says Dad's only in the mild stages of dementia and might stay that way till he dies.' She paused. 'It's not worth wasting time on anyway. My brothers will object as soon as the court notifies them that I've put in the application.' She fell silent again.

'Why?'

Amy gave a bitter little smile. 'They're only interested in what they're going to inherit. It's no skin off their noses if Dad squanders his pension, but the house is worth about twenty times what he paid for it in 1970. They don't care how difficult it is for me as long as their inheritance isn't sold to pay for a nursing home.'

Beale eyed the unhappy slump of her shoulders, wondering

how blunt he could be. 'Has your father told you what he's spending his pension on, Ms Tutting?'

Either she misinterpreted the question or the tentative note in Beale's voice suggested he knew the answer already. A look of resignation crossed her face. 'Will it get into the newspapers?'

'I can't say at this point.'

'It's *so* disgusting. Why would an eighty-two-year-old man want to do that kind of thing? It's only a couple of years since Mum died.'

'Maybe that's why,' said Beale.

'I suppose he's told you he doesn't *do* anything with them . . . just wants a chat now and then because he's lonely.' She didn't wait for an answer. 'It's not true. They all know the more they play with him the richer they'll be. I've found mugs with sperm in them. It's revolting.'

'Difficult for you.'

'He's so senile he forgets if he's paid them. All they have to do is ask for money upfront and money at the end . . . and he just keeps opening his wallet. He must be the easiest touch in Bermondsey. I told the doctor, Dad's become a free banking service to every little tart in the area . . . and do you know what he said?' The resentful lines around her mouth scored deeper into her skin. 'It's probably good for his prostate.'

Twenty

FOLLOWING HER FIRST HOUSE call of the evening, Jackson went on the attack about Daisy. As ever, Acland was lounging against her car when she returned. 'You look like shit,' she said severely, abandoning her earlier attempts to persuade him to talk about Jen. 'It doesn't do my image any good to drag an unshaven gorilla around with me.'

He stroked his stubble. 'I'd have frightened Daisy if I'd appeared looking like this.'

'She says you're acting like a stalker.'

'I know. I heard you arguing in the kitchen yesterday morning. That's why I thought you needed some time to yourselves.'

He had an answer for everything. 'You shouldn't have listened.'

'I didn't have much choice,' he said mildly. 'Daisy's voice goes into overdrive when she's angry.'

'This isn't easy for her.'

'Only because the boot's on the other foot for once.'

Jackson frowned at him. 'Meaning?'

'I'm spending too much time with you, and that's not the way it's supposed to be. She's jealous.'

Jackson gave a surprised laugh. 'Of you? Give me a break! She's been jealous of the odd woman in the past . . . but it wouldn't cross her mind to be jealous of a man.'

Acland came close to a smile. 'It's nothing to do with sex . . . it's about being the centre of attention. The only interest you're supposed to attract is fear when she calls on you to act as a bouncer. She'd see off a dog if it wagged its tail too vigorously every time you came home.'

'So now you're a psychiatrist.'

He shrugged. 'I'm happy to stare at her tits all day if it'll make your life easier. It's what every other bloke in the bar is expected to do.'

'She doesn't do it for fun,' said Jackson, irritably popping the locks and dumping her medical case in the boot. 'It's good for business.'

'End of discussion, then.' In what appeared to be deliberate provocation, Acland opened the driver's door. 'I'll jog back to the pub and join the fan club.'

Jackson glared at him as she eased herself behind the wheel. 'Get in,' she said crossly, jerking her head towards the passenger seat. 'I'd rather have you attached to my hip than scaring the life out of Daisy by ogling her breasts.' She waited while he walked round the bonnet and climbed in beside her. 'What's the deal on this? What's she done to make you dislike her?'

'Nothing. It's the other way round. *She* dislikes me.'

'You're as bad as each other,' said Jackson with a frustrated sigh, tapping her fingers on the steering wheel.

Acland gave another shrug. 'If you want the truth, she scares the shit out of me. I don't feel comfortable with the way she dresses . . . I don't feel comfortable when she plays with her hair . . . and I sure as hell can't stand the way she puts her hands on people.'

Jackson turned to look at him. 'Would you do anything to hurt her?'

'I might if she tried to touch me,' he said truthfully, buckling his seat belt. 'That's why I'm avoiding her.'

*

DI Beale tapped on the glass panel in Ben Russell's door to attract the superintendent's attention, then waited outside for Jones to appear. He caught a glimpse of one of his uniformed colleagues taking notes by the window, and a full view of his boss's irritable expression as the door closed behind him. 'The kid's giving yes or no answers and the bloody solicitor's protecting him at every turn. He threatens to pull the plug every time the miserable little wretch yawns.' He moved away from the door. 'Tell me some good news.'

'You were right about prostitutes. If the daughter's to be believed, Walter's been entertaining most of the working girls in south London over the last six months. She's short on detail – doesn't know names and can't describe any particular girls because she's never seen any of them – but she's adamant that half a dozen see her father as an easy touch.'

'How did she come up with a number if she's never seen them?'

'Walter let it slip when she told him he was a fool to think a drug-addicted tart would give a damn about him. He said it wasn't just one, it was more like six.'

'Why didn't she tell us this before?'

'The usual,' said Beale, flicking the pages of his notebook. 'We didn't ask . . . she didn't think it was important . . . she thought her father had said it was a man who'd attacked him.' He isolated an entry. 'I mentioned that none of the fingerprints in Walter's house matched anything we had – and I said it was odd because I didn't believe her father had picked on the only six prostitutes in London who didn't have convictions – and her answer was, "I told him I wouldn't come back if he didn't clean up after himself."'

'So where's the evidence of prostitution? You said, "if the daughter's to be believed". Are guesses all you've got?'

'He's been paying them. According to Ms Tutting, he's so senile he coughs up two or three times for a single session. She says the girls use him as a free banking service every time they need a fix. She even thinks he's given his PIN to one or two of them.'

'Anything else?'

'A list of examples of how disgusting Walter's been.' Beale kept his voice deliberately matter of fact. 'Semen in mugs . . . dirty underpants . . . the smell of cheap perfume round his trouser fly . . . fag ends in the sink. Apparently, he masturbates in front of Ms Tutting when he forgets who she is.'

Jones pulled a grimace of distaste. 'Is she telling the truth?'

'I'd say so. She's had some ding-dong rows with her father about money and he hasn't denied that he's spent it on prostitutes . . . claims it's his right to do what he likes with it. I'll check with his bank tomorrow, find out how much he's withdrawn in the last six months.'

'Why six months?'

'Ms Tutting found a stack of unpaid bills dating back to February. It could be longer. She says he's been acting weird since his wife died two years ago.'

'Weird as in sexually active?'

Beale shrugged. 'Sexually curious, at least. She claims to have seen a telephone bill from last year which shows he racked up five hundred quid on 0900 lines in a single quarter.'

Jones frowned. 'Why haven't we found that? 0900 numbers should have been ringing alarm bells for days.'

'Walter threw everything away when Ms Tutting threatened to have him certified as financially incompetent. That was two or three weeks ago.'

'How long's she known about the prostitutes?'

'For certain? Not much longer. A month at most . . . from the time she found the unpaid bills and challenged him about them. She's been trying to persuade him they're robbing him blind and he's not to open the door if one of them rings.'

Jones rubbed his hands vigorously over his face. 'I've a damn good mind to have the idiotic woman arrested for obstruction.' He thought for a moment. 'Does she know how he contacts these girls?'

Beale shook his head. 'She says it's the other way round. They seek him out whenever they need cash.'

'He must have contacted them in the first place. Did she have any ideas on that?'

'The only things she's sure about are that he doesn't know how to work a computer and he's been having a drink in the same pub every night for thirty years.' He consulted his notebook again. 'The Crown. It's a couple of streets away from Walter's house. Do you know it?'

Jones shook his head.

'I've a nagging feeling at the back of my mind that it's come up before in this inquiry . . . but I can't remember where. I'm wondering if it's one of the places that had a mini-cab arrangement with Harry Peel?' He raised enquiring eyebrows. 'Strike a chord?'

'No. Has anyone checked it out since the attack on Walter?'

'I don't know. Ms Tutting said she mentioned it when she was asked about her father's habits, but it didn't come up when I spoke to one of the team earlier.' He watched the superintendent's expression darken. 'It won't be anyone's fault, Brian. Walter's been on a back burner because of Kevin Atkins's mobile. Do you want me to call in to the Crown on my way back?'

Jones looked at his watch. 'Give me ten minutes and I'll come with you.' He jerked his thumb at Ben Russell's door. 'Is there anything Ms Tutting told you that might wipe the smile off laughing boy's face?'

Beale hesitated. 'Nothing specific, but she has huge issues with teenage girls – the sister was bang on the button about that. I listened to a two-minute rant on how the only thing feminism has created is a generation of sexually active, celebrity-mad, half-naked, binge-drinking wannabes . . . then another two minutes on how easy they've made it for teenage boys to take advantage of them.'

Jones smiled slightly. 'So? Any copper on the beat will tell you the same.'

'Agreed, but it made me wonder about Ben. He wants us to think Chalky's his only friend in London and that he still holds a candle for Hannah in Wolverhampton . . . but I'd say that's a little unlikely, wouldn't you? He's been here a while, and presumably he was a healthy sixteen-year-old before the diabetes kicked in.'

'You think he knows Walter's prostitutes?'

Beale shrugged. 'It's a reasonable bet. They're the same age group, and I can't see letters from an absent girlfriend keeping a sexually active sixteen-year-old on the straight and narrow for long . . . or not one with Ben's capacity for dodging and weaving.'

*

'Ten minutes,' Jones agreed with the solicitor as he resumed his seat, nodding to the WPC to resume her note-taking. 'Just a few more questions and then we'll call it a day.' He studied Ben's bored expression for a second or two. 'You might prefer your mother to leave the room,' he murmured, 'unless you're happy to discuss your sexual activities in front of her.'

He was rewarded with a flicker of alarm, but the solicitor jumped in before the boy could say anything. 'We agreed that questions would relate only to those items in Ben's rucksack that he has freely admitted stealing, Superintendent.'

Jones nodded. 'But we believe your client received or stole those items from teenage prostitutes, Mr Pearson, and I'm interested in the relationship he has with these girls.'

Pearson gave a perfunctory smile. 'If you put those questions individually, Mr Jones, I will advise Ben to answer them. If you insist on linking them, I won't.' He paused. 'Perhaps you'd prefer me to do it.' He turned to the boy. 'Ben . . . have you ever received stolen items . . . or stolen items yourself . . . from teenage prostitutes?'

'No.'

'To your knowledge, have you ever had a relationship – sexual or otherwise – with a teenage prostitute?'

'Not unless Hannah was one.' He sniggered at the solicitor's frown. 'It was a joke, for fuck's sake. I've never been with a prozzie in my life.'

'Please continue, Superintendent.'

Jones studied the man's face and wondered what he really thought about his client. Mid-forties and well spoken, Pearson seemed an unlikely champion for a foul-mouthed Wolverhampton lad. 'Irrespective of those answers, Mr Pearson, I intend to continue this line of questioning. Ben has a history of predatory behaviour on vulnerable under-age girls. Hannah was twelve when he first had sex with her. He was fifteen.'

'We've dealt with this issue, Superintendent. Hannah's parents have declined to take the matter any further.'

Jones pulled a sceptical smile. 'They can't do anything else. Their daughter refuses to make a statement. She has a romantic notion that a frayed photograph and some semi-literate letters will keep an absent lover faithful.' He turned his scepticism on Ben. 'What's wrong with girls of your own age? Are they too intelligent to do what you tell them? Less easy to mould?'

'You wish.'

'How will Hannah react when she finds out you've been hanging around with prostitutes? Will she take it well, do you think?'

Ben flashed him a look of dislike. 'None of your fucking business.'

Pearson cleared his throat. 'My client said he's never been with a prostitute, Superintendent.'

'That's right,' said the youngster. 'I don't even know any girls in London.'

'You prefer boys?'

Ben lined up his pistol hand and pointed it at Jones. 'Fuck off.'

'So in all your time on the streets here, the only friend you've made is Chalky? Is that what you're telling me?'

'Yeah . . . and if it's Chalky you've been talking to, he doesn't know his arse from his elbow most of the time. He probably meant shirt-lifters . . . calls them "girls" and "ladies" and spits on the ground behind their backs. He showed me the alleyway to get me away from them. He hates gays.'

Jones nodded. 'So you said the first time we interviewed you. You seem very keen for us to see this only friend of yours as a died-in-the-wool homophobe.'

'If that's a gay hater, then that's what Chalky is.' He swivelled the pistol hand towards the window and performed a mock recoil. 'He said if he still had his gun, he'd shoot the buggers.'

'Are those your views, too?'

'Sure. Shirt-lifting's unnatural, innit?'

'But sleeping with twelve-year-olds isn't?'

The boy looked immediately to his solicitor to rescue him.

'We've covered this area already, Superintendent.'

'I don't think we have, Mr Pearson. It's the under-age girls your client's been bedding in London that I'm interested in.' He leaned forward. 'We didn't get our information from Chalky, Ben, and there was no confusion about the kind of girls that were being talked about. Young prostitutes with drug habits.' He watched the youngster's face for a reaction and thought he saw one. 'What's your role in the operation? Pimp?'

'Like hell!' Ben shifted his attention back to the solicitor. 'He's talking crap. I don't know any prozzies.'

'Where's this leading, Superintendent?'

'To Walter Tutting,' answered Jones, keeping his eyes on the boy, 'the elderly man who was beaten half to death last Friday . . . lives at 3 Welling Lane in Bermondsey. He regained consciousness a few hours ago.'

The speed of Ben's response suggested he'd rehearsed his answer. 'Nothing to do with me. I was puking like a dog on Friday . . . wouldn't have ended up in here otherwise.'

'Mr Tutting was attacked at lunchtime,' Jones said, 'and you were functioning well enough to climb over some railings twelve hours later. Would you like to tell me where you were and what you were doing between eleven and one on Friday?'

'Can't remember.'

The solicitor weighed in again. 'Ben told you during his first interview that he has no clear recollection of details from Friday,

Superintendent – nor, indeed, from a couple of weeks before his admission – other than that he was regularly sick and may have passed out a couple of times. His consultant confirmed these symptoms as typical of type one diabetes and the further complication of ketoacidosis.'

'I'm aware of that, Mr Pearson. I also recall that the consultant mentioned mental stupor as a precursor to coma, and I'm wondering how a boy in a dazed state –' he introduced sarcasm into his tone – 'which appears to prevent him remembering *anything* – managed to find his way around Covent Garden in the dark.'

'I was probably on auto-pilot,' said Ben, observing Jones through half-closed lids. 'If you go to a place often enough, you can find it in your sleep. Don't remember doing it, though.'

'Do you remember being in the Bermondsey area at lunchtime?' Jones asked.

'Don't reckon I was. Never been there in my life as far as I can tell . . . don't even know where it is.' He scowled at his solicitor. 'Is he allowed to do this? The doctor's told him how sick I was, and it sure as hell ain't got nothing to do with the stuff in my rucksack.'

'Do you have any evidence connecting Ben with the attack on Mr Tutting, Superintendent?'

'Not directly, but we believe he knows who was involved. His position will be a lot stronger if he confirms that for us now.'

'Is this a fishing trip, Superintendent?'

Jones shook his head. 'Far from it. At this stage, the only thing that's preventing Ben from being interviewed under caution as a suspect in the assault on Mr Tutting are the constraints his illness puts on me under the Police and Criminal Evidence Act.' He glanced at Ben's mother, who was sitting with her habitually bowed head. 'Whoever attacked Mr Tutting has a deep contempt for the elderly. First the poor old fellow was fleeced of his savings, then he was tossed aside as of no further value. It's a miracle he's still alive.'

Mrs Sykes stirred. 'My Ben wouldn't do a thing like that. Would you, love?'

'Course not. I like old people. Chalky's old. My stepdad's old. May have had the odd row with 'em, but I'd never hit 'em.'

'Is that where you draw the line?' asked Jones.

'What line?'

'It's OK to steal off an old person, but not to hit him.'

'I ain't never stolen off an old person.'

'According to your stepfather, you have. You used his Switch card to take three hundred quid out of an ATM the day before you ran away. He also found other withdrawals of lesser amounts when he went back through his bank statements. He blames himself for recording his PIN in his diary and giving you the impression that stealing was easy.'

'That's different.'

'How?'

'Stealing off family's different from stealing off strangers.'

'Meaning what? That it's a lesser crime or it's easier to get away with?'

'Mum and Barry know why I did it.'

'And that makes it acceptable?' Jones asked drily, eyeing the woman.

She raised her head. 'It was a difficult time for him. He did some things he regrets. Barry and I understand that.'

Jones studied her face with interest. 'Does your understanding extend to the cell phones Ben has admitted stealing in the last four months? He uses interesting terminology when he refers to his victims . . . he calls female victims "bitches" and male victims "mother fuckers". Both suggest disdain for the people he robs.'

'None of them was *old*, though,' said Ben with a gleam of satisfaction in his pale eyes, as if he'd scored a point. 'I wouldn't call an old bloke a mother fucker . . . I'd call him a geezer. In any case, you don't see that many of 'em flashing their mobiles around in the street, so they ain't that easy to rob.'

'It's not a moral issue, then, it's a practical one. If a frail eighty-two-year-old made it easy for you, you'd treat him the same way you treat a teenager.'

'Think what you like,' the boy said dismissively. 'It don't make no difference to me if you twist what I say.'

'An elderly black lady was punched and kicked not so long ago for her mobile phone. She was so badly injured, she had to be hospitalized.'

'Nothing to do with me.'

'For the record,' the solicitor interjected, consulting his watch, 'my client, Ben Russell, said he doesn't steal from old people, nor does he refer to them in derogatory terms. I am also drawing Superintendent Jones's attention to an earlier interview where the phrases "bitch" and "mother fucker" were discussed at length. These are recognized street slang for young females and males respectively, and in no way suggest contempt on the part of my client.' He tapped his watch. 'We agreed ten minutes. I shall have to insist that we end the interview now.'

'By all means.' Jones bared his teeth in a wolfish grin. 'What are we keeping you from, Mr Pearson? The opera?'

The man's mouth curved in a faint smile. 'I don't write the rules, Superintendent. I am merely obliged on behalf of my client to remind you that they exist.'

'Then I suggest you remind your client similarly. As an over-worked taxpayer, I presume I'm in the ludicrous position of both investigating this self-confessed thief –' he gestured towards Ben – 'and paying you to protect him.'

'I'm afraid so,' the solicitor agreed. 'The French would call it the theatre of the absurd, but it's the price we pay for living in a civilized democracy.' He turned an unsympathetic gaze on his client. 'I do understand your frustrations, however. I've never met a policeman yet who would describe what he sees on a daily basis as civilized.'

*

Jones waited until he, Beale and the WPC were clear of the building before he asked the female officer what she'd made of the solicitor's parting remarks. 'Did you get the impression Pearson was trying to tell us something?'

'Only that he doesn't like the kid. He doesn't like the mother either. While you were talking to Nick outside, the pair of them kept whingeing on about compensation for police harassment. I could tell from Mr Pearson's body language that the whole conversation was making him angry.'

'What did he say?'

'That he could see no basis for such a claim but they were within their rights to pursue it through another solicitor if they chose.' The woman laughed suddenly. 'He suggested they go to Grabbit and Runn in Litigate Street and keep their fingers crossed that a malicious suit didn't result in Ben being charged with multiple counts of theft.'

Twenty-one

FOR A WOMAN WHO prided herself on her common sense, Jackson felt a superstitious spike of alarm when she returned after a second patient visit to find her car deserted. *Now what?* She stared up and down the well-lit road, but there was no sign of Acland anywhere, nor was there a message under the windscreen wipers to indicate where he'd gone or why. She wasn't even sure what had spooked her unless it was her lingering suspicion about what he'd been doing the previous night.

She called Daisy on her mobile. 'Hi . . . no, everything's fine except that Charles seems to have vanished again. Is he with you?'

'What do you mean "again"?' Daisy sounded annoyed. 'Did he come back?' The noise of customers was loud in the background.

'He was waiting by the car when I went out. He said he'd been walking all night.'

'Oh, for goodness' sake! You've got to stop this, Jacks. It's ridiculous. He's not your responsibility.'

Jackson stifled a sigh. 'We'll talk about it later. I just wondered if he was there, that's all.'

'Not that I know of . . . unless he's in his room. Do you want me to take a look?'

'No,' Jackson said sharply. 'Let him be.'

Daisy's voice grew clearer, as if she'd moved out of the bar into the corridor. 'What's going on?' This time her tone was suspicious. 'Why are you so worried about him suddenly? You're not his *mother*, Jacks . . . though I'm beginning to wonder if that's what this is all about.'

Jackson watched a lean figure emerge from behind a transit van fifty yards away. 'Forget it,' she said curtly. 'I'll talk to you later.'

'That'll be a change,' came the acid reply. 'I hardly get a look-in these days.'

Jackson's expression was grim. 'Give it a rest,' she snapped. 'I hate this kind of thing at the best of times, but it really gets on my nerves when there's no reason for it.'

'Then tell him to stop treating me as if I don't exist,' Daisy hissed. 'That's what's getting on *my* nerves . . . in case you hadn't noticed.'

'You're too touchy-feely for him. He feels threatened by you.'

'Is that what he's told you?'

'Yes.'

'And you fell for it?'

'I certainly took on board that he has no idea how to respond to a sexy lesbian with a cleavage,' Jackson answered. She lowered her voice as Acland drew nearer. 'He's on his way back. I shall have to stop in a minute.'

'Well, tell him, if he thinks I'm going to dress in a burkha, he's got another think coming,' Daisy said crossly. 'It's my blasted house, for Christ's sake. If he doesn't like the way I do things, he can take himself off.'

'Which is precisely what he does when he comes with me,' Jackson murmured, 'but you don't like that either.' She flipped the mobile closed and waited for Acland to come within earshot. 'I'm not a taxi service, Lieutenant. Another time, I'll drive away without you.'

'You should have done it this time,' he told her. 'Your next patient's only two streets away. I'd have met you there if you hadn't waited.'

'Thanks for telling me,' she said acerbically. 'Couldn't you have left a message . . . saved me the bother of trying to track you down?'

He gestured towards the transit van. 'I could see you from over there. If you'd climbed straight into the car, instead of making the phone call, I'd have come running.'

She opened the boot and put her bag inside. 'Why didn't you, anyway?'

Humour lines appeared around Acland's good eye. 'Perhaps I was testing you. Perhaps I wanted to see how long you'd hang around.'

'Cut the crap,' she said impatiently. 'I'm not in the mood for jokes.'

He eyed the mobile which was still in her hand. 'Daisy been giving you a hard time again?'

'No.' She tucked the gadget into her pocket. 'What's with the van?'

'Nothing. I was using it as cover, that's all.'

'For what?'

'To look into one of the flats in that block.' He jerked his chin towards a modern brick construction opposite the parked transit.

'Great! So now you're a Peeping Tom as well as a stalker?'

The humour lines deepened round Acland's eye. 'It's Jen's flat, and some of the stuff belonged to me. I wondered if any of it was still there. I moved it in when we got engaged.' He shook his head at Jackson's expression. 'Nothing to see. The curtains are pulled.'

She held his gaze for a moment, recalling his insistence that everything he owned was in his kitbag. Like the police, she'd questioned how anyone could exist on so little. 'I didn't think you had any property in London, other than what you carry with you.'

'I don't, not any more. Jen appropriated the lot. I was just curious to see if she'd kept any of it. There were some artefacts that I got from South Africa a few years back—' He broke off, as if he'd said too much.

'Are you sure you weren't trying to catch a glimpse of Jen?' Jackson asked as she took her place behind the wheel.

Acland shook his head. 'I saw her leave in a taxi about fifteen minutes ago. That's why I went down for a look.' The side of his mouth lifted slightly. 'She had a punter with her . . . fat little fellow about so high –' he raised his palm to shoulder height – 'I couldn't see too well, but it was probably a Jap. She always said Japs were the most gullible.'

'About what?'

'The difference between Uma Thurman and a cheap whore.'

*

Jones gave Beale a summary of his interview with Ben as they headed for the Crown. 'He was ready for questions about the attack on Walter Tutting, jumped in PDQ with reasons why he couldn't have done it.'

'You think he was involved?'

'Not necessarily. He may just be scared he's going to be charged with something he didn't do. It depends what he thinks he needs to defend himself against. He's been plugged in to his TV set since he arrived and Walter certainly featured on the news over the weekend.'

'Along with a rape in Richmond Park, a stabbing in Leyton-stone and assorted brawls outside pubs,' Beale said reasonably. 'Why would he expect questions about Walter and not about the other assaults?'

'That's what we need to find out. If he wasn't responsible for the attack, he may be able to point us in the direction of who was.'

'Did you ask him?'

'No,' said Jones with sudden weariness. 'I need something a lot stronger than guesswork to prise information out of the little toerag.' He fell silent for a moment. 'Have we had any luck with Chalky? Any sightings?'

'Not yet. Khan located the women that Charles Acland told us about, but they haven't seen him for weeks.'

'Which women?'

'Five lesbians who hang around Docklands,' Beale told him.

'According to Khan, they said Chalky was lying if he claimed any kind of friendship with them. They avoid him as far as possible . . . He's frightening when he's drunk and verbally abusive when he isn't. The last time they saw him was about three months ago.'

'What about the hostels and the drop-in centres?'

Beale shook his head. 'Same story. We've left contact details in case he turns up, but they all said he never comes in during the summer. He's a bit of a loner, by all accounts. We can't find anyone in the homeless community who claims to spend time with him.'

'What about the alleyway?'

'A patrol's been looking in twice a night every night. He hasn't shown up there either.'

'Is he still in London?'

'No idea . . . but we've put out a general alert to the neighbouring forces and we've had nothing back. He appears to have dropped off the radar completely.'

'Have you checked the hospitals?'

'Only the London ones. Shall I extend the radius?'

Jones seemed unduly pessimistic that evening, as if the long hours were finally taking their toll. 'I'm not sure it's worth the effort. What's Chalky going to say if we do find him? He told Dr Jackson he'd only known Ben for a month, and Ben didn't put it much longer. Six weeks at most.'

'Assuming either of them is telling the truth.'

'Why wouldn't they be? Ben doesn't know what Chalky told Dr Jackson.'

Beale shrugged. 'I can't get my head round the relationship. Why would an antisocial drunk even notice if a kid was being propositioned by gays?' He flicked his indicator to turn off the main road towards the Crown pub. 'It would make more sense if it was the other way round, and it was Ben who took pity on Chalky.'

'Why?'

'Chalky's the one who gets pissed on.'

*

Jackson was taken aback by Acland's casual reference to Jen being a 'cheap whore'. It seemed as out of character for an intensely private man – *calculatedly out of character?* – as his earlier willingness to discuss his parents. She recalled the end of her conversation with Robert Willis when he mentioned something Susan Campbell had told him.

'According to the police, Jen's a high-class prostitute. They asked Susan if Charles's reasons for wanting to marry her were because he wanted to save her.' The psychiatrist paused. 'I suggest it's the other way round . . . that he had no idea what she did and only found out late in the relationship that he'd been sharing her with her clients. He wouldn't have handled that well.'

'Not many men would.'

'Indeed,' said Willis, 'and I imagine quite a few in the same situation would have taken the sort of revenge that Charles took. Sex is a major issue for him – probably because it was offered and withheld at whim.'

'That doesn't make him safe,' said Jackson. 'What if he's developed a taste for rape?'

'All the evidence points the other way,' said Willis. 'He wouldn't be so ashamed of himself if he felt comfortable with what he did. Frankly, I'd be a lot more worried if you told me he sat in the bar all day staring at Daisy without saying anything. Predatory rapists have strong sexual appetites and tend to use pornography and Peeping Tom activity to support their fantasies . . . but that's not a description that fits Charles.'

No, thought Jackson, reaching for the ignition and turning the key. The most apt description was the superintendent's 'monk'. She put the car into gear. 'Are you saying Jen's a prostitute?' she asked Acland, as if it was something she didn't already know.

'She bills herself as a hostess, but it amounts to the same thing.' He sounded indifferent.

'What does she need the money for?' Jackson asked, pulling out into the road.

He stared dispassionately through the windscreen. 'She lost her meal ticket. I used to pay for everything until I wised up.' He gave a small laugh. 'I thought she was a struggling actress who couldn't afford her rent. Some joke.'

'What was she really spending the money on?'

'Take your pick. She was freebasing on crack the last time I went to the flat.'

The day of the rape . . . ? 'What happened?'

'She told me to snort some coke myself and loosen up.'

'Did you?'

Acland shook his head.

'When was this?'

'End of September . . . the weekend before I went to Iraq. In a funny sort of way it was a relief. It's easier to accept things if you can blame a drug.' He lapsed into silence.

'What things?'

'Being an idiot. She was the most confident person I'd ever met at the beginning. Nothing fazed her. It was like winning the jackpot . . . looks and personality all wrapped up in one.' He made a sound in his throat that sounded like a laugh. 'I should have realized it was too good to be true.'

Jackson flicked him a sympathetic glance. 'What do you know about cocaine addiction, Charles?'

'It destroys people.'

'It certainly alters aspects of the personality,' she said calmly. 'It can produce a variety of responses – euphoria, heightened sexuality, overwhelming confidence – but you wouldn't assume those were drug-induced traits unless you were told. The downsides are aggression and paranoia, particularly in long-term users.'

Acland didn't say anything.

'When did you find out?'

'About what? The drugs or the prostitution?'

'Either.'

'The day I told her it was over.'

'At the end of September.'

Acland shook his head. 'Closer to the beginning. She didn't like me being the one to end it. A man doesn't walk out on Jen . . . not without being made to look a fool first.'

Jackson pulled up outside her next patient's house and killed the engine. She found the timeline, and details, of when and how he ended the engagement confusing. 'Why did you go back at the end of September?'

Acland set to squeezing his knuckles again. 'To fetch my stuff. She wasn't supposed to be there. The agreement was I'd use my key and leave it behind when I left. She reneged on that the way she reneged on everything else.'

'I'm surprised you thought you could trust her.'

He stared at his hands. 'I didn't. I just hoped she'd show a bit more sense.'

*

Beale drew his Toyota into a parking space in front of the Crown and leaned forward to watch a woman emerge from the side of the pub. 'Do you see the blonde?' he asked Jones. 'That's Jen Morley . . . Charles Acland's ex . . . the call girl Khan and I interviewed the other night, the one who fancies herself as Uma Thurman.'

The superintendent followed his gaze and took in the swept-back hair and high-necked, figure-hugging outfit that the girl was wearing. 'She could pass for her tonight. I've seen a lot worse.'

They watched her walk to a waiting cab where a small, portly man climbed out of the back and held the door open for her.

'Did you check to see if she's on file?' asked Jones, watching the vehicle pull away.

'She was arrested a couple of years ago during a blitz on crack houses in south London. She fell into the bracket of users who picked the wrong time to visit their dealers. She was given a caution, but not charged. I couldn't find anything else.'

Jones glanced towards the unlit passageway at the side of the pub again. 'What are the odds on a supplier being down there?'

'High,' said Beale matter-of-factly. 'From what Khan and I saw the other night, she's pretty far gone. I can't see her getting through a couple of hours with a client without some assistance.'

London Evening Standard – *Wednesday, 15 August 2007*

Body Found in River
The body of a man was recovered from the Thames in the Woolwich area this morning. His identity is unknown but he's described as bearded with greying dark hair, of average height and build and wearing a brown overcoat. Police are investigating the circumstances surrounding his death.

Twenty-two

THE CROWN WAS SMALLER, darker and less noisy than the Bell, although it wasn't short of customers. Their average age appeared to be older than the twenty-somethings Daisy attracted, and the place had an atmosphere of respectability rather than the boisterous buzz that the Bell's younger clientele inspired. As soon as they walked in, both Jones and Beale questioned whether teenage prostitutes would want to frequent it, or even be allowed through the doors if they did. There was a prominent sign on the bar saying: 'It is illegal to sell or serve alcohol to under 18s. Proof of age may be requested.'

If the publican recognized the two men as policemen, he didn't show it. He broke off from a conversation with another customer and approached them with a smile. 'What can I get you, gentlemen?'

Jones took out his wallet and nodded to one of the draught taps. 'I'll have a pint of the Special. What about you, Nick?'

'The same, thanks.'

The man watched them while he drew beer into the first glass. 'Any news on Walter?' he asked pleasantly. 'We've all been rooting for him. There's a rumour going round that he's regained consciousness. Is that true?'

Jones took a fiver from his wallet and placed it on the counter. 'It is,' he said equally pleasantly. 'I'm Superintendent Brian Jones and this is Detective Inspector Nick Beale.'

'Derek Hardy. I've been wondering why we haven't seen any of you in here before. Walter hasn't missed a night in thirty years, or that's what he tells me anyway. Everyone knows him.'

'You didn't think about phoning us with that piece of information? We've only just learned ourselves.'

Hardy placed the first glass on a mat and started to draw the second. 'Not my fault, mate. I called the hotline the day after the poor old sod was mugged and I haven't heard a dicky bird out of you since.' He nodded towards the man he'd been speaking to. 'Old Pat did the same. He says he's called twice and both times he's been told the information's been noted . . . then nothing happens.'

Jones frowned. 'I'm sorry.'

'The wife said you're probably getting loads of calls. She reckoned I should go in person to the station.' He placed the second glass on the mat and smiled at them. 'I was planning to do it tomorrow, then you two show up. How's that for timing?' He took Jones's note. 'Four forty-eight, mate. Anything else?'

'No thanks.' He waited until the man returned with his change. 'What's so important that you'd come to the station in person?'

'I don't know if it's important or not,' Hardy confided, putting the coins into Jones's hand, 'but it's a bloody odd coincidence.' He folded his forearms on the counter. 'A guy called Harry Peel was a regular here until he was beaten to death close on twelve months back. It was before my time – the wife and me took over as managers at the beginning of the year – but Walter talked about it once or twice . . . said you've never found the guy who did it.'

'We haven't.'

'Well, after Walter got beaten up last Friday, Pat's started worrying that he's next on the list.'

'What list?'

'Whoever had it in for Harry and Walter. The three of them were good friends.'

Jones looked towards the elderly man at the other end of the bar. 'Is that Pat?'

'Yeah. Will you talk to him?'

'Sure.' He turned to Beale when Hardy was out of earshot.

'Do you want to check the Gents? It's probably a waste of time but there might be some cards in there.'

'Now?'

'Might as well. It'll be a good five minutes before the old boy gets into his stride. He looks in worse shape than Walter.'

*

It wouldn't have surprised Jackson to find Acland gone again when she returned to the car. He hadn't been willing to explain what he meant by Jen showing more sense and showed no inclination at all to open up about the relationship. It was more of a surprise that he *was* there and that he reintroduced the subject of Jen of his own accord.

'We never went anywhere in Bermondsey,' he said suddenly. 'I'm getting to know the area better with you than I ever did with Jen.'

'Was there a reason for that?'

'I booked a table at a restaurant in the high street shortly after we met – I was trying to persuade her that a soldier's life's fairly normal at weekends when he's not on manoeuvres or fighting a war – but she made me cancel when I told her where we were going. She said she had enough trouble with blokes in the street trying to chat her up, without adding waiters to the queue. I was naive enough to believe her in those days.'

'And what do you believe now?'

'That she was afraid we'd run into a dealer or a client. She wouldn't come out with me unless it was in my car or in a taxi. We never used the tube, never used buses, never walked anywhere from her flat together –' he shook his head – 'and it took me a long time to question how peculiar that was.'

'I'm not surprised if you were only there at weekends,' Jackson pointed out. 'It would have been obvious much sooner if you'd lived with her permanently. What was the plan for when you were married? Did you ever talk about that?'

'She kept sizing up properties in Chelsea on the basis that my mother did a *grande dame* act the only time she met her. Jen thought it meant my parents were loaded and would give us a hand with the finances. I tried to tell her she'd got the wrong end of the stick, but she wouldn't believe me.'

'Does she have family of her own?'

He crunched his knuckles. 'I don't know. She said she was an only child and her folks had died, but I don't think it's true.'

'Why not?'

'She forgot which background she'd invented for them. Her father started out as a bank manager and ended up as a hot-shot lawyer.'

'She was trying to impress you.'

'Then she should have been honest,' he said shortly. 'It wouldn't have worried me what her parents do.'

Jackson believed him. He certainly wasn't the snob that his mother appeared to be. 'So where were you going to live?' she asked, returning to her previous question. 'It doesn't sound as if Jen wanted to stay in Bermondsey.'

'She didn't. She wanted a ticket out and I was the sucker who was supposed to provide it. That's the only reason she latched on to me.'

His tone had an edge to it that sounded like pain and Jackson wondered how to respond. What kind of reassurance did he want? That he hadn't been suckered as easily as he thought?

'It wouldn't have been so black and white,' she said slowly. 'You said you liked the person she was at the beginning, so her feelings for you must have been genuine. She may even have tried to kick her habit for you.' She gave him time to answer, and went on when he didn't. 'She's a user, Charles. Most of them are deeply sincere about their desire to give up – they don't like how it impacts on the people they love – but only a tiny percentage succeed without professional help.'

He pressed the back of his thumb against his eyepatch. 'Then go and do the business yourself. You know where she lives. You might even prefer her to Daisy. She'll be all over you as long as the first rush hasn't worn off.'

Jackson allowed a pulse of silence to pass. 'I didn't deserve that . . . and, just for the record, I don't fancy addicts – they're too damn twitchy for my liking. *But*,' she continued over his muttered apology, 'even if I did, I wouldn't turn myself into a martyr over one of them. So Jen initiated sex during cocaine rushes. What's the big deal?'

He didn't answer.

'Does it hurt your pride? Are you thinking she only fancied you with chemical assistance?'

Acland leaned forward abruptly to grind the knuckles of his left hand into his eyepatch. 'You need to stop,' he said through gritted teeth.

She glanced at him, saw his pallor. 'There's a sick bag in the dashboard pocket,' she said unsympathetically. 'I'll stop when it's safe to do so.'

'No.' Acland's right hand shot out and grasped the steering wheel, veering the car to the left. 'You're doing my fucking head in! *Women* do my fucking head in!'

Jackson stamped on the brakes and used her own strength to keep the BMW from ploughing into a line of parked vehicles. 'Take your hands off!' she snarled. 'NOW!'

For a moment his grip seemed to slacken, then, with a sudden reversal of pressure, he turned the wheel to the right, using the force Jackson was already applying to steer the car towards the other side of the road. It happened so fast, and the combined strength of both their pulls was so powerful, that any attempt on her part to redress the drift came too late. She watched a lighted bollard in the middle of the road race towards them, felt the offside front tyre strike the kerb, and the only thought she had was that he was trying to kill her.

Her reaction was automatic. She took her left hand from the

steering wheel, chopped the point of her elbow into the side of his jaw, then used her forearm to slam his plated cheek against the passenger window . . .

*

'Harry was Bob Peel's eldest . . . did a stint in the army, then followed his dad into dockwork . . . until Maggie Thatcher took agin the unions and sold off the wharves to property developers.' Pat took a thoughtful slurp from the beer Jones had bought him. 'Me and Walter always knew Harry was a bit AC/DC . . . very dapper . . . liked his clothes . . . but it came as a shock to Bob. He hoped the army would knock some sense into Harry . . . and, when it didn't, he married him off to Fred Leeming's lass.'

'Debbie.'

'That's the one. They never had any kiddies, which was a shame. Bob blamed it on Harry's nancy-boy ways, but Harry told me in private that it was little Debbie who had the problem. She had a fair few women's problems . . . fibroids and such . . . ended up with a hysterectomy before she was forty.' He lapsed into silence, as if he'd forgotten what he was talking about.

'You said you saw more of Harry after he and Debbie separated,' Nick Beale prompted.

'That's right. He was lonely, poor lad. His dad died twenty years back but his mum passed away the night of the millennium . . . never got to see the new century. Good thing, too, some would say. It would have broken the old girl's heart to know her boy got murdered.' He bent his head for another mouthful of beer. 'Walter and me did what we could to keep him chipper. He drove his taxi most nights, but he'd usually find time to drop in here around six for an orange juice and a quick chat. He was a good lad . . . not my generation, of course . . . I was his dad's friend.' He smiled vaguely at the superintendent. 'Did you know Bob Peel? Worked down the docks . . .'

Derek Hardy broke in. 'They want to know about Harry, Pat. You need to tell them about the men he took back to his bedsit.'

'Thieving bastards, more like,' said the old man, his mouth curving down in disgust. 'I don't say I approved of what Harry got up to . . . poor old Bob'd turn in his grave if he knew . . . but Walter said there were some things you couldn't help . . . and I reckon he should know. He's a bit that way himself. Him and May got on well enough, but they weren't exactly soul mates.'

Jones stirred. 'They had three children.'

'I'm not saying he didn't do his duty . . . just that he left the bedroom stuff alone once it was over. The missus said May wasn't particularly bothered about it . . . in them days, sex wasn't the be-all and end-all of existence . . . you just got on with the hand you were dealt.' He took another swallow of beer. 'Him and May were happy enough, but there's no denying Walter'd rather sit in here with me and Harry than stay at home with his old lady. Don't reckon May knew it, though. Walter'd never have hurt her by telling her as much.'

Jones had heard this refrain before. His team had spoken to at least fifty men who hadn't wanted their families to know they were leading double lives. Kevin Atkins's wife had been particularly poignant about her husband's discretion. 'If he'd loved us less he'd probably still be alive. He went out of his way to keep his gay side secret . . . just to avoid embarrassing the kids.'

'Did Walter and Harry get together after May died?' he asked Pat.

'None of my business . . . never asked.'

'What about other men?'

'You talking about Walter still?'

Jones nodded.

'Doubt it . . . reckon he was scared off by what happened to Harry.'

'The murder?'

'Before that . . . Harry got taken for half a grand. Never seen the poor bugger so scared. Said he was frogmarched to a cashpoint with a knife to his throat and made to take out two lots of two fifty, one before midnight and the other after.'

'Did he report it?'

Pat shook his head. 'Told him to, but he was scared out of his wits they'd come after him. All he could think about was leaving the place he was in and going back to Debbie . . . Reckon it put him off fagging for good.'

Jones sorted the various pieces of information in his head. 'When did this happen?'

'A month or so before he was murdered.'

'You said "they". How many people were involved?'

'Not sure . . . two, I think. Far as I remember, Harry said the lad he took home let a second one in soon as business was completed . . . could have been more, though.'

'Into Harry's bedsit.'

Pat nodded. 'Gave Harry the scare of his life by all accounts . . . he was half-asleep and naked when he found a knife at his throat.'

'Did he know who these people were? Did he describe them?'

'He said they were black . . . reckon that's why he was so frightened. He thought they were going to take his money and stab him anyway. It's the kind of thing that type does, isn't it?'

Jones ignored the remark. 'Afro-Caribbean? Nigerian? Somalian?'

'Dunno.'

'Age?'

'The first one was a youngster, I know that, but I'm not sure about the other. Harry guessed they'd run the scam before . . . went straight to his wallet, took out his card and said they'd report him for sex with a minor if he didn't come up with a grand.'

'Did he say where he met the youngster?'

The old man shook his head. 'Probably a fare . . . he was damn wary who he let into the cab after. Do you reckon they're the ones who killed him?'

Jones avoided the question. 'We could have done with this information a bit earlier, Pat. Did you report it after Harry was murdered?'

'Certainly *did*,' said the old man in an affronted tone. 'Me and Walter both. A couple of uniformed coppers took statements from everyone in here the day after Harry was found. We told them you should be looking for blacks . . . but nothing's been done. Sometimes wonder if you lot are as afraid of them as the rest of us.'

The superintendent took a sip from his own glass. 'You'll have to accept my apologies on this one, Pat,' he murmured diplomatically. 'It seems that none of your information has got through. You have my word I'll look into it.'

'No need to cause a ruckus. You've got it now.'

Jones nodded. 'Except I'm having a problem understanding why Harry would invite the same young black man back to his bedsit a month after he stole money from him.'

'Who's saying the boy was invited? Maybe him and his mate came back for a second helping.'

'Harry's bedsit was on the second floor of a block. He had to use an intercom to let people in and he had a spyhole in his door. We are as sure as we can be that his killer was there by invitation.'

'Never went to his place. Didn't know that.'

'What about Walter? Would he invite a black man into his house after what happened to Harry?'

The old man shook his head. 'Can't see it.'

Jones nodded. 'What about a young white guy? You said Walter was scared off by what happened to Harry . . . but would that have applied to *all* young men, irrespective of colour?'

In the absence of an answer from Pat, who seemed to flag when his long-held belief that blacks were responsible was undermined, it was Derek Hardy who spoke.

'He brought a lad in here one time,' he said. 'The kid wanted a lager but I refused to serve him alcohol because he didn't look eighteen and he didn't have any ID on him.' He nodded to the notice on the bar. 'Walter was pretty annoyed about it and took him away.'

'How long ago was this?'

'Not sure. A couple of months?'

'Can you give me a description of the lad?'

'Ginger hair . . . bit of a beanpole . . . fifteen or sixteen at a guess. He may have been one of Walter's grandchildren. They seemed pretty close and the kid was carrying a rucksack. I got the impression he'd come to London on a visit.'

*

It was arguable who was more put out when Jackson suddenly appeared at the other end of the bar and signalled to Derek Hardy – she, Jones or Beale. Certainly, none of them looked pleased to see each other. Jackson cursed herself for not recognizing their back views as she came in, and Jones cursed the fact that she was the one who'd interrupted his conversation with the landlord. He wondered how much she'd heard before they noticed her.

'Drinking on duty, Doctor?' he asked sarcastically.

'I might ask you the same, Superintendent.'

There was a brief, uncomfortable silence.

Hardy glanced from one to the other with a look of curiosity on his face. 'What can I do for you, Jacks? If it's Mel you're after, she said she'd be back by ten.'

Jackson glanced at the clock above the bar but seemed in two minds about what to do.

Jones, who thought of her as a decisive woman, couldn't resist a barbed comment. 'Would you like us to move to a table so that you can speak to this gentleman in private?' he asked. 'Presumably it's something you don't want the police to hear.'

'You have a suspicious mind, Superintendent. You'll draw the wrong inferences whatever I do.'

He watched her for a moment. 'I'll admit to being curious about where the lieutenant is. According to Dr Campbell, he's safe as houses . . . couldn't possibly harm anyone . . . because *you* never go out without him. Should I be concerned that you're on your own?'

'He's in my car.'

'Then we don't have a problem.' Jones glanced at his inspector.

'Invite the lieutenant in, Nick. I'd hate Dr Jackson to think I inferred anything from Charles's absence.'

Jackson gave an abrupt sigh. 'He's vomiting into a sick bag . . . and my car has a crumpled offside wing and a flat tyre,' she said. 'As things stand, I can't change the wheel unless someone helps me lever out the wing. I'm running late, I don't have time to wait for the AA, and I was hoping Derek would lend me a hand. I also need to report a damaged bollard fifty yards down the road that's likely to cause an accident.'

'All of which sounds right up our street,' said Jones with a smile as he eased off his stool. 'We'd better take a look, hadn't we?'

Twenty-three

WHILE DI BEALE WENT to check on the bollard, the superintendent accompanied Jackson to the BMW, which was parked on a double yellow line beyond the Crown. The passenger door was open and Acland was sitting immobile in the seat, with his hands in his lap and his head pressed back. The fact that he'd put his jacket back on was of no interest to Jones, who was unaware that he'd ever taken it off, but Jackson noticed it.

She raised her voice unnecessarily. 'Best I could do on the parking front, Superintendent Jones,' she said loudly. 'All the other spaces were taken.'

Jones watched the lieutenant's head jerk away from the seat rest and turn to look at them, but the sudden movement set him heaving into the bag he was holding. There was no question he was ill. The undamaged areas of his face were deathly white, making the grafted skin of his tapering scar seem more prominent than usual, and his hands shook visibly as he lowered the bag into his lap when the bout of nausea ended.

Jones squatted in the open doorway to take a closer look. He thought he could make out areas of bruising around the young man's jawline – a faint blue flush under the skin – although Acland's growth of stubble created its own shadow. There was certainly no mistaking the diagonal weal of the seat belt on the left-hand side of the neck, or the raw split along his bottom lip where his teeth had sliced the flesh. 'You seem to have come off rather worse than the doctor, Charles. She doesn't have a mark on her.'

Jackson spoke before Acland could. 'He didn't know it was going to happen,' she said, propping her hand on the side of the car and dropping to her haunches beside the superintendent. 'He couldn't see the bollard from where he was sitting.'

'Have you called an ambulance?'

'Not yet.'

Gingerly, Acland opened his mouth. 'I don't want an ambulance,' he slurred. 'It's migraine.'

'You look as though you could do with a hospital trip to me. What do you say, Doctor?'

Jackson addressed Acland direct. 'I'd be happier if you went for an X-ray,' she told him. 'That was quite a bang you took to the side of your head. I'd hate to think there are any more fractures in that cheek of yours.'

His mouth lifted in a ghost of a smile. 'Hardly felt it.'

She shook her head. 'I'm not taking you with me,' she said firmly, as if to pre-empt any such request on his part. 'The choice is a trolley in A&E or a bed here for the night . . . assuming Derek agrees to put you up. I can give you an anti-emetic before I go, and you can make your own way to the Bell in the morning. But I'll have to tell Derek you'll need watching. You understand that, don't you?'

Acland nodded. 'Nothing will happen.' He drew a cross on his chest. 'I promise.'

Jackson straightened abruptly, but Jones thought he saw annoyance – *incomprehension?* – in her face before she stepped back. 'People can die from inhaling vomit,' she said to neither in particular. 'It's important to keep an eye on them.'

'You're the expert,' Jones remarked lightly, using the armrest on the door to push himself upright. 'Shall we take a look at the wing?'

The damage wasn't as bad as he was expecting. The collision had been absorbed by the BMW's front offside impact unit, although it was clear that the side of the car had scraped along the bollard for several feet before Jackson managed to steer it free.

The bodywork was dented and scratched from the front wheel arch to the rear door, but to Jones's eye the problems were cosmetic. The flat tyre was genuine, but he was highly doubtful that an untidy chassis would have prevented Jackson from changing the wheel.

'You hit the kerb good and hard,' he said, pointing to a four-inch distortion in the alloy rim. 'A tyre can't hold air when the rubber loses contact with the metal.'

Jackson took a breath. 'I'm aware of that,' she said, struggling to keep the irritation out of her voice.

Jones smiled. 'Interesting accident, Doctor. The lieutenant has some strange injuries for an offside collision. Nearside or front-on, I might accept because of the seat-belt burn –' he touched the left side of his own neck – 'but *offside*? If the impact was hard enough, he should have spilled to the right.'

She shrugged. 'I expect he did initially. I wasn't looking. I was more interested in trying to control the car.'

'Trying?'

'Controlling the car,' she corrected herself. 'What I was *trying* to do was avoid the bollard.'

'Naturally, but why were you driving towards it in the first place?'

She didn't answer.

'Doctor?'

'Temporary loss of concentration,' she said, 'for which I hold my hands up. I was looking at Charles when I should have been looking at the road. I'll inform my insurance company and the council that any damage to public property is my responsibility. Do you want me to take a breathalyser to prove that I was competent to drive?'

'Not my area,' he said with an amused smile, 'but if Inspector Beale's called the traffic police, you may have to.' He bent down to inspect the wheel arch. 'You're lucky the bollard wasn't concrete or you wouldn't have driven away from it. Which bit needs levering out?'

'It's not as bad as I thought.'

'No. More of a scrape than a collision, wouldn't you say? The only real damage is to the wheel rim . . . and to Charles's face, of course.' He straightened again. 'I think the best thing we can do is take him off your hands. Will Ms Wheeler have any objection to keeping an eye on him if we return him to the Bell?'

'She won't be able to. She's running the bar.'

'The same applies to Mr Hardy.' He paused, waiting for an answer. 'It's a genuine offer. The inspector and I can drop the lieutenant off on our way back to the station.'

'He'll need help getting upstairs.'

'I'm sure we can provide that.'

'He needs to lie down as soon as possible. If you're really willing to help, then give me a hand getting him into the Crown. I don't have time to debate alternatives.'

Jones smiled slightly. 'Why do I get the feeling you don't want to leave Charles alone with your partner, Dr Jackson? What are you afraid he'll do?'

'I'm a lot more worried about how Daisy will react,' she said tersely. 'If we end up in another row over the stresses Charles is putting on our relationship, I could find myself homeless.' She bared her teeth in a sarcastic smile. 'It's a lesbian thing, Superintendent.'

*

Beale's reaction to the damaged bollard echoed Jones's view of Jackson's car. Not as bad as he'd been expecting. It was on a raised island in the middle of the road, one of two indicating a pedestrian crossing point between them, and if its twin was anything to go by it had been illuminated before Jackson hit it. The white plastic casing had split longitudinally and the steel structure underneath leaned drunkenly to one side. But it was hardly a hazard to the irregular passing traffic.

He phoned the information through as a low priority, then, much as his boss had done, read the accident from what he could see. Visible tyre tracks before the still-intact bollard suggested Jackson had been braking hard as she approached the first island; fresh scarring along the concrete kerb suggested contact with one or both of her offside wheels; while the state of the second bollard suggested the car had still been steering to the right when she impacted with it.

Intrigued, he approached a young couple who were standing at a bus stop on the other side of the road. 'How long have you been here?'

'Long enough.'

'Did you see a car hit that bollard?'

They both nodded. 'It was two blokes fighting,' said the girl.

'What kind of fighting?'

'The guy who was driving smashed the other one in the face.' The girl shivered. 'We'd be dead if he hadn't. The car was coming straight for us.'

Beale phoned Khan as he walked back towards the Crown. 'Ahmed? Yes, yes . . . still with the boss. I need a couple of favours, mate. Can you get hold of Dick Fergusson and find out if he knows of any crack operations in Kitchener Road? Alongside or behind a pub called the Crown. Right . . . ASAP. The next one's a long shot. Have you ever seen the film *Gattaca*? No? Then you'll have to Google it for me. G – A – T – T – A – C – A. Put in Uma Thurman and bring up her movies.'

He came to a halt while he waited. 'That's it. You should have a cast list with Jude Law and Ethan Hawke at the top. Great. What's the name of the character Uma Thurman plays? Irene Cassini? How's the Cassini spelt?' He listened for a moment. 'Yes,' he agreed slowly, 'that's what I've been wondering. The boss and I saw her an hour ago and she was wearing an identical outfit to the one Uma Thurman wears in the movie. Right . . . try the hostess sites first.'

He was about to ring off when Khan spoke again.

Beale sighed. 'No, of course I haven't read the *Evening Standard*. I've been working non-stop since I left the house twelve hours ago.' He listened again. 'Chalky? Only the description Dr Jackson gave us. Dark-haired . . . bearded . . . mid-fifties. I can't remember the rest of it but it's on the computer. I put out a general alert to the neighbouring forces.'

His face tightened with irritation as Khan went on. 'And you're seriously telling me you only know about this body because you read it in a *newspaper*!'

*

The superintendent was alone when Beale resumed his seat beside him. Pat, the elderly man, had left, the only member of staff on duty was serving a customer at the other end of the bar and there was no sign of Jackson, Hardy or Acland. Jones pushed Beale's untouched pint towards him. 'Drink up,' he said, 'we may have something to celebrate. The doctor parked the lieutenant on a seat over there before she and Mr Hardy took him upstairs, and Pat recognized his undamaged side. Says he saw him in here several times last year when Harry Peel was still alive.'

His number two took a tentative mouthful of beer, expecting it to be flat, and it was. 'With his girlfriend?'

Jones shook his head. 'Always alone, but Pat's fairly sure he would have spoken to Harry. Harry used to hand out cards for his taxi service, apparently . . . claimed face-to-face contact was the best advertisement.'

'What are we going to do? Take him back to the station?'

'He's in no fit state to go anywhere at the moment, and not just from migraine either. He's sporting a cut lip and a seat-belt burn.' Jones raised a questioning eyebrow. 'How hard did they hit the bollard?'

'More of a glancing blow. They can't have been going very fast. The doctor was braking hard enough to leave rubber on the road.' Beale repeated what the young couple had told him. 'At a rough guess, I'd say the lieutenant grabbed the wheel and the only way the doctor could regain control was to punch his lights out. They missed one bollard and hit the other.'

299

Jones nodded. 'I came to the same conclusion. Any ideas on why he'd want to grab the wheel?'

'He doesn't react well to migraine?' Beale suggested. 'He seems to lose his temper when the pain first starts. He lost it with the Pakistani in the pub and he lost it with you. It's only when the retching begins that he becomes incapacitated.'

Jones shook his head. 'He lost it with me because I touched him . . . The same was true of the Pakistani. He may be less able to control his anger when he has a migraine, but I don't think it's the reason he kicks off. He didn't have a migraine outside the bank when Walter poked him, but he still reacted angrily.'

'And walked away without doing anything stupid, Brian,' Beale pointed out. 'Maybe the migraine isn't the initial trigger, but it sure as hell contributes to the violence of his responses. He needs to carry a warning sign . . . steer clear when my head hurts.'

'He's in a bad way at the moment,' said the superintendent thoughtfully. 'The doctor's pumped him full of an anti-emetic and gone off to change her tyre. I think he's expecting her to wash her hands of him.'

'Is that likely?'

'It depends whether she thinks he was trying to kill her. She's covering his arse at the moment by claiming it was her fault – probably because she knows she provoked him – but she may change her mind by the morning. She's mighty pissed off . . . and *very* reluctant to leave him alone with her partner.'

Beale used a finger to stir the beer in his glass, hoping to energize some fizz. 'I had a mate who tried to kill himself in a BMW,' he said idly. 'He drove into a brick wall at forty miles an hour, and walked away without a scratch. Claimed afterwards that he forgot about air bags and didn't know that BMWs were built like tanks.'

'You think Acland was trying to kill himself?'

'He's a mess . . . bit like my friend . . . Can't handle what's happened to him. According to Dr Campbell, he's been trying to end it for months through slow starvation while kidding himself it's a lifestyle choice. Maybe he opted for the more direct approach tonight and decided to take Dr Jackson with him.'

Jones didn't say anything.

'You don't buy that?'

'Some of it,' the superintendent said. 'He's certainly a mess and it wouldn't surprise me if he ends up dead somewhere, but I wouldn't expect it to be through suicide. One day he'll take on someone who's angrier and more messed up than he is.' He paused. 'You could describe that as a death wish, I suppose.'

'So he was taking the doctor on? He wanted her to punch him?'

'Not exactly. I think he wanted to *test* her . . . see how she'd react if control was taken away from her. I'm beginning to wonder if that's why he put a half nelson on me. Pay-back for depriving him of his liberty for six hours.'

Nick Beale was doubtful. 'What was he planning to do if the doctor lost control?'

Jones shrugged. 'Pull on the handbrake . . . Hold the wheel steady . . . Prove his nerve was stronger than hers. They can't have been going more than twenty, not from the damage I saw, and he's been trained to drive a Scimitar at high speed across rough terrain.'

'Then by rights we should notify traffic and tell them a criminal offence has been committed. Whatever his reasons, Acland interfered with the safe operation of a moving vehicle. He's damn lucky the doctor did what she did before they ploughed into those kids at the bus stop.'

'All in good time,' said Brian Jones, pressing his thumb and forefinger to the bridge of his nose. 'At the moment he's under my jurisdiction and I want it to stay that way.'

*

For Derek Hardy the superintendent's 'jurisdiction' was becoming uncomfortable. Having run rural pubs for twenty years before he and his wife were offered the management of the Crown, he was more used to the village bobby showing up in his shirtsleeves for a game of darts than a detective superintendent turning his bar into a new base for operations. Another two policemen had arrived, and Derek and Jackson watched the four men swap information on the CCTV monitor in the kitchen.

'What's going on?' Jackson asked curiously, using a wodge of paper towel to turn the tap in the sink to avoid smearing the chrome.

'You probably know better than I do,' Derek said irritably. 'Everything was fine till you showed up with sonny boy. What's he done?'

'Nothing to concern that lot.'

'Why don't you want Mel going near him?'

Jackson washed her oily hands and wrists at his sink. 'He has a problem with women being nice to him.' She pulled a wry face at his alarmed expression. 'You don't need to go into the room, Derek. Just check from the door that he's breathing. A couple of times should do it. Once the retching stops, he'll go to sleep.'

'You're making me nervous.'

'No reason to be. He gave me his word he'll stay in his room and not bother anyone.' She used the paper towel again to turn off the tap, then wiped the sink with it to remove the last traces of oil. 'I'm more worried that he'll do something to himself, particularly if he knows that lot are still around.' She nodded at the monitor.

'Is he the reason they're here?'

'I don't see how. They didn't know we were coming,' she reminded him. 'What were you talking about when I first walked in?'

'The old boy who was clobbered the other day. He's one of our regulars.'

'Walter Tutting?' Jackson ran off another length of paper towelling. 'They've already interviewed Charles about that assault and he was able to prove he was three miles away when it happened.' She dried between her fingers as she watched Ahmed

Khan pass a piece of paper to Brian Jones. 'It has to be something you told them.'

'Pat Streckle did most of the talking. He and Walter knew the cab driver who was killed.'

'Harry Peel?'

Johnson nodded. 'He used to come in here before Mel and I took over. Did you know him?'

'No.' She folded the towel and put it in the rubbish bin. 'What did you tell them about Walter Tutting?'

'Me? All I did was describe a lad I saw with him once. They were more interested in Pat's views on whether the old boy was a closet gay or not.' He paused. 'Pat recognized your friend. Maybe that's what they're excited about.'

'Charles?'

Derek nodded. 'He told the superintendent he'd seen him in here before.'

Jackson frowned. 'When?'

'Last year . . . said he sat at the bar a few times on his own. Before we arrived,' he added, as if Jackson's frown was an accusation of customer-poaching. 'He doesn't ring any bells with me.'

She pulled her sleeves down and buttoned her cuffs. 'Ever seen a girl who looks like Uma Thurman in here?'

Derek shook his head. 'Who is she?'

'Good question,' said Jackson with a frustrated sigh. 'Charles swore blind to me that he'd never used any of the pubs round here. If he can lie about that, he's almost certainly been lying about his girlfriend.'

Hardy folded his arms and studied her for a moment. 'How the hell did you come to be involved with this bloke?'

'Because I'm a fool,' she said crossly, 'and I'm damned sorry to have wished him on you and Mel. He should sleep through the night, but I'll take him off your hands first thing . . . assuming he's still here.'

'Why wouldn't he be?'

She glanced at the monitor. 'He makes a habit of being in the wrong place at the wrong time,' she said cryptically, 'and it's looking less and less like coincidence.' She moved towards the door. 'He's not your responsibility, Derek. If they transfer him to hospital because they want to question him, then that's something Charles will have to deal with himself. He wouldn't be here at all if he hadn't acted like a prize idiot.'

*

DC Khan, one of the officers who'd joined Jones and Beale in the bar, placed a couple of printouts in front of the superintendent. 'This –' he touched a page – 'is Dr Jackson's description of Chalky, the other gives the details of the man the river police pulled out of the Thames this morning. I've had a word with a chap called Steve Barratt and he's blaming paperwork for why no one made the connection. He said they checked missing persons, but there was no one matching the description.'

Jones leaned forward to scan the pages. 'So what else has dropped through the net? We have phone calls that haven't been followed up . . . statements that haven't been read –' he smacked the back of his hand against Jackson's description – 'and now this. What are we running here? A chimpanzees' tea party?'

'We distributed Chalky's particulars across the whole network, sir.'

'But you didn't think to list him as a missing person?'

'No,' Khan admitted. 'Just that he was wanted for questioning.'

Jones looked irritated. 'What else did this Barratt tell you? Have they done a post-mortem?'

Khan shook his head. 'Not a full one. A pathologist took some blood and temperature readings and had a look at the external features, but there were no signs of foul play. There's a high level of alcohol in the blood. He concluded the man was a vagrant who drowned in the river some twelve hours before his body was recovered . . . and they gave the case a low priority. According to Barratt, vagrants are the hardest to identify. It usually takes months, and no one cares when they finally come up with a name.'

Jones wasn't interested in anyone else's problems. 'What about fingerprints?'

'They weren't planning to run a check until tomorrow, but I've asked Barratt to advance that process and call me when he gets a result.'

'You mean *if* he gets a result. There's no guarantee this dead man was ever convicted of anything.'

'The chances are good, sir.'

'Even so . . . a name isn't going to help us. It still won't tell us if this man was Chalky. We need someone to identify the body.'

DI Beale glanced towards the window. 'Shall I have a word with Dr Jackson before she goes?' he asked. 'I think she's still around and she's the obvious person to do it.'

'Why not?' Jones agreed slowly. 'I'd like to know how she reacts. The lieutenant seems to bring misfortune on everyone he meets.'

*

Beale called out to Jackson as he emerged from the front door and saw her about to climb into her car. She flashed him an exasperated glance and toyed with pretending she hadn't heard. 'What do you want?' she demanded. 'I really need to get on.'

'I'm aware of that.' He handed her the details that Khan had printed out. 'This man was pulled from the river this morning. We believe it might be Chalky but we need someone to identify the body. Would you be willing to help us out? We can wait until you've finished your shift.'

She stooped to read the page by the BMW's internal light. 'Is there any doubt about when he died? It says here that the body temperature suggests late last night.'

'We've no reason to question it.' He studied her expression. 'Why do you ask?'

The struggle she was having with herself showed in her face, but she avoided a direct answer. Instead, she handed the paper back to him. 'The conclusion at the end says the man fell in and drowned while heavily intoxicated, and there's no evidence of foul play. Is there any doubt about *that*?'

Of course Beale was suspicious. She wouldn't be asking the questions if she didn't have doubts. 'We won't know till tomorrow. The pathologist hasn't done a full post-mortem yet.' He folded the page and tucked it into his pocket. 'What aren't you telling me, Doctor?'

'That I might not be as good a judge of character as I thought I was,' Jackson said cryptically. She stared past his shoulder towards the Crown's façade, before giving an abrupt sigh. 'I have no idea where Lieutenant Acland was between midday yesterday and late this afternoon, Inspector. The last time I saw him was outside a squat in Bread Street . . . which is down near the docks . . . and I think he was looking for Chalky.'

Twenty-four

FROM DEREK HARDY'S PERSPECTIVE there seemed to be a period of calm after Jackson's departure. The two detective constables left, and Jones and Beale moved to a vacant table, giving up beer in favour of coffee and sandwiches. They were friendly enough to the landlord and his staff, but they rebuffed any attempt to find out why they were still there. After half an hour, Derek decided they'd abandoned work for the night like any other customer and went to check on Acland.

To avoid waking the man, he eased the door open quietly and looked towards the bed, but a lighted table lamp showed that it was empty. Derek's response was to step into the room and look around, and his stomach lurched uncomfortably when he saw Acland, fully dressed, standing in the shadow behind the door.

'Jesus Christ! You gave me a bloody shock! You all right, mate?'

'What do you want?'

Derek spread his hands to demonstrate his peaceful intent. 'Just doing what Jacks asked me to do . . . making sure you're still breathing.' He started to back out. 'Sorry for the intrusion. I didn't want to make a noise in case you were asleep.'

'Are the police with you?'

The older man shook his head. 'There's a couple downstairs still.'

'I thought you were them.'

'I guessed. You sure you're all right?'

'Yes.'

'Well, you don't look it,' said Derek bluntly. 'You should follow doctor's orders, son, and stay in bed. Jacks said she'll be back for you tomorrow morning.' He watched the young man's shoulders relax slightly. 'Can I get you anything?'

'No, thank you, sir, everything's fine.'

Perhaps it was the courtesy 'sir' and the obvious contradiction between the words and the pallor of Acland's face, or perhaps, like Willis, Derek saw how young the lieutenant really was. In either event, he reached out a fatherly hand. 'Come on,' he said kindly, taking Acland's arm. 'You need to lie down.'

There was a movement in the doorway behind him. 'I wouldn't do that if I were you, Mr Hardy,' said Jones. 'I think you'll find the lieutenant prefers to make his own way.' He walked into the room and looked at Acland's rigid posture. 'That's right, isn't it, Charles?'

'Yes.' He freed his arm and backed into the corner.

Jones nodded pleasantly to the publican. 'Your bar steward gave us permission to follow you up here.' He indicated Beale in the doorway. 'We wanted a quick word with you before we left.'

'What about?'

'It'll wait.' He shifted his genial attention to the lieutenant. 'I hadn't realized you'd be up and about, Charles. We've a couple of questions for you, too, if you can spare us a few minutes. That's not a problem, is it?'

DI Beale watched Acland respond exactly as the superintendent had predicted. 'He'll agree,' Jones had said. 'There's something in his character . . . a bloody-minded determination never to back down . . . that'll push him to confront us however ill he feels.'

'What if he does?' his number two had retorted. 'Anything he says will be discounted as unreliable. The CPA will rule the circumstances oppressive and refuse to admit the evidence.'

'Only if it's incriminating and Charles refuses to repeat it under taped conditions.'

'Why gamble? Why not wait until tomorrow morning and do it properly?'

'Because we're more likely to get the truth out of him tonight.'

'And jeopardize a prosecution in the process,' Beale said with sharp criticism. 'At least consider the rest of the team before you go charging in like a bull in a china shop. We've all worked damned hard on this inquiry and no one's going to thank you for a botched job at the end.'

'Including you?'

'*Especially* me,' the inspector said with emphasis. 'I'll even put on record that I object to any interview with Charles Acland tonight . . . and warn you that, if you insist on going ahead with it, I shall advise the lieutenant to keep his mouth shut.'

Jones ran a thoughtful hand up the side of his jaw. 'You should have been a lawyer, Nick. You're even more of a stickler for the rules than Pearson is. As a matter of interest, what incriminating confession are you expecting Charles to make? Impeding the safe operation of a vehicle on one of Her Majesty's highways?'

Beale refused to be drawn. 'I'm not playing guessing games, Brian. I've told you what I think.'

Jones sighed impatiently. 'But that's all we've been doing for months . . . *guessing* . . . and you're the expert on it, my friend. How many new ideas have you run past me tonight, eh? Ben Russell might have been the ginger-haired lad who came in here with Walter . . . Walter's daughter might have imagined the cheap perfume . . . the prostitutes might have been boys . . . Charles Acland might have pushed Chalky into the river last night after a row over a duffel bag—' He broke off. 'What the hell does that bag have to do with anything?'

*

Derek Hardy shifted uneasily as Beale joined Jones in the room and the two men ranged themselves on the other side of the bed from the lieutenant. 'I'm not sure you should be doing this,' he said. 'You can see the lad's poorly.'

'It's up to Charles,' murmured Jones. 'If he doesn't feel well enough to speak to us, he only has to say so.' He lowered himself on to a hard-backed chair, as if to demonstrate that he knew Acland's mind better than Derek did.

Beale studied the young man's face which, despite its pallor, was set in grim determination to accept the superintendent's challenge. 'You're under no obligation to talk to us now, Lieutenant,' he said firmly. 'If you prefer, you can come to the station tomorrow. Indeed my advice would be to do that. I agree with Mr Hardy, you don't look well enough to answer questions.'

'I'm OK. I'd rather do it now.'

'At least let him lie down,' Derek protested. 'Dr Jackson said he should be in bed.'

'Would you like to do that, Charles?' the superintendent asked. 'No.'

'I didn't think you would.' He smiled. 'And just to reconfirm for these gentlemen's benefit, you're quite willing to answer a few questions? It's purely for background information. I estimate ten minutes or so. Is that acceptable to you?'

'Yes.'

Jones glanced at the landlord. 'Thank you, Mr Hardy. We'll take it from here. Would you mind closing the door as you leave?' He waited until Derek's footsteps had vanished down the corridor. 'There's no requirement to stand to attention, Lieutenant,' he said. 'You're not on parade.'

'You'll think less of me if I don't.'

Jones eyed him with amusement. 'It's certainly more usual to see signs of nerves in the people we interview. Don't you have anything to feel guilty about, Charles? You're a rare man, if so.'

'Nothing that concerns you.'

'Is that right?' Jones crossed his legs and made a play of consulting a notebook that he took from his pocket. 'So why does your name keep cropping up in this inquiry? We've been told you used this pub on a few occasions last year. Is that true?'

'Yes.'

'You always sat alone and cold-shouldered anyone who tried to talk to you.' The inflection of the superintendent's voice took on a judgemental note. 'That suggests you were antisocial even *before* you went to Iraq.'

'If you like.'

'Then I'm genuinely confused. Why would Dr Campbell lead us to believe it's your disfigurement that's caused you to be wary of people?'

'She wouldn't know. She didn't meet me until after I had surgery.'

'She said your commanding officer described you as friendly and outgoing until the accident.'

'He was a good man. I got on with him.' Acland abandoned his rigid posture to press his palms against the wall to support himself. 'And the attack on my Scimitar was *not* an accident, Superintendent. It was a targeted explosion that killed two of my troopers.'

'I apologize,' Jones said immediately. 'It wasn't my intention to belittle what happened . . . or your part in it. To call it an accident is to suggest that two brave lives were wasted through negligence.' He met the lieutenant's gaze. 'And that would certainly be something to feel guilty about.'

Acland stared back at him. 'You don't even know what bravery is.'

'Then tell me.'

But Acland shook his head.

'Is it about proving you have bigger balls than the person next to you? Is that why you tried to steer Dr Jackson off the road tonight? To see what she's made of?'

A spark – *an acknowledgement that Jones was right?* – glinted in the younger man's good eye. 'Is that what she's told you?'

Jones ignored the question. 'Why did you need to test her? What did she do to provoke you?'

'Talked too much.'

'About what?'

'Sex.'

Jones lifted an eyebrow. 'With whom?'

'No one in particular. She was telling me about the types she fancies and the types she doesn't.'

'So it was a discussion about gay sex?'

'I wouldn't describe it as a discussion.'

'A lecture?'

'Something along those lines.'

Jones was sceptical – he couldn't imagine Jackson delivering a monologue on same-sex relationships to anyone as fastidious about the subject as Charles Acland – but he didn't press the issue. 'Did Dr Jackson know you'd used this pub before when she brought you here?'

'I wouldn't think so. I haven't mentioned it to her.'

'Did you ever come across a man called Harry Peel in here? Taxi driver . . . five feet ten . . . late fifties . . . dark curly hair . . . London accent. Ring any bells?'

Acland shook his head. 'I came in here to get away from things, not to talk to people.'

Jones noted the '*get away from things*' but let the remark go for the moment. 'That wouldn't have prevented Harry from approaching you,' he said. 'He was one of the regulars. Everyone describes him as a friendly sort who'd strike up a conversation with anyone. He used to hand out cards for his taxi service. Are you certain you don't remember him?'

A flicker of something showed in Acland's face – *recognition?* – but he gave another slow shake of his head.

'He sat at the far end of the bar with a couple of older men and only drank orange juice because of his job.'

'I vaguely remember some older men – I think they were always there – but I don't remember anyone else.'

Jones watched him closely. 'Do you recall seeing either of those men outside the pub?'

'No.'

'One of them was the old fellow at the bank . . . Walter Tutting. Are you sure you didn't recognize him when he started poking you?'

'No,' said Acland again, frowning at the superintendent in what appeared to be genuine puzzlement. 'I thought he was a complete stranger.'

'Then you're either very bad on faces or you had a lot to think about when you were sitting at the bar.'

'It was a long time ago,' said Acland. 'I came in here maybe four or five times during June and July last year. A lot's happened since.'

Jones nodded. 'You said you wanted to get away from things. What kind of things?'

The lieutenant didn't answer immediately. He bought himself some time by running his tongue across his lips and feeling at the cut on the right-hand side of his mouth. 'We were heading off to Oman for desert training throughout August. The logistics of organizing something like that does your head in after a while. It helps to have some space to get away from it.'

He was a bad liar, thought Jones. 'Didn't your girlfriend give you space?'

'She wasn't happy about me going to Oman.'

Jones nodded. 'So it was Ms Morley, rather than logistics, who was doing your head in?' He paused. 'Is that why you were always alone?'

Acland didn't answer.

'Harry Peel was murdered on or around 9 September 2006. Do you recall if you were in London that weekend, Charles?'

Beale watched the lieutenant brace his legs to support himself against the wall. To his eyes, Acland looked close to collapse and he was intrigued by the need the man seemed to have to demonstrate his toughness to the detective superintendent. He had a sneaking feeling that it was being done out of respect, but whether the respect was for Jones or for the power he exercised as a policeman, Beale couldn't tell. Nor was it clear if Acland had even understood the question, because he continued to look at Jones with the same mystified frown that he'd worn when he'd said he hadn't recognized Walter Tutting.

'Will your regiment have records of your weekends out?' Jones asked.

Acland nodded. 'But I can tell you myself. I *was* in London that weekend. I returned from Oman three days earlier on 6 September.'

'So you came to see Jen after a month's absence?'

'Yes.'

'Was she glad to see you?'

Silence.

Jones checked another date in his notebook. 'What about 23 September?' He looked up. 'Were you in London then as well? If it helps to jog your memory, it was the weekend before you went to Iraq.'

Both men expected him to ask why that date was important, but he didn't. Instead, he gave another nod. 'I was at Jen's flat on the Saturday. I went back to my base in the evening.'

'What time did you arrive at the flat?'

'Midday.'

'How long were you there?'

'A couple of hours.'

'Where did you go afterwards? You must have spent time somewhere else if you didn't return to your base until the evening.'

'The Imperial War Museum.'

Jones looked sceptical. 'Is that the recommended way to prepare for war?'

'It was my way.'

'Which exhibitions did you see?'

'The Holocaust . . . a film about crimes against humanity.'

'Heavy stuff,' murmured Jones. 'You can't get much closer to the dark side of man's nature than films about the brutality of war. So why did you need to remind yourself that soldiers don't always behave with honour, Charles?' He paused briefly. 'What happened between you and Ms Morley that day?'

'We decided to go our separate ways.'

Jones turned a page in his notebook and tapped his thumb

against a paragraph. 'Before or after you buggered her?' The question was blunt enough to cause a reaction.

Acland's hands shook visibly against the wall as he stared at the superintendent. 'Is that why you're here? Is that what these questions are about?'

'Rape is a serious accusation, Charles . . . more so when the victim's a woman and the man's taste is to bugger her.'

DI Beale stirred. 'You'd be well advised to take that on board, Lieutenant. If you're wise, you'll refuse to answer any more questions without a solicitor present.'

Acland glanced at him with a look of bewilderment, as if he'd forgotten there was anyone else in the room. 'How's a solicitor going to help me? You'll believe Jen whatever I say.'

'Why assume that?' Jones asked.

'The police always take the woman's side.'

The superintendent shook his head. 'The stats prove the opposite. Only a third of cases ever make it as far as court. The other two-thirds drop out at the police stage. It's very difficult for a woman to substantiate rape . . . particularly months after the event.' He eyed Acland thoughtfully. 'Unless the man admits it, of course.'

Twenty-five

IT WASN'T UNTIL JACKSON had finished her second house call after leaving the Crown that she opted to save time and cut security corners by putting her case into the back of the BMW rather than into the boot. As soon as she opened the door, she saw the duffel bag on the floor. Whatever was in it wasn't big enough to fill it and the bag was collapsed in on itself, lying on its side, half-wedged under the driver's seat. Jackson's understanding of what it was, and how it had arrived there, was immediate. She recalled Acland's effete pose with his jacket and a knot of alarm tightened in her gut as she made the inevitable link with the body in the Thames.

Her first instinct was a craven desire to slam the door and pretend she hadn't seen it. There was no reason why she should have done, except that she'd chosen to stow her case on the back seat. If she continued with her shift, only she would know that she didn't spot the bag until the early hours and the imperative to do her job was a great deal stronger than the less attractive imperative of making another trip to Southwark East police station.

Her second instinct – governed as much by curiosity as by common sense – was to check the contents. The shape inside the canvas folds suggested a conical object and she had no intention of spending an hour explaining to a bored policeman why the bag might be important . . .

. . . only to be told she'd handed in an empty wine bottle.

*

Acland repositioned himself against the wall, retreating as far as he could into the corner. 'What does my relationship with Jen have to do with your taxi driver?' he asked Jones.

'Who says I'm talking about the taxi driver? A civil servant called Martin Britton was killed the weekend of 23 September.' He could see from the lieutenant's expression that he wasn't telling him anything he didn't already know. 'He worked for the MOD. Perhaps you ran into him at the Imperial War Museum.'

'I didn't.'

The superintendent shrugged. 'You were angry that weekend. You might have lost your temper with anyone.'

Acland shook his head.

'You lost it with Jen.'

'The anger was all on her side.'

'Why?'

'She was happy to take my money but she didn't enjoy what I did to her.'

Jones frowned. 'You paid her for sex?'

Acland nodded.

'Why would you treat her like a prostitute, Charles?'

'Because that's what she is.'

Jones didn't argue the point. 'And you thought payment constituted consent?'

'That was the agreement.' His mouth twisted. 'She made the deal and told me to do my worst. She was laughing at the beginning . . . wasn't so keen afterwards.'

'When did you find out she was on the game?'

'The day I ditched her.'

'Which was when?'

'Three days after I returned from Oman.'

Jones eyed him curiously. 'The weekend of the 9th?'

'Yes.'

'You must have been angry that day as well, Charles. It doesn't do anything for a man's confidence to find out he's been sharing his fiancée with every Tom, Dick and Harry in town.' He paused, waiting for an answer. 'Did you rape Jen that day as well?'

'No.'

'Too shell-shocked to do anything? Couldn't believe you'd been so gullible?'

Silence.

'So you went back two weeks later and punished her with the roughest sex you could think of. It doesn't work that way, Charles. Prostitutes have rights, too, you know.'

'Not when they take your money and refuse to honour the contract they don't.'

'How does telling you to go ahead and do your worst constitute refusal?'

'She wasn't planning to go through with it.'

Jones looked enquiringly at DI Beale. 'Are you following any of this?'

'I think the lieutenant's saying there were two different agendas operating. His and Ms Morley's. For whatever reason, he was willing to pay for a sex act . . . and, for whatever reason, she thought she could pocket the money without obliging him. I'm guessing, because of the relationship they'd had, she believed she knew him well enough to assume he wouldn't demand his rights as a client.'

'Is that correct, Charles?'

'Pretty much.'

'Why did she think she could get away with it?'

'She thought she knew me.'

The superintendent's frown deepened. 'What were you doing in her flat that day? Was your only intention to have sex?'

'No. I went to collect my stuff before I went to Iraq. She wasn't supposed to be there. I still had a key.'

'So she broke her word twice?'

'Three times. There was nothing to collect. She'd destroyed most of it.'

'And that made you angry?'

'Everything about her made me angry. I hated her . . . she repulsed me.' Acland spoke with real loathing. 'I didn't even want to touch her. I sure as hell didn't want her touching me.'

Jones was less perplexed by the ambiguity behind this statement than some of the others Acland had made. The line between love and hate was a thin one. 'So you decided to punish her instead . . . and paid for the right to do it?'

'Only to show her how it feels to be treated like a laboratory rat.'

'What does that mean?'

'If you press the right button you get a reward . . . if you press the wrong one you get an electric shock.'

*

Jackson stooped to pull the duffel bag upright. It was softer than it looked, made of hemp rather than canvas, and the contents were heavier than she was expecting. If there was a bottle inside, it was full. She untied the strings at the top and pulled the opening wide to disclose a plastic carrier bag loosely wrapped around a rigid object about twelve inches long. With belated caution, she swivelled the hemp bag to allow the object to lean against the back of the driver's seat in order to retrieve some medical gloves from her case, but as she let go of the opening, the hemp fabric, unsupported, fell in folds over further objects at the bottom, at least one of which was visible.

At first glance, she thought it was a mobile telephone, until she noticed the two strips of embossed metal at the top and knew she was looking at a stun gun.

*

Beale felt instinctively that his boss had taken the wrong route when Jones chose to ask Acland how Jen had rewarded him. There was a slight relaxation of the lieutenant's stiff posture when the superintendent homed in on sex as a currency within the relationship. 'Did you have to negotiate for intimacy? Did Jen only sleep with you when you behaved the way she wanted?'

'More or less.'

'Most men would find that demeaning.' He watched Acland for a moment. 'More so if she had to get high just to go through the motions.'

No response.

'We saw her outside the pub earlier. She had a client waiting in a taxi and we think she was on her way back from her dealer.' Jones pulled what passed for a sympathetic smile. 'It's not easy to get excited about sex when you're only doing it to feed a habit, Charles. You shouldn't have taken Jen's lack of enthusiasm to heart.'

It was a deliberate needle but Acland met his gaze unflinchingly. 'I didn't. I got out.'

'You punished her.'

'Not as much as I wanted to. You asked me the other day why I travelled so light . . . well, that's why. There was nothing left after she slashed my clothes and trashed the rest. I had a new laptop. It was in pieces on the floor.'

DI Beale stepped in when his boss didn't say anything. 'What did she use to smash it, Lieutenant?'

There was a slight hesitation. 'Probably a hammer. I kept a tool box at her flat.'

Beale nodded as if the matter were of little importance. 'She obviously has a violent streak,' he said idly. 'Did she use ever the hammer against you?'

Acland's expression closed abruptly. 'No.'

'Are you sure? You called yourself a laboratory rat earlier . . . talked about pressing the wrong buttons. Did you discover too late that you'd signed up to a coke-addicted bunny-boiler instead of an Uma Thurman fantasy?'

*

Jackson stared down at the exposed wooden club. She was no expert in African artefacts but the polished rounded head and stock reminded her of a picture she'd seen of a Zulu knobkerrie. There was no reason for her to place any particular significance on it – the police hadn't shared their forensic findings with her – but the hairs on the back of her neck bristled anyway. She'd read enough of the newspaper coverage to know that the three victims of the 'gay killer' had been beaten to death.

Of rather more weight in her decision to step away, leave everything as it was and call the police to come to her were the two mobiles lying beside the stun gun, one of which had a strip of Dynotape stuck to its front . . .

. . . saying 'Harry Peel'.

*

Jones uncrossed his legs and leaned forward. 'I think it was *you* who was the abuser, Charles. You've got a real temper on you when you're angry, and we all know how undignified it is having to beg for sex.'

Acland moved his palms to gain a better purchase against the wall. 'You obviously know more about that than I do.'

Jones smiled slightly. 'I've never been reduced to raping a woman because I couldn't get it any other way. And I don't go looking at Holocaust exhibitions to wallow in misery over my own behaviour either. Did that make you feel better . . . salve your conscience . . . because the Nazis had done worse to the Jews?'

Acland took a shallow breath and put his head back. 'That's not how it was.'

'Oh, yes, I forgot. You and Ms Morley had a business deal . . . compensation for a broken laptop. That's some revenge from a man who claims not to care about possessions.'

'You don't know the first thing about it.'

'I know this much, you don't behave like a man who's at peace with himself. What are you ashamed of? That you regularly beat her . . . or that you allowed her to do it to you?'

Silence.

'I'm guessing you came in here to drown your sorrows . . . to *think* about things.' He put a cynical stress on the words. 'Did you target Harry Peel because he annoyed you? You wouldn't be the first pussy-whipped man to take out his frustrations on a complete stranger.'

Beale made another move to intervene. Jones's relentless belittling provocation was driving the lieutenant deep into the corner. His pallor was catastrophic. Even his lips were bloodless. 'You have to stop, Brian. This is too much. He needs a doctor.'

With an irritated sigh, Jones stood up and shoved his chair in front of Acland. 'For God's sake, sit down before you fall over. What makes you think a trained soldier is any better equipped to deal with a violent woman than the rest of us? If we fight back, we give her the opportunity to paint herself as a victim . . . If we don't, we're in danger of taking a knife between the ribs. Why would you want to defend her?'

Acland ran his tongue around the inside of his mouth to generate some saliva but, even so, his voice sounded brittle when he spoke. 'I'm defending myself.'

'Against what?'

'Whatever your next accusation's going to be.' His tongue rasped against his dry palate. 'Last time it was Mr Tutting . . . This time you started with a taxi driver who was murdered . . . then a civil servant . . . Now it's rape and humiliation.'

Jones pointed to the chair. 'Sit down,' he ordered peremptorily. 'I'm damned if I'll end up in another fight because I have to force you.' He watched Beale pour a glass of water, then perched on the side of the bed as Acland lowered himself on to the chair. 'I want to know why you came back to Bermondsey and why you're involved in this investigation.'

Acland took the water with a muttered 'Thank you' and drank it at one swallow, before bending forward to place the glass on the floor then pressing his left hand to his eyepatch. 'Maybe you should ring Dr Campbell and ask her to explain synchronicity to you.'

'I don't follow.'

'If you look for meaning in random events, you'll probably find it.'

*

Jackson's call was put through to DC Khan. As he listened to what she had to say, he was reading an email on his monitor.

> 'Re urgent request for fingerprint identification on body taken from river this a.m. Match found with Paul Hadley, 68. Awaiting trial on indecent assault charges against a minor. Registered address 23 Albion Street, Peckham SE15. No known family. Photograph attached.

He clicked on the attachment and stared at the mug shot of Paul Hadley.

'I hear what you say, Dr Jackson, and I understand your frustrations, but first I'd appreciate confirmation of a photograph I have on my computer. I think it has a bearing on what you've found in your car. Do you have a 3G mobile? I'd like you to confirm whether the man in the photograph is the one you know as Chalky.'

*

'Why should I accept that any of this is random?' asked Jones. 'You drank in the same pub as Harry Peel . . . you were in possession of Kevin Atkins's mobile . . . and you spoke to Walter Tutting a couple of hours before he was attacked. I'm looking for connections, not meanings.'

'It amounts to the same thing.'

'Not in my book it doesn't. Anyone can invent meaning after the event – it depends how irrational you're prepared to be – my job is about understanding causes.'

'I didn't know you'd be here tonight,' Acland pointed out, 'so this interview is entirely random . . . and all in your favour. It wouldn't be happening if I'd let Jackson take me back to the Bell.'

'Why didn't you?'

'I needed to think about things.'

The irony wasn't lost on Jones and he gave a low laugh. Leaning forward on their respective seats – the superintendent on the bed and the lieutenant on the chair – their heads were only inches apart, and they seemed in thrall to a mutual respect rather than a mutual enmity. 'So you decided to steer Dr Jackson's car towards the Crown.'

Acland shrugged. 'Even if I did, I still didn't know you were going to be here. Chance works in different ways for different people, so you and I will never take the same meaning from anything.'

'We might if we agree that the end result is satisfactory.'

Acland raised his head slightly. 'And if we don't?'

'The only way that could happen is if you're the person we're looking for,' the superintendent said reasonably. 'Or you're shielding someone.'

A tiny smile lit Acland's eye. 'Or I don't *give* a shit. We're just rats in a cage . . . you, the inspector and me . . . acting out our alpha, beta and omega roles. Maybe I'm bored with the whole stupid game.'

'You've got quite a thing about rats.'

'Only the caged ones.'

'So who's the omega? You? On what basis? That you're passive in every situation . . . or that you allow alphas to dominate you?'

'You and the inspector are doing a pretty good job at the moment.'

Jones gave a grunt of genuine amusement. 'We're doing a lousy job, Charles. An omega would have run for cover as soon as we entered the room. We see that type all the time. They hide behind solicitors, lie their heads off and duck into the nearest bolt hole the minute we turn our backs.'

'Maybe I'm just keeping my head down while you throw your weight around. That's pretty standard omega behaviour.'

'Is that how you dealt with Ms Morley?'

Acland held his gaze. 'Why are you so interested in Jen?'

'I'm far more interested in you, Charles. You react violently in certain situations and I want to know why.'

'I'm angry about what happened to me and my men.'

'Rightly so . . . but that's not what makes you fire off when you're touched. You'd be getting into fights all the time if resentment was your driving force.'

'Except you've already cleared me of the attack on Mr Tutting, and I can prove I was back on my base by the early evening on both the dates you mentioned.'

Jones stared at him, wondering why he'd waited so long to offer a defence. Was everything a test of nerve with Acland, a need to see how much pressure he could absorb before he issued a challenge of his own? 'We'll certainly check on that,' he said. 'Presumably your regiment keeps records—' He broke off as his mobile started ringing. 'Excuse me.' He straightened and took the phone from his pocket.

The caller was DC Khan but, after giving a clear indication that he wasn't able to speak freely, Jones let the constable do most of the talking. Bar a couple of requests to clarify information, the superintendent's longest speech came at the end. 'Agreed. Send a couple of uniforms here. The inspector and I will wait. Just make sure nothing's moved until we get there. We'll be with the SOCO team in thirty minutes max.'

He tucked the mobile away and turned his concentration back on Acland, staring at him intently for several seconds. 'What's Dr Jackson ever done to you, Charles?'

'Nothing. I like her . . . rather a lot as a matter of fact. Has she found the bag?' He gave a hint of a smile at Jones's expression. 'I could have got rid of it, you know. I carried it around for twenty-four hours before I put it behind Jackson's seat. Hasn't she worked that out yet?'

'Not by the sound of it. According to DC Khan, she's furious about having to cancel her patient list again. Why did you leave her to find it? Why didn't you hand it to me when I came to the car?'

'I wasn't ready.'

Jones could just about accept that. 'You could have told Dr Jackson at least.'

Acland focused his attention on the carpet in front of him. 'I was trying to. I just hadn't got round to it. I thought she'd be less spooked if she found it herself. One of things in the bag belongs to me.'

'So you know what's in it?'

'Yes.'

Jones rose to his feet. 'Then I won't be asking you any more questions tonight.' He stared down at Acland's bent head. 'Are you well enough to spend the night in a cell? The alternative is to sit on a chair in a waiting room until I'm ready for you.'

'A cell will be fine.'

'You won't be under arrest, but I will be placing you in the charge of two uniformed officers. If for any reason you feel you're not fit enough to travel in the back of a police car—'

Acland straightened. 'I'm OK, sir. You don't need to worry about me.'

Jones gave a sigh of pure frustration. 'You're a flaming bloody nuisance, Charles. I don't know whether to admire you for your guts or despise you for your stupidity. What am I supposed to believe here? That you're the victim of another unfortunate coincidence?'

Acland's mouth twisted into an approximation of a smile. 'It sure as hell looks that way,' he said.

Twenty-six

JACKSON WAS LEANING AGAINST a pillar box, playing chess on her mobile, when Jones and Beale drew up behind her car. She acknowledged them with a nod, but showed no impatience when they spent fifteen minutes with the three-man SOCO team who were working on the contents of the back seat. Whatever irritation she'd felt earlier seemed to have evaporated.

'I'm sorry about this, Dr Jackson,' said the superintendent, finally walking over to speak to her. 'I realize we're making your life difficult.'

'Not your fault,' she said, closing out the game. 'Not mine either . . . but I wouldn't blame you if you thought otherwise. I seem to be making a habit of bringing hot telephones to your attention.'

'Courtesy of Lieutenant Acland.'

'He's the only other person who could have put the bag in the car. I'm assuming he left it for me on purpose, otherwise he'd have told you about it at the pub. I was hardly going to miss it. I only had to open the back door.'

'Why would he do that, do you think?'

'Fear?' she suggested. 'He was terrified when I identified Atkins's mobile . . . wanted to abandon the whole idea of reporting it because he thought he'd be first in the firing line. I imagine he feels the same about being associated with Harry Peel.' She paused. 'I've been wondering why he didn't dump the bag as a matter of fact. He could have distanced himself immediately if he'd left it for someone else to find.'

'Or thrown it in the Thames and got rid of it altogether?'

Jackson nodded. 'That, too. I don't say I'm happy to be landed with the responsibility, but he deserves some credit for doing the right thing . . . even if it was in a roundabout way.'

'He told us he walked around for twenty-four hours before he put the bag in your car. Is that a likely time-frame?'

She frowned. 'Have you questioned him already?'

'Briefly. It's a significant find, Dr Jackson.'

'That's no excuse to badger a sick man.'

'I agree,' said Jones with a blatant disregard for truth, 'which is why we kept the questions to a minimum. When did you leave him yesterday?'

'Midday.'

'And you're sure he had the bag with him when you met up again this evening?'

'Pretty sure.'

'He said something in it belongs to him. Have you any idea what that might be?'

Jackson shrugged. 'I haven't seen all the contents. I backed off as soon as I spotted Harry Peel's phone. Is there a wallet? Maybe that belongs to Charles.'

Jones shook his head. 'I didn't get the impression he'd added anything to the contents. I think whatever he was referring to was already there.' He glanced at Beale who'd just joined them. 'Would you agree?'

The inspector nodded. 'He seemed to think you'd be spooked by one of the objects. He says it belongs to him.'

Jackson looked surprised. 'Surely he'd be more worried about your reactions.'

'He was answering a question from the superintendent about why he'd kept you in the dark. He said he'd been working round to telling you.'

'The stun gun might have spooked me,' she admitted. 'I'd question the motives of any man who carried one of those little bastards. Can you think of an easier way to overpower a woman than to have her twitching on the ground for fifteen seconds, unable to defend herself?'

Jones nodded. 'We're interested in the stun gun,' he agreed. 'The other objects are a wooden club – we think a Zulu knobkerrie – two mobile phones – one of which would appear to be Harry Peel's – a packet of baby wipes and some throat lozenges. Might any of those belong to the lieutenant? Did he say anything that might have given you a clue?'

Jackson looked from one to the other. 'He said he'd left some African artefacts in his ex's flat,' she said slowly, describing how Acland had gone to look through Jen's window. 'I've been wondering about it ever since I found the knobkerrie. Do you think he was checking to see if his was still there? If he could spot it in her room, it would mean *that* one –' she nodded towards the car – 'had nothing to do with him.'

Jones looked sceptical. 'What makes you think he wasn't setting you up to repeat a convenient lie? It sounds like smoke and mirrors to me. How many knobkerries are there in London? Wouldn't he have recognized his own as soon as he saw it?'

'It wouldn't stop him checking. *I'd* have checked if I'd found something I thought was mine next to a mobile with Harry Peel's name on it.'

'Or you'd have spent twenty-four hours working out a story. The lieutenant's not a fool. If he says he left a knobkerrie in Ms Morley's flat – backed by your interpretations of his actions – and she says he *didn't*, then we're no further forward.'

Jackson eyed him curiously. 'I'm obviously way off-beam here. I thought this was Ben Russell's bag, the one that Charles said Chalky nicked.'

Jones spread his hands in a gesture of bafflement. 'We're as confused as you, Dr Jackson. For all we know, the bag has always been in Lieutenant Acland's possession.'

She studied him for a moment. 'No,' she said with sudden

conviction. 'You wouldn't know it existed but for Charles. First he told you Chalky had taken it . . . then he left it for me to find. Why would he keep drawing attention to it if it ties him to Harry Peel?'

'Smoke and mirrors,' said Beale, echoing his boss's earlier statement. 'Unless you noticed the bag yourself last Friday – which you say you didn't – we've only Charles's word that it was ever in your boot. He's accused both Ben and Chalky of handling it, but the only way we'll know if he was telling the truth is if we find their fingerprints or DNA on any of the objects. If we *don't* –' he shrugged – 'if we only find Charles's – he'll be able to claim they got there when he searched the bag yesterday.'

It was Jackson's turn to look sceptical. 'If that's the way your mind works, I'm not surprised he wanted me to turn the stuff in. He didn't have to do it at all . . . He could have dumped the lot and walked away from the responsibility.' She searched their faces. 'Why tempt fate if he's guilty? It doesn't make sense.'

'He enjoys taking risks,' said Jones thoughtfully. 'He's obsessed with chance, feels there should be meaning in random events.'

'You would be, too, if you'd lost your eye, your career and your crew in an indiscriminate explosion that was aimed at the first vehicle that passed a particular point,' said Jackson bluntly. 'He understands malign fate extremely well . . . probably because he's suffered quite a lot of it in the last few months.'

Jones eyed her curiously. 'Why have you changed your mind, Doctor? You looked close to washing your hands of Charles earlier . . . and DC Khan said you were blowing a gasket when he spoke to you on the phone.'

'The wonders of modern technology,' she said, opening her phone again and scrolling through her menu before turning the screen to the superintendent. 'This isn't Chalky. The face is too thin . . . and the beard and hair too grey. I'd describe this man as a goatee-wearing professor type. Chalky was more of a grizzly bear

. . . wild beard with a square, heavy-featured face. I've told DC Khan I'll confirm it formally by looking at the body later, but I guarantee this isn't the man I saw in the alleyway.'

'It was dark,' Jones reminded her.

'He was a passenger in my car for twenty minutes. Even if I hadn't had a good look at him when he climbed in beside me, I had a clear view of his profile during the journey. Chalky's nose was broken. This guy's isn't.'

Ahmed Khan had already passed this information to Jones. 'I hadn't realized you were so worried about what the lieutenant might have done to Chalky,' he murmured. 'You obviously think Charles is capable of violence.'

Jackson tucked the mobile into her pocket. 'I know he is,' she said matter-of-factly. 'I saw what he did to you at the station, and to Rashid in the pub . . . but he didn't kill either of you, and the only weapons he used were his hands.' She placed a meaty elbow on the top of the pillar box and stared towards her car. 'Why are you so interested in the stun gun?'

'For the same reason you gave. That particular model packs a million volts. Anyone touched by it would be unable to defend himself for two or three minutes . . . possibly longer. They're illegal in this country, so it must have been smuggled in from abroad . . . which may well rule out Ben and Chalky.'

'Meaning it's Charles's?'

'It's a possibility. He's laying claim to something in that bag that he thought would worry you . . . and the first thing you nominated was the stun gun. You said you'd be very suspicious of a man who used an electric pulse to subdue a woman in order to rape her.'

Jackson shifted her attention back to the superintendent. 'Are you suggesting Charles would do that?'

Jones shrugged. 'You tell me, Doctor. All I know is, he has a real problem talking about the last time he saw Ms Morley . . . and that was shortly after he returned from a training exercise in the Middle East. It wouldn't be hard to hide a stun gun in a kitbag.'

*

Jackson wasn't amused to be informed by DI Beale a few minutes later that her car would have to be towed to a laboratory for examination under controlled conditions. He talked apologetically about contamination. 'Two of the people who might have handled the bag have travelled in your car – Chalky and the lieutenant – so we need to be very precise about the location of DNA evidence. We also need to look for fibres in the boot. If we find a match with the bag, it will go some way to substantiating Charles's claim that Chalky took it.'

'Only some way?'

'He could have put it there himself when you came into the pub.'

'And taken it *out* again?' she asked sarcastically.

'It's a possibility.'

Jackson gave an impatient sigh. 'You seem very set on Charles's guilt. I don't give much for his chances with you and the superintendent against him. Are you even *looking* for anyone else?'

*

Chalky opened a bloodshot eye and blinked into the beam of the torch that was shining in his face. 'You'd better not be who I think you are. I *hate* cops!'

DC Khan turned the torch to illuminate the two uniformed constables beside him. 'I'm afraid you're out of luck, Chalky. We've been searching all over for you. Are you willing to cooperate or are we going to have to arrest you? Either way, you'll be coming with us.'

'Who let you in?'

'Your lady friends.'

'Two-timing bitches!' The corporal raised his voice. 'You *hear* me, you fuckers! This is the last time I do favours for dykes.'

Avril spoke from the doorway. 'Seems to me it's us who's done you the favour. A bit of shoplifting, you said . . . no harm done. So how come we get served with a search warrant, eh? And how come there's four more of these bozos downstairs guarding the exits. What you been up to, Chalky?'

He covered his face with his arm to block out the light. 'Took the word of a bloody officer,' he said. 'Arrogant bastard! Should have known he couldn't be trusted.'

*

'I'm afraid we need to impose on your time a little longer,' said the superintendent as he and Jackson stood side by side, watching her BMW disappear down the road on the back of a recovery vehicle. 'Chalky – or a man we believe to be Chalky – was picked up ten minutes ago from a squat in Bread Street. It would be helpful if you could identify him for us.'

'The ladies' squat? How come they let you in?'

'They didn't fancy the alternative,' Jones told her with a small laugh. 'Given the choice between handing over the man tonight or having every inch of their property searched tomorrow under an official warrant, they traded Chalky. They don't seem to like him very much.'

'The woman who runs the squat doesn't like people she can't manage . . . and I imagine Chalky's a bit of a nightmare when he's drunk.' She stooped for her medical case, which had only been released from the car after she threatened to sue the Metropolitan Police for depriving her of her livelihood. 'Is Charles still at the Crown?'

'No. He was removed about an hour ago after agreeing to spend the night in a cell. You're welcome to check on him back at the station. He's not under arrest and I don't have a problem with you talking to him.'

Jackson eyed the superintendent thoughtfully. 'Why so gener-ous suddenly? What if I repeat your suspicions to him?'

'I wouldn't advise it, Doctor. If he changes his story now, he'll be digging an even bigger hole for himself.'

*

Chalky was already in the interview room when Jones and Beale returned with Jackson. They watched him on the monitor as he sat swearing at the uniformed constable who was in the room with him. 'He's not happy,' said Khan. 'He's claiming wrongful identity . . . harassment . . . false imprisonment . . . and anything else you can imagine. I've offered him legal representation, but he doesn't like solicitors either.'

Jones turned to Jackson. 'Doctor?'

She nodded. 'That's the man I know as Chalky.'

'Is he drunk?' Jones asked Khan.

'Claims he isn't. It's one of his beefs as a matter of fact. He says the women keep hiding their bottles and cans, and he hasn't had a decent bevvy in days.' He paused. 'Apart from a bottle of vodka that the lieutenant gave him yesterday.'

'So he admits meeting the lieutenant?'

'Not in so many words. He mentioned taking the word of an arrogant bastard officer . . . then a little bit later he said the arrogant bastard had bribed him with a bottle of vodka. I'm assuming he was referring to the lieutenant.'

'Mm. Well, I suggest we don't make any assumptions at this stage . . . except that he's sober. You're not going to tell me different, are you, Doctor? He looks fit enough to answer questions to me.'

'If you want a professional opinion that you can use in court, then you'll have to let me examine him.'

'That's not a bad idea. It'll be interesting to see how he reacts to you. I wouldn't mind him knowing his card's been marked by someone who can recognize him.'

*

The smell in the room was ferocious. 'Don't you know anything about hygiene, Chalky?' asked Jackson amiably. 'You're stinking worse than the last time I saw you.'

He glared at her. 'What you doing here? Where's the lootenant? Fucking bastard conned me . . . gave me his word he wouldn't let on where I was.'

'He didn't,' she said. 'It was me who suggested you might be at the squat.'

Chalky spat on the floor. 'Bloody interfering women . . . Can't let a man alone . . . Got to be at him all the time. How's the kid?'

'Still in hospital but doing all right.'

'He's the one they should be talking to. What the fuck do *I* know? You do a favour for a little toerag and the next thing you're banged up in the sodding nick. It ain't fair. I was planning on hoofing it down to Brighton tomorrow . . . Get me some R&R by the sea.'

'Let's hope you still can,' said Jackson pleasantly. 'As I understand it, you're not under arrest.'

'Amounts to the same bloody thing. Me and the cops don't see eye to eye on much.'

'Then the sooner you're out of here the better. They've asked me to assess whether you're sober enough to answer questions. What's your opinion?'

He looked at her through narrowed lids, a calculating gleam in his eyes. 'Wouldn't know what it feels like . . . Haven't been sober for twenty years. Can't answer questions in the state I'm in.'

'You might find the alternative worse,' Jackson warned him. 'You'll suffer withdrawal symptoms if the police keep you on ice until the alcohol's out of your bloodstream. You seem pretty alert to me and I'm willing to give them the go-ahead now, but I'm equally happy to test your blood for alcohol if you'd rather delay.'

Chalky held his palm parallel with the table. 'Shaking like a fucking leaf. It's alcohol I *need*. Tell 'em that. I'll be a damn sight keener to give the bastards what they want with a drop of liquor inside me . . . stands to reason.'

*

Whether by design or accident, Jones allowed Jackson to watch the monitor while Chalky was interviewed by DC Khan and a second detective whom she hadn't seen before. The door to the viewing room stood open and she stepped quietly inside after a visit to the cells, where she'd found Charles asleep. Two other members of the inquiry team were gathered around the screen, but there was no sign of Beale. If anyone noticed Jackson's arrival they didn't comment on it.

Most of Chalky's statements contained long, complaining monologues against the police, bossy dykes, lying officers, ungrateful teenagers and the inhuman brutality of 'denying a bloke a bevvy'. But in essence his story corroborated Jackson's and Acland's in relation to the events in the alleyway and the subsequent drive to St Thomas's.

'Do you remember how many bags Ben brought in with him, Chalky?'

'Just the two . . . a black rucksack and a Londis carrier.'

'And how many did the lieutenant have?'

'Reckon he had two as well . . . a kitbag and a duffel.'

'Are you sure about that?'

'You calling me a liar?'

Khan shook his head. 'Just getting a few facts straight. Is it true you took the Londis bag? We've been told it had cigarettes and alcohol in it.'

'What if I did? The kid can't use it in the hospital. I'll pay him back next time I see him.'

'What about the duffel? Did you take that as well?'

'Course not. It wasn't mine.'

'So what happened to it?'

'The lootenant took it.'

Khan studied him for a moment. 'Meaning what? That he never removed it from the doctor's boot?'

Chalky looked as if he was about to spit on the floor again, then appeared to think better of it. 'Don't ask me, mate,' he said indifferently. 'I wasn't looking . . . But the lootenant's the one that's got it. It sure as hell ain't nothing to do with me.'

Khan nodded. 'That's pretty much what we thought.'

'So what am I doing here?' Chalky asked belligerently. 'The likes of me have rights, too, you know.'

'We're aware of that and we're grateful for your assistance. You've confirmed an important piece of evidence for us. Up until now, we only had the lieutenant's word that the duffel bag was ever in the boot. The doctor never saw it and, for all we knew, the lieutenant had reasons of his own to invent a bag that didn't exist.'

Chalky's black eyebrows drew together in a ferocious frown. 'I ain't confirming nothing.'

Khan consulted some notes on the table in front of him. 'Why did you hole up in Bread Street, Chalky?'

'None of your sodding business.'

'Did you open the duffel and take fright when you saw what was in it?'

'I want a lawyer. I ain't answering no more questions without a brief in the room.'

'Sure,' said Khan easily. 'Do you have a solicitor of your own or would you rather take one of the duty paralegals? If you choose a paralegal, it'll be a couple of hours before they get here. You're welcome to sit in this room with a cup of tea and a biscuit until they arrive.'

'I'll take a beer.'

'This isn't the Hilton, Chalky. We don't do alcohol.'

He hunched forward over the table. 'I should've tossed the bloody thing in the river,' he grumbled. 'Damn near did as a matter of fact. Only took it in the first place because I thought it had a bottle in it. It's the kid you should be talking to. His head's fucked.'

'Why do you say that?'

'He's a vicious little bastard . . . Got his girls to give me a kicking not so long ago.' Chalky tugged at his matted beard. 'He didn't like me telling 'em they'd do better without a good-for-nothing pimp living off 'em.'

'The pimp being Ben?'

'Right.'

'So how come you let him sleep in the alleyway with you?'

'Didn't know what he was like the first time I met him. All I saw was a skinny kid taking a kicking himself. He told me the guy was a faggot after a rent boy . . . but I reckon it was someone he'd fleeced. Got stuck with him after that. He used the alleyway as a bolt hole whenever he thought people were after him . . . only reason he kept the location to himself.'

Khan folded his hands over his notes. 'Weren't you frightened of him after he attacked you?'

Chalky gave a growl of disgust. 'Him and his bitches caught me asleep. Told him I'd break his fucking neck if he tried it again. Didn't see hide nor hair of him till he turned up that night. The lootenant reckoned he was sick . . . Me, I thought he'd been on the receiving end of another thumping . . . Even more so when I looked in his fucking bag after I'd split with the doctor.'

Khan made what he could of this. 'The duffel bag? Had you seen Ben with it before?'

'Wouldn't make any difference if I had or not. He had it that night . . . and in my book that makes it his.'

'Why did you hang on to it?'

Chalky flicked him an assessing glance, as if to measure how gullible he was. 'Because I read the newspapers, that's why. Do you think a meths drinker doesn't know what's going on in your piss-ant world? The army's not good for much – it drops you like a hot potato when you've done your bit for Queen and country –

but it doesn't take you on if you're stupid. Recognized the name, didn't I?'

'Harry Peel?'

'That's the one. Put it together with the doctor telling me the kid had a murdered bloke's mobile in his rucksack . . . and knew I'd shot myself in the bloody foot. I should have stuck with the booze and fags and left the duffel bag alone.'

'All the more reason to dump it somewhere.'

'Not if you have a conscience, it isn't,' said Chalky in an injured tone. 'What makes you think I like killers any more than you do?'

'The fact that you never brought the evidence to us,' said Khan with a faint smile. 'I'm betting you thought Ben would pay to get it back.'

Twenty-seven

BEALE REACHED FOR HIS radio as a taxi drew up alongside the transit van. 'Go,' he said quietly. He made a note of the time – 03.17 – then eased his Toyota door open as Jen Morley emerged from the back of the cab and walked towards the door of her apartment block.

She stopped as two plain-clothes policemen converged from the shadows at the side of the building into the light shed by a low-wattage lamp inside the hall. They moved in front of her to stop her entering, holding up their warrant cards. 'I have a rape alarm,' she warned.

'Metropolitan Police, Ms Morley,' said one. 'We're investigating an attack that occurred last Friday in the neighbourhood of Gainsborough Road and we believe you may be able to assist us by answering some questions. We're happy to do the interview in your flat or, if you prefer, you may accompany us to Southwark East police station.'

She stared him down with surprising coolness. 'Do I look as if I've got "mug" stamped across my forehead?' she murmured. 'I can't even read your cards from here.'

On instructions not to crowd her, both officers stayed where they were. 'If you have a mobile,' said the same man, 'I'll give you a number to call so that you can verify our status.'

'The only number I'll be dialling is 999,' she said, removing a slimline device from her pocket. 'Are you sure you want me to do that?'

'Indeed, Ms Morley,' said Beale from a couple of yards behind her. 'Ask to be patched through to Detective Inspector Beale and you'll find yourself talking to me.' He held up his own mobile. 'We spoke a few days ago if you remember.'

She swung round to face him, then backed away a few steps. 'You're too close and you're frightening me,' she snapped. 'I want to go into my flat and make the call from there.'

She looked in better shape than Beale had been expecting – make-up still in place and hair rolled neatly in the pleat behind her head – and he wondered if her client had had his money's worth. 'That's not a problem . . . as long we accompany you.'

Her eyes narrowed. 'Why would I take three strange men into my flat when I've already said I'm afraid of you? Either I go in alone or I'll sue the Metropolitan Police for intimidation.'

Beale smiled good-humouredly. 'So you do recognize me?'

She shrugged. 'Whatever. Any court will agree that it's un-reasonable to surround a woman in the middle of the night when all you want to do is ask her questions. I'll make an appoint-ment to talk to you tomorrow.'

'Can't do that, I'm afraid. Would the presence of a woman constable set your mind at rest?'

He watched her made a quick calculation in her head as she tested her options. 'Not if it means I have to stand out here waiting for her. I'm cold and I'm tired and I need to sit down.'

Beale held up his mobile again. 'We can sort this very quickly if you dial 999 now, Ms Morley. I understand your concerns, but we believe you have information that will assist our inquiry.'

'I don't even know what inquiry you're talking about.'

'An elderly gentleman was assaulted outside his home in Ber-mondsey last Friday.'

She looked at him in surprised disbelief, her huge eyes widening like a little girl's. 'You mean the old chap who was taken to hospital? How would I know anything about that? What time did it happen?'

Her surprise seemed genuine, thought Beale. 'Midday.'

'Then I wasn't even in Bermondsey. I left here at about eleven-thirty to meet a friend for lunch in central London.'

Beale smiled pleasantly. 'No one's suggesting you were involved in the attack, Ms Morley. The questions relate to certain items that may be connected to the inquiry. We believe they were in your possession at one time.'

'What items?'

'I have photographs to show you.' He gestured towards the front door of her block. 'May we come inside?'

There was something very wrong inside her flat, he thought, judging by the way she kept computing different courses of action. She tried a tired smile. 'I can't do it tonight,' she said, placing a slender hand against her belly. 'I've been having really bad period pains for two hours. I'm sure my solicitor would say it's unfair to question me under those circumstances.' She offered him the wide, innocent gaze again. 'I truly am perfectly willing to come to the police station later.'

'Is that a refusal to cooperate, Ms Morley?'

'Only on the grounds that what you're asking is unreasonable.'

'Then you leave me no choice but to invoke stop and search powers, Ms Morley. DCs Wagstaff and Hicks of Southwark East police station—'

The change in her demeanour was immediate. Her face blazed with sudden fury. 'That's a cheap threat,' she broke in angrily. 'I've given you no reason at all to suspect me of carrying illegal drugs.'

'A suspect can be stopped and searched on the basis of a tip-off, Ms Morley. Shortly before midnight a man called Lemarr Wilson, also known as Duane Stewart, was taken into custody. He made a statement which leads us to believe you are in possession of a class-A drug. DC Wagstaff will explain your rights before the search commences.'

'You're lying.'

'He gave a very good description of a woman who bought five hundred milligrams of cocaine off him at around eight-thirty last night. He knows you as Cass.' Beale smiled slightly. 'You're very distinctive-looking, Ms Morley. Too distinctive. I saw you myself after you'd made the purchase. That's what led us to Lemarr Wilson.'

Something like fear flickered in her eyes, but she made an effort to compose herself. 'I'll answer your questions at the station. That's what you came for, isn't it?'

Beale ignored her. 'Should a class-A drug be found on your person, Ms Morley, you will be arrested. In addition, your premises will be searched under the extended powers that such an arrest allows.'

'I can refuse to be searched by men,' she hissed. 'You should have brought a woman with you.'

'You only half know your law, Ms Morley. Nevertheless –' he raised his hand and beckoned to a passenger in his car – 'WPC Barnard will conduct the inspection as soon as you've placed your bag and the contents of your pockets on the ground in front of you and stepped away from them.'

Jen watched the woman police officer approach and a smile suddenly transformed her face. 'Hi,' she said with easy friendliness. 'I'm sorry about this. I didn't much fancy being patted down by your male colleagues.'

The WPC, who was carrying a small holdall, came to a halt beside Beale. She was a sturdy forty-year-old with fifteen years' service and she eyed Jen with amusement. 'Each to his own,' she said lightly. 'In your shoes I'd have chosen the men. Same-sex searches are a lot more thorough.'

Beale nodded to DC Wagstaff to read Jen her rights. When the officer had finished, the DI said, 'Everything on the ground, please, Ms Morley, including the object in your hand.'

Jen uncurled her palm to look at it. 'It's only a rape alarm.' She opened her leather shoulder bag, put the device inside it, along with a tissue from a pocket, then pressed the flap closed and lowered the bag to the pavement. 'That's all there is,' she said, stepping backwards.

The WPC eyed her for a moment, then knelt down and took a square of plastic sheeting from the holdall, which she unfolded on to the pavement. She snapped on some gloves and, using a foot-long grab-stick to hook the strap, she dragged the bag on to the sheeting.

'Most of these guns are effective through heavy clothing,' she told Beale, 'so leather won't prevent an accidental discharge.' Avoiding the metal catch, she caught the edge of the flap between the grab-stick claws and flipped it open to expose the contents. 'It's definitely a stun gun,' she confirmed. 'This one's called a Small Fry and packs a million volts. The red light means it's primed and ready to go.' She leaned away to allow Beale to look over her shoulder.

'How do you turn it off?'

'There should be a switch at the side – but it'll be safer if I empty everything on to the sheeting. I don't fancy sticking my hand in and hoping for the best . . . even to amuse Ms Morley.'

She grasped the edge of the sheeting and gave it a flick, tumbling the bag towards Jen. As the stun gun fell out, a deafening, high-pitched electrical siren screamed into the night air. The woman grinned as Jen jumped backwards. 'Most guys with any sense do a runner the minute they hear the siren,' she said, stretching forward to flick the switch. 'The ones who don't end up on the floor for ten minutes.'

Using her grab-stick, she caught the bottom of the leather bag and upended the rest of the contents over the sheeting. From among the detritus, she isolated an empty biro tube and a small gilt compact. 'No imagination,' she said, popping the catch and showing Beale the white powder inside. 'Nine times out of ten, women disguise their stash as cosmetics.'

She stood up and beckoned Jen forwards. 'Legs apart and arms out to the side, please. When I'm satisfied that you have nothing else in your clothing, you will be taken to a police station, where you may be asked to undergo a more intimate search.'

For a moment, Jen looked as if she was about to comply with the woman's brisk, no-nonsense manner, then she abruptly raised an open hand to slap her. This time the WPC's smile was dismissive as she easily caught the swinging hand and twisted it behind the girl's back. 'I told you you should have chosen one of the men,' she murmured, grabbing Jen's other hand and snapping on a pair of handcuffs. 'They might just have been fool enough to take that.'

*

Acland was awake the second time Jackson went to check on him. He was sitting cross-legged in the corner of the bed, his back resting against the wall, and he nodded as she appeared in the open doorway of the cell. 'I'm sorry,' he said simply.

'What for?'

'Everything . . . the damage to your car . . . the duffel bag . . . involving you again. It wasn't fair on you or your patients.'

Jackson leaned her shoulder against the jamb and folded her arms. 'Then why did you do it? I don't even have a car at the moment. It's been towed to a lab for forensic examination.'

'Sorry.' He made a move to stand up. 'Would you like to sit down?'

'No, thanks . . . and don't keep saying sorry. It's the most infuriating word in the English language. Just a cheap way to behave badly, then shelve responsibility by putting the onus on the other person to be forgiving.'

He knew her well enough by now to know that her bark was worse than her bite. 'It wasn't deliberate,' he said. 'I got stuck with the damn bag and I didn't know what to do with it.'

'Why didn't you hand it in to the nearest police station? That's what a normal person would have done.'

'A normal person wouldn't have gone looking for it in the first place.' A glint of self-deprecating humour appeared in his good eye. 'And neither would I if I'd known what was in it.'

'What did you *think* was in it?'

He shrugged. 'More of Ben's possessions. It annoyed me that he denied knowing anything about it.' He put his head back to stare at the ceiling. 'Chalky couldn't get rid of it fast enough. I should have suspected something at that point.'

'You'd still have taken it,' said Jackson. 'You'd have been too curious not to.'

Acland acknowledged the point with a nod. 'I wouldn't have paid for it, though.'

'How much?'

'Fifty quid.'

She gave an abrupt laugh. 'You shouldn't be allowed out alone. Chalky says you got it in exchange for a cheap bottle of vodka. How come the dykes let you back in?'

'I didn't try. I waited at the end of the terrace until Chalky came out. It didn't take long. He said he hadn't had a drink in twelve hours.'

'How did you know he was in there?'

'While we were there I heard a man hawking phlegm up in the room across the corridor. I didn't know for a fact it was Chalky but it seemed worth a try.' He held her gaze for a moment. 'Thanks for telling the police he was there.'

'You could have done it yourself. You had the perfect opportunity when the superintendent spoke to you outside the Crown.'

'I gave Chalky my word I wouldn't.'

Jackson's smile was cynical. 'That's Pontius Pilate stuff, Charles. How long were you planning to sit on the bag before you chose a side?'

'That's not what I was doing. I was trying to work out—' He broke off on a sigh. 'Chalky said the bag belonged to Ben. Is that what he's told the police?'

'In a manner of speaking. His view seems to be that as Ben brought the bag into the alleyway, it must be his . . . on the basis of possession being nine-tenths of the law.' She saw the doubt in Acland's face. 'The police aren't convinced.'

'I wouldn't expect them to be.'

'Then I suggest you come up with some credible answers about how you knew the bag existed. From what I remember, you told the superintendent you only *thought* it did.'

*

Apart from a glass crack pipe on a coffee table in the open-plan sitting room with a kitchen at one end, it wasn't immediately obvious why Jen had been so reluctant to allow the police into her flat. If she'd entered first and palmed the pipe, Beale doubted that he or his detectives would have noticed. The room was in some disorder, with various outfits slung across the back of a sofa and different pairs of shoes littering the floor.

'Looks as if she couldn't make up her mind what to wear,' said Wagstaff. 'I wonder what the bedroom's like if she had to bring the choices in here.'

'More to the point, what's in here that had her so twitched? This is the only room we could reasonably have entered if she'd been willing to come with us.'

DC Hicks nodded towards a flat screen on a desk against one of the walls. 'Her computer's still on. I can hear the fan working. She may not have had time to close out before she left.' He walked over and nudged the mouse with the tip of a gloved finger. 'Bloody hell!' he said with amusement. 'She's seriously up her own arse if she has to admire her own pictures.'

Beale and Wagstaff joined him to gaze at the naked and half-naked images of Jen on the screen. They were standard soft-porn poses – fully naked on hands and knees with her arse raised provocatively, bare-breasted on a chair, cutely provocative in high heels and a bikini bottom.

The text beside the pictures read:

Cass's STAR profile

Cass is BEAUTIFUL with the look of a movie goddess. You'll find out that a date with her will be pure class. Her European heritage and soft Italian accent add even more to her allure.

Cass is IRRESISTIBLE but BE WARNED! Her passionate Latin nature will make her unforgettable and your body will crave her for a very long time.

Incall
1 hour: £150
2 hours: £280
Outcall
1 hour: £200
2 hours: £350

'What's with the soft Italian accent?' asked Beale. 'It sounded more like Estuary English to me when Barnard put the cuffs on her. Doesn't anyone regulate this crap?'

Hicks grinned. 'Shall I go back one? It'll probably bring us to the home page of her escort agency.'

Beale nodded.

The detective gripped the mouse between the points of his gloved thumb and forefinger and steered the cursor on to the 'back' arrow before using a pencil to depress the 'click' button. He took out his notebook and jotted down the name 'Party Perfect' and the telephone details. He nodded to the photographs of other girls running down the side of the page. 'Look at the names. I should think most of them are Eastern European . . . unless they're using pseudonyms.'

'Try minimizing it,' Beale told him. 'Let's see if there's another window underneath.'

Hicks moved the cursor to the other side of the screen and clicked with the pencil again. 'Microsoft Outlook. Three messages in the inbox. Do you want me to open them?'

Beale ran a thoughtful hand round his growing stubble, wondering how much leeway they had on this search. 'Not at the moment. Click on "contacts". We've a legitimate interest in looking for Lemarr Wilson or Duane Stewart.'

All three of them stared at the displayed page. Top left was 'Robert Allan'. Bottom right was 'Timothy Gains'. A third of the way down the second column was 'Kevin Atkins' and an inch below in the third column was 'Martin Britton & John Prentice'.

Hicks pointed to an icon at the bottom of the screen. 'She uses a cell-phone synchronizer to feed in information from her mobile. That's why so few of the names have email addresses. All she's recording are telephone numbers.'

'In Britton's case, there's no number, just his address in Greenham Road.'

'Maybe that's all she knew.' Hicks clicked on 'P'. 'No Harry Peel.'

'Try "T" for taxi,' said Beale. 'If the gods are smiling on us, we'll find Walter Tutting as well.'

Twenty-eight

BEN RUSSELL'S PROTESTS about being woken at six o'clock in the morning to be taken to Southwark East police station for questioning under caution were noisy and prolonged. He was sick. He wanted his doctor. He wanted his mother. He wanted his solicitor. The police were fascists.

He turned his ire on the ward sister. 'You should fucking stop them,' he snapped, pointing his pistol hands at the two uniformed constables.

'I've no reason to,' she told him. 'Dr Monaghan feels there are no medical grounds to prevent you going. You've been given all the tools to manage your condition and you've been doing it successfully for several days now. We'd have discharged you yesterday if you'd agreed to live with your mother.'

'Bitch!'

The sister ignored him. 'There's a doctor at the police station who will monitor your regimen during the interview. Your mother and your solicitor will also be there. You will be allowed regular rest periods, and both the doctor and your mother will ensure that you follow your instructions on blood testing for glucose levels and that you administer your insulin the way you've been taught.'

He stared mutinously at his hands. 'You can't make me go if I don't want to.'

'You're due to be discharged this morning anyway. You will continue on Dr Monaghan's list and attend for outpatient visits, but social services have found a place in a hostel where a qualified staff member will keep an eye on you. This was all explained to you yesterday.'

'I'm not fucking going to a hostel.'

'You'll need support for a few months yet.'

'Why can't I get it here?'

'You will . . . as an outpatient . . . but you can't take up a hospital bed for the rest of your life just because you have diabetes. You know all this. Dr Monaghan has told you several times that a hostel placement is your only option if you refuse to accept your mother's help.'

'I like being here.'

The sister smiled slightly. 'You could have fooled me,' she said. 'I thought you were in a hellhole run by bitches and mother fuckers.'

*

'We'll give your client as much latitude as he needs,' Superintendent Jones told Pearson.

The solicitor was sitting across the desk from him, as dapper at eight o'clock in the morning as he'd been at eight o'clock at night.

'It would help if Ben understands that the interview will be shorter and less stressful if he answers our questions frankly and honestly.'

Pearson leaned forward to look at the bagged items on Jones's desk. 'You asked him if he took a canvas bag into the alleyway. This one's too soft to be canvas.'

'At that time, we could only go by Lieutenant Acland's description. Both he and Terence Black – the man Ben knows as Chalky – have since identified it as the bag your client brought into the alleyway.' He paused. 'It's not in Ben's interests to deny it, Mr Pearson. His fingerprints are on both mobiles and on the plastic carrier that was wrapped around the knobkerrie.'

'I can see that one of the mobiles has Harry Peel's name on it. Have you identified it as his?'

'We have.'

'May I ask if you know who the other one belonged to?'

'Martin Britton.'

'A full house, then ... if we include the one belonging to Kevin Atkins that you claim was in Ben's rucksack.'

Jones's Rottweiler personality had him leaning forward aggressively. 'There's no "*claim*" about it, Mr Pearson. Your client never disputed that he had the Nokia in his possession. He said he stole it between two to four weeks before his admission to hospital.'

The solicitor nodded. 'We both know he was lying.'

'Indeed.'

'Would you be willing to tell me how you think he's involved in your inquiry?'

Jones propped his elbows on the desk and folded his hands under his chin to stare at the other man. 'If it'll help influence the way you advise him, we don't believe he was involved in any of the murders.'

'But you're not ruling him out of involvement in the assault on Walter Tutting?'

'Not at the moment.'

'Meaning your decision will depend on when and how he came by the bag –' he tilted his chin towards the knobkerrie – 'and, more specifically, the weapon?'

'It will certainly help to clarify a few details.'

'Ben's told you several times that he has no recollection of what happened that day, Superintendent. His consultant endorsed the possibility of deep confusion prior to his collapse.'

'I'm aware of that.'

'Which may explain why he denied taking this bag into the alleyway. If he wasn't aware that he had it, he wouldn't have recognized the description you gave. By the same token, he may not be able to recall how he came by it.'

Jones shrugged. 'Then I shall have to assume he was telling the truth about Kevin Atkins's mobile. He was vague about who he stole it from but not at all vague about carrying it around for two plus weeks.'

Pearson gave a faint smile. 'I thought we agreed he was lying about the Nokia. May I suggest the scenario went something like this? Ben acquired the bag at some point on Friday afternoon, rifled through the contents and transferred the only phone that might be worth something to his rucksack. Harry Peel's has Dynotape stuck to it and Martin Britton's is a "pay-as-you-go". The fact that my client was still carrying the bag when he entered the alleyway is the best evidence you have that he wasn't thinking straight afterwards. On any other day, he'd have dumped it.'

Jones shook his head. 'You can't have it both ways, Mr Pearson. If Ben was compos mentis enough to recognize a halfway decent mobile . . . then frightened enough of how he came by it to spin us a convoluted yarn about a man in Hyde Park . . . my educated guess is he remembers *exactly* what happened.'

'Do you have a suspect for the murders?'

'Is that another way of asking if we'll know when your client's lying?'

The solicitor smiled. 'Possibly.'

'Advise him to be frank with us, Mr Pearson.'

METROPOLITAN
POLICE

WITNESS STATEMENT

Witness:	Benjamin Russell (16)
Interviewing officers:	DI Beale, DC Khan
Present:	Mr H. Pearson, Mrs B. Sykes, Dr J. Jackson
Date:	16.08.07
Incident:	Assault on Walter Tutting on 10.08.07

I, Benjamin Russell, agree that the following is a true record of statements made by me during an interview today with DI Beale and DC Khan.

I've known Walter Tutting a few months. We got friendly because I used to hang out around the pub he uses. Some girls I know have a dealer close by. Walter was pretty lonely and he liked me because I was the same age as his grandson. He told me he hadn't seen the boy since his wife died.

At first I thought it was me Walter was keen on, but when I told him I wasn't into that kind of thing, he said it was the girls he liked. He wanted to know if any of them would be willing to spend time with him. He told me he was making calls to a sex chat line for a bit of company but it wasn't the same as having a woman to cuddle.

Walter was pretty old, so it took a bit of persuading to get
one of the girls to go. None of them fancied the idea much.
The girl who went said he didn't do anything, just wanted a
chat, and gave her thirty quid at the end. After that, they
were all up for it. I went a few times myself. When one of
the girls volunteered to wank him off one night, he gave her
a hundred quid.

He was always a bit twitched about anyone seeing us go in.
He said his daughter wouldn't like it if she found out. We
used to sneak down an alley behind his terrace and get in
through the back. He was always pleased to see us, even
told me his PIN on his card so that I could get cash out at
night-time if he was short. We were good mates so I never
took more than he said. I used to buy fags and booze for him
as well.

Everything changed about a month ago. Walter started
locking his back door and telling us to go away. The girls
were upset because they were fond of Walter. They asked
me to wait for him in Gainsborough Road one day to see if I
could find out what was wrong. We had a bit of a row
because he said we'd been stealing off him. I told him it
wasn't true. He said his daughter had found out about it
and was going to put him in a nursing home. I think his
brain had gone a bit. He said he wasn't allowed to let
anyone in any more. After that we left him alone.

When I woke up on Friday, 10 August, I was feeling really
sick. I hadn't been well for a few days but I thought it was flu.
I'd spent the night down by the river and I knew there was a
drop-in centre in Gainsborough Road. I decided to go there
and ask for a doctor. One of the girls said she'd come with me.
We had to go down Harris Road to get to the centre.

The time was about eleven o'clock and there was no one around. We saw a woman come out of an apartment block and stand at the edge of the pavement. She looked as if she was waiting for a lift. She was about five foot eight and thin but we couldn't see her face. She was wearing a baseball cap and had her head down. I think she was blonde. She was carrying a duffel bag and I snatched it off her and ran down the road. The girl with me pushed the woman over to stop her following us.

I know it's wrong to steal off people but we'd done that kind of stuff before. It's easy when there's no one else around. I tucked the bag under my jacket and turned down West Street. The girl split off in the opposite direction. I don't know if the woman screamed. The running made me sick so I wasn't concentrating on anything else.

I was stupid to go anywhere near Walter's house, but he lives in a cul-de-sac off Gainsborough Road. I thought it would be a good place to check what was in the bag before I went to the drop-in centre. The only thing worth taking was a Nokia mobile. I put it in my rucksack and left the rest in the duffel bag. I needed somewhere to ditch it and Walter has a couple of flower tubs outside his door. I thought I'd squeeze the bag in behind one of them.

He came back just as I started. I was kneeling on the ground and he hit me round the head with a carrier bag he was holding. I grabbed it off him and we had a bit of a scuffle. I told him he was senile and that made him more angry. He put his key in the door and said he was going to call the police.

I was feeling very sick by then and I don't remember exactly

what happened next. I think it may have been me who
turned the key and pushed him into the hall. We were both
angry. Walter hit me with a walking stick so I swung the
duffel bag at him. I was holding it by the strap. I know I
missed the first time but I think I hit him twice afterwards.

I was shocked when he fell over. I never intended to hurt
Walter Tutting. I wouldn't have tried to defend myself if he
hadn't hit me first. I believe most of my actions on Friday,
10 August, happened because I am suffering from type one
diabetes. I remember leaving Walter's house with my
rucksack, the carrier bag and the duffel bag, but I don't
remember anything that happened afterwards.

I confirm that the bag shown to me by the police was the
one I stole in Harris Road and subsequently took to Walter
Tutting's house. I confirm that the carrier bag in Walter
Tutting's possession was a Londis bag.

I do not know the real names of any of the prostitutes who
took money from Walter Tutting. I do not know the name of
the girl who was with me when I stole the duffel bag.

I do not know the name of the woman in Harris Road and
cannot give a more accurate description of her. I would not
be able to recognize her if I saw her again.

Signed,

Ben Russell

Benjamin Russell

Twenty-nine

JACKSON SHOOK HER HEAD when Pearson asked if she would be accompanying Ben to the juvenile court. 'Not my area,' she said. 'If you or Mrs Sykes have any concerns when you get there, you'll have to put your request through the court system. You won't have a problem. The magistrates have been notified of Ben's condition and they've agreed to push the hearing through as fast as possible.'

Mrs Sykes's expression was sour. 'It shouldn't be allowed. He's a sick boy.'

'Not as sick as Mr Tutting,' said Jackson.

'My lad was only defending himself.'

Jackson exchanged a glance with the solicitor. 'Look on the bright side, Mrs Sykes,' she said cheerfully. 'At least Ben's agreed to be bailed to your address. If the magistrates allow it – which they certainly will because of his condition – he should be well in charge of himself by the time he comes to trial. With your help, of course.'

The woman's mouth became an inverted horseshoe. 'It shouldn't be allowed,' she said again. But whether she was referring to her son being charged with grievous bodily harm or the fact that, as his mother, she was about to become responsible for his health and whereabouts wasn't clear to either the doctor or the solicitor.

*

'Will you get a conviction?' Jackson asked Jones. She'd joined him in the monitoring room, although he'd leaned forward to switch off the screen as she came in.

'Unlikely. Too many "ifs". If Walter's competent to give evidence . . . if he's willing to admit getting excited about teenage prostitutes . . . if his daughter allows it . . . if he has a rebuttal to Ben's self-defence plea—' He broke off. 'I'm a great believer in natural justice. The kid will remember Walter every time he injects himself with insulin.'

Jackson shook her head. 'I wouldn't bank on it. I read a paper the other day that said Brazilian scientists are working on a stem-cell cure for type one diabetes. If Ben's lucky he'll be injection-free in ten years.'

'You're a ray of sunshine, Doctor. How's the lieutenant?'

'Resigned to a long wait.'

Jones nodded. 'Has he told you anything that you feel you can repeat to me?'

'I'm happy to repeat the entire conversation, but it won't add anything to what you already know.' She paused. 'I've worked out why he has a phobia about being touched.'

The superintendent eyed her thoughtfully. 'I suspect we all have.'

'I can't see him talking about it,' Jackson warned. 'He's had everything stripped away from him in the last few months. Pride is all he has left.'

Jones shook his head. 'My guess is his reticence is more about stalling for time than wounded feelings, Doctor. He wants to know what Jen says before he offers us anything.'

'Or he feels partly responsible. Nick Beale said Charles had a row with Jen before each of those men was killed. That's a heavy weight for anyone to carry on his conscience.'

'Are you asking me to feel sorry for him?'

Jackson gave a small shrug. 'To recognize that none of this is easy for him, at least.'

'I wish I could be that generous,' Jones said honestly, 'but I need Charles's evidence. I want to know why he went after the bag when he claims he had no idea what was in it or who it belonged to.' He smiled sympathetically at Jackson. 'He knew what the contents were before last night, Doctor.'

She didn't say anything.

'If Jen can put the blame on Charles she will. She's perfectly capable of painting herself as an abused woman. He needs to understand that.'

Jackson sighed. 'Try narcissist with a developing cocaine aggression. It's a potent mix. A woman who demands constant admiration . . . is preoccupied with fantasies about how special she is . . . and has a grandiose sense of her own importance. She'd react badly to anyone who rejected her. Not just Charles.'

James Steele, the psychological profiler, had said more or less the same over the telephone earlier.

'I can advise you better when I've had a chance to watch her, Brian, but meanwhile I suggest you focus on her apparent belief that she's entitled to behave the way she does. I'm interested in her reaction to the female officer. Leaving the stun gun active, and attempting to slap the woman suggest a contempt for other people that isn't normal.'

Jones looked up at Jackson. 'Have you ever seen Ms Morley?' he asked her.

'No.'

He reached out to switch the screen back on. 'She's waiting for her solicitor,' he said. 'You wouldn't think butter would melt in her mouth, would you?'

Jackson studied the delicate face with its wide-eyed stare and slightly puzzled smile. 'Only because she has baby features,' she said matter-of-factly. 'Big eyes appeal to the care-taking response, which is why we describe women like her as beautiful. There's plenty of literature on the subject.'

'You don't find her attractive?'

'Not particularly,' said Jackson honestly. 'Too damn willowy for my liking. I'd be afraid of breaking her.' She paused to watch Jen smooth her hand over her skirt. 'Is she alone in there?'

'There's a female officer by the door.'

'But she knows there's a camera on her?'

Jones nodded. 'She's already attacked one policewoman, so she was told she'd be monitored by CCTV to prevent her doing it again. As a result, she's behaved impeccably since she's been in there.'

'What does she look like when she's in a temper?'

'Not much different, according to Nick. There are no obvious signals to alert anyone she's about to lose it.' He blanked the screen again. 'That's why we need Charles's evidence, Doctor. If we know what triggers her rages, we'll have something to work on.'

'Are you asking me to persuade him?'

'He'll listen to you.'

Jackson shook her head. 'I doubt it. The last time the subject of Jen came up, he drove me into a bollard.'

Thirty

ACLAND HADN'T MOVED from his place in the corner of the bed. He sat in the same position with his disfigured profile towards the door, staring at the wall opposite and apparently oblivious to the comings and goings outside. Jackson watched him for a second or two. He had a capacity for stillness that was quite extraordinary, she thought.

'Were you born with patience or did they teach it to you in the army?' she asked.

He turned to look at her. 'I learned it as a child. There wasn't much point getting worked up about sitting alone in my room when nothing I did was going to make a difference. Now it comes naturally.'

'Did you know it was me at the door?'

He nodded. 'I recognized your footsteps.'

She moved into the room. 'Have you been told that Jen's been arrested?'

He nodded again.

'They're waiting to interview her.' Jackson gestured towards the end of the bed. 'May I?' She took his silence for assent and perched on the end, leaning forward with her elbows on her knees. 'The superintendent wants to question you first. How do you feel about that? Would you like me to stall him . . . give yourself a little more time?'

'What for?'

'So that you can decide how quickly you're willing to cooperate. Mr Jones needs it all, I'm afraid – every *i* dotted and every *t* crossed – and he'll just keep going until he gets it.' She glanced sideways. 'We've all worked out why you react so violently to being touched, Charles. I doubt you've many secrets left.'

'I wouldn't bet on it.'

'How many times did Jen use the stun gun on you?'

'It depends whether you count repeated hits,' he said. 'If she zapped me every five minutes she could keep me on the ground for as long as she liked.' The humour lines appeared around his good eye. 'A man would have to be pretty stupid to get caught more than once, wouldn't he?'

'Is that what embarrasses you? That you think you were stupid?'

'It doesn't say much for my army training. Soldiers are supposed to be ready for surprise attacks.'

Jackson smiled. 'From the enemy, maybe . . . not from friends.'

'I didn't even know she had it the first time she used it. She said it was an accident and only zapped me the once. The second time, I fell asleep in a chair when we were supposed to be going out. She said it was to teach me a lesson about taking her for granted.' He fell into a brief silence. 'It was shortly before I went to Oman and she said she only did it because she was upset about me going . . . so I took the damn thing off her and smashed it with a hammer.'

'But she bought another one while you were away?'

Acland nodded.

'They're easy to come by, Charles. Daisy's been offered several by touts in the back streets. You shouldn't beat yourself up over it.'

He didn't say anything.

Jackson straightened. 'What happened?'

'I told her I'd had time to think it all through in Oman and the engagement was over. She didn't take it too well.' He gave a small laugh. 'I turned my back on her. Pretty naive, eh?'

'How many hits?'

Acland shook his head. 'I gave up counting. Every time I tried to get up, she used it again. The charge does something to your head . . . makes you lose coordination. Repeated charges scramble everything.'

'Which is why they're illegal in this country. In the hands of someone like Jen they could kill you. The body can only take so many shocks.'

'She thought it was funny.'

Jackson heard the hatred in his voice. 'How did you stop her?'

'She took a phone call . . . and it lasted longer than she realized. When she came back I managed to lock on to her wrist and turn the gun on her.' He fell into another brief silence. 'I came damn close to killing *her*. I could have done it easily and she knew it.'

'Why didn't you?'

'Because I'm better than that.'

Like your father, she thought. 'Did Jen use anything other than the stun gun on you?'

'Nothing I want to talk about.'

Jackson shook her head. 'Mr Jones won't accept that. He needs to know if she hit you with the knobkerrie.'

There was a small hesitation. 'She didn't have to stun me to do that. It was her favourite weapon. It started as a joke . . . a tap on the wrist if I was late. It turned nasty around July, when I told her about the month's training in Oman. She damn near broke my arm on one occasion.'

Jackson glanced at him again. 'When did she first use the knobkerrie? Before or after the engagement?'

'I'm not a complete idiot. *After*,' he said with another wry laugh. 'She was fine up until then.' He paused. 'I thought maybe I'd pushed her into something she didn't want to do, but it made her worse when I said we didn't have to go through with it. I made myself scarce whenever she kicked off . . . but she didn't like that either.'

'At the Crown?'

He nodded. 'I told the superintendent I never spoke to the taxi driver, but I think I may have done. I remember being given a card one time which I passed on to Jen. She goes everywhere in cabs.' He lapsed into another silence.

'So what makes Jen angry?'

'The same thing that fires my mother up . . . not getting her own way. As long as you agree with her, she's fine. It's when you say no that the trouble starts.'

'Some people can't function without constant approval. Any disagreement is seen as the equivalent of rejection, and they react angrily because they feel degraded and betrayed. Does that describe Jen and your mother?'

'Apart from the things you've left out.'

'Like what?'

'The fact that they live in fantasy worlds about how sweet-natured and beautiful they are . . . The fact that the more approval they're given the worse they get . . . The fact that they don't give a shit about anyone else—' He broke off on a sigh. 'Jen wasn't always like that, you know. She was great at the beginning.'

'And probably still is when she wants to be,' said Jackson calmly. 'People with personality disorders don't lack charm. They employ it whenever they want to manipulate a situation to suit themselves . . . particularly if they think of themselves as special in some way.'

The humour lines appeared around Acland's eye. 'Tell me something I don't know.'

'All right,' she agreed. 'Your father deserves your admiration and not your scorn. From what you've told me, he seems to have gone to immense trouble to break the cycles of abuse within your family, both by controlling his own responses to your mother's aggression and by shielding you from the worst of it. That's not an easy thing to do.'

The humour vanished. 'It didn't work, though, did it?'

Jackson eyed him thoughtfully. '*You* tell me. I know of only two occasions when you retaliated against Jen – the last time you went to her flat and the day she visited you in hospital. Were there more?'

'Three, if you count turning the stun gun on her.' He squeezed one fist inside the other. 'If I'd been more like my father, those men would still be alive. The dates all fit.'

'That doesn't make you responsible. It's just as likely that having you helpless on the floor gave her a perverted sense of power and she re-enacted it because she enjoyed it.' She watched his writhing hands. 'You said I shouldn't bet on knowing all your secrets. What else did she do to you?'

He avoided a direct answer. 'Jen wouldn't have taken the knobkerrie with her if she hadn't meant to humiliate those men.'

Humiliate . . . ? 'How?'

His expression was bleak. 'The same way she humiliated me,' he said.

*

Jones and Beale listened to Jackson in silence. 'He told us last night that he buggered her as punishment,' Jones remarked when she'd finished. 'It makes more sense now. Was that his real reason for going back to her flat? To pay her out in kind?'

'I suspect it was six of one and half a dozen of the other. He says he sent her a text warning her to make herself scarce, but I'm sure he knew she wouldn't take any notice of it.'

'Is that why he feels responsible?' asked Beale.

'I imagine so,' said Jackson with a touch of sarcasm. 'He didn't become a monk for religious reasons.' She paused. 'One way and another, he has a lot on his conscience.'

'The deaths of three men,' agreed Beale drily.

'Two,' she corrected him. 'His troopers . . . and that's all in his head anyway. I don't believe he's remotely to blame for Peel, Britton and Atkins. He could never have predicted that Jen would take out her anger on strangers.'

'He still played a part,' said Jones, 'even if unwittingly.'

'You could say the same about Harold Shipman's wife. Being in a relationship with a disturbed personality doesn't mean you set them on the route to crime.'

Jones acknowledged the point with a nod. 'But something Charles did seems to have a triggered a psychotic reaction. All three murders followed a meeting with him.' He paused. 'Do you have an opinion on that?'

'Why do you care what I think if you have a Cracker on tap?'

'You're closer to Charles than the rest of us.'

'Even if that's true, it's Jen you need to understand, and I don't know any more about her than you do . . . except what Charles has told me.'

'I'm listening.'

Jackson shook her head. 'I'm a bog standard locum, not a specialist in forensic psychology.'

'If there's anything bog standard about you, then I'm in the wrong bloody job,' said Jones sarcastically. 'It's your impressions I'm after, Doctor, not a thesis on sociopathy.'

Jackson grinned. 'I might do that rather better.' She raised her hands in a pacific gesture. 'OK, OK!' She thought for a moment. 'The obvious trigger is that he kept rejecting her . . . but she was also excited by having a man helpless. She used the stun gun on him twice before, so she clearly enjoyed the power it gave her.'

'He should have left her after the first occasion.'

'Do you think Charles doesn't know that? Everything's so damned easy with hindsight. He's extremely ignorant about women. The only thing his upbringing taught him was not to get into arguments with them . . . and nothing could have suited Jen's personality better. In some ways he was the perfect partner for her.'

'Would she have recognized that?'

Jackson shrugged. 'Probably. I suspect her feelings for him were a lot stronger than he realized.'

'So why attack him in the way she did?'

'During the stun gun episode? Because he'd given her her marching orders and she wasn't prepared to accept them.'

Jones looked sceptical. 'And she thought ramming a knobkerrie up his backside would persuade him to change his mind?'

'She was angry and she wanted to hurt him. Logic goes out the window when a red mist descends.' Jackson shrugged again at Jones's expression. 'Look, what the hell do I know? Maybe Charles is right and her fantasies are all about humiliation.'

There was a short silence.

'The two views aren't mutually exclusive,' said Beale. 'Rage usually takes the form of putting an opponent down . . . either verbally or physically.'

'So why didn't she go the whole hog with the lieutenant when she had him at her mercy?' Jones asked. 'Why let him live?'

'Because she loved him,' said Jackson. 'The dynamics of domestic abuse are as much about powerful attachment as they are about control and manipulation.'

'You seem very convinced Jen's feelings were genuine. Does the lieutenant agree with you?'

'No. He thinks she saw him as a meal ticket.'

'Why doesn't that persuade you?'

'Because Charles was the one who cooled. He wanted an equal partner – the opposite of what he perceived his parents' relationship to be – and he started to lose interest when he realized how demanding Jen was. That's when her aggression surfaced. She was more intent on keeping him than he was on staying.'

'Perhaps her real character only came out after she had a ring on her finger,' said Beale.

Jackson nodded. 'That, too . . . and the drugs wouldn't have helped. It's possible she made an attempt to kick her habit at the start of the relationship, then slipped back when she began to understand the reality of a soldier's life. Charles being away for long stretches of time wouldn't have suited a woman who craves constant attention. I'm sure her visit to Birmingham was about proving to him that he couldn't live without her. She must have believed it herself or she wouldn't have gone. I can't imagine hatred was the response she was expecting.'

'He demonstrated hatred when he raped her,' Jones pointed out.

'You and I might think so, but I doubt Jen would. It was a sex act and that's an area she knows well. You need to put yourself in her mindset. She's beautiful and desirable and Charles showed he still wanted her. He wouldn't have been able to achieve an erection otherwise.'

'He said he paid for it.'

'That doesn't make her any less desirable. Some men will have paid a lot more to sleep with her.'

'Not recently,' said Beale. 'We can find only one agency still advertising her through their website and they've had no requests for her for weeks. Word gets round, apparently, and she has a bad reputation with clients. Light-fingered and not compliant enough.'

Jackson frowned. 'Charles said he saw her with a Japanese.'

'We did, too . . . probably the same one . . . but it's almost certainly a private arrangement, a man who's employed her before. We think most of her work is coming that way at the moment. Her drug dealer says her earning capacity has taken a dive in the last six months.'

'Then perhaps Charles is right. He's convinced the only reason Jen went to the hospital was to get her hands on his disability compensation.'

'Why doesn't that persuade you?' Jones asked again.

'It might have done if she'd turned up in sackcloth and ashes with tears running down her cheeks, begging for a second chance. Instead, she came as her favourite fantasy, even to the extent of wearing the same outfit she wore the day she used the stun gun on him.' Jackson arched a rueful eyebrow. 'And the knobkerrie wasn't the worst of Charles's problems, you know. For most of the time, she was holding a bread knife to his penis and threatening to castrate him.'

'Go on.'

'The only meaning I can take from that is that Jen thought Charles had been as excited by her dominatrix act as she was.'

Jones smiled cynically. 'That's a big leap of imagination.'

'I'm not saying it's rational, Superintendent. I'm saying it's what an intensely egotistical woman might think.'

'Yet according to Dr Campbell, Jen told Charles's psychiatrist in Birmingham that she hoped his amnesia covered the end of the relationship. She sent him a series of love letters that didn't even mention the rape, let alone how close he came to castration.'

'But he didn't read them and he didn't reply.'

'So?'

Jackson shrugged again. 'If you were Jen what would you take from that?'

'That the letters never reached Charles.'

Jackson nodded. 'And what do you take from the fact that the contents were anodyne and only mentioned how good the relationship was?'

'That she hoped he'd forgotten?'

'Or she was afraid a nurse would have to read them to him because she didn't know what his injuries were.' She paused. 'The more interesting question is why Charles was willing to hand them unopened to his psychiatrist when he was so resistant to revealing anything about the relationship.'

'Go on.'

'He knew Jen would do what his parents have done all his life . . . keep their secrets under wraps. He prefers it like that. The only way he knows how to deal with pain is to absorb it.' She sighed. 'He's said all along you were out to crucify him . . . and that's what you'll be doing if you force him into court to support a prosecution. He's carrying too much baggage to cope with having all this dragged into a public arena.'

Jones shook his head. 'You underestimate him, Doctor. If I've learned anything about the lieutenant in the last few days, it's that he's a great deal more determined to face his fears than you and I are.'

METROPOLITAN
POLICE

INTERNAL MEMO

To: ACC Clifford Golding
From: Det Supt Brian Jones
Date: 20 August 2007
Subject: Interview procedure

Sir,

Re Concerns expressed by Jennifer Morley's legal
representative

Please find attached a copy of Morley's custody record,
showing that she was charged well within the 36-hour time-
limit allowed under PACE.

In the view of the interviewing officers and myself, the
'breakdowns' cited by Morley's legal representative were
determined attempts to run down the detention clock.
Morley employed fainting spells, panic attacks and constant
requests for healthcare assistance to disrupt her interviews.
Despite these delays, she was charged at 11.45 on Friday,
17 August 2007, with the murders of Harry Peel and Kevin
Atkins, making a detention time of 32 hours and 15
minutes. She appeared before magistrates three hours later
and was remanded to HMP Holloway.

The custody officer is entirely satisfied that we had
reasonable grounds for detaining Morley, and that all
interviews were conducted in accordance with Codes of
Practice. She was allowed several rest periods, including a
sleep break, and was given appropriate assistance and
monitoring at all times together with regular offers of food
and beverages. Most of these were declined. A copy of her
custody record was made available to her legal
representative.

The following is a brief summary of events

DI Beale and DC Khan pursued a line of questioning,
proposed by James Steele (psychologist), which was
designed to persuade Morley that she had control of the
interview. As Steele predicted, this led her to offer easily
disputed alibis about where she was and who she was with
over the murder weekends. In the first two cases (Peel &
Britton), she claimed to have been in London in the
company of Lt Charles Acland; in the third (Atkins), to have
been in a hotel in Birmingham, following a visit to Lt
Acland in hospital.

Morley's first fainting spell occurred after DI Beale showed
her the register from Lt Acland's base, and read parts of his
statement, detailing her violence against him. Thereafter,
the 'breakdowns' became more frequent as new evidence was
disclosed. On the insistence of her legal representative,
Morley was given time to recover after each occasion.

In her next interview, she denied assaulting Lt Acland and
made counter-accusations that he'd brought the stun gun
and the knobkerrie into the relationship in order to assault

her. She portrayed herself as an abused 'spouse' with
battered-wife syndrome. When asked if this had given her a
fear of men, she agreed that it had, although she refused to
comment on information retrieved from her computer that
suggested a continued willingness to put herself in danger
from men in the role of prostitute/escort. This information
included the names and/or telephone numbers and
addresses of Peel, Britton and Atkins.

Following a two-hour break at the request of her solicitor,
she offered drug dependency as a reason for her
prostitution. She further claimed that her victim status as
an abused spouse had driven her to self-medicate on
'uppers' in order to treat her depression and low self-
esteem. She blamed Lt Acland for her dependency, laying
prolonged stress on his violent and jealous behaviour. As
explanation for having Peel/Britton/Atkins's contact details
on her computer, she claimed to work part-time for a sex
chat line.

On James Steele's advice, DI Beale and DC Khan allowed
these statements to go unchallenged and 'rewarded' Morley
with an overnight sleep break. She was woken at 06.30 and
given an opportunity to perform basic ablutions and apply
make-up. Breakfast was offered, but declined.

Morley's demeanour remained upbeat until she was shown
the forensic evidence obtained from two different sets of
clothing in her flat. Blood-spot DNA traces on a dark jacket,
linking her to Atkins, and similar DNA traces on a pair of
shoes, linking her to Peel. In addition, FSS made matches
with fibres taken from a woollen scarf in Morley's apartment
to fibres found on Atkins's premises.

After another 'breakdown' and a lengthy consultation with her legal representative, Morley admitted involvement in the deaths of Peel and Atkins. She offered self-defence and 'battered-wife syndrome' as justification, saying both men became aggressive under the influence of alcohol. She claimed to have lashed out in a panic with the first thing she could lay her hands on. In the case of Peel, a table lamp base. In the case of Atkins, an unopened bottle of wine.

Morley was then shown the hemp duffel bag and its contents and was asked to account for the stun gun and the knobkerrie. On the advice of her legal representative, she refused to answer further questions, and I took the decision to charge her with the murders of Peel and Atkins.

The detailed investigation of Morley's property continues, and FSS are confident of linking her to Martin Britton's premises and murder.

Three strands of hair found on the inside of the hemp bag have provided a DNA link with Morley, although this will certainly be contested in court. It is feasible, if unlikely, that Lt Acland carried them on his clothes for several months and transferred them unwittingly to the duffel.

The ongoing examinations of Morley's computer and mobile telephone, also Peel's and Britton's phones, continue to produce evidence. Information retrieved and followed up to date shows that Morley had had previous contact with all three men.

- Harry Peel in his role as taxi driver – Morley was an occasional customer.
- Martin Britton through his partner, John Prentice –

Morley was commissioned for at least two photo-shoots of silk fashion in a chinoiserie room at the Britton/Prentice house. (Prentice said the slender Uma Thurman look suited his company's designs.)
- Kevin Atkins as a builder – his company carried out maintenance work on Morley's apartment block in 2004.

All contacts in Morley's email folder and cell-phone address book are being traced and questioned. From interviews conducted so far, a picture is emerging of erratic behaviour over a period of years. Morley has had no contact with her family since punching and kicking her younger sister during an assault in 2001. Her mother admitted to being afraid of her.

Two ex-boyfriends, who dated Morley for less than a month each, have described stalker-type behaviour following break-up – threats, late-night visits, nuisance phone calls. A theatre company sacked her after two days for 'anger issues'. Three escort agencies have taken her off their books because of client complaints.

A high percentage of the telephone numbers recorded in Morley's computer have been disconnected. Three, including the ex-boyfriends, have been tracked through their servers and interviewed. All cite harassment from Morley as the reason for the disconnection. The third, who lives in Newcastle, admitted to using her services during a business trip to London. 'I told her she wasn't worth the money. She sent fifty obscene texts during the following two weeks.'

Despite Morley's claim that it was Peel and Atkins who approached her 'for sex', there is no evidence to support this. Both men's cell phones have listings for 'Cass' under a number that was discontinued around the time Morley met Lt Acland. We believe the initial contact came from Morley, either via a pay phone or by turning up 'on spec' at their houses, and that a need for money was the driving force. (Steele argues that Morley's drug dependency/cravings would have become critical following the encounters with Lt Acland.)

If her intention had been to find a client for the evening, she may have tried other contacts before receiving a green light from her victims. (This might explain her use of a pay phone to avoid her name appearing and giving the recipient a chance to ignore the call.)

Steele's theory is that all three murders were 'opportunistic' – i.e. various factors collided to create a 'killing' environment. He suggests the following scenario:

- Morley was angry/destabilized by Lt Acland's refusal to continue the relationship and/or support her financially.
- If Morley was rejected by a number of potential clients, this would: a) frustrate her need for cash; b) fuel her anger; and c) persuade her to adopt a different approach.
- Her first victim, Harry Peel, was easily accessible as a taxi driver and only accepted payment in cash. This would have been known to Morley. If her initial request was for his taxi service, he was unlikely to refuse her.
- Her second victim, Martin Britton, was described by everyone who knew him as 'courteous'. Britton's brother believes Martin would have invited Morley in because of the connection with his partner. From her previous visits to the house, Morley may have known that the two men kept cash on the premises.

- Morley's third victim, Kevin Atkins, may be the only one who responded to an offer of sex. His ex-wife says, 'He hated being on his own, particularly at weekends. We used to do things as a family and he missed that terribly.' Atkins preferred to be paid in cash for 'VAT and tax reasons' and kept it in a 'roll' until he could get to a bank.
- Despite inviting Morley on to their premises, Steele believes all three men reacted negatively afterwards. Either by questioning the value she put on herself or by refusing requests for money.
- Lt Acland's evidence offers a pattern of how Morley uses a stun gun to exercise control. He was told he'd be allowed to recover as long as he followed her orders – 'crawling naked round the floor pretending to be a dog' – but any show of disobedience would result in another hit.
- Lt Acland refused to comply, but it's doubtful that less fit, older men would have been willing to do the same. They may also have believed that being instructed to dress in bathrobes and lie on their beds was merely a device to prevent them following her when she left.
- Because her victims lived alone, there was no bar to Morley's behaviour. She did what she did because she could.

Conclusion

My team and I have come to know Harry Peel, Martin Britton and Kevin Atkins during the months we've worked on their cases. These were good, decent men who deserve better than to allow their killer to plead self-defence or diminished responsibility.

All efforts are now being directed at proving that Morley's motive was financial gain, and that she was prepared to murder her victims because they knew her and could identify her.

I trust this deals with your concerns.

Best wishes,

Brian

Detective Superintendent Brian Jones

Thirty-one

DAISY APPEARED QUIETLY in the open bedroom doorway and watched Acland pack his kitbag. Everything he owned was laid out neatly on the bed and, like others before her, she was struck by how little he had. To her, the most poignant articles were the single mess tin and mug which spoke of a life that wouldn't be shared with anyone else.

She shifted her position slightly to draw attention to herself. 'Jackson doesn't want you to go,' she murmured quietly to avoid her voice carrying downstairs, 'but I don't think she'll tell you herself.'

'Has she actually said that?' Acland asked, folding a T-shirt.

'Not in so many words . . . but I'm sure I'm right.'

He glanced at her with genuine warmth in his expression. 'I don't think you are, Daisy. Jackson's a realist. She knows there's no way I can suddenly redefine myself as an anonymous paying guest . . . not if she keeps watching me for migraines and you keep trying to feed me.' He tucked the T-shirt into his kitbag. 'Thanks for saying it, though.'

'Will you keep in touch?'

'Sure.'

Daisy didn't believe him. 'I know you think Jacks is strong-minded and tough, but most of that's a front. She worries about everything underneath. She'll worry about *you*.'

Acland pushed the T-shirt to the bottom of his kitbag. 'She can always find out where I am from the police. I have to report in on a weekly basis in case I'm needed for further questioning.'

'I can't see you doing that either,' said Daisy with sudden conviction. 'You'll disappear and leave everyone wondering where you went and what happened to you.'

Acland eyed her for a moment. 'It worked for Chalky,' he said.

*

Jones had expressed the same doubts as Daisy when Acland sought him out on Monday morning to tell him he was planning to leave the Bell the next day. With his bail conditions lifted, he was free to travel again. 'Are you about to do a runner on me, Lieutenant?'

'No.'

'How good is your word?'

'As good as it's ever been.'

The superintendent nodded. 'But I'd like to be sure you really understand what's at stake here. We'll get a conviction of some kind without you . . . but I doubt we'll have justice. Any accusation Jen chooses to fling at you will go unchallenged if you're not in court to defend yourself.'

'I won't be the one on trial.'

'But your good name will, along with the reputations of Jen's three victims . . . and dead men don't have voices. The blacker she paints you the better her chances.'

Acland hesitated. 'You might do better without me,' he said. 'In a contest between Quasimodo and Uma Thurman, I can't see the jury believing Quasimodo.'

Jones looked amused. 'You're the wrong body shape for Quasimodo, Charles. Dracula, possibly.'

'Same problem – Beauty versus the Beast – and I'm not sure my name matters that much to me, Superintendent. It hasn't done me any favours so far.'

'Then here's where we part company,' said Jones, 'because I have a lot of respect for Lieutenant Acland.' He looked for a response in the younger man's expression and shook his head when he didn't find it. 'The doctor's right. You're far too keen on martyrdom, my friend . . . and it's your least attractive quality. Your forte is fighting.'

'I'm not allowed to do that any more.'

'There's more than one way of skinning a cat. Pick a legal fight. Become a champion.'

'Of what?'

'Three dead men would be a start. Justice doesn't come automatically. It has to be fought for.'

Acland wondered if Jones realized that he was using the same kind of language that politicians use to justify wars. In the end, the only satisfaction was to settle one's scores for oneself. 'Isn't justice the job of the police?' he asked without emphasis.

'Certainly,' the older man agreed, 'but we can't do it on our own. You'd have been called as a witness whatever happened, you know. Your association with Jen would have come under scrutiny as soon as we fixed on her.'

'Only because I gave her to you. If I hadn't come back to Bermondsey, you'd still be in the dark.'

Jones smiled slightly. 'We'd have got there eventually. We found the name "Cass" on Kevin Atkins's mobile.'

'I gave you that as well . . . and the duffel bag.'

'You didn't know it was Jen's.'

For the last time Acland toyed with keeping to himself the only secret he had left, but Jackson had urged him to be fair. 'You can't destroy all the evidence,' she had said. 'At least give the police a chance with the Harry Peel photos . . . even if you don't like Jones much.'

She was wrong about that. Acland had a great deal of respect for the superindentent. He'd recognized the man's strength the first time he met him, just as he'd recognized Jackson's. With a sense of regret that he was about to lose Jones's sympathy, he shook his head. 'I was watching from across the road when Ben snatched the bag off her,' he admitted. 'I always knew it was hers.'

The superintendent didn't bother with surprise. 'Did you know who Ben was?'

Acland nodded. 'I recognized him as the kid who set his girls on Chalky. Jen didn't make a sound, just got to her feet and stood there as white as a sheet. It made me wonder what he'd stolen.'

'Why didn't you tell us this before?'

'I did. I said several times that I thought a bag existed.'

'You *knew* it existed, Charles.'

'Not for certain. I couldn't see what Ben was carrying when he arrived in the alleyway. He collapsed almost immediately, and it was so dark I wasn't even sure he was the kid I wanted until I shone a torch in his face and checked his breathing. I think that's when Chalky buried the duffel in one of his own bags.'

Jones tapped his forefingers together. 'You could have told us you'd witnessed the theft.'

'There was nothing to tell. For all I knew, Ben had stolen a pile of magazines.' He saw the irritation in the superintendent's face. 'I hoped the bag contained something I wanted. That's the only reason I went to the alleyway. I thought Chalky might be able to tell me where the kid usually hung out.'

'What's the something you wanted?'

Acland hesitated. 'These,' he said curtly, putting his hand into his jacket pocket and placing a couple of USB flash drives on the desk. 'It wasn't Jen who smashed my laptop, it was me. That's why I went back to her flat two weeks later. She'd loaded some photographs on to it that I didn't want anyone to see. I hoped that was the end of it till she sent me a letter the day I went to Iraq with one of these memory disks in it.' He squeezed his temples between a thumb and forefinger. 'She said she'd made copies before the laptop was destroyed.'

Jones looked at the two small rectangular objects. 'Why did you think they were in the duffel bag?'

'I didn't . . . it was a possibility, that's all. Jen was carrying a memory card in her handbag when she came to the hospital. I took it and ran it through Susan Campbell's computer the next day.' He shook his head at Jones's questioning expression. 'Publicity shots.'

'What were you doing outside her flat last Friday?'

The good side of Acland's mouth lifted in a wry smile. 'Working out how to get in. I could have done it if she hadn't been so shell-shocked by the theft. A minicab turned up a few seconds later, but she cancelled it and went back inside. That's what made me curious about the contents of the bag.' He paused. 'I had no idea there was anyone else involved. I truly believed it was all about me.'

Jones wasn't impressed. 'You must have wondered when you found Kevin Atkins's mobile in Ben's rucksack.'

The lieutenant shook his head. 'Not at the time. I assumed Ben had nicked it along with the iPods and the BlackBerry. I might have guessed if he'd transferred the stun gun.' He fell silent.

Jones studied him for a moment. 'Perhaps you didn't want to believe there was a connection?'

Acland shook his head, but whether in agreement or denial Jones couldn't tell.

Out of habit, he used the tip of his pen to pull the USB flash drives towards him. 'Were you searched when you were brought here from the Crown?'

'Yes.'

'Why weren't these on you then?'

'They were under the mattress in the bedroom. I needed to see what was on them before I handed them in.'

'And?'

'One's blank and the other has some photographs of someone who might be Harry Peel. I think Jen may have loaded them on to my laptop before I destroyed it. If she took pictures of Britton and Atkins, they'll be on her own computer.'

'We haven't discovered any.' Idly, Jones moved the USB disks again. 'You should have trusted me, Charles. We wouldn't have put pictures of you into the public domain. These are worse than useless if you've contaminated the evidence.'

Silence.

'Whose computer did you use to download and delete your images? Dr Jackson's?'

Acland shook his head.

'Are you going to force me to serve her with a subpoena?'

'You'll be wasting your time. There's no way you'll be able to retrieve anything, either from the disk or from a hard drive. Will you trust *me* on that?'

'Why should I?'

There was a brief pause before Acland drew himself to attention. 'Because you're the person I wanted to keep the photographs from, sir. There's no way you'll ever see them. I'd rather have your respect than your pity.'

'You're a pain in the arse, Lieutenant,' said Jones with a growl. 'You'd have had my respect either way.' He stood up abruptly and held out his hand. 'Will you give me a personal promise that you'll come to court?' He saw the hesitation in Acland's face. 'You told Inspector Beale you'd never betray a friend. If you refuse to shake on it, should I take that as a compliment?'

Humour creases appeared around Acland's eye. 'Not necess-arily.' He grasped the other man's hand. 'I prefer enemies. At least I know where I am with them.'

*

Jackson was straddling a chair at the kitchen table, head bent over some accounts, big shoulders hunched forward. She flicked an amused glance at the lieutenant as he appeared in the doorway with his packed kitbag, and he saw with relief that she wasn't proposing to be sentimental about his departure.

'You owe Daisy a fiver for breakfast,' she said, tapping the top page, 'otherwise you're up to date.'

Acland took out his wallet. 'She force-fed me a horse in case I starved.'

'It's her way of saying goodbye,' said Jackson, folding the note he handed her.

'What's yours?'

She reached over to open the money drawer. 'A fifty-quid fine for making me reformat my hard drive. You're lucky I'm a computer whiz.' She watched him sort through his remaining notes. 'On second thoughts, you can make it a hundred. I hardly had any sleep over the weekend because I had to reinstall my own data afterwards.'

Acland placed five twenties on the stash that was already there. He didn't think the drawer had been emptied since the last time he'd paid a fine. 'Who are you planning to give it to?'

'I'm a businesswoman. What makes you think I hand out gifts?'

'Intuition,' he said with a gleam of a smile. 'I've discovered I have a feminine side.'

'You're making progress, then.' She watched him sling his kitbag across his shoulder. 'Do you want me to come to the door and wave you off?'

Acland shook his head. 'You'll only pester me about whether I'm going to keep in touch.'

'Not my style,' she said firmly. 'Either you will or you won't . . . but I'm damned if I'll massage your ego by asking.'

His smile deepened, pulling his scar into something approaching a laughter line. 'According to Daisy, you'll worry if you don't hear from me occasionally.'

Jackson placed his five-pound note in the money drawer. 'You'd better believe it,' she said.